THE COLOR OF JUSTICE

Center Point
Large Print

Also by Ace Collins and available from Center Point Large Print:

The Yellow Packard
Darkness Before Dawn
The Cutting Edge

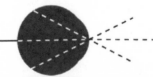

THE COLOR OF JUSTICE

Ace Collins

CENTER POINT LARGE PRINT
THORNDIKE, MAINE

This Center Point Large Print edition is published
in the year 2015 by arrangement with Abingdon Press.

The text of this Large Print edition is unabridged.
In other aspects, this book may vary
from the original edition.
Printed in the United States of America
on permanent paper.
Set in 16-point Times New Roman type.

ISBN: 978-1-62899-415-5

Library of Congress Cataloging-in-Publication Data

Collins, Ace.
The color of justice / Ace Collins. — Center Point Large Print edition.
pages ; cm
Summary: "A complex thriller that fuses the past and present with two
controversial court cases steeped in racial prejudice"—Provided by
publisher.
ISBN 978-1-62899-415-5 (library binding : alk. paper)
1. African Americans—Crimes against—Fiction.
 2. Trials (Murder)—Fiction. 3. Race relations—Fiction.
 4. Mississippi—Fiction. 5. Large type books. I. Title.
PS3553.O47475C65 2015
813'.54—dc23
                                                    2014037689

To all the good Samaritans
who have touched my life.

THE COLOR OF
JUSTICE

1964

1

Saturday, June 20, 1964

As her vision became accustomed to the dimness of the rural night, sixteen-year-old Wendy Adams gazed through the windshield, lifted her eye-brows, frowned, and then glared at Frank Baird. The Justice High School senior simply wouldn't give up. This was his big surprise! This is why he'd told her to keep her eyes closed for the past five minutes. Leaving the VFW dance early had all been a ploy to get her alone and to this spot.

As Frank inched closer, Wendy shook her head and apprehensively hissed, "You're pretty sure of yourself. Do you honestly believe getting me up here will somehow change the rules? This is beneath even you. Now, let's turn the car around and go home."

"Ah, come on, Babe," Frank begged, switching off the long, sleek, '63 Pontiac's motor and moving across the wide bench seat to where his lips were just inches from hers. "Just a few minutes out here in the moonlight will change your life forever! Besides, with your body, those blue eyes, those full lips, and your perfect chin, you're

11

wasting what every other girl in school wishes she had. I mean you're as close to Sandra Dee as Mississippi has ever seen."

He was attractive. He did have a certain animal charm. So, as he dipped his head even lower, she was tempted to meet him halfway, to give in to his will and compromise her own, but the thought of sitting beside her mother at church the next morning caused her deeply ingrained moral fiber to once more wrestle control from her suddenly fluttering heart.

Pushing herself up against the passenger door, she hesitantly announced, "We're going home now."

"Not unless you're walking," he replied with a grin. "And it's a long way back to town. Just might wear those heels out before you get there."

Even as she glared at him, he edged closer, never taking his eyes off hers as he reached over and switched on the radio. Suddenly, the strains of Lesley Gore's "It's My Party" filled the Pontiac's interior. A few moments later, his lips once more within inches of hers, Frank whispered, "And it's our party, too."

Ricky Nelson couldn't have charmed her using such a cheap line. It not only ruined the moment, it reset Wendy's moral radar. Reaching for the door handle, she yanked it, spun to the right, and stepped out into the warm summer night. Slamming the Pontiac's door behind her, she took a half-dozen steps down toward the creek before stopping to lean up against a century-old elm tree. As her blue eyes stared down into the barely moving water, she heard a car door open, close, and then footsteps in the grass behind her. She was hoping he was coming to apologize, but those hopes were quickly dashed.

"Wasted trip," Frank barked as he took a spot on the other side of the eighty-foot tree. "I guess I'm just not your type. In fact, I don't think you have a type. You shoot every guy down before the game even starts. Last fall, you were crowned the homecoming queen, and tonight you won the title of the ice princess."

She moved forward and glanced around the elm's large trunk at Frank. He was tall, a bit over six-foot, lean but toned, his shoulders wide and hips narrow. He had deep brown eyes and wavy black hair. He was not handsome in the way Hollywood defined it, but he did have rugged good looks that made him stand out in a crowd. Sadly, those gifts framed an attitude proving he believed himself to be God's gift to the world. It was his attitude that canceled out his myriad positive traits, as well as shaking all desire from her head and heart. And his smug brashness was the reason she found the strength to coldly declare, "You've accomplished nothing more than proving you're not a gentleman."

"Never claimed to be one," he shot back.

13

At least he was honest. She'd hand him that much. He didn't want to be the school's best citizen. He never claimed to walk the straight and narrow. He only wanted what was in front of him at the moment.

Tearing her eyes from his lustful gaze, Wendy tried to understand her own convoluted feelings. Why was his pull so strong? Why, when every boy in school dreamed of going out with her, did she say yes to Frank? Why did she have to be the good girl when she wanted something no good girl should want?

Pushing herself off the tree, Wendy took two steps forward and glanced around at the place the kids called Lovers Park. She had to admit, in a cheap sort of way it was romantic. The moonlight, the breeze rustling through the trees, and the gurgling of the slow-moving creek did create a natural setting for intimacy. Though there were some clouds, it was still clear enough that the stars did offer something to wish on as the solitude brought about a false sense of independence and maturity. Even nature seemed to be whispering, "Give in to your desires." While she was tempted, she couldn't listen—at least not tonight and surely not with Frank. But each second she was mute, as each moment went by with no words spoken, it likely convinced him that this trip had not been for naught. Even now, he probably thought she was reconsidering. So, she had to say something, no matter what it was, to prove she was in control.

"I don't know about wasted," she began, trying to be forceful and bold, "I mean, I've always wondered what this place looked like. I've heard whispers at school, you know, from *those* kind of girls, but all of my friends are a bit too proper to visit this spot."

"They're not *that* proper." Frank grinned. "They just don't admit they've been here."

She ignored both his insinuation and the fact that he'd once more closed the distance between them. As she felt his breath on her neck, she knew she had to restart the conversation or face fighting him off again.

"Isn't this where you had the hot dog cookout I heard about a month ago?"

"How did you hear about it?" He pulled back, seeming genuinely surprised. "And besides, it was more than two months back."

Wendy grinned; she'd gotten him to back off. "Well," she sang out, "Becky admitted to me she was here, and it wasn't really a cookout, but rather a make-out session."

"Yeah," he admitted, "and Becky was a willing participant."

"That's not the way she told it," Wendy shot back, fearing she had once more lost control.

Frank laughed. "We didn't roast hot dogs, but we were doing some cooking and we did have a fire. Want to see where it was?"

"I'm not sure I need to get any farther from the car," she replied apprehensively.

Moving closer, he reached out to touch her left hand and, in a suddenly assuring tone, "You can trust me. I won't make you do anything you don't want to do."

She hesitated, took a deep breath, and shook her head just hard enough for her blonde ponytail to bounce. "Nobody makes me do anything I don't want to do."

"I kind of got that," he replied.

Wendy took his hand and allowed him to lead her down by the creek and deeper into the shade of a half-dozen sixty-foot trees. When, after only a dozen steps, he put his arm around her shoulder and draped his hand dangerously close to her chest, she wondered if this had been such a good idea.

"That's where the fire was," he said, using his right hand to point to a spot down by the water.

The moonlight was just bright enough to see where the rocks had circled the space. As her eyes grew accustomed to the shadows, she noted there were still a few charred logs piled in the center.

"It must have been a pretty big blaze," she observed.

"Big enough," he explained. "But not so big anyone came up here wondering what was going on. And your friend looked beautiful in the flickering light. I do remember that."

Trying to ignore what he was implying, Wendy observed empty bottles thrown down by the creek. She'd heard that some drinking had fueled the party, and she wondered if Becky, the president of her church youth group, had been a part of it, too.

As Wendy's eyes moved from the bottles up to the creek bank, she spotted a few large trees fallen at least a generation before. She imagined they'd offered places where couples used to sit, snuggle, and kiss. Her curiosity was about to completely overwhelm her principles, when her eyes caught something obviously out of place.

"What's that?" Wendy asked, pointing out the object to her date.

His eyes followed her fingers until he saw it, too. Dropping his arm from her shoulder, he jogged over to the spot, leaned closer, and picked up what she had spied. Pushing it back toward her, he proudly exclaimed, "Someone must not have gotten home with all her clothes. Wonder how she explained it to her parents, and wonder when she lost it."

Wendy quickly moved across the ground to where the smirking Frank stood holding the prize. "Let me see it." She held up the light blue blouse, moving it out of the shadows and into the moonlight. The monogrammed *B* immediately gave away the garment's owner. "It's Becky's," she sighed.

"I'd thought she was almost as icy as you are," he sniped. "I guess someone else may have found the defrost button."

"Not funny," Wendy protested, tossing the blouse back his way. "We don't really know what happened, and I need to talk to Becky before you breathe a word of it to any of your friends."

"My silence can easily be bought," he shot back. "And it doesn't take money. Come here and kiss me."

"You're disgusting." She sighed, even as he pulled her into his arms.

"You can't be sure until you kiss me," he bragged, bringing his lips to hers.

"Wait," Wendy whispered, pushing her hands against his chest to hold him back.

"What?" he groaned. "Wendy, it's 1964! You need to get with the times. Being a good girl died a generation ago."

She ignored his vocal jab and pointed out into the darkness. "What's on the other side of the log?"

"You're a bigger iceberg than the one that hit the *Titanic*," he complained. "No more stalling, kiss me."

"No," she said, jerking free of his clutch, "there's something over there."

Even in her pumps, she quickly covered the twenty feet to the log and peered into the dark shadows. There was something there. She'd seen it a few seconds before.

"Over here!" she almost screamed as she pushed her wind-blown ponytail back over her shoulder.

Frank slowly trudged through the grass to her side. "Boy, I've heard of excuses before, but this one tops it. I bring you to the most romantic spot in the area, a place where generations have come to make out, and you freeze up like ice cream. This is going to be our last date. If all the girls in town move away and you're the only one left, I will never take you out again."

He folded his arms and glared into Wendy's eyes before following her gaze into the darkness. He surveyed the scene for a few disgusted seconds, then noted, "I don't see anything, Wendy." Shaking his head, he added, "I know when to give up. I'm waving the white flag now. The money I spent on flowers, the dance, and gas has been wasted. So, Miss Adams, let's go on home."

"Wait," she pleaded, reaching out and putting her arm through his to hold him in place. "Just keep looking out there until the wind blows, the tree branches move, and the moonlight reveals what I spotted. I tell you, something is right over there. Just about twenty feet from the big oak tree."

Neither of them had to wait long. A few seconds later, the wind was strong enough to not just move the branches but to almost push the two teens sideways.

"Storm coming," Frank noted with urgency. "We really ought to get home. Dad will be steamed if I get mud on his car."

"There it is!" Wendy exclaimed.

Dropping her arm from his, she rushed to and climbed over a log, then raced through the grass into the darkness and shadows. She finally stopped when she was sure she was near what she had seen. Suddenly, clouds covered the moon, the night was plunged into pitch blackness, and a large raindrop struck her cheek. She could now smell the rain and even hear it peppering the leaves above her. As the moments passed, she stared out into the darkness as the falling water soaked through to her skin. Curiosity, not common sense, held her in place.

"Come on, Wendy," Frank called out. "We've got to get back to the car and get out of here."

"Just a second," she yelled back.

"Wendy!" He moaned.

With the strong, wet breeze blowing her hair and pleated skirt, the most beautiful girl in Justice stubbornly fixed her gaze on the dark ground. Her concentration was rewarded when a bolt of lightning lit up the night. Frozen in place, her eyes locked onto a sight too ghastly to fully comprehend. As the image flooded into the deepest recesses of her mind, she tried to catch her breath, but it refused to come. Fear paralyzed her throat and threatened to possess her body, too. Even though the night was still warm, she was chilled to the bone. Suddenly there was no wind, rain, or storm. Reality had somehow turned a dream date into a nightmare, and whatever romance or temptation had lured her heart—to places she had once feared to tread—had now evaporated. Terrified, Wendy raised her hands to her mouth and tried to scream, but nothing came out. Lightning struck a tree less than a hundred yards away. The noise was deafening, the ground shook like an earthquake, and the smell of burnt wood filled her senses, but she still couldn't move.

Every fiber in her lithe form screamed at Wendy to turn away. *If you don't see it, it doesn't exist! Don't look and it will fade away; dissipate like a nightmare!* Yet she couldn't follow the demands of her heart or mind. Again, she had to view the ghastly scene just a few feet in front of her. And a five-second jolt of electricity snaking from one horizon to the other gave her the chance.

Becky Booth's body was bloody and pale, grotesquely twisted, her lips blue, her eyes open but seeing nothing. Around her, where she was lying but not really resting, were a saddle oxford shoe, her favorite red scarf, and a purse. The grass flattened into a path, and a trail of blood could be seen on the ground, ending at the place where Becky's twisted form had been dumped. This was it, there was nothing more to see, but so much to forget.

Not waiting for another burst of lighting to reveal what she now wished she'd never viewed, Wendy glanced back toward the still-confused Frank. It was obvious from his frustrated expression he hadn't seen anything. If he only knew how lucky he was. Willing strength into her weakened limbs, she raced with purpose over the distance separating her from the boy. Hurdling the log as if she was an Olympic sprinter, she hurried to his side and pushed herself deeply into his chest as if he would or could keep her safe from the monster who brutalized her best friend. As his arms wrapped around her, she sobbed.

"What is it?" he asked, a sense of urgency now even apparent in his tone.

What she had seen was too horrible to think, much less speak, but she had no choice. She had to share the horror with someone, even if saying it made it real. "It's Becky," she sobbed. She could force no more from her lips as the unrelenting rain pelted down from the now angry skies.

Not wanting to, but somehow unable to stop, Wendy pulled from Frank's grasp and turned back toward the spot. When lightning once more lit the dark sky, when for a few seconds night became day, she once more saw her friend's dead body, bloody and broken, lying in the grass.

Though she hadn't even kissed Frank Baird at Lovers Park, Wendy had nevertheless lost an innocence never again to be found.

2

A troubled Cooper Lindsay walked from his desk to the window of his second-floor law office. Death was a numbing occurrence, but when it happened brutally to a young person whose whole life lay ahead of her, it moved from numbing to gut-wrenching. And yet, in spite of this tragedy the world kept turning, and in so many ways, it was just another sunny Monday morning around the Justice, Mississippi, town square.

Tom Miller was sweeping the sidewalk in front of his Western Auto Store, Virginia Rankin was rearranging the display in her flower shop, and just like they had on almost every weekday for twenty years, Mayor Johnson Goodly was visiting with Walter Green in front of the city offices. Just beyond them, a half-dozen folks were tromping up the marble steps and filing into the red-brick courthouse, and about the same number were making their way into the Sunshine Café on the square's far corner. Not far from a Civil War memorial statue, Jacob McBride and Aaron Carver were sitting at a table studying a checkerboard. Coop, as his friends and family called him, wondered how many games those two old men, the grandsons of slaves, had played and who was actually ahead. Yep, it was another day just like any other and would likely be repeated tomorrow, the day after, and the day after until time itself stopped. Except in this case, tragedy tempered the normal routine. The cloud of despair created by Becky Booth's murder would likely hover over Justice for days, if not weeks, and Coop was sure it would haunt him, the father of three, for years.

Moving his right hand through his thick black hair, Coop ambled slowly back to his large oak desk. Like the filing cabinets, the green leather office chairs, and even the walnut bookcases, the desk had been handed down from generation to generation in the Lindsay family. A hundred years before, a time when the Civil War was winding down its final bloody days, John Jacob Lindsay had used this desk in the office at his sawmill. Then, Jefferson Lindsay had lugged it over to First National Bank where he served as president for more than four decades. Finally, Coop's dad, Abraham, had used the massive oak desk when he'd pastored the Justice Methodist Church. He'd been working on a sermon when a massive heart attack struck him down. His secretary found him with his head resting on the place where Coop's legal pad now set. The desk had then gone to the

Lindsay's home until a few months ago, when Coop's mom, Agnes, died. On her deathbed, she'd made him promise he'd use the desk in his practice. It seemed much easier to move his wife and family to Justice than move the heavy desk to Nashville. So here it was and here he was, too. Though he'd never intended to, he'd come home.

He'd grown up under the gaze of all 4,252 folks who called Justice home. They'd watched him from his days as an infant crying during his father's sermons to his fabled exploits on the gridiron and ball fields. They'd even waved when he headed off to Ole Miss to earn his under-graduate degree in journalism. Later, at Vanderbilt University, in Music City, he not only earned a law degree, but also found a bride. And after six years of working for the Tennessee Supreme Court and fathering a boy and two girls, the only child gave up his plan and dreams of staying in Tennessee to come home and help his cancer-ridden mother. Sadly, no sooner had he moved his family to Justice than Agnes died.

Now, three months of living in the sleepy community where five generations of his family had called home had proven two things to the lanky, dark-haired man. The first was something he liked: Justice was the same quaint town he remembered from his youth. The second was something he hated: Justice was still the same quaint town he remembered from his youth.

How could a person both despise and embrace the same thing? For Coop, it was about history and progress. Initially, there was a comfort found in shopping in the same stores and seeing the same people he'd known all his life. There was also a familiar and somehow soothing and comfortable rhythm here. The smells, the food, the unchanging traditions, and the Southern twang were almost like a baby's security blanket, and he loved having them back in his life. Not only that, but the fact that the Lindsay family had called Justice home for more than a century meant work immediately came his way. In so many ways, he had found the perfect life. How could he ask for anything more?

Yet, while on the surface things were seemingly wonderful, beneath the top layer of his new old life there was something troubling Coop more each day. He'd never noticed it growing up. It had never concerned him then. But now, the racial divisions so accepted in Justice ate at him like the cancer that had killed his mother. A generation after Jackie Robinson had integrated baseball, this town still functioned the same way it had for decades. Blacks and whites coexisted but didn't mingle. Negroes worked for whites, but whites never worked for Negroes. Even after Rosa Parks's bus ride and Martin Luther King's speeches, there was an accepted double standard in Justice no one dared challenge. Though it was a part of everyone's life, no one seemed to notice except him.

Since he'd opened his office, not one black person had knocked on his door. Yes, they'd speak to him on the street, always calling him "Mr. Lindsay," but they didn't feel comfortable visiting his office or seeking his advice. People of color also didn't attend the church his father had once pastored or eat in any of the community's five restaurants. So while they lived here, essentially confined to their own part of town, and while their money was accepted for goods in stores, they weren't really citizens. They had no representation and no opportunities. In some ways, it was like the way society had flourished before 1860 and was still very much alive a hundred years later. And for the lawyer who had once been a minster's son, this reality left him cold. He simply couldn't reconcile his faith with the culture. Hence, he felt very much like a stranger in a town where he was revered, and that was why he just couldn't fully embrace the seemingly perfect life he had been given by coming home.

A knock on his inner office door made him feel like a boxer saved by the bell and kept him from sinking into another round of wondering if making the move to Justice had been the right one for him and his family.

"Come in," he wearily announced. He then

27

looked toward the entry to see who would be opening the large, oak door.

Abby Simpson, the fifty-year-old spinster who served as his secretary-receptionist almost apologetically pulled her rail-thin form into the room. She checked her bun with her right hand and pushed her dark-rimmed glasses up her long, narrow nose before saying, "Mr. Lindsay, there is a Negro woman here to see you." The sentence's strained tone revealed the woman's discomfort with even voicing the news.

Coop shook his head, raised his eyebrows, and shrugged. "What did you tell her?"

Abby balled her hands together, dipped her head, and looked down at her long gray skirt. Clearing her throat, she apologetically said, "I told her to wait and I'd see if you were in."

"And am I?" Coop asked with a smile.

"I figured you wouldn't want me to say you were," came the earnest reply.

"And why is that?"

"Because she's colored," Abby whispered.

"Is it catching?" Coop teased.

"What?" the confused woman asked, completely missing the point the lawyer was trying to make.

After giving Abby a few seconds to puzzle on his question, he inquired, "What is the woman's name?"

"I didn't ask her," she replied honestly.

Shaking his head, his gray eyes sparking,

the lawyer said, "Usher her into my office."

"Are you sure you want to see her in here?" she quizzed.

"Yes," he resolutely replied, "if she is a client, she is welcome in here. In fact, she is likely more welcome in here than she is in front of your desk."

Unable to fully grasp what Coop had implied, the thin woman quietly turned and went back through the door, pulling it shut behind her. As he waited for his unexpected guest to make her entrance, the lawyer looked down at the black-and-white framed photo of his family set on the right corner of his desk. Judy was far more beautiful than any of the local girls he'd dated and a lot smarter. Maybe a part of her beauty was because she'd traveled, seen the world, had a college degree in philosophy, and a desire to go back to college for her Master's, but even without the brains, she was a knockout. And thankfully, Dina and DeDe looked like their mother. Clark, meanwhile, was the spitting image of his old man. Coop's finger was tracing the three-year-old boy's head when he heard a quiet knock on his door.

"Please come in," he said rising to his feet.

A few seconds later, a large, ebony-skinned woman, dressed in a blue maid's uniform complete with a white apron, hesitantly stepped into the entryway of the attorney's office. She waited at the door for a few moments before softly asking, "Do you have time to see me, Mr. Lindsay?"

"Of course," he quickly answered. "You are more than welcome here."

Moving from behind his desk, Coop stepped over to his guest, surprised her by gently taking her right hand, and led her to one of the two chairs reserved for guests and clients. After she'd taken a seat and smoothed her apron with her hands, he eased down in the chair next to hers.

"What can I do for you?" he asked.

When she didn't immediately answer, Coop took the time to study his unexpected guest. She was likely about five-and-a-half feet tall and he guessed her weight at around one-seventy. Her hair appeared short, pulled into a bun set on top of her head. She wore dark stockings and plain black shoes. Her lower lip showed a slight quiver and her left eye a twitch. It was apparent she was nervous and uncomfortable as she had immediately pushed her hands together and forced them into her lap where she worked them back and forth like a major league pitcher doctoring a baseball.

"I'm Cooper Lindsay," he said, breaking the silence. "But I'd rather you call me Coop."

Keeping her eyes on the floor, the woman spoke so softly he had to lean forward to hear her words. "Mr. Lindsay," she began, then paused a moment to correct herself, "I mean, Mr. Coop, I know I shouldn't bother an important man like you with my problems, but you see, we don't have no lawyers on our side of town."

"I understand," he assured her. "And it is no bother." Even as his words faded, she still hadn't looked up. Instead, she kept her gaze on the floor and her continually fidgeting hands in her lap.

"What is your name?" Coop asked.

"I'm Hattie Ross," she answered politely, still not looking his way.

"And how can I help you, Hattie?"

She paused, as if searching for either courage or words or both, then quietly asked, "Did you hear about the white girl who got herself murdered?"

"You mean Rebecca Booth?" he asked.

"Yes sir, that'd be her."

"I did hear about it, Miss Ross." He paused a moment, trying to understand how Hattie Ross connected to Becky Booth. "I knew her family. It was a tragic loss. I found out about it yesterday after church. It's hit the community very hard."

Finally lifting her head, her eyes moist and her lips trembling, Hattie continued, "I worked for the family. I had been their maid for more than twenty years. She was like a daughter to me. I even nursed her from my own breast after I lost my own little girl. I couldn't have loved Miss Becky any more if she had been my own."

"I'm sorry for your loss," Coop broke in.

"It is more than that"—Hattie sobbed, her

31

voice now shaking—"they've arrested my boy for killing Miss Becky." Suddenly, as if a dam had ruptured, her words spewed out so quickly Coop had problems keeping up. "They claim he did it, Mr. Coop. And my boy wouldn't have done it. He's a good young man. He just got back from his first year at college. And I know in my heart, he didn't do it. You see, Calvin is a gentle soul, just like my daddy was. He's like a lighter-skinned version of his grandfather, even to the way he walks and talks. He's a good boy. There ain't no bad in him. None at all."

The large woman's bosom heaved as she brought her hands to her face. Coop let her alone with her grief until her tears subsided. Then he posed his first probing question.

"Hattie, how do you know Calvin didn't do it? Do you have any proof?"

She sadly shook her head. "If you're asking if I knew where he was Saturday night, he told me he was home. And I have no reason not to believe him. He's never lied to me before. Never! Not even when he was just a little shaver."

Coop nodded. "Were you there with him?"

"No, sir, I was at church preparing for our annual Founder's Day singing. I lead the choir, and we was preparing our numbers. I didn't get back until almost midnight. But he was home then. In fact, I ginned him out for not doing the chores I asked him to do before I left. He was just too busy reading, I reckon. You see, he just loves to read."

"Hattie, was anyone else at home with Calvin that night?"

She shook her head. "It's just me and him at the house. We're all who lives there. But he told me he was home, and like I told you, reading. You see, he wants to be a preacher someday, and he gets ideas for sermons from books. And he'll make a fine preacher, too. I just know he will."

Coop got up, moved back behind his desk, and sat down. As the woman's large, brown eyes locked on him, he picked up a pad and pencil and posed his next question, "Has Calvin been arrested?"

"They gots him in the jail now," she quickly answered. "They came to the church during our evening service and took him away. I mean they marched right into God's house and just grabbed him. They didn't say why or even give us a chance to ask any questions; they just put those handcuffs on his wrists and marched him right out into the night."

"So they didn't tell you they suspected him of the murder?" Coop asked.

"They didn't say nothing. But I went back to see him in the jail today, and they must have pretty much beat him all night. His face is swollen like nothing I've ever seen, his eyes are almost shut, and they even knocked out a couple of teeth. Calvin told me they were trying to get him to confess, but he didn't. No sir, no matter what they done to him, he wasn't going to tell a lie to make them quit."

Coop eased back in his wooden swivel chair, brought his left hand to his mouth, and ran his thumb and forefinger over his lips. He had no way of knowing if Hattie was telling him the truth, but it was easy to tell she believed it.

"Mr. Lindsay," Hattie whispered, "I mean Mr. Coop, I ain't got no money. I don't have much of anything. It's just me and Calvin, and I pretty much spent all I had just getting him raised. But we need a lawyer, one who's fair and don't look at black skin and see only guilt. So if you'll take this case, I'll clean your house, wash and iron your clothes, do your cooking, and take care of your kids for nothing for as long as I live. I swear on a Bible I will."

As Coop looked into the woman's bloodshot but hopeful eyes, he recalled a sermon his father had given on the good Samaritan. Those words were meant to wake up a community to the sinful nature of prejudice, but so many years ago the message had fallen on deaf ears. Now, a decade later, Coop once more heard the lesson, but could he embrace it?

"So will you take the case?" Hattie asked.

He looked back into her eyes. What sounded good in his head wasn't so easy in real life. He lived in Justice, and there were lines not to be crossed. If he dared challenge the unwritten rules of society, there would be consequences. And his visitor knew it, just as well as he did, but still she had hoped he would somehow look past tradition and hear her pleas. And for the moment, with the two of them alone in his office, he couldn't break her heart by trying to explain why a white man in Justice couldn't betray his own kind.

"Let me visit your son first," Coop finally explained. "After I see him at the jail, I'll come by your home and we'll talk about it."

"My home?" She asked in disbelief. "White folks don't come over there unless they're collecting rent."

"I will." He smiled. "What's the address?"

"Our streets don't have names," she explained. "My home is the only light blue one on the other side of the tracks. It is about a half mile after the pavement ends. There's a shack behind us that we use for chickens. As Miss Becky's mom fired me this morning, I ain't got no place else to be, so I'll just go home and wait for you. We can sit out on the porch so no one talks about you badly. I don't want to ruin your fine reputation. It just wouldn't do. No sir, it wouldn't do at all."

"It will be fine," Coop assured her. "I'll find your place and then we can discuss what we need to do for Calvin. Until then, just go home and try not to worry."

She pulled herself from the chair, smoothed her dress, and nodded. With tears filling her eyes, she looked up and once more studied the man behind the desk. After a moment she declared, "You is every bit the man your father prayed for you to be. I knew him. I cleaned up your church when you was just a little child. Your daddy was a fine man. He didn't look at me like I was beneath him. He made me feel real special, like I was a lady. He gave me—what did he call it?—yeah, value."

As she departed, Coop once more considered the man his father had been and the legacy he'd left. For the moment, he was not sure either was working in his favor.

3

After a few minutes spent unsuccessfully trying to recall Hattie's working as a maid at the church, Coop got up and moved once more to the window overlooking the square. Pushing his hands into his pants pockets, he glanced back out onto the streets. Things had somehow changed from the first time he'd looked out today. Now he felt as if he were a prisoner and those below were the jury. If he took this case, then the jury might well rule him unfit to even live in their town. So how was the best way to handle it? A knock on the door interrupted his considering more questions he didn't want to pose or attempt to answer. Turning slowly he asked, "What is it?"

Abby opened the door and glanced apprehensively around the room, as if the Negro guest's presence had somehow permanently altered something. After assuring herself they were alone, she asked, "What did she want?"

"My advice," Coop quickly replied.

"You know that boy who lives with her is a murderer, don't you?" Abby chimed in.

The man lifted his eyebrows. "Has the trial already taken place? Has the jury already reached a verdict?"

"No," she spat, "but they got him good. He knew Becky well, and the two of them were seen together Saturday afternoon talking outside the Western Auto. Can you believe it, he was talking to one of our own?"

"Amazing," Coop answered, the sarcasm dripping from his voice.

"And that's not all," she continued, "they found his bloody knife beside the body. He wasn't even smart enough to get rid of it. He left it right there."

"Yep, Abby, it's pretty stupid all right. Kind of makes you wonder how the young man got into college."

"Well," she explained hurriedly, her blood pressure and her energy level both elevated, "he went to one of those black schools. He wouldn't have made it into a white university. We teach at a much higher level. Those Negroes just can't learn like we can."

"We actually don't know for sure, do we?" he shot back. "I mean, we wouldn't let him into one of our schools anyway! So how can it be measured?"

As his stinging words hung in the air, Coop shook his head and strolled back to his desk. Once there, he perched on the corner, crossed his arms and posed a question, "So you think if a white boy had done the deed, he'd have gotten rid of the weapon?"

"Of course," she resolutely answered. "But a white boy would have never killed and raped Becky in the first place."

Coop leaned forward. "So she was raped, too? I hadn't heard it."

"Well," the woman admitted, "no one has said so, but you know those black boys."

He paused a moment, took a deep breath, and then asked, "Abby, where did you work before I hired you?"

"I was a secretary at the title company," she explained.

"Then why don't you clean out your desk and go see if they have an opening," he suggested.

"What?"

"I think you heard me," Coop said. "I want you out of here in the next five minutes."

"Why?" she asked.

"First of all," he explained, "I'm an attorney, and I practice in a country where every person is innocent until proven guilty. It doesn't matter if they are male or female, young or old, white, black, or green. Those who work with me must adopt the same viewpoint."

He sharpened his glare and continued, "Secondly, this is a nation where supposedly all men are created equal. That means Miss Hattie Ross is just as good as you are. At this point, I would actually put you well behind her in a two-woman race for character and value."

Coop paused, unfolded his arms, and pointed an accusing finger in the woman's direction. "And finally, as the son of a minister, I can't devalue any human life. In God's eyes, we are all the same."

He studied the woman's growing frown before adding, "So because you are so quick to judge, because you feel superior just because of the color of your skin, and because you believe someone of a different race has less value than you do, I am dismissing you. Good-bye!"

"You're no better than they are!" she snarled.

"Who are they?" Coop asked.

"Coloreds," she snapped back. "You're just like 'em!"

"Finally you have said something I agree with." He laughed. "I am no better than black folks, and I am proud to be just like them—one of God's children."

As he fumed, she turned and slammed the door behind her. A few moments later, he heard her forcefully close the outside door and clomp down the stairs.

For a second, he considered how she must feel. Had he been too hard on her? After all, she was just a product of her culture. From her birth she had been conditioned to believe what she believed. But it sure felt good telling at least one person what he thought about the most troubling aspect of life in Justice. Still, while it was easy to dress down a frail, old spinster would he be so strong when confronting a jury in a courtroom? Even Coop didn't know the answer to his question.

4

The Justice jail was an ancient structure even by the standards of the old South. Built in 1899, the red brick two-story building had a dozen cells, one restroom for whites only, no conference rooms, a small office for the sheriff, and an even smaller one for his two deputies. Roaches, mice, and even rats were obviously more than happy to call the jail home, but for men, this hotel for the accused was a hell on earth. There was little heat in the jail's cells in the winter and no air conditioning during the summer. Even on the hottest summer day, fans were not allowed. It was not a place where even the most hardened souls would want to spend a few hours, much less weeks.

After pausing to observe either a small rat or large mouse scurry from a dogwood tree, race across the parking lot, and dart through a hole in one of the outside wall's bricks, Coop entered the smaller office reserved for deputies. As no one was currently seated behind either the table or the desks, he wandered across the room to Sheriff Wylie Estes's office. The attorney knocked, but as he knew the lawman well, Coop didn't wait for a greeting to enter.

Estes, a tall, balding man in his mid-forties, glanced over the rims of his black-framed glasses and smiled. Swinging his well-scuffed cowboy boots off his desk, he rose, stuck his hand forward and, after Coop heartily grabbed it, said, "Well, I haven't seen you since yesterday in church and wasn't expecting to see you until next Sunday. What brings you over to my part of the woods? Your pretty wife get fed up with your snoring and asked you to seek other accommodations and this is all you can afford?"

"I don't snore," Coop bluntly replied, "and I came here on business. So can I have a seat?"

"Well," the sheriff said, "I've got one extra besides mine. Why don't you take it and I'll slide back into the chair I was keeping warm." After sitting down, Estes crossed his arms over his bulging tummy and declared, "Sure glad we got rain this weekend. Boy, we needed it."

"Yeah," Coop replied, "but it seems the only time I remember our back porch leaks is when it pours. I need to get up there and fix that, but I never think about it when the sun is shining. Besides, I think you promised you'd help, too."

"Did I say that?" Estes laughed. "Funny, I don't remember doing it. I'm not real good on ladders." The big man paused for a second and then noted, "You haven't come over to my office to visit since I was your coach in Little League."

Coop smiled. "Those were the days. We almost won state."

Estes rubbed his left hand over the top of his head and frowned. "Don't remind me. I should have pitched you in our last game rather than Bobby. You could have held those bats from Montgomery down."

"I don't know," the lawyer replied honestly. "They had some big boys." He paused a moment, took a deep breath, and then looked directly into his host's eyes. "I'm not here to jaw about old times. Got something a bit more serious on my mind."

"I figured," came the reply. "So just spill it.

You were never any good at small talk anyway."

Coop shrugged. "What can you tell me about Rebecca Booth's murder?"

"Been trying to forget what I saw," Estes sadly admitted. "Haven't viewed anything like it since my days in the Pacific in World War II."

"Yeah," Coop cut in, "nothing like it happened during my days growing up in Justice." He shook his head and sighed. "Can't imagine losing a child. I don't know how you ever get over something like that."

"Me either," the sheriff replied. "My Kathy is just a couple years older than Becky. This morning I was scared to let her leave the house and go to work at her summer job at Jessup's Drug Store." He stopped a moment, rubbed his chin, and then quietly asked, "You didn't see her there, did you?"

The lawyer smiled. "She was working behind the counter when I got my coffee and newspaper. She's fine."

"Good. I've wanted to call, but I didn't want her to think I was an overprotective dad."

Coop nodded. "It has to be tough raising a kid by yourself. Especially a daughter."

Estes sighed. "Sally was a special lady. She was so good to me. But cancer doesn't pull any punches. It sure took her from us in a hurry. Found out about it one week and she was dead the next. Didn't really have time to say good-bye."

"Wylie, I'm sorry I wasn't there for you."

"You were in college," the sheriff said. "You likely didn't find out until the service was over. You know your dad did a great job. His words were a real comfort."

Coop nodded. "He always did say the right words at the right time. I still remember things he told me that caused me to steer my life in directions I don't think I'd have taken if it weren't for him."

"Don't we all," Estes agreed.

"Well," Coop continued, "Kathy should be fine from here on in. After all, I understand you've caught the guy who killed Becky. So we really don't have anything to worry about, or do we?" The lawyer looked into his friend's eyes. "I mean the killer's off the streets. You're sure of that, aren't you?"

"Guess so," Estes quietly answered. Not sounding nearly as positive as Coop had hoped.

"You mean you don't think the Ross kid did it?"

The sheriff shrugged. "I don't know. I mean the colored kid was seen talking to her, and it made Brent Booth so mad he ordered Ross to back off. I guess you heard they had words. The folks who witnessed the confrontation said the boy is uppity. And then there's the knife we found at the crime scene. He had his name carved in the handle, and it was covered with blood. And Becky was cut up really good. So there was a lot of rage in the attack, and she didn't have an enemy in the world. It just had to be revenge for her father's berating the kid in public. I mean, it's all I can figure and the only thing to make sense."

"But," Coop asked, "why would a young man as smart as Ross leave the murder weapon at the scene? He was a college kid, wasn't he? After so many viewed the confrontation, wouldn't he have made sure he covered his tracks? And how did he get Becky to go out there with him?"

"I don't know," Estes replied, "I figured the boy was smarter. But it's where the knife was. Maybe he just didn't think we'd find it, or maybe he just dropped it because he panicked."

The sheriff took a moment, stared off into space, and without returning his gaze to his guest, added, "I do like the boy's aunt though. She literally cooked for us for nothing after my wife's death. She wouldn't accept a dime. Said she was doing the Lord's work. I don't know if I could have made it without her. I hate to see her go through this."

"His aunt?" a puzzled Coop asked. "Who is the aunt?"

"Hattie Ross."

"I thought she was his mother."

"Oh," Estes replied as his eyes fell back to Coop, "she raised him and thinks of herself as his mother, but the boy was a product of one of her

45

older sister's affairs. So the kid never had a daddy or mother, just Hattie."

Thrown off track by the explanation, Coop leaned forward. "Where's his real mother?"

"She died about fifteen or sixteen years ago in a house fire. Somebody set it; we never found out who did it. But it was definitely arson, no doubt of that. She was likely passed out drunk when the blaze took hold. Hattie was coming home from working at your dad's church or maybe the Booths, I don't remember which. But no matter, when she got there, the shack was already in flames. Witnesses said she never even paused to think about herself; she grabbed a blanket or something off the clothesline, dipped it in a mud puddle, and just rushed in. Somehow, and I sure don't know how, she managed to get Calvin out." Estes shook his head. "It was quite a feat of heroism. Not a man watching the shack burn would get close to those flames, and Hattie just charged right into the inferno. A few seconds later, she broke out a window and jumped down to the ground. And now it looks like it was all a waste."

"Why?" Coop asked.

"Because they're sure to send Calvin to the chair." Estes shook his head and sighed. "If he'd died in the fire, Becky would still be alive, and my job would be a lot easier."

Kind of a dim way of looking at things, but

when it came to murder there was no bright side. Yet as what-ifs didn't matter and facts did, it was time for Coop to dig a bit deeper.

"My secretary said Becky had been raped."

The sheriff shrugged, "It's not in the medical examiner's report, but you know town gossip. For as long as I can remember, everyone always thought black men just lived to assault white women."

"Yeah," Coop sadly acknowledged. "A lot of things we were taught were nothing more than lies."

"Yep," Estes replied, putting his boots back up on his worn, metal desk. "Now it is my turn to put you in the witness stand. Why are you so curious about all this? I know you well enough to know you don't get any morbid thrills by wading in others' misery."

Coop carefully considered his response. Should he admit he was thinking of representing Calvin or just chalk it up to professional snooping? While the latter was safer, it was hardly the honest way to go. And he'd never lied to Estes, even back when telling the truth had cost him a chance to pitch in a playoff game. So he needed to be up-front and honest, no matter what it meant to his standing with his old coach.

"Hattie came to my office," Coop finally explained. "I guess you know what it means."

"You aren't thinking of representing the boy,

are you?" The sheriff's slight frown and wrinkled brow showed his genuine concern.

"Yeah," Coop replied, "if I think he is innocent, I might do it."

Estes pulled his feet from the desk, spun out of his chair, and ambled a few steps closer to his guest. Leaning forward, he whispered as if he were scared someone would overhear, "Are you kidding? Do you have a brain in your head? Do you know what it will mean to you and your family?"

"I think so," the lawyer replied. "But it might be good for me to hear what you think it would mean. Just tell me in your own words. Let me have it right between the eyes."

Taking a seat on the edge of his desk, Estes folded his arms and began, "If you represent this boy, the folks in this town would turn on you in an instant. In their eyes, he is guilty. They want to string him up in a tree right now. I'm not sure some of them might not get liquored up over the next few days and try it, too. And they'd hate you even worse than Calvin if you were to represent him. You'd be better off being a leper than the attorney on this case."

"Why?" Coop asked, as if he didn't know. He then poignantly added, "And I want you to spell it out to me."

"Because you're white and you'd be turning your back on your own kind. Nobody here will cotton to you doing any such thing. They'd call you a . . ." The sheriff stopped before finishing his thoughts.

"A what?" Coop demanded.

"You know!" Estes barked back, his eyes aflame.

"Say it!" Coop challenged, sticking his finger at the other man's face. "Say the word. Everybody else does. It is said in churches and schools. It's one of the first words babies learn. People build jokes around it. So just go ahead and say it."

Estes swallowed hard. "Coop, I don't have to say it; you know what they would call you." He looked up and sadly added, "And even if I didn't say the word, you heard it in your mind. You know it was on my lips. Are you satisfied?"

"No," the lawyer replied as he leaned back in his chair, "I wanted you to say it just to prove to me that time hasn't marched on over the past century."

"Think of Judy and your kids," Estes begged. "They will be treated just like you. Somebody will likely even burn a cross in your yard before this is all through. Can they take that? Is it fair to them?"

The room grew silent as both men peered off into space. Finally, after a minute seeming more like an eternity, Coop posed a very simple question.

"Do you think Calvin is guilty?"

Estes eased up, circled his desk, sat down in his

chair, and shook his head. "No, I don't. My gut tells me someone else did it. He's not that kind of kid. But the only evidence I see means he is just a walking dead man. He's got no chance."

"If he were white, would the evidence condemn him?" Coop asked.

"No!"

"So it is his skin color?"

"Yeah," the sheriff admitted.

"Then I have to at least speak to him," Coop said. "Because if I don't take this case, some incompetent fool will, and the kid won't have a chance. I have to know in my heart he is 100 percent guilty before I walk away from this."

"But, Coop—and I am begging you now—you have to think about what it would do to your family."

The lawyer grimly smiled. "I guess in your mind my family trumps the kid dying in the electric chair. After all, what is a black man's life in comparison to a white lawyer and his family taking the easy road to prosperity?"

Estes sadly shook his head. "Why don't you forget about what is right and wrong this time and do what is best?"

"Because I am my father's son."

"I know you are," Estes replied sadly, "but win or lose, you will be a pariah in your own town."

Coop shrugged. "So was the good Samaritan, but it didn't keep him from doing the right thing."

He paused for a few seconds, letting the lesson his father once tried to teach take root in a new time and place. As he stared off into space, he was sure for a second he could almost hear his father's rich baritone voice. When the moment passed, he looked back to his host and asked, "Can I see Calvin Ross now?"

5

Even though it was just past ten in the morning, the temperature in the jail was likely over eighty, and it would only go higher as the day went on. The eight-by-eight-foot cell was at best dark, dank, and foreboding. The only light was a sixty-watt naked bulb hanging from the middle of the ceiling. One small metal chair sat on the right side of the room; an ancient iron bed frame covered with a thin mattress was pushed up against the left wall. Two metal buckets were in the back corner. One contained water; the other served as a toilet. The walls were dirty red brick, and the floor, dingy concrete. As Coop walked up, Calvin Ross was sitting up in the bunk looking mournfully toward the one-by-one-foot bar-covered window at the top of the back wall.

"You've got a visitor, Calvin," the sheriff dolefully announced.

The prisoner studied the unfamiliar white man as Coop made his way through the now open door and into the tiny cell. He continued to size up the lawyer as Estes pushed the door shut and relocked it.

"I'll be down at the end of the hall," the sheriff announced. "Just yell when you want me to come let you out."

Estes had only traveled four steps when the guest spoke, "My name is Coop Lindsay. Do you mind if I have a seat?"

The prisoner shrugged. Taking it as an affirmative, Coop eased down onto the metal chair. He sat there for a moment, allowing his eyes to get used to the dim light. When he could fully focus, he assessed the situation.

The slightly built Calvin Ross was of medium height and likely weighed about a hundred and fifty pounds. His hair was cut close and his skin was somewhere between butterscotch and caramel. His eyes were large and expressive, and his fingers thin. His light blue, short-sleeve shirt revealed powerful arms, likely due to years of working in fields. Except for the sad look in his badly swollen eyes and the bruising around his jaw and cheeks, he appeared to be the picture of health.

"They must have worked you over pretty good," Coop noted. He waited a full minute for a response, but when none came, he tried again.

"Your mother told me you kept quiet the whole time. You didn't tell them anything."

While his eyes never left his visitor, Calvin still remained as silent as a mime.

"This conversation seems a bit one-sided," Coop noted, trying to lighten the mood. When that didn't work, he added, "I was hoping to actually get to know you a bit. I promised Hattie I'd see if I could help you out."

The prisoner slowly moved his eyes back to the window while keeping his lips firmly together.

Taking a deep breath, Coop leaned back in the chair and began to whistle a tune. As the melody echoed off the walls, Calvin looked back toward his guest.

"You know the name of the tune?" Coop asked.

The young man shook his head.

"It's called 'The Prisoner's Song', and it was a big hit when my father was a boy. It's about a man who wished he was a bird and could somehow fly through the bars and away from his troubles. Well, son, you can't just fly away. You're going to have to have someone help you to get out of this mess. And it's why Hattie asked me to come see you. I'm a lawyer and my job is to find the truth and make sure those who are innocent don't waste their lives in places like this."

Calvin's eyes locked onto Coop, but he still remained mute.

"Listen," the now-frustrated lawyer continued,

"I need to know your story. I need to hear it from your own lips. You need to tell me the whole truth, and you need to trust me."

The young man's mouth formed a slight smile, as he deliberately shook his bruised head. Then he finally revealed his baritone voice. "Trust you? I'm no field hand; you can't sell me a worthless bill of goods. I know what the white man's trust means, and I know what you think of those whose skin is as dark as mine."

Coop allowed the hate, anger, and hostility obvious in those words to sink in before grimly admitting, "You've got every right to feel that way, son."

"I'm not your son," the man spit back, "and if I had any rights, I wouldn't be here. If I had any rights my face wouldn't be swollen, and I'd still have all my teeth. But for me to have any rights, I guess my skin would have to be the same color as yours. So don't talk to me about rights; I found out early on that my only rights were to watch my step and stay in my own place."

Coop nodded. "You're likely on target, Calvin. But I'm not interested in the way things have been or the way things are; I'm interested in the way things ought to be. And it means if you're innocent, then you need to be able to prove it in a court of law, walk out of this jail, and never look back."

"Why do you want to represent me?" the young man shot back, hostility still dripping from his lips. "You feel the need to make up for a couple of centuries of enslaving my kind, or are you just trying to be noble? Or maybe it's all a game. You're just trying to get me to open up now so you can sell me up the river in a few weeks in court. Or how about religion? Did you go to a revival recently and God laid some kind of burden on you about racism? Is that it? Just tell me what's in it for you?"

Coop licked his lips. It was time to be completely honest. It was time to show this young man, who at this time he neither liked nor felt sorry for, what this case really meant.

"There's a lot in this for me," Coop firmly explained. "A lot more than you know. If I represent a Negro in a case like this, the whole town's likely going to turn against me. My wife and kids will be cursed at and likely spat on. Folks likely won't talk to me on the streets. And my business is going to suffer and likely die. And if I get you off, then I'm probably going to have to move to another town and start all over again. Yeah, there are a lot of rewards waiting for me."

Coop slowly pulled himself off the chair, covered the few steps separating the two of them, pushed his finger in the young man's chest and added, "And moving is not what I'd like to do. You see my family has called Justice home for more than a century."

"You said your last name was Lindsay?" Calvin asked, rage still evident in his tone.

"Yeah."

"Did your people have a spread outside of town back in the days before the Civil War?"

The lawyer nodded, "Yeah, my great-great-grandfather moved from North Carolina and built the farm with his bare hands."

Calvin smiled grimly. "Actually, it was my people who built it. You see, I come from the line of slaves your great-great-granddaddy owned. So while my family name is not as well known or respected as yours, when it comes to our history in Justice, my people and your people go back to the very same moment. Yep, we built your dreams together, and then those dreams turned into nightmares for us."

As Coop studied the man's angry eyes, he suddenly felt a guilt he'd never before known. His own kin, those men and women he'd heard heroic stories about as a kid, had owned slaves. Thus, his heritage played a part in racially dividing a world to the point where Negroes were still devalued to this day. He had come into this jail feeling noble for reaching out to a black man, when in truth if it hadn't have been for a courageous Negro woman's visit to his office, he would have never considered Calvin's case or even questioned his guilt. The good Samaritan didn't need someone to push him to do the right thing, he didn't need anyone to point out the path he should take, but Coop sure did. Without Hattie's pleas and his father's sermons, he wouldn't be here right now. And what did it say about him? Was he really any better than his ancestors who bought and sold men like Calvin?

The prisoner's mocking voice woke Coop from his guilt trip. "You can't help me! And why should you? Just live in your world built on the backs of folks like me, and then pretend you are somehow better because God made you white."

6

Awash in a suddenly overwhelming sense of insecurity about himself and his motives, Coop moved back to the chair and took a seat. Running his hands through his hair, he glanced toward the room's only window and tried to think. If he took this case, if he proved this young man innocent, then Coop and his family would be trading places with Calvin. They would be inside a prison. That prison wouldn't contain bars or walls, but it would still exist. They'd be outcasts in Justice. Their friends wouldn't trust them, and there would be no way to make a living. In a sense, if he took this case, he would be trading Calvin's life for his family's freedom. It was a very steep price, one his father might have paid, but Coop was a different man.

Pulling himself off the chair, the lawyer called down the hall, "Wylie, I'm ready."

"So I take it you aren't going to represent me," Calvin sarcastically noted. "I'm just a little too dark for you."

Coop glanced back toward the young man as the sheriff unlocked the cell. Standing in the open doorway, the lawyer took a deep breath before forcing out an all-too obvious, feeble excuse. "I can't represent someone who won't be honest with me."

As the lawyer stepped outside, Estes locked the door and Coop walked briskly toward the exit with the lawman close behind. They were in the sheriff's office before either spoke.

"Coop," Estes announced with a relieved smile, "you made a wise decision. And this will actually play well in the community. The mere fact you talked to the young man shows just how much of a Christian gentleman you are, and white folks and black folks will respect that. Everyone will admire your compassion. The fact you didn't take the case will also keep you in good standing with those who matter in this community. You will come out of this looking noble and smelling like a rose."

"Not so sure about that," Coop sheepishly replied, the sheriff's view stinging worse than any hornet could. Still, in an effort to find the words to convince himself and the sheriff that he simply couldn't represent Calvin Ross, he added, "The kid couldn't trust me. It tells me he either needs someone else or he's guilty."

"Where you heading now?" Estes asked.

"I have to go back to the office," the lawyer explained. "I have two wills to put in final form for a couple of area businessmen, and there is a property sale I need to work on. And then I also have to replace the secretary I fired this morning."

"You fired Abby?"

"Yeah," Coop admitted, "I didn't like her tone." The words had no more left his mouth than he realized he and Abby really weren't so different. They might even have been cut from the same piece of cloth. And if it was the case, maybe he should fire himself, too.

He walked out of the jail offices and got in his car, and except for the shadow created by Becky Booth's death, life again seemed normal. And because of the normality, a half-dozen people smiled and sang out their greetings. Countless others waved from their cars or trucks, making sure they showed the popular hometown boy how much they loved him. After he'd parked and got out of his car, the mayor even tried to persuade Coop to take a break and eat lunch with him at the Sunshine Café. It was as if nothing had changed. He was still the golden boy, the all-American kid who had grown up here and would maintain the values making Justice the special place it was for everyone who happened to look like Coop.

Marching up the steps to his office, he resolutely made his way through the other room and opened the door into his private chambers. Moving to the window, he looked back down on the town he called home. Earlier he had been fresh and feeling noble, but now he suddenly felt a bit dirty. Worse yet, he knew no amount of soap was ever going to remove the stench off a man who would so easily trade right for wrong, who would so readily take the easy road rather than the proper but less-traveled path. There was nothing like selling out to put a face on one's priorities. And what an ugly face it was. In one brief moment, a moment in which he'd sold his moral fiber for security and acceptance, his whole life had changed. His decision—one few would even know about—would define him from this day forth. It would shape who he was and his sense of values. Like the mark of Cain, it would greet him every time he looked in the mirror.

7

It was late in the afternoon when Coop closed his office and made his way over to the other side of the tracks. Among the fifty or so houses and shacks strung out along three dirt roads, he had little trouble picking out Hattie's home. As there was no driveway, he pulled up in front of the tiny house and studied its sagging roof and peeling blue paint. A strong wind could take the whole place down. It was a shotgun structure and likely had three rooms and a small bath. There was stoop for a front porch with just enough room for two metal lawn chairs. In front of the porch, there were maybe a half-dozen rose bushes surrounded by a myriad of multicolored flowers. There was an almost futile irony in seeing beauty in a place so depressing. Why should anyone care enough about this dump to try to spruce it up?

Hattie had been sitting in one of the porch chairs when he had driven up in his shiny blue 1963 Ford Galaxie 500. When he pulled himself out of the car, she smiled and waved. "Mr. Coop," she called out hopefully, "did you see my boy?"

Shoulders sagging, he made his way slowly up the worn, wooden steps and looked sadly into the woman's dark eyes. He figured his expression was the reason she dipped her head, turned, and stared in the other direction down the muddy street leading to a dozen more shacks folks called homes. The two stood there for a moment until she finally broke the silence.

"It's kind of lonely here now. I should be used to it. I mean, he was away for months at college, but I'd just gotten comfortable with him being home again." She turned back to Coop, tears in her eyes. "It's not really much of a home, is it, Mr. Coop? I mean white folks probably wouldn't keep their chickens in our place. I wish I could have done better for Calvin, but a maid don't make much. I did the best an old black woman could do."

"You did fine, Hattie." Coop almost choked on his words. He dropped his chin to his chest and muttered, "I do wish things were different for you."

"Things are what they are," she sighed. "I've lived in worse places. This ain't so bad. But I sure wish he had better. He deserves it, you know? My goodness, he is a fine boy." She shook her head. "No, he not a boy anymore. He is a young man, and he deserved so much better than what I gave him."

"I'm sure he did," Coop quietly assured her. Glancing to his left, the lawyer noted three children, the oldest likely not more than four years old. He raised his hand in friendly greeting, but rather than wave back, they turned and ran into a shack down the street.

"Don't mind them," Hattie suggested, "the only white folks who come over here mean trouble for us. So you kind of scared them." She took a deep breath and with obvious effort sighed. "You ain't going to take the case, is you?"

Too ashamed to face the woman, he locked his eyes onto the house where the children had disappeared. He wondered, as he looked at the roof patched with an old Coca-Cola sign, how many folks lived in the tiny structure.

"I didn't figure you'd be able to help us," Hattie continued sadly. "Can't blame you. You can see I got nothing, and a big, important white man like you deserves to be paid. If I was young and still had my figure, I'd offer you my body, but I'm years past being someone even poor black men wants. But my talk shows you just how desperate I is. I gots no shame left. When it comes to Calvin, I'd do pretty much anything. And maybe I should have done a lot more."

Coop glanced back to Hattie. It was the first time he'd really looked at her since the office. She was no longer in her maid outfit; now she wore a simple, red-checked, short-sleeved dress. Her bare arms revealed a series of ugly scars running from her wrists to her shoulders.

"I heard about the fire," he said.

"Oh, these." She shrugged, glancing at her right

arm. "It weren't nothing. I was really blessed, Calvin didn't get burned anywhere. I guess the good Lord was looking out for him then." She paused, tears welling up in her eyes, and added, "But He's not looking out for him now, is He?"

"I don't know," Coop answered as his stomach pushed a foul taste into his mouth. Swallowing hard, he added, "I just don't know."

The lawyer's belly was not all that was burning. So was his head. Sweat first beaded on his brow before running down and stinging his eyes. This was even worse than he had expected. Just reciting the lie he had so carefully rehearsed made him feel small and weak. Only after easing into the chair nearest the stairs did he attempt to make his case. "I went by to see him, but he wouldn't talk to me. He doesn't trust me, Hattie. I don't think he could trust any white man."

She shook her head and looked out into the street, her eyes still avoiding her guest. "Guess he's got no reason to. He'll go to his early death hating, but maybe it's better than living a full life always hating. Hate just destroys everything it touches. His mother hated everyone and everything, and so it was truly merciful when she died. You see, the night of the fire, the hate in her was killed, but I guess it's rising up again in her son. Just wish I knowed how to get rid of hate. Yes, sir, just wish I did."

Hattie stopped and bit her lip. "But I want you

to understand, I knows in my heart he didn't kill the girl. He wouldn't do it. So when they put him in the chair and pull the switch, it won't do nothing about the hate in the person who actually took Becky's life. The hate will still be alive, and it will still be destroying folks. I knows that as surely as I knows my name." She balled her hands up in her lap and nodded.

Coop turned to study the woman sitting three feet to his right. She wasn't angry, just defeated. She was born with a bad hand and never got a chance to get any more cards.

"No reason for me to live, Mr. Coop," she sobbed. "I lost one child just a few days after she was born, I lost another child I loved when Becky was killed, and I will lose the last one when Calvin is murdered by the state. Forty-eight years of hard times, and only the promise I saw in those young people kept me going. Nothing to keep me going now; they might as well toss me in the Mississippi mud and cover me up."

She yanked herself from the chair and made her way to the front door. As she reached for the handle, she looked at her guest and said, "God bless you, Mr. Coop. Thanks for seeing my boy. Thanks for at least listening to me. And thanks for coming to my house to tell me face to face you tried but just couldn't find a way to help Calvin."

Coop watched her disappear into the tiny shack

before slowly making his way down the steps. He lingered beside his car taking in the poverty and desperation where a couple hundred of God's children called home and wondered how they managed to find any hope or peace. After all, their world was one without promise. Was there anything any sadder than a life without enough hope to even generate dreams? His friends, those folks on the other side of the tracks, would assure him what happened in this world was not any of his business. And maybe they were right. At least it was what he needed to believe right now. But deep down, he couldn't find a way to rationalize the way things were with the way things should be. And there was no rationalization for what he'd just done; it was just pure cowardice.

Opening the door, he turned the key and brought the V-8 to life. Slipping the car into reverse, he backed up into an open lot, pushed the shifter into drive, and headed in the direction of his home. As he picked up speed, he looked back at the dusty scene in his rearview mirror. The three kids were once more in the street. The white boogieman was leaving and they again felt safe.

8

"What's wrong, Dear?" Judy asked as she wandered into the living room from the kitchen. "You hardly said anything at supper, and here I find you staring blankly at a TV show you don't even like. Something must be on your mind."

Tall and thin, Judy Lindsay was blessed with a model's figure and classic high cheekbones. Her lips were full, her skin fair, and her eyes a deep blue. Her brunette shoulder-length hair had natural body and always looked fixed. In fact, Coop often joked that she always looked so perfect, the wind must blow around her.

Taking a seat in the overstuffed brown chair that matched the couch where her husband had perched, Judy paused, took a deep breath, and studied the twenty-by-fifteen-foot room. Two dolls and a kick ball had found their way under an oak rocker, and a coloring book along with three broken crayons—blue, red, and orange— had been pushed under the TV. At least the green area rug was clean, the family photos on the far wall were straight, and the coffee table and end tables were free of dust. It was as good as it was going to get with three kids.

Reaching forward, she picked up the latest

copy of *Good Housekeeping* and pretended to scan an article on bathroom remodeling, which their sixty-year-old home actually needed, before finally tossing the magazine back onto the table, snapping her fingers, and blurting out, "What is it? I haven't seen that look on your face since the day your mother died."

"It's nothing," he fibbed.

"Oh, yes, it is," she softly argued, not for a second buying his response. "And whatever it is, you need to talk about it. So why don't you turn off the TV and lay your problems on the line."

"Not sure I want to tell you," he quietly explained. "It shouldn't be bugging me like it is. It's not a big deal, and with a good night's sleep, I should be able to forget it. I've just got to face that there are some things I can't change."

Judy smiled, got up, pushed the seventeen-inch Zenith's power button, and then walked back over to take a place beside her husband on the couch. Though talkative and inquisitive by nature, she vowed to say nothing until he decided what direction to take the conversation. Still, the next ten minutes of listening to him breathe all but caused her to break out in hives.

"Where are the kids?" he finally asked.

Crossing her right leg over her left knee, she straightened her pencil skirt and announced, "Clark's asleep, and Dina and Dede are playing in their room."

"Good," he mumbled. "How was your day?"

"I took care of the kids, washed some clothes, and did the week's shopping, so it was nothing out of the ordinary. Oh, I did shoot a bear in the backyard. I had to borrow a gun from the Smiths. It only took me three shots to bring him down. I pulled it up on the back porch. Do you think we should have it mounted, and how do you feel about bear steak for supper tomorrow?"

"Fine," he said, and added, "You just do what you think is best."

She grinned. He hadn't heard a word she had said. So why not keep the mix of truth and fable going? "Yes, it was a nice day. I think the high was in the mid-eighties, so it was a bit sticky, but it's cooling off nicely now. I think the heat actually wore the bear out, too. Maybe that's why he didn't charge the kids when they were out taunting him. I think Clark thought he was a pony. He tried to ride him."

Coop took a deep breath and nodded. "I bet they had fun."

Tired of playing games, Judy stood up and moved directly in front of her husband. "Coop, everybody's talking about what happened to poor Becky Booth. You know I visited with her last week at church about babysitting for us when we go to the Chamber Banquet next week. I called her mother today, but Martha was just too broken up to talk." She paused a moment before finally asking, "Is Becky's rape and murder what is troubling you?"

"She wasn't raped," Coop quickly shot back.

"It's what everybody is saying," she quickly explained.

"It's a rumor," he quietly assured her. "It's not as if people need to add gossip to a tragedy already too large to comprehend."

"It's just the way folks are," she added. "They want to believe the worst."

"Judy, I don't know what I'd do if something like that happened to one of our kids."

She fully understood. She'd been thinking the same thing all day. Resting her hand on his arm, she asked, "So, is this all about Becky?"

"Yes and no," he admitted. "I can't believe she's dead. I can't believe someone would brutally murder such an innocent young woman. I can't even fathom evil like that existing, but . . ."

"But what, Coop?"

"Judy, what else are folks saying about the crime?"

She sat back on the couch and turned to where she was facing him. After folding her hands in her lap, she shrugged. "Just that they caught the person who did it."

"You mean Calvin Ross?"

"That's the name I heard," she replied. "He was the son of the family's maid. I heard they found the murder weapon at the crime scene and it has his name on it."

Rubbing his forehead, Coop asked, "What else are folks saying?"

"You know how folks around here are," she answered.

"What do you mean?" he demanded.

"Almost everyone is blaming it on the fact he's a Negro, and they keep saying there is just a mean streak in black men. When they see a white woman, they just can't help themselves."

He nodded. "Do you believe it, Judy?"

"You mean about Negroes?" she asked.

"Yeah. Do you believe what they say about them?"

"Coop, you know me better. I went to school with black kids in Ohio. They were my friends growing up. They weren't any different from you and me. But why is what I think important now? Why make me reassure you how I feel and how I think? We've talked about the shallowness of prejudice going back to our second date. You know where I stand, and I thought you felt the same."

He took another deep breath, pulled himself off the couch, and looked out their picture window into the dark night. Folding his arms across his white dress shirt, he sighed. "Judy, I don't know what to think anymore. After today I'm not sure what really matters to me. I always thought it was justice, not the town, but the legal term. I always believed I was a man who had the courage to stand up for what was right. Now I'm thinking I might be a coward." He shook his head. "No, I'm not thinking that; I know I am as yellow as lemonade."

He jumped a little when she stood and placed her hand on his shoulder. "You need to get whatever is on your mind out in the open."

"Maybe I do," he answered quietly, "and maybe I don't."

Putting her arm around his waist, she whispered, "Only you know."

"How much do you like living in Justice?" he asked.

"I like living anywhere with you."

"That's not an answer," he snapped.

"Okay," she replied, "I liked Nashville better, and if I had my druthers, I would really rather go back to Dayton. I guess I'll always be an Ohio girl at heart. Go Buckeyes!"

"So," he said, his eyes still focused on the scene outside the window, "if we had to leave Justice, you wouldn't be too unhappy?"

"Did you get a job offer somewhere?" she asked. "Is it what's eating at you?"

"No," he explained quietly, "I got a job offer here. It pays nothing and carries with it the assuredness that lepers would be more welcome on the streets in Justice, Mississippi, than I would be."

The room filled with an awkward silence, and Judy moved in front of Coop, encircling him with both her arms. As she did, he dropped his left hand to her shoulder and leaned his head down on top of hers. He let it rest there until she finally spoke.

"You've been asked to represent Calvin Ross?"

"His mother asked me," he admitted. "Actually, Hattie Ross is his aunt, but she's raised the boy and she swears he didn't do it. Even the sheriff has his doubts. And the family doesn't have the money to hire a good lawyer."

"The state will assign one," she suggested.

"Yeah," he answered, "and whoever that is, he won't have the experience or desire to do anything more than show up and wave good-bye to the kid as he is shipped off to death row."

"But you don't want to take the job," Judy said. "And I think I know the reason."

"Tell me why I'm hesitating?" he asked while dropping his arms and digging his hands deeply into his pockets.

"Because you're worried about me and the kids. You think we have this peaceful, picture-book-perfect life, and it is somehow more important than a capital case involving a Negro. And yet, if you were single and we weren't in the picture, you'd take it in a New York minute. And then there's the fact that Becky was a part of a family your family has known for generations."

He yanked his hands from his pockets, pulled free from her arms, and moved out the front door to the porch. She followed him step for step. He spoke only after they'd both taken a seat on the swing.

"I've known the Booths all my life," he sighed. "Gosh, I remember when Becky was born. But it is more than just knowing them. I'm a part of this culture. My people helped make Justice what it is today. If I take this case, I will be going against everyone who has ever supported me. I will be seen as worse than Benedict Arnold."

"I don't really think it scares you," Judy said. "I mean, the young man I met at Vanderbilt didn't mind swimming upstream. You were an idealist then. I figure some of your idealism still exists."

"Maybe," he replied grimly, "but I was in a different city; no one really knew me. I could easily stand up for what I believed, because I wasn't going to be there forever. It's different now. If I defend Calvin, I will be hated. If I get him off, I will be hated even more. And you and the kids will be hated, too. I don't think there is any coming back from doing this. I won't have a practice, we won't have any friends, and I'm afraid I might even be risking our lives."

"Risks are a part of living well," she assured him. "And I like to live well!"

He shook his head. "Risks with the chance of good returns are worth taking sometimes. But there is no good return on this investment. Right or wrong, I will lose and you will, too."

"But what about the young man sitting in jail?" she asked.

Coop shook his head. "The odds are so stacked against him in Justice, he might have one chance in a hundred, even if I were to represent him."

Judy drew him closer and whispered, "It's one more than he would have if you don't take the case."

"It would ruin us in Justice," he assured her. "They'd run us out of town on a rail."

She patted his back. "I think you'd like Dayton."

"Do they have bears there?" he asked with a lopsided grin.

"Have I ever told you that you look just like a young Clark Gable?"

"Yeah, a few dozen times." He laughed. Then, his face suddenly serious, "This doesn't mean I'm taking the case. My dad always said to think things over before making a move that could change your whole life. I need to consider this for at least a day."

"How you going to work out that answer?" she asked.

"Going to a pond," he announced. "Not going to the office tomorrow, just going to do some fishing, some thinking, and maybe a bit of praying."

9

Wednesday, June 24, 1964

The morning sky was nickel gray, and the humidity was close to ninety percent. It was a day made for staying in cool, dry places and drinking big glasses of sweet iced tea. The last place anyone would want to be this morning was at the sheriff's office battling mice for the breeze created by the building's six-inch oscillating fan. But at just past nine, it's where Cooper Lindsay was. Parking his blue Ford outside on the gravel parking lot, he nervously scanned the streets to see who might be observing his visit. Due to the fact that the building was two blocks from the nearest business, he was relieved to find he had the street and the parking lot to himself.

Opening the door and stepping from the car, he was surrounded by a sense of dread even darker than the clouds. He had been thinking about nothing else for two days, and yet he still didn't want to do what he was doing. He would have rather been digging ditches with a chain gang than marching into this ancient brick building. And he wouldn't have been here if his sense of

76

guilt didn't outweigh his fear. And right now, as he hesitantly made his way up the cracked concrete sidewalk, he truly wished he had been born a coward.

Grabbing the knob, he twisted it and opened the door. As the outer office was once more empty, he quickly made his way to where Wylie Estes spent a good portion of his days. This time he didn't knock.

"I'm surprised to see you again," the sheriff said as he looked up from his desk and watched Coop walk into his lair. While his words professed some shock, Estes's tone indicated just the opposite.

"I'm a little surprised myself," the lawyer admitted.

"What do you need this time?" Estes asked. "I mean, two visits in one week! Wow! I feel honored! I might even put you on my Christmas card list."

"I went fishing yesterday," Coop explained.

"Catch anything?" the sheriff asked.

"Never put the line in the water," the guest explained. "I just needed to do some soul searching." He shrugged. "Guess it was my way of putting off what I knew had to be done."

"I've done some of that kind of fishing myself," Estes admitted.

Coop forced a smile before muttering, "I need to see the Ross kid again."

"I wouldn't advise," the lawman said with a stiff grin. "He's an angry boy today."

"Wylie," Coop sighed, "I don't care if he's angry or not, I want to see him."

A large yawn, accompanied by the dark circles under his eyes proved the lawyer had slept little since Monday. And now, if he followed through on his plans, he would likely sleep even less over the next few weeks.

Estes shrugged. "Well, I guess it is your funeral." After retrieving his keys from the desk, the khaki clad lawman got up and headed to the door at the back of the room.

For the second time, Coop followed the sheriff into the jail area and back to where the city's now most-hated man was housed. He watched as Estes unlocked the cell door, and after it swung open, he apprehensively strolled in with all the enthusiasm of a condemned man heading to his execution. He waited until the sheriff left before finally looking at the young man he'd come to see.

As Calvin stood against the back wall of his cell, the rage still showed in his battered face. He looked as if he were ready for a fight, and though Coop was taller and outweighed the kid by thirty pounds, he still felt intimidated. At this moment, with his energy level only slightly higher than his enthusiasm for his job, if a battle of fists did break out, the lawyer would place his money on Calvin. As the young man continued to stare holes through Coop, the latter attempted to defuse the awkward situation.

"Yeah, you thought you ran me off on Monday. After our meeting, you probably figured I'd be joining the group who wants to determine your fate without a trial. And if I were as smart as my grades in law school indicated I was, I would have joined the group. But I can't go there. If you're innocent, then you need to at least have a fighting chance, and I'll give you a better one than whomever the state would assign to your case."

"What's in it for you?" Calvin snarled.

Coop smiled grimly. "Let's just say, if there is a lynching party and they only have one rope, they'd likely choose me over you."

The young man tilted his head to the right as if considering Coop's words and then pointed to the metal chair. After the attorney grabbed a seat, Calvin eased down into a sitting position on his bunk.

"Can I ask you some questions?" Coop began.

The prisoner shrugged.

"The first one is obvious, but I need to get it off the plate before we do anything else. It doesn't matter which way you answer, I will still be your attorney, but I need to hear the answer from your lips, and you have to shoot straight with me. You get that?"

"Sure," the young man answered.

Coop took a deep breath, "Someone murdered Becky Booth. Was it you?"

Calvin didn't move. He didn't open his mouth or even blink. He just resolutely stared at his visitor.

As he patiently waited for the reply, Coop leaned back in the chair until the front legs left the floor and he felt metal contact the brick wall. Then, for all practical purposes, time stood still. After two full minutes, the impatient lawyer broke the silence.

"You have to answer. I have to know one way or the other. If you did it, then I will prepare for a defense to save you from execution. If you didn't do it, then I have to move heaven and earth to prove you are innocent."

Dropping the chair's front legs back to the concrete floor, Coop leaned forward and brought his hands together while resting his elbows on his knees. This time he vowed he would wait until Calvin spoke even if it took all day.

As the seconds became minutes and as he attempted to put himself in the kid's place, Coop's eyes found the floor and considered what he knew about the case. Before the girl's murder, Calvin was profanely dressed down by her father for daring to even speak to Becky. The day after her death, he'd been dragged out of church, handcuffed, taken to jail, and obviously beaten.

Plus, all his life he'd been told to watch his place, to play the role of the good Negro and to never question any white's authority. He couldn't eat in nice restaurants or live in a part of the town with city services and paved streets. He had gone to a school with ancient desks and leaking roofs. And he had been told time and time again that he would never be treated with respect by anyone whose skin was fair. So why should he trust Coop? After what he'd been through in his nine-teen years of living, why should he trust anyone who was white?

Coop glanced back across the narrow cell, trying to again gauge Calvin's mood. Nothing obvious was written on the young's man swollen face, but the eyes, which had been burning in rage two days ago, now told a much different story. They were lifeless. Coop was looking at a man who had no hope. The prisoner had taken all he could; he looked up and read the scoreboard, and victory was so far out of his reach, nothing mattered anymore. He had given up.

As time continued to drag by and ten silent minutes became twenty, the lawyer shifted his attention to the cell itself. The tiny area was dirty and smelled like an outhouse. There was mold on the walls and grime on the floor. The mattress was ripped, stained, and obviously lumpy. A filthy, torn blanket served as the only cover. And then there were the insects and rodents, including one large roach crawling up the wall toward the barred window.

"It's not so bad, you know," Calvin quietly observed. "Maybe to you it is, but not to me. If it wasn't for the bars and the locked door, I've stayed in worse. Hattie and I lived in a chicken coop for a few years."

Coop's eyes moved back to the no-longer-mute kid.

"Mr. Lindsay," he continued, his voice now showing none of the wrath it had during the previous meeting, "I didn't do it, but it really doesn't matter. If I did or didn't, the case is decided and the kind of justice I've seen all my life will be dispensed after the farce of a trial is over."

Calvin paused for a moment, looking toward the light coming through the window, then sadly noted, "You don't need to defend me. Battles you can't win aren't worth fighting. Believe me, being black, I know. So there is no use in you giving up your life just to fruitlessly try to save mine. I can take being hated; I've grown used to it, but there is no reason for hate's shadow to fall on you just because of me."

"Calvin," Coop cut in. But before he could put his own thoughts into words, the young man continued.

"We can't help the way we were born. You were born white and I was not, and it gives you the advantage. Through fate or luck, your kind makes the rules and controls the game of life. And if Jackie Robinson, Nat King Cole, Rosa Parks, and Martin Luther King haven't changed it, then you and I can't either. There is no miracle cure for this kind of thinking. It has been rooted in man for thousands of years. Those folks who are your friends see me for what they have been told I am. They see me as a sex-starved animal. They see me as an evil to be eliminated."

Calvin looked back to the window before adding, "So thank you for your time, but it's just not right for you to be taken down with me. It's just not right."

Coop smiled. "The other day you pegged me."

Calvin shrugged. "Not sure I get what you mean."

"The man I was the other day is just what you described," Coop explained. "I was a coward who didn't want to and wouldn't stand up to the powers in this town. Today I'm a man you can trust and who'd rather have your respect than any other person in this whole town, except for maybe my wife, kids, and Hattie."

"Just words," Calvin replied with a sly smile. "You almost had me a while ago, but white folks only do stuff like this when there is something in it for them."

"Maybe," Coop answered, "history does kind of prove you're right. But white or black, what is a life filled with guilt? It's worthless. I found it out when I tried to go to sleep the last two nights. Besides, I'm doing this as much for my father as I am you. You've got no choice. I'm entering this fight. And maybe my reason for doing it is because I can't live with the guilt if I don't."

Coop pulled himself off the chair and slowly crossed over to the young man. He stared down at him for a moment before making a request. "Would you stand up, please?"

Calvin pushed himself off the bunk and stood before the lawyer. They looked into each other's eyes for a few seconds before Coop made another request. "I want to shake your hand."

The young man refused the request, keeping his hand close to his side.

"My handshake is as good as any legal document," Coop assured him. "Once you take my hand, you and I are now a team. The team's goal is save your life."

"Not going to," Calvin replied bluntly. "No use shaking a white man's hand. You might be one of the better white men; in fact, I kind of think you are, but still, I learned a long time ago, your word is no good. You might look at me as a person in here, one on one, but when a group of whites is around you, you will change. I know because history and time has proved it. And if you look in a mirror, you'd admit it, too."

Coop took a step back and shook his head. He

was about to post an argument, but the prisoner cut him off. "I still don't trust you. There is something wrong with this whole setup. Important white folks in Justice don't do this sort of thing."

As Calvin crossed his arms and once more glared at the visitor, Coop shook his head. The rage was back. Just when he'd thought he'd found a bridge of trust, it had been blown up again. Nothing about this case was going to be easy.

10

Calvin had almost allowed himself to be sucked into thinking that the white lawyer might be on the up and up. His desperation had almost given way to hope. But then a dozen memories of promises whites had made to him in the past leaped from the dark recesses of his mind and back into the present. Those experiences framed this moment, and thus, the lawyer's pledge suddenly rang hollow. Why should he trust him?

"Wylie," Coop yelled down the hall.

"You ready to get out in the fresh air?" the sheriff yelled back.

The fresh air was something Calvin was sure he'd never smell again. There were a lot of other things gone now, too. No more fishing. No singing with the choir or dancing in one of those blues clubs they had in Memphis. There would be no more of Hattie's butter beans and cornbread served on the front porch on hot August nights. In fact, there wouldn't be many more days for anything. And here was the man who asked him to trust him, the guy who said he'd be on his team, making the promise and now calling the sheriff and walking out before he'd even asked him about the case. So Lindsay wasn't really interested in making sure Calvin got a fair shake; he was just another part of the white justice system signed on to make this *appear* like the colored boy had gotten a square deal, before they took him down and fried him in the chair.

As Estes finally made it to the cell door, Calvin studied the two men. Neither of them would have had the positions they had if they had been black. Neither of them would be worth a plug nickel in Justice if they had been Negroes.

"Wylie," the lawyer announced, "I don't need out, but I do need my briefcase. It's in my car. Would you mind getting it for me?"

"No problem," the sheriff replied.

This was interesting. Why was the lawyer sticking around? Was there a chance he actually was on the up and up? Calvin really wanted to believe it, but he still wanted to believe in Santa Claus, too.

As Estes departed on the errand, Coop once

more turned back Calvin's way. "We are going to go over in detail the day Becky Booth died. I need to know everything you did and everywhere you went. I have to know who you talked to, what you said, and even how you reacted. Let's start with what time you got up."

"Why?" Calvin barked.

"Because I need the facts," Coop barked back.

"And you really want to do this? You really want to represent me?"

"Nope," Coop replied, "I really don't want to do it, but the only way I can go back to your house and look your mother in the eyes is to take this case and do my best. Like it or not, you've got me in your corner."

"She's really my aunt."

"You can call her what you want," Coop shot back. "I've got a question for you."

"So?" Calvin sneered. "Asking it might make you feel important, it might even make you think you're doing me a favor, but it doesn't mean I'll answer it."

"Fine," Coop said, "but I'm asking it anyway. Do you love Hattie?"

He was caught off guard. Why did the lawyer want to know?

"What does that have to do with anything?" Calvin asked.

"A lot," the lawyer assured him as he reached up to loosen his tie and open his shirt collar. "If you don't love her, then I can feel pretty good about walking away from you. Because if you don't love that woman after all she's done for you, then you don't deserve anyone's help. Now, do you love her?"

"Yeah," Calvin answered softly, the anger suddenly passing from his heart. "I love her."

How could he not love the only woman who had ever had real faith in him? She was his rock, his cheerleader, his defender, and the one person who always saw the best in him.

"Okay then," Coop explained, "I'm doing this for her. You need to understand this. And because you love her, you are going to work with me as I try to save your neck. You are going to help me, because you owe her. Do you understand?"

Calvin nodded, but warned, "But let's get this straight, I still don't really trust you. You're up to something."

"Okay," Coop said, "believe what you want. We'll work through that later. For now, let's talk about the day Becky Booth died. Listen, I need you to tell me everything as it happened from the moment you got up until the time Hattie got home from the church at night."

Calvin eased back on the cot and considered the request. Could he remember everything about Saturday? At this moment, it was just a blur. And even if he were able to piece together the details, could he come up with anything to help the attorney in finding something to put suspicion on someone else? This was a tall order. And what if he gave the man that information? Was he sure the lawyer wouldn't just bury it in order to bury him? As he was still trying to organize his thoughts and bring the events of that day into sharp focus, Estes returned with the lawyer's briefcase.

"Here you go, Coop, but before I open the cell, I will have to look through it."

"I understand," the lawyer agreed. "It's not locked, but be careful and don't let anything fall out. There's some stuff that could easily break in there."

A now curious Calvin watched as the sheriff propped the dark brown leather case against the cell door and popped the latches. Estes quickly glanced through the contents, seemingly satisfied all was in order, before he snapped it shut and slipped it through the cell bars to Coop.

"Thanks," the lawyer said, "It might take me a hour or so to make some notes and get the information I need. I'll yell when we are finished here." Coop said nothing more until the lawman made his way back down the hall and into his office.

"Okay, what time did you get up?" Coop asked pulling a legal pad out of the case and a pen from his gray suit jacket pocket.

Calvin shrugged. Like it or not, there were no

other options. He was going to have to trust some-one, and this was the only man who was even offering him a chance. Besides, maybe Santa Claus was real!

Leaning back on the cot until his back touched the cool, damp bricks, Calvin began this story: "Not sure of the exact time, but it was just before dawn. I'd promised to help our neighbor on the back side of our house butcher a couple of hogs. His place is across a creek, through a patch of woods, and his name is Joe Green. It took some time. I didn't finish up to about eleven or so."

Coop jotted down the information and without even looking up posed the next question. "What did you do then?"

"I came home and ate some cold biscuits and leftover sausage and then went down to the creek and cleaned up. As it was Saturday and I had nothing else to do, I walked downtown to see what was happening."

"Is that when you saw Becky?"

"Yeah, Mr. Miller was having problems hanging a sign outside his store, and I climbed up onto the ladder and tied it off for him. He's almost seventy; I thought he'd fall if he tried to do it by himself. Becky was walking down the sidewalk when I stepped down from the ladder."

"And," Coop asked, "you talked to her?"

"Yeah," Calvin admitted, "I did. It's not like I normally talk to white girls—I know better—but

Becky and I have known each other all our lives. So when she said hi, I answered. Then she asked me how my first year of college at Hillman had been. I was telling her about a girl I was sweet on, when her dad came out of the Western Auto. He pulled her to one side and then pushed me back against the store's show window. I hit the glass so hard I thought it might break. He then cussed me out royally for not knowing my place."

Coop looked up from taking notes. "Did any-one see this confrontation between you and Brent Booth?"

"There wasn't any confrontation," Calvin explained, "I said nothing; I just let his tongue wag. And, yes, there must have been a dozen or more folks who watched it take place, including one rich, white woman who I know hates black men."

Coop looked up and asked, "Who was that?"

"Linda Maltose," Calvin explained. "She thinks she is really something."

The lawyer shrugged, glanced back to his legal pad, and continued, "So you didn't threaten Brent Booth?"

"I'm not stupid," Calvin replied. "I just took it, and when he got done yelling and took his hands off my shirt, I hustled on back to our house. Once there, I pulled out a book, sat out on our porch, and spent a few hours reading. I still had my nose in that novel when Hattie came home."

"What time was it?"

"Maybe two."

"Where had she been?" the lawyer asked.

"At the Booths," Calvin explained. "She works about a half day on Saturday getting their meals ready for the weekend and making sure all of the clothes the family needs for the next two days are washed and ironed."

"So," Coop continued, "what did you do next?"

"Hattie had me help her straighten up the house, and then I watched as she trimmed one of the pieces of meat Joe had given me for helping him. It was a butt ham. I remember her tossing the trimmings into a pot of pinto beans, adding some water, and putting them on the stove to cook."

"Was it for supper?" Coop asked.

"No," Calvin answered, "it was for lunch at church the next day. It's why the beans were on low; they'd have been on high if we needed them for supper. We had leftovers at night from our main meal. A bit of roast and some turnips."

"Then what happened?"

"We sat on the porch and talked a bit before Claude and Mamie Johnson came over. They live next door. Our houses are so close they almost rub up against each other. I guess you could say we have no secrets from the Johnsons and they have none from us. They can smell what we're cooking almost as soon as we put it on the stove, and we can listen to their radio as clear as if it was in our kitchen."

"Yeah," Coop said, "I noticed when I went to see Hattie yesterday."

Calvin was shocked. "You went over to our side of town?"

"Yes," the attorney replied, "and got a new perspective being there, too. Now, we don't have much time, pick up your story."

"Well, first Claude showed us a new instant camera they'd gotten as a gift from their son. He even took a picture of Hattie and me, and a minute later he pulled back the paper and there it was! The first instant picture I'd ever seen. He gave it to us, and Hattie carefully put it in her Bible. We then killed some time talking about everything from the weather to community gossip, and before I realized it, it was five. Hattie and I went inside and ate early because she had to be at the church getting things ready for the big all-day Founder's celebration taking place the next day. I could have gone with her, but I decided to stay home and finish reading. Sure wish I had gone now."

The lawyer looked up, traced his lips with the top of his ballpoint pen, and then asked, "Did Hattie tell you anything before she left?"

"Only to clean up the clothes I'd been wearing when we worked on the hogs. I'd left them on the front porch along with my big knife I'd used that morning. Then she and Mamie headed off to church."

"So," Coop verified, "you cleaned up the stuff and then stayed home and read."

"Well," Calvin admitted, "you're partially right. I stayed home and read, but I didn't clean up anything. When Hattie got home at night, she whooped and hollered about my not doing my chores. I guess I was too wrapped up in *The Shoes of the Fisherman* to remember to do what she'd asked. It didn't sit too well with her."

"It's a good book," the lawyer acknowledged, "I can see how you would get lost in it." Coop looked back at his notes before posing the next question, "You said only Mamie Johnson went to the church. What did her husband do?"

"Well," Calvin smiled, "he stayed home. He told her he was going to do a bit of Bible study, but she had no more gone than three of his buddies came by to shoot some dice. I could watch the game and hear the conversation through our front room's open window. I could also smell the homebrew that Deacon Thomas had brought along. I found it amusing that a bunch of fifty-year-old men were acting like misguided teenagers."

"So all you did was read?"

"Practically all. I also had to add water to the beans." Calvin stopped as the evening suddenly drew into even sharper focus. "Yeah, and I talked to Big Mike Morgan and two of his friends for maybe fifteen minutes. They wanted to know if I'd come along with them to spin some disks at Sweet Ray Elliott's."

"Spin disks?" The lawyer asked as a confused look crossed his face.

"You know, play records."

"And who is this Sweet Ray?"

Calvin shook his head. "It's a place, a jive joint, kids hang out there, dance, smoke, and play music."

"Got it," Coop replied. "And what time did this"—he glanced back to his notes—"Big Mike come by?"

"Must have been about nine-fifteen to nine-thirty."

"You didn't see anybody else?"

"Not until Hattie and Mamie got home about eleven. We talked for a few minutes, then she put the food for tomorrow's potluck away and we went to bed. She was in her bedroom, and I slept on the couch like I always do." Calvin smiled. "Oh, and she did put her finger in my face for not doing anything with the stuff I'd been wearing to butcher the hog. She was still ranting about it the next morning when the Johnsons picked us up in their old gold Dodge to take us to church. We all laughed about it until Claude slipped on the knife as he stepped off the porch. Then, I guess just because he was so proud of his new toy, he took another picture of Hattie and me. Once again, she put it in her Bible."

The lawyer glanced back through his notes, took a deep breath filling his cheeks, and slowly pushed it out. Setting his legal pad onto the floor, he reached down, picked up his briefcase, opened it, and pulled out a camera exactly like the Johnsons' Polaroid. After retrieving some flash-bulbs, he stood up and studied his client.

What was this all about? Why did the lawyer need photographs to prepare his case? Calvin didn't have to wait long for the explanation.

"I want to take some pictures of you. I want to record every bruise we can still see on your body. I want to be able to document what they did to you in trying to get a confession. So stand up, take off your shirt, and let's get this taken care of."

Calvin stood and began unbuttoning the work shirt. As he did he felt a need to explain something to the attorney. "It was Mr. Fredrick that ordered the deputies to do this."

"The district attorney?" Coop asked. "K. C. Fredrick?"

"Yes, sir," Calvin replied as he pulled the shirt from his shoulders, "but you need to know, Sheriff Estes wouldn't have any part of it. When he couldn't stop it, he left the room. He's been good to me."

The lawyer snapped the flashbulb in place,

moved closer to his client, and took the first photo. The bright light in the dark room caused spots to fill Calvin's eyes. He could barely see Coop pull out the first shot to let it develop, insert another bulb, move to another spot, and snap another picture. He continued this exercise until he'd used up two packs of film and twenty bulbs. After studying each of the photos, Coop dropped them and the legal pad into the briefcase and watched as Calvin put his shirt back on. After the young man was once again dressed and his vision was clearing, the lawyer posed a final question.

"Would you mind if I look at your hands and arms?"

What a strange request! What did it have to do with anything? Nevertheless, rather than question the visitor, Calvin held them out.

"This cut on your finger," the lawyer asked, pointing to the left ring finger, "how did you get it?"

"When I was helping to butcher the hogs."

"Okay, hold your bare arms up, I need to take one more picture." After retrieving the camera, loading in a new pack of film and snapping on a final flashbulb, Coop took the last shot.

"This is a good start," Coop assured a still somewhat unwilling client. "I've got something to work on. We'll have a preliminary hearing tomorrow morning. Then the judge will likely set the trial for three weeks."

Calvin was shocked. Was it going to be so soon? It meant if he were found guilty, he might be put to death even before the year was out. Maybe even before his birthday in August.

"Wylie," the lawyer called out, "I'm ready." He then looked back to Calvin. "You understand everything?"

"Yes, sir," Calvin lied. He really didn't understand much at all. Starting with why Cooper Lindsay was representing him. There still had be a trick up his sleeve.

"Can we shake hands now?" the attorney asked.

With a ton of reservations, Calvin reached for the other man's right hand. When they clasped their hands together, he looked Coop in the eye, but the answers he needed could not be read there.

After the door had once more opened and closed and the mysterious lawyer left, Calvin sank back onto his bunk, closed his eyes. Had he given away too much? Had he paved his own doom by trusting this man? But what difference did it really make? He was sure the jury was only going to spend fifteen minutes before deciding the black boy needed to die.

11

Koffman Curtis Fredrick was just a touch over five-and-a-half feet in height. His skin was pasty white, his eyes dark, and though he had not hit the half-century mark, his salt-and-pepper hair was retreating for much higher ground. He was almost as round as he was tall, taking after his mother, Mable, who had been the librarian at Justice High for five decades. Yet his inability to keep his mouth shut for more than a few seconds at a time came from his father, a barber everyone called Wordy Will. K. C., as he had been called since infancy, was in one sense a meek milquetoast, a man who never challenged his mother, wife, or those in the Elks Club. But on Monday through Friday, when he embraced the title of Common County District Attorney, he morphed into a tyrant, flashing his power as if he were a light-house for truth, justice, and the American way, when in actuality he cared very little about any of those three virtues. It was the macho version of Fredrick who waddled into the sheriff's office at just past noon on Wednesday.

"Well," he spat through thick lips, "you taking good care of our murderer?"

Estes looked up from his desk and nodded. "He's being fed and tended to."

"Good," Fredrick smiled as he rubbed his hands together. "I want him healthy when he makes his last walk down death row."

"He'll be fit," the sheriff assured his guest. "Though I have my doubts we've got the right man."

"We've got the boy we need," Fredrick shot back seemingly not caring if what he said revealed his lack of character. After plopping down in a wooden chair and pulling his right leg over his left, which took considerable effort, he posed his next question. "Has he had any visitors?"

"Hattie's been here a couple of times."

"Fine," the DA replied. "She'll go back to the other side of the tracks with what she's seen, and it will help us keep the rest of those bucks in line."

Estes shook his head before announcing, "And he's had another visitor as well."

"Well, isn't he popular?" Fredrick laughed as he slapped his knee. "I suppose he's got a girlfriend who's worried about him."

"No," the sheriff replied casually, "he's got an attorney."

Fredrick grinned, as it was news he had expected, but still there was no reason to worry. The only lawyers who'd work this case were colored boys from Mobile and Atlanta, and they wouldn't have the means to investigate or put together any kind of defense. Besides, winning with both a Negro defendant and attorney would be like taking candy from a baby. A jury of whites wouldn't cotton to it at all.

"So, Wylie," Fredrick said, allowing his lips to smack with each new syllable as if relishing his own diction, "I'm guessing one of the colored churches raised the money to bring in one of those educated Negroes from out of town. Well, you treat him fine. You give him all he wants. I don't want us to come off as being anything but fair and accommodating in this case."

"Oh, don't worry, K. C.," Estes smiled, "I've treated him with the same respect I treat anyone else who comes into my jail. But you're wrong on a couple of counts."

The guest ran his short, stubby fingers over the top of his balding head before asking, "How am I wrong?"

"For one thing, K. C., the attorney is working for nothing"—Estes paused and smiled before icing his verbal piece of cake—"and the guy who is defending Calvin is white."

"What?" Fredrick asked disbelievingly.

This was certainly news he hadn't expected. Had Martin Luther King and his ilk gotten news on this matter and brought in some high-powered talent from the likes of Washington, New York, or Chicago? If it happened, then it would mean the national media would get involved and would spell nothing but trouble. The last thing he needed was one of those young network reporters like Dan Rather coming into town and giving Justice a black eye. After chewing on the prospect of an easy case suddenly getting complicated, the DA glanced back and demanded, "Where's this guy from?"

"Here," came the steady, emotionless reply.

"Who?"

"Coop Lindsay."

"You're joshing me, son. Coop's one of us. He grew up here. He'd never represent someone like Calvin Ross."

The sheriff smiled. "I'm not kidding, and if I were you I might start getting my act together. This is not one of those times when you can show up, point to the color of the guy's skin, and land another conviction. You're about to be challenged, and even if you win, I have a feeling you're not going to look very good as you take your bows."

"Coop is doing this to me?" Fredrick gasped.

"Not to you, K. C.," Estes explained, "he's doing it for Hattie Ross and probably for Calvin, too. I get the feeling Coop thinks the boy is innocent just like I do. The only difference is, I'm not brave enough to stand up for what I see might be a miscarriage of justice, and old Coop is."

Fredrick pulled a handkerchief from the inside pocket of his seersucker suit and used it to wipe his brow. Why would any man in his right mind upset the natural balance of things? Coop knew the rules; he understood how things worked in Justice. What was his game? The only outcome that could result during the trial would be for Coop to be cast in a horrible light in the community. Unless . . .

The DA quickly moved his eyes back to the sheriff. "Do you suppose Coop might have some kind of inkling who killed the girl?" When he fully realized the gravity of his words and the fact that they sounded like an admission, he tried to temper them by adding, "I mean, if by some chance Ross didn't do it. And I am sure he did."

Estes raised his feet, leaned back in his chair, and plopped his boots down on the top of his metal desk. He smiled for a few moments, shrugged, and asked, "Do you really have an inkling of who did it?"

"The Ross boy did it," came the quick but unsure response.

"I hope you're right."

"Come on, Wylie," a suddenly worried Fredrick begged, "does Coop have anything to make us look stupid?"

"I honestly don't know," the sheriff replied, "but you better make sure you've got the right boy. If you don't, and he does have something you missed when putting together this case, then you can kiss your job good-bye."

Had he missed something? Was there evidence pointing to someone else? Without even a wave or nod, a suddenly uncomfortable Fredrick awkwardly pushed himself to his feet and hurried to the door.

12

Fifteen minutes after leaving the jail, a winded district attorney pushed the doorbell at the antebellum home of John David Maltose. A few seconds later, a small, elderly black man dressed in a suit opened the door.

"Moses," Fredrick barked, "I need to see John David."

The servant stepped to the side as the fat man entered and then announced, "Mr. Maltose is in the study."

Walking over the tile floor and under a huge chandelier imported more than a century before from France, the DA's short legs rushed down the hall toward a room he knew well. As his leather heels clicked on the tile's surface, a maid looked up from polishing the dining room's wood walls. "You're in a powerful rush, Mr. Fredrick. You better slow down before you get yourself a case of high blood pressure."

Without stopping, Fredrick glanced over at the

caramel-skinned woman and nodded disdainfully. She was right, but he'd have to worry about his physical health later. For the time being, he had something far more important on his mind.

Not bothering to knock, the DA opened the twelve-foot high oak door and marched into the forty-foot square, bookshelf-lined room. Maltose was seated in an oversized, dark blue leather-backed swivel chair behind a massive mahogany desk talking on the phone. He looked up from the call long enough to point to a chair and then went back to his conversation.

"I don't care what you have to do, you get me the property. I like to fish on the private lake there, and I want to own it. Money is no object."

Fredrick found his seat, took a deep breath, and tried to relax and convince himself he had nothing to worry about. After all, John David could fix anything. This would be a walk in the park for the millionaire.

Glancing around the huge study, the DA studied the works of art hanging on the walls and resting on shelves. How much had it cost the thirty-eight-year-old businessman to amass all of these treasures? Probably more than K. C. would ever make in a lifetime. And then there was the antique furniture, like the large library table and chairs from Germany and the divan supposedly from one of Henry VIII's castles. Even the flasks, glasses, and decanters at the corner bar were obviously worth more than the hundred-year-old whiskey they held. Fredrick was still trying to guess the values of the items in this one room of the twenty-two-room mansion when he heard his host bark another order and hang up the phone.

As their eyes met, the tall, dark-eyed, powerfully built man smiled wickedly and said, "The only time you visit me is when you're in trouble, so what is it?"

Fredrick took a breath, swallowed hard, and meekly explained, "Probably nothing."

"Then leave," came the quick reply. "I don't have time to be bothered by people who have nothing on their mind."

"Let me rephrase," the DA suggested softly. "It might be something we need to address."

"Spit it out," Maltose demanded, rising from his chair and moving to the bar. As he poured a glass of scotch, his guest found a voice.

"The Booth murder, we might have hit a snag."

The tall man took a long drink, letting the liquid slide slowly down his throat before setting the crystal glass on a round walnut table. He smoothed the sleeves on his white dress shirt and checked the shine on black Italian loafers before looking back at his guest. As Maltose's accusing stare fell on Fredrick, the short man wished he'd opted to handle this situation on his own. But it was too late now; he'd opened the door, and now he had to walk in.

"What is it, man?" Maltose demanded as he closed the distance between them. "What have you messed up now? I thought you told me this was an open-and-shut case."

"You know who we arrested?" Fredrick asked.

"I haven't paid any attention to the details," came the reply. "All you told me was you got some Negro for the crime."

As Maltose's six-foot-four-inch frame hovered over him, Fredrick stammered out an explanation. "Cooper Lindsay is representing that colored boy."

"Isn't your evidence solid?" the big man demanded.

"We have enough to convict a Negro," came the explanation.

"Well," Maltose replied, while smoothing his mustache, "then it would seem to me you have nothing to worry about."

"Well, I hope not," Fredrick worriedly answered. "I mean it shouldn't be very hard to hang the Ross kid."

The host's eyes suddenly popped wide open, "Ross, you say?"

"Yeah, Hattie's nephew, that uppity boy who is going to college. Though I don't know how he got the money."

Maltose glanced toward the window, ran his right hand over his hair, and sighed. "So you arrested Calvin Ross?"

"Yeah," the DA shot back.

The host turned back to his guest and snapped out an order. "I don't want to see Calvin get the chair."

"But the Booths will expect—"

Maltose cut Fredrick off. "You heard me. I don't want to see Ross executed. And besides, why couldn't you find a better goat to frame?"

"Are you suggesting I'm framing someone?" the DA meekly asked.

"Let's not go there," Maltose shot back. "Now tell me about your problem."

As his host backed up and perched on the corner of his desk, Fredrick quietly asked, "Why would Coop take the case if he didn't have enough evidence to get Ross off? That's what worries me."

Maltose tilted his head as if puzzling on the question before folding his arms and grinning. "Did you ever read Sherlock Holmes? He's a detective in stories by Sir Arthur Conan Doyle."

Fredrick shook his head. What did the words of a dead English author have to do with anything?

"Well," the big man continued, "when things get interesting, Sherlock always says, 'The game's afoot.' It seems you are now in a race. If Coop does have something, then he will use this trial to get something else he wants. Maybe he wants your job or perhaps a bit of national publicity. He is too smart to take a case that is not a sure win. There is too much at stake. After all, he is risking being run out of his own town just for considering a murder case with a Negro defendant. No man without something really big to gain rushes into a situation like this."

"I feel the same way," Fredrick admitted. "So what do we do?"

"You make sure it never comes to trial," Maltose suggested.

"How do I do it?"

"Get to Ross and make a deal now. Get him to admit he did it in exchange for time in jail. I think he'd rather be in prison than go to the chair. I'll take care of things afterward."

"But what if he doesn't go for it?"

"Then you come back to me," Maltose explained. "I'll drum up a few things to make it either very hot for Mr. Cooper Lindsay or very profitable. The weather is perfect for this sort of thing." He looked down at an obviously confused DA and grinned. "You just aren't real deep, are you?"

"What?" Fredrick asked.

"Just get back to the jail and turn the temperature up on the Ross boy. Hold his feet to the fire. Get him to cop a plea or put the finger on one of his friends. In the meantime, I will be readying a backup plan, just in case your power of persuasion falls short. I'm not going to let the state execute someone you framed, even if he is a Negro!"

Fredrick nodded, stood up, and extended his hand toward his host. Maltose raised his eyebrows but didn't bother unfolding his arms. For a few uncomfortable moments, neither man moved. Finally, the DA awkwardly pulled his arm down and pushed his hand into his pants pocket.

"Thank you," Fredrick said.

"You know the way out," Maltose said dryly. "And close the door when you leave the room. I don't need to have any more trash blow in here today."

The words stung, but not deeply enough for Fredrick to protest. The wealthy man who owned so much of Common County owned people, too, and the DA would be a willing slave to the man's wishes for the rest of his life. There was no escape. The only satisfaction was in knowing he wasn't alone, and as long as he played the game, he also would never lack for cash in his pocket.

13

The ringing pulled Coop's attention from the papers and photographs on his desk. Putting down a black and white eight-by-ten shot of the crime scene, he reached over and picked up the office desk phone.

"Coop Lindsay."

"Good to know you are alive," came Judy's quick reply. "Supper has been ready for more than an hour. I finally got tired of waiting and let the kids eat."

Glancing across the room to the old school-house-style clock on the wall, the attorney noted the time. 6:35! He'd been so immersed in his work, he'd lost three hours.

"Sorry, hon," he sighed. "Wylie finally got me all the evidence files. It took a while to get copies made of the photographs, then autopsy results were delivered about mid-afternoon, and I had to copy those as well. With the preliminary hearing tomorrow, I'm just trying to get my ducks in a row and I must have lost track of time."

"So do I need to put things in the oven or the fridge?" Judy asked.

"No reason to leave them out," Coop replied. "I need to use all the time I have before I go to court tomorrow. Once I walk into the courtroom and sit at the table with Calvin, the cat will be out of the bag. Everyone will know who is representing him. Initially, I fear the news will cause my phone to ring off the wall, and then that will be followed by no one talking to me at all. So, for a few days, it might be hard to work."

"Coop," Judy said, "I've been thinking about it. Maybe the kids need to go and spend a few weeks with my folks in Ohio. Mom and Dad

111

have been begging us to have them for part of the summer. What do you think?"

"I think it is a great idea," he assured her. "In fact, why don't you call them tonight? Get it set up. I'd rather the children not see and hear what I fear will happen." He paused and looked back at a stark image of Becky Booth lying in the field. "Maybe you might want to stay with them, too."

"No way, Mr. Lindsay," she quickly replied. "I will be here with you each step of the way."

He knew there was no use arguing with her. She had a mind of her own, and once she set on doing something, no one could talk her out of it. And he had the feeling she could likely withstand the heat just as well as he could. "Okay, Judy, have it your way, but please get the kids out tomorrow morning. I want them a hundred miles north of here by the time the hearing starts. And why don't you at least drive them all the way? I think it would be better for our trio of munchkins if you were there at your folks the first night. It would help them settle in."

"So how long will you be?" she asked. "I'd like to see you tonight."

After glancing at his desk and then the legal pad where he had scribbled a few dozen pages of notes, he leaned back into the receiver. "Maybe an hour, maybe two."

"Love you," she said.

"You, too," he answered and hung up.

As he again turned his attention to the photo of the body at the crime scene, something didn't ring true. Maybe it was the angle, but something just looked obviously wrong. While there was a blood trail leading to the spot, there wasn't enough blood pooled around the body.

Reaching to the autopsy report, he studied the findings of the state examiner. The wounds had been numerous and had left the body all but drained of blood. So where was it? He could only come up with one answer. She must have been killed somewhere else and dragged to Lovers Park. Thus, he was going to have to retrace Becky Booth's steps the day of the murder. Right now, beyond knowing where she had been when she'd run into Calvin downtown, he had nothing.

As he tried to assemble a plan for mapping out Becky's last day on earth, something else he'd overlooked hit him. Why hadn't the local officials tracked the information down? Why had they not put together this timeline in order to run down all possible suspects? And why was there no mention in their report of the murder taking place some-where else and the body being disposed of at Lovers Park?

Picking up the report and going back through it again, he was next confused by the depth of the wounds. They varied from just a few inches in some places, while in others they went almost clear through the body. Some were ragged and others were clean. It made no sense why was there so much variance from place to place on her body.

Grabbing the phone, Coop dialed a number he'd known since childhood. On the third ring, a familiar male voice picked up. "Hello, Dr. Willis here."

"Hey, John," Coop began, "this is Coop Lindsay, and I have a medical question for you."

"One of the kids sick?" came the quick reply. "I can grab my bag and be right over."

"No, no one's sick. I'm looking at the autopsy report and photographs in the Becky Booth murder. And something is bothering me."

There was a long pause before the doctor came back on the line. "Why?"

Coop took a deep breath, said a short prayer for acceptance and understanding, then launched into his explanation. "I'm going to represent Calvin Ross. I just don't think he did it. I don't have proof yet, but Hattie swears he is innocent and she's pretty convincing."

This time the doctor didn't make Coop wait for a reply. "Hattie is one of the finest women in this county, white or colored. I've often said I'd rather have her on my side, praying for me and supporting me, than my own pastor. But you're not doing yourself any favors by taking on this case. Folks around here aren't going to take kindly to it at all."

"Yeah, I know," Coop admitted, "but, John, what would my dad have done? After all, you and he grew up together. You remained best friends until he died."

This time the response took a few seconds. "You are your father's son. He would not worry about what was the expected thing to do; he would consider what was the right and moral thing. If Calvin was innocent, he'd be in his corner." The doctor paused and then asked, "Now what do you need?"

"Did you see Becky's body?"

"No, I didn't, as she was already dead when they found her and took her to the funeral home. Then it was decided to ship her to the capital so the state's medical examiner could do the autopsy. So I can't help you there."

"I have some photographs," the lawyer explained, "and the report of the state's medical examiner. What I am seeing in this stuff just doesn't add up in my mind. I need to see if it makes any sense to a medical professional."

"Well," the doctor answered, "I take it you want to put me on the stand. I don't feel real comfortable with doing so. I mean, I'm not as noble as your father was and as you apparently are. When I was a kid, I didn't even color outside the lines."

"No," Coop shot back, "I wouldn't ask you to do that. I can bring in a doctor from Nashville or someplace if I need them in the trial. But before I consult others, I at least need to ask a couple of questions."

"Well," Willis answered, relief evident in his tone, "what are you seeing that you don't understand?"

Coop glanced back at the report from the state medical examiner. He found the notations he wanted and posed his first question. "Some wounds are deep and some are shallow. Some have ragged edges and others are smooth. Some are only an inch wide and others are three inches or more. What does it tell you?"

The line went silent for a few seconds, and when he came back on, the doctor's tone showed a hint of confusion. "Without examining the body or photographs, I couldn't be sure, but it sounds to me as if the deep, clean wounds would have been made after she had passed out."

That made sense. Maybe the murderer was simply making sure he had finished his work. Glancing back to the autopsy notes, something else jumped out. One of the smaller wounds severed the spine just below the shoulders. At that point, Becky would not have been able to fight back. Thus, the doctor's thoughts fit in with such a scenario.

"John," Coop continued, "why would there be almost no blood found around or under her body. The crime photos of the site after the body has been removed seem to show little or none."

"Could be several reasons." Willis's quick answer showed he was more than willing to weigh in on this observation. "First, we had a strong storm that night, and it could have washed a lot of it away. Second, the blood might have pooled inside her body rather than flowing out. And finally, she could have been killed elsewhere and then taken to the scene."

"Thanks, John," Coop quickly replied, "and you don't have to worry about me telling anyone where I got the information."

"I appreciate it," Willis assured him. "And even though I can't afford to be vocal about it, I do hope if Calvin didn't do it, you can find a way to get him off. I hate to see an innocent person executed, even if he is a Negro."

The doctor no doubt meant his last line as proof of his real character, but what it really indicated was his mind-set. By qualifying his remarks, it had shown that even he had not been able to fully escape his feelings of racial superiority. And it was the same mind-set most of the prospective jurors in this case would carry into the court-room. So to have a chance at getting a not-guilty verdict, Coop was going to have to pull a Perry Mason and come up with enough evidence to convince even a KKK member that his client was innocent. The attorney wondered if somewhere in these stacks of papers was a rabbit he could pull out of a hat.

14

Deputy Buford Stafford was snoozing at his desk when K. C. Fredrick opened the door and quietly entered the office. The DA studied the short, slightly built twenty-five-year-old for a few seconds before kicking the man in the shin.

"What are you doing?" Fredrick screamed. "Is this what we are paying you for?"

A confused Stafford literally fell out of his chair and onto the floor. Still half-asleep but now scared to death, he got his bearings, struggled to his feet, and tried to yank his gun from his holster. He had the revolver halfway out before recognizing his visitor. "Mr. Fredrick," he mumbled.

"Put the gun away," the DA barked.

The embarrassed deputy held the pistol in front of him and said, "It doesn't matter. It's not loaded."

"Figures," Fredrick replied.

After slipping the weapon back in its holster, Stafford glanced over to the wall clock. "Mr. Fredrick, it's past midnight, what are you doing here?"

"I want to talk to the Ross boy."

"Now?"

"Right now, so get the keys and lead me back there. And be quick about it."

Stafford turned and led the heavyset man through the outer room and into Sheriff Estes's office. Opening the middle desk drawer, he pulled out a set of keys and motioned for the DA to follow. Unlocking the door to the jail, Stafford signaled for the visitor to trail him down the corridor and to the row of cells.

"What's going on?" A man in the second cell grumbled. "Who turned on the lights?"

"Just me, Howard," the deputy answered. "Have you slept it off yet?"

"No," came the reply, "I'm still pretty lit up."

"Okay then, go back to bed."

Fredrick shadowed the deputy as Stafford moved along until he came almost to the end of the hall. The young man then kicked a cell door and yelled out, "Wake up, boy, you got a guest." He glanced back to the DA. "You want me to unlock the door and let you in, or do you want to just talk through the bars?"

"I'll talk through the bars," Fredrick replied with a wave. "And you get lost. I don't want you hearing any of this. I'll meet you in the office in a bit."

After Stafford cleared the corridor, the DA looked back into the cell. Sitting in the bunk, with the dim light illuminating his forehead and cheeks, was the person he'd come to see.

"Hello, Calvin."

He was greeted with silence.

"Boy, I came here tonight with a deal for you," Fredrick continued. "My conscience has been bothering me. You see, I just don't like to see anyone go to the chair. I can't sleep nights when I think about the fact that I would be the man who put him there. So I'd like to offer you a deal. What do you think, boy?"

The prisoner didn't move or say anything, and his lack of reaction made Fredrick very uncomfortable. He only waited for a few seconds and then changed his tone.

"Listen, boy, when an important white man talks to a colored, he answers. I know you got a tongue, so use it."

Calvin glared back but remained mute.

Grabbing the cell door and shaking it, the DA shouted, "I'm offering you a chance to live, you fool. I'm giving you a ticket out of the electric chair."

The room grew quiet for a few more seconds before Calvin's lips finally parted. "I don't think I'd buy anything you're selling. After all, you were the one who told them to beat me into a confession. And you smiled each time they hit me. What makes you think I'd trust you now?"

Releasing the bars, Fredrick stuck his hands into his slacks' pockets and clenched his fists. After taking a series of deep breaths, he once more gained some control over his emotions and explained, "All you have to do is admit you killed Becky Booth and I'll make sure you don't get the death penalty. Then, someday down the road, you'd have a chance of getting your freedom again. It sounds like a pretty good deal to me. You can probably even complete your college degree behind bars. I can make it happen."

Calvin quickly yanked himself off the bed and leaped over to the cell door. He grabbed the bars with both hands and pushed his face as close as he could get to the visitor. As a shocked Fredrick stepped back, the prisoner smiled. "You're scared. You're hiding something, and now you are afraid it will come out and ruin you."

Pushing further from the caged man until he felt the bars from the opposite cell rubbing his back, Fredrick stammered, "No, I just wanted to give you a break. And if you didn't do it, then give me the name of someone who did. Maybe the buck they call Big Mike decided to butcher a white girl for fun. Just tell me you saw him do it, and I'll get you out of this can. You got my word. I really feel for you, boy."

"I told you before, I'm not buying anything you are selling," Calvin quickly replied, "so listen to me and listen good. You know I'm innocent. You knew it when you picked me up. It means you might actually know who did it, and you're afraid Cooper Lindsay will find out your secrets. It's hot tonight, I've been sweating up a storm in this jail cell, but I get the feeling you'll be sweating a lot more in your fine air-conditioned house. I'm not going to make this easy on you. Not now, not ever. And if I do get out, if Lindsay does get me off, make sure you always look over your shoulder when you're walking alone."

A stunned Fredrick glanced into Calvin's eyes. He saw such rage—even though there were bars between them—it scared him to death. Turning, he hurried down the corridor toward the exit. As he passed the second cell, the occupant pleaded, "Maybe now I can get some sleep."

Rushing through the two offices and out into the street, K. C. Fredrick wished for the same thing, but he was fully aware that on this night sleep was not coming.

15

Thursday, June 25, 1964

Coop watched Judy and the kids pull out of the driveway at five, headed north. And while he hadn't convinced her to stay with her folks in Dayton until this mess was over, she had given in to spending a couple of days in Ohio before driving back. It would at least keep her away from the initial blast created when the locals found out he would be representing Calvin Ross. And it gave him a bit of peace of mind.

As Coop sipped on a lukewarm cup of black coffee and munched on bacon, he mentally planned his day. First, he was going to make a trip out to the crime scene. Though there would likely be no evidence left to see, he still wanted to refresh his mind on the lay of the land. After all, he hadn't been to Lovers Park since his high school dating days. After the trek into the woods, he planned on stopping by the jail to prep Calvin on what would be happening in the preliminary hearing. Then he would head back to the office, decide what he needed to take to the courtroom. Finally, it would be home, shower, change into his new gray suit, and make his way to the courthouse.

Pushing his chair back from the kitchen table, Coop set his empty cup and plate into the sink and hurried into the living room. He paused for a moment to catch the black-and-white images of *The Today Show* flicking on the TV before pushing the off button. Grabbing his keys and billfold, he was almost out the door when the phone rang. Reversing course, he made his way back into the kitchen just in time to answer before the third ring.

"Hello."

"Is this Cooper Lindsay?" a deep male voice inquired.

"It is."

"Coop," the man continued, "it has been a while since we have visited."

He didn't answer; instead, he tried to put a face to the caller's voice. He sounded familiar, but who was it?

The caller quickly ended the guessing game. "Anyway, Coop, this is John David Maltose, and I want you to come out here right now and visit with me. There is something we need to discuss."

This was just like Maltose. He never went to see anyone; everybody came running to him. He snapped his fingers and the world trembled—at least Justice did. He was worth millions, all inherited from his father, and he felt his wealth made him a king. It seemed most folks in the area agreed. But his kind of thinking didn't faze Coop.

"I can't imagine what we'd need to talk about," the lawyer answered. "But if you want to see me, you can make an appointment and come to my office."

"Now listen, boy," Maltose's tone was obviously agitated, "if you know what's good for you, then you'll drop what you're doing and drive out here right now."

"I have a life to live," Coop replied, "and right now it doesn't include making a trip to your place. Why don't you come by my office tomorrow morning about ten?"

"I know you're playing with fire," Maltose warned. "I can put the fire out before you get burned."

"Smokey the Bear and I are good friends," Coop quipped. "I'll let him put out the fires in my life."

Coop knew no one talked to the big man in this fashion, but he'd learned a long time ago that bullies thrived on fear, and when fear wasn't shown they got uncomfortable. He sensed by the silence on the other end of the line that Maltose was starting to get an uncomfortable feeling right now.

"Listen, Cooper, I can fix it where no one uses your legal services. You've got no family money, so I can pretty much starve you out in just a few months. You need me to stay in business, and if you play the game my way, you can make more money than you can imagine. After all, a man like me always needs a good lawyer. In fact, I need a team of them. You could head up my team. And if you don't play the game my way, well then, you won't be able to even get a job cleaning out septic tanks."

A day ago, the threat might have shaken the attorney, but today, with Judy and the kids likely out of state by now, it failed to lift a single hair on the back of his neck. Besides, the case he was taking was pretty much going to end his practice long before Maltose could put his plan into action. So Coop had nothing to fear, and the big man's threats were meaningless.

"Listen, John David, as I told you a while ago, I have things to do today. My calendar is full. If you need to visit me, you have two choices. The first is to come into my office tomorrow at ten. I'll likely be in. The second is to drive over to Lovers Park in about thirty minutes. I'm going to spend a few minutes there doing some research. But I'm not coming to see you, today, tomorrow, or next week."

"You're a fool," the caller snarled.

"No doubt," Coop replied. "Good-bye."

Not waiting for a response, the lawyer not so gently placed the phone into the cradle, rushed back through the house, and out the door. As Judy had taken their Galaxie, Coop slid into the '57 Studebaker his mother left him in her will. For the next few days, the yellow-and-green President would be his means of getting around.

16

Lovers Park had changed little since the days when Coop had visited it as a teen. The dirt road leading to what some kids called the Passion Pit was washed out and filled with ruts, the ditches along the road were littered with bottles and the big oak where at least two generations of teens had carved their initials was still standing.

Parking the Studebaker in the six-inch grass along the side of the road, Coop walked slowly up into a meadow. He paused a moment to get his bearings before turning right, strolling under a century-old elm, and making his way to the creek. Looking past a fallen pine, his eyes fell upon a small open area where the grass had been trampled. Bingo!

Moving beyond the log, he approached the spot where, according to the crime scene photos, Becky Booth's body had been found. In spite of the rain, he could still see a few bloodstains. Bending over, he touched a bloody spot with his right hand and looked back toward where the kids usually parked their cars. If he was right, and she wasn't killed here, then the person or persons responsible for the crime would have had to carry the body about sixty to seventy feet. Becky was not large, maybe 115 pounds, but it would have still taken one pretty strong man some effort to bring the body to this point.

Pushing himself upright, he surveyed the area for any other possible ways to bring the body to the clearing. The creek was too shallow for boats, the only road was the one he drove in on, and the woods behind the clearing were so thick even hunters avoided them. So it was just as he had remembered, only one way in and one way out.

With that in mind, why bring her here? Why take a chance on being caught in an area with no real alternate means of escape? There had to be a reason.

Moving through knee-deep grass, Coop strolled up to the place the teens always parked their cars. Once there, he looked back into the clearing. He was starting to believe there was something symbolic in the way this all played out. He was rolling a couple of different theories over in his head when he heard a vehicle motoring up the hill leading to Lovers Park. Turning his gaze to the place he'd left his car, he watched a new white Cadillac ease up and stop. A few seconds later, John David Maltose yanked his tall form from the driver's seat and purposefully walked up the slight grade toward the meadow. His set jaw seemed to prove he was none too happy to be there.

17

"Well, you must have really needed to visit with me," Coop announced with a grim smile.

Maltose stopped and glared, but said nothing. Instead, he paused to pull a burr from the cuff of his no-doubt imported black slacks.

"You didn't dress for this place," Coop noted.

"A silk shirt and Italian shoes are a bit too stylish for Lovers Park. You'll note I'm in jeans and a work shirt."

Maltose frowned, his contempt obvious, before continuing his trek until he stood directly in front of the attorney. Almost like a boxer just before the first bell, he sized his opponent up for a moment and then barked, "I came here to warn you."

"You wasted your trip," Coop snapped.

"You don't even know what I'm talking about," Maltose replied, pointing his finger into the slightly smaller man's face.

"Okay, tell me."

Maltose nodded, dropped his hand back to his side, and in a firm tone ordered more than said, "You're going to dump this case. You're not going to do any more work for that Ross kid."

This didn't make sense. Why was the local kingpin so worried about Coop defending Calvin? There was nothing Maltose was going to gain or lose, no matter which way the verdict went. He didn't have any kind of relationship with the Booths, and there was no money to be made if the kid was convicted and none to be lost if he walked. Yet here was a man who never went to see anyone, suddenly so concerned that he was making a trip down a dirty road in a new Caddy just to issue a warning. With that in mind, Coop needed to keep this conversation going.

"Why should I quit?"

"There are ten thousand reasons in a briefcase in my car," came the quick response.

"So you think I can be bought off?" Coop asked as he glanced beyond the man to the Caddy.

"Every man has a price," came the resolute response.

"But, John David, you don't buy worthless junk. My defending this boy has some moral value for me, but there is no financial upside for you. This isn't art you can hang on your wall or a fine wine you can share with out-of-town guests. This is just a Negro boy, not even accepted as a full member of society. There is something else at play here for this to be worth your time and money."

Maltose immediately shot back, "Cooper, if you ride this thing to the bitter end, you'll be ruined in this town. Right now, you have value. With your looks and your background, you can go places. The kid has no value to me, but you might. You're worth the money and the risk."

On the surface, the explanation made sense. Maybe the big man did have plans for him possibly in politics, but the timing of this revelation stunk. He'd been back for months, and during that time Maltose had never once even contacted him. So as Coop dug below the surface, this again smelled. This had to be all about the case and whatever it was the big man was so scared would come out. What was so important that he had his wallet open and was willing to make a big-time deal?

Coop grinned. "The Hollywood actress from the thirties, Jean Harlow, often gets credit for saying, 'If you lie down with dogs, you get up with fleas.' I'm thinking in this case, she was right."

Maltose grinned. "Come on back to the car; I'll give you the money. I told K. C. you'd see it my way."

Coop dug his hands into his pockets and laughed. A few seconds later, the big man joined in and slapped the lawyer on the back. For a few awkward moments, both men appeared happy.

"You fooled me, didn't you, Cooper?" Maltose announced with a smile. "Not many men can run a bluff on me. I admire you. How much do you want? What's your price?"

The lawyer shrugged, but said nothing.

"And," the tall man continued, "I get your Harlow statement, too. You'd have picked up some fleas you'd have never gotten rid of if you stuck with this case. You'd lose everything. Your legacy would be ruined, and your future would be worth nothing at all. So coming to work with me is what you'd planned all along. How did you know Fredrick was in my hip pocket and you entering the case would force him to come to me to buy you off?"

The lawyer didn't know if he'd been insulted or complimented, but he was sure the big man was not going to like what he heard next.

"John David, I certainly don't want to spend the rest of my life scratching fleas. But you're the one who missed the point."

Suddenly Maltose's grin faded. As it did, the lawyer laughed, "You're the dog I'm not going to lie down with. You've got the fleas; Calvin doesn't."

"What?"

"You heard me. And as you drive off with your tail tucked between your legs, take a long look at my legacy. My father was not named after the biblical Abraham. No, he was named after the president who tried to right a wrong you seem to want to perpetuate."

Maltose set his jaw and glared. "You remember what happened to Lincoln?"

"Yeah," Coop quickly replied, "I sure do."

"Well, son," his voice was now as cold as a February wind, "maybe you need to take note of history. This isn't a threat; it's a promise. If you take this case, I can't fix anything for the boy or you!"

He said nothing else, just whirled around and marched back to his car. He only glanced back once, flashing a hateful stare hot enough to melt ice at the North Pole, before jumping in the Caddy and driving off.

The dust from the road was still hovering in the air as Coop turned back to look again at the place where Becky's body had been found. What in the world had he walked into, and why was it worth ten grand or much, much more?

18

Because of the nature of the crime and the importance of the young woman who had been murdered, the courtroom's two hundred spectator seats must have been filled by noon with scores of others waiting in the hall. As he observed from his office window the throng descending upon the scene, Coop noted that many from Justice's most elite upper crust had turned out to support the Booth family, but they were joined by a horde of common everyday folks who must have been drawn to the uniqueness and brutality of the crime. So almost every facet of Justice society was turning out for the drama, and the one thing those going into the courthouse all had in common was the color of their skin.

Those of another color were there, too, but they were milling around on the courthouse lawn. None of them dared walk through the doors to mingle with the whites in the three-story, red-brick structure. They knew their place and they were staying in it.

With his briefcase in hand and wearing his newest gray suit, a white shirt, and dark blue tie, Coop walked away from the windows and across his office. Pausing only to lock his doors, he then made his way down the steps and out onto Front Street. Word was evidently not yet out that he was defending Calvin, as a half dozen folks either spoke to him or waved. He sensed those friendly greetings would soon become a part of his past.

After making his way slowly across the street, he stopped on the steps leading up to the courthouse entrance and studied the Negroes waiting under the walnut trees providing shade for the lawn. There was a sense of apprehension evident in their body language; their faces seemed to reflect fear, and their hushed tones indicated worry. Even the town's checkers champs, Jacob McBride and Aaron Carver, had put away their game board and were standing looking up at the building's second floor as if expecting a nightmare to blow through the courtroom windows.

"The darkies have come out en masse today."

Coop immediately recognized the voice of the man who'd made the observation. Though he hadn't seen him walk up, Coop knew that standing beside him was seventy-year-old Oscar Fields. Fields was a retired judge who had been born in Justice and, except for college and law school, had never left. His grandfather had been an officer in the Civil War and his father one of the area's most successful businessmen. The local grocery story still bore the Fields's name. In a town priding itself on having an established upper crust, Oscar was only slightly below John David Maltose in power and prestige.

"How are you today, Coop?" Fields asked as they made eye contact.

"Fine," the lawyer fibbed. He was anything but fine. He was nervous and unsure of the way he should deal with the fallout that was about to happen. After all, if things went the way he expected, it would be as if he were planning his own death and funeral.

"Pretty much open-and-shut," Fields continued, "I mean the case, not this heavy front door."

"Don't know about that," Coop replied.

"Really?" The man probed. "K. C. told me they have the boy dead to rights. He even left his knife at the scene."

Coop shrugged. "Well, K. C. thinks he has the whole world figured out. Maybe we should just send him to Washington and let him deal with the Russians."

Fields laughed. "It's a thought, but I'm not sure he could even find his way to DC."

Glancing back to the crowd, Coop noted Hattie Ross standing with a few other folks about her age under the largest of the trees. Dressed in a black dress and carrying a purse the size of a small suitcase, she projected an air of confidence. But when he caught her eyes, he noticed they were swollen and red and showed her real mood. Sensing a need to bring her up-to-date on the case, as well as offer some assurance and comfort, he stepped down from the steps and into the crowd.

"How you doing, Hattie?" he asked reaching his hand out to take hers. It was then that he noted her white gloves. Even the maid held on to the past in some ways.

"I've been a lot better," she replied quietly.

As a host of folks, both black and white looked on, Coop leaned closer. "Are you going in?"

"No, sir," she replied slowly shaking her head. "Only black person in the courtroom today will be Calvin. I took him some good clothes to wear. So he should look fine and respectable."

"Today doesn't mean much; this is not the real deal," Coop assured her. "What we need to focus on is about three weeks from now."

"Do we have a chance, Mr. Coop?"

"I hope so"—he smiled as he pushed those three words through his lips—"but you still need to be doing some powerful praying."

"I will," she assured him.

After patting her on the shoulder, he turned and trotted up the steps, through the ancient heavy doors and into the courthouse. It was packed. The last time he'd seen this kind of crowd was at a bargain basement sale in a Nashville department store four years before. Pushing through the curious swarm gathered in the foyer, Coop made his way up the stairs and into the hall just outside the main courtroom. Forcing past another mass of humanity, he finally got to the door guarded by two Common County deputies. One of them held up his hand and caught Coop on the shoulder.

"Sorry, Mr. Lindsay," Buford Stafford announced, "there's no more room."

"There is a seat saved for me," Coop assured him.

"Where?" the officer asked.

"Beside the defendant."

A half dozen people gasped, and the deputy's jaw dropped. As the news filtered through those who were crammed shoulder to shoulder in the hall, everyone quit talking and looked toward the entry to the courtroom. Suddenly, there were hundreds of eyes staring at the attorney, each seemingly waiting for him to tell the world he'd just been joking. Feeling their questioning gaze, Coop turned his head and glanced into the shocked faces.

"Did I hear you right?" the deputy asked.

"You did." Coop then raised his voice and declared, "I'm representing Calvin Ross. He is my client, and I intend to prove him innocent."

A short, heavyset, middle-aged woman in a

dark blue flower-print dress shook her head and spat at Coop's feet.

"You have a problem with me, Jessie Lou?" he asked.

She didn't hesitate to share her thoughts. "You ought to be ashamed. You are dishonoring your name and your race. I'm glad your mother is dead. I'd hate for her to see this."

A man in the back yelled out, "Don't matter who represents the boy. Every nig—"

"Don't say it!" Coop warned. "I don't want to hear that word ever again."

The man paused, puckered his lips, studied the tense attorney, and finally all but shouted, "Every colored put on trial for murdering a white in the fifty years this courthouse has been standing has been found guilty."

"We'll see," Coop replied. He then looked back to the woman who'd just berated him. "Jessie Lou, you're wrong. My mother would be more proud of me for representing this young man than you could even begin to imagine. You see, unlike you, she didn't just listen to my father's sermons; she took them to heart. So I suggest you go home and read the tenth chapter of Luke and see what you missed."

Coop took a final look at the now silent but hostile throng before turning and making his way through the doors and into the main courtroom. As he slowly walked the aisle to the front of the room, everything grew church-like quiet. When he placed his briefcase on the defense table and took a chair, the murmurs began. He didn't have to turn around to see the revulsion being tossed his way; he could feel the heat from the hateful glares on the back of his neck.

19

Coop sat alone for ten minutes as the clock ticked down to the most anticipated preliminary hearing in the history of Common County. There could be little doubt those ten minutes spent pretending to study his notes were the longest of his life. Behind him were people he'd called friends for a lifetime. Now most of them were likely looking at him as if he were the devil himself, or the most generous ones might have figured he'd simply lost his mind. Either way he'd become a person to be avoided.

Out of the corner of his right eye, Coop spied Brent and Martha Booth. Brent locked onto him the moment he'd sat down at the table and had not moved his gaze for an instant. Martha, her eyes hidden behind dark glasses, had never even looked his way, treating him as if he were invisible. He didn't know which was worse.

Trying to forget those seeing him as Judas, he

focused on the surroundings. The room's pressed tin ceiling went up two stories. The walls and all the furniture were oak. The six light fixtures, covered by brass-trimmed glass bowls at least four feet across, dangled eight feet below the ceiling and were held in place by gold chains. The judge's desk sat six feet above the floor, and the witness box rose half the height. Carved into the wall above the judge's bench was the state seal. A large standing Mississippi flag on one side and an American flag on the other set off the final patriotic touch needed to make this facility a place where fairness reigned. Still the grand trappings did little to inspire Coop's confidence that justice could be found here for a young Negro man named Calvin Ross.

At 1:01, according to the courtroom clock hung just to the right of the jury box, Calvin Ross was ushered into the room through a side door. Wylie Estes escorted the slightly built young man to his chair behind the table and beside Coop and unlocked his cuffs. Then the sheriff moved about six feet to the left and took his place in another chair against the wall.

After Calvin was settled, the lawyer leaned close and whispered to his client, "How you feeling?"

"Okay, I guess," he whispered back.

"This shouldn't take long," Coop explained. "We will plead not guilty. Shouldn't be any witnesses called, and then the judge will set the trial date for about three weeks from now, likely starting in mid-July. I believe it gives me time enough to prepare."

Calvin glanced back at a crowd who seemed ready to get out a rope and find a tree, before once more speaking to his attorney. "Mr. Coop, you better finger the person who did this and have photographs of the attack because nobody here is rooting for the colored guy."

If only it was so easy. If only there was a way to unmask someone and present so much proof even the people of Justice would have to admit their misjudgment and celebrate an innocent man's freedom. But this wasn't a TV courtroom drama, and Coop was no detective. The best he could likely hope for was finding a way to prove there was not a way in the world Calvin could have done this. Anything short of that would probably mean failure.

"All rise," Walt Atkins, the chief bailiff announced. "The District Court of Common County is now in session in the matter of the State versus Calvin Ross with Judge Hyrum Metlock presiding."

Metlock was a nice-looking fifty-year-old man who had grown up in Mobile. With bright blue eyes and still-dark hair, his passion, outside of the law, was tennis. If the temperature was above forty and the sun was out, he would find a way to hit the courts at least once a day. When he had this hearing behind him, he'd likely be heading directly over to the park for another match, ready and willing to take on all comers, no matter their age.

As Metlock took his seat, the rest of those in the court followed. The judge remained quiet for a few moments as he studied a piece of paper on his desk. He looked up, first at K. C. Fredrick and then over to Coop and Calvin.

"Gentlemen," he began, "as this is a capital case, I will be accepting no requests for bail, so let's not even go there. And as this is a preliminary hearing, I assume neither of you will be calling any witnesses nor presenting any evidence other than what I have already seen."

"The state will not present any evidence or call any witnesses in this matter until the trial," Fredrick announced.

Coop looked to the bench, slightly dipped his head and, without ever taking his eyes off the judge, announced in a strong voice, "The defense will also wait until the trial to present our case."

"Okay," Metlock replied. "Then let's get to the business at hand and be on our way." The judge looked to the defense table and asked, "Will you rise?"

After Calvin and Coop stood, the judge continued, "Mr. Ross, do you understand the charges against you?"

"Yes, sir," the young man answered in a surprisingly strong voice.

"In the matter of the murder in the first degree of Rebecca A. Booth, how do you plead?"

Calvin glanced to Coop and, after the attorney nodded, looked back to the judge. Standing tall in his black suit, white shirt, and thin blue tie, he announced, "Not guilty, sir."

Metlock looked down at his desk, paused for a moment, and then moved his gaze to the DA. "K. C., could the state be ready to go to trial on July 13? It is a Monday."

"We can and will be, Your Honor."

The judge then looked over to the defense table. "What about you, Coop?"

"I will do my best," came the honest reply.

Metlock nodded, scratched his head, and looked out on those in the gallery who had gathered to observe this short exercise in law. After studying the spectators for a moment, his gaze returned to Coop. "If you run into any problems fully gathering the materials to be ready to go to trial by the date I have chosen, please ask for a hearing and a continuance. As this is a trial of great magnitude to this community and the defendant, I want to make sure we don't move so quickly that either side in this matter is at a disadvantage."

"Thank you, sir," Coop replied. "And, if needed, I will ask for one. But I am not anticipating needing more time than has been given to us."

The judge nodded. "Any other court business?"

Both attorneys shook their heads.

"Then we are dismissed until the thirteenth." He brought his gavel down, stood, and left for his chambers.

"That's all there is to it?" Calvin asked.

"Yes," Coop said, as those behind the pair began to talk, "now the real work begins."

"Do we have a chance?" the young man asked as Sheriff Estes walked up to the table and took his arm.

"Yeah," Coop assured him. "This case is full of holes, and I just realized a possible way to make sure what we present is viewed fairly without prejudice. If I can make it happen, we should win."

Coop watched the sheriff lead his client away and then glanced back to the scene behind him. He felt like a treed bear. No one had left and almost every eye in the room was on him. Picking up his briefcase, he slowly ambled to the aisle and, accompanied only by the muttering of a few in the crowd, made his way to the hall. Standing between him and the stairs was Jessie Lou.

"Excuse me," Coop said with a smile.

She stared at him for a few seconds before puckering her lips and spitting directly into his face. As everyone around the woman looked on, the attorney reached into his pocket, pulled out a handkerchief, wiped the moisture from his cheek and softly cracked, "Jessie Lou, you're getting pretty good. You might need to enter the spitting contest at the next county fair. You could do your family and Justice proud."

Coop stepped by the woman and pushed through the mass of humanity to the stairs. Keeping his eyes aimed forward, he navigated the twenty steps and was just about to the outside exit when someone behind him brought a fist into his right kidney. With pain searing his side, he pushed forward, showing not a hint that the blow had done any damage. Once out the door and onto the steps, he stopped and glanced out to the faces of those from the other side of the tracks. He nodded once and then strolled across the lawn to his office. After marching up the steps, he closed and locked his door.

Leaning against the wall, he reached back to where the blow had landed, but vigorous rubbing did nothing to ease the searing pain. As he tried to catch his breath, a thought hit him. The first battle was over, but the war had just begun, and on the surface, the odds looked longer than the ones Crockett and Travis faced at the Alamo. But the idea he'd come up with while observing the judge just might even things up a bit.

20

Coop's evening was anything but peaceful as a constant stream of cars slowly drove by his sixteen-hundred-square-foot frame home. None of them stopped, nothing was shouted; they just kept coming, one, then another, and then another. After a while, he began to feel like a dying animal, struggling to walk across the desert while vultures circled above watching his every move. For this reason, and a thousand more, he was glad that Judy had taken the kids to Ohio. None of them needed to experience this.

After closing the shades, he moved to the kitchen and put his briefcase on the table. Once more, he pulled out the crime scene and autopsy photos. As no person, black or white, had been with Calvin during every moment Hattie was at the church, these photos and the autopsy reports would have to provide the foundation for the young man's innocence.

Coop picked up a picture where the perspective presented Becky's body from her head looking down toward the feet and clearly showed the brutality of the crime. There were even stab wounds on her face. Hence, this crime had to be driven by either hate or revenge. And as Becky was one of the most popular young people in Justice, the theory offered a real problem. Calvin's confrontation with Brent Booth cast the boy as the only one with a real motive to fuel such rage.

After shuffling through a dozen more photos taken from every possible angle, Coop turned his attention back to the sheriff's notes. Wylie Estes had always been a stickler for details. Even as a Little League coach, he'd studied the opposition so closely he knew each player's weaknesses on offense and defense. So his writings covered every facet of the crime scene from the blood trail leading from the meadow above Lovers Park to the way the body was lying on the ground. It was obvious the latter had bothered the seasoned lawman as he had put a question mark beside those particular notations.

The body was not just dropped on the ground; it was positioned in such a manner as to indicate the murderer took time arranging it. It was almost as if she was folded into a V-shape with one of the legs crossing from one side of the V to the other.

Looking up from the notes, Coop glanced back to the photographs. What the sheriff had noted then, now jumped out at him. Except from this angle it looked more like an A rather than a V.

The lawyer considered this unique quirk for a few moments, trying to put a reason for anyone taking the time needed for this action, before he turned his attention back to finishing the sheriff's notes. What he found there helped very little, but it's what wasn't in the writing that struck Coop as being the foundation he needed to build his defense.

Picking up the crime scene photos, he examined each of them one by one. Over and over, he looked at them from every possible angle. Once again, Estes's mind-set for details was evident when instructing his deputy or the local press to shoot pictures of the scene. There were even shots of one of Becky's shoes lost between the parking spot and where her body had been dumped. There were also photos of her discarded blouse. But one thing not there verified something Calvin had told him upon their initial discussions about the evidence. Pulling the notes of the conversation from his briefcase, Coop smiled. This wasn't the key to unlocking the cell door, but it might be just what he needed to spring, when Fredrick made his case.

A sharp thump against the picture window pulled his attention from the pictures to the front of the house. Several more similar noises followed. Getting up, he made this way across the dark living room and peered from the side of the curtain just as another projectile struck. Glancing out to the street, he observed maybe a dozen teenage boys armed with eggs. They were using Coop's house as a target. He continued to watch the kids until they finally ran out of ammunition and dashed off. As long as it didn't go beyond this, he was fine. Eggs weren't going to hurt him, but his gut told him the next volley in this war would be a bit more serious.

21

Friday, June 26, 1964

Coop parked the Studebaker about half a block from the Methodist church. As it was misting and it looked as though there might be a full-blown storm on the way, he would have much rather found a spot in the main parking lot. But with only twenty minutes left before the start of Becky Booth's funeral, it was full.

Pulling himself from his car, he hurried down the walk past the Green's and Smith's stately two-story brick homes before getting to the church's well-manicured grounds. It was there the trouble began. A male quartet, all dressed in suits, stood on the front walk glaring at Coop. As he drew nearer, the biggest one, a hulking figure who owned the lumberyard, stepped forward.

"What are you doing here?" Troy Bedlow demanded.

Coop stopped, studied the man's drawn expression, and replied, "Same thing you are. I am coming to mourn the loss of an outstanding young woman."

"The Booth family doesn't want you anywhere near the church," Bedlow barked. "And we are here to make sure those wishes are followed."

"I don't want a fight," Coop announced, holding up his arms.

"You're already involved in one," the big man snarled.

"Listen, Troy," the lawyer calmly replied, hoping his tone would bring down the temperature a bit. "Do you sell building supplies and materials to Negroes?"

He nodded.

"Okay, I'm not doing anything more than you do. I'm just representing a young man who I feel is innocent."

"You're the only one," another man shouted from behind Bedlow. "The rest of us know who did it, and we know why."

Coop tilted his head, caught the little man's eyes in his gaze. "Ernie, you haven't heard the evidence yet. How can you judge?"

"She was a beautiful, innocent white girl," the man shot back, "and he was nothing more than a lousy, dirty—"

"Don't say it," Reverend Martin Clements ordered. The preacher, an athletic, white-haired man in his forties dressed in a black suit, white shirt, and dark tie, stepped from the church entry and hurried to a point between the angry quartet and Coop. "You men just get inside and prepare for the service. I'll take care of this."

Coop and Clements watched as the four enforcers turned and slowly walked up the steps and into the building. When they disappeared, the preacher looked back to the lawyer.

"Coop, didn't they build this new sanctuary when your father was leading this flock?"

"Sure did," the lawyer answered as he studied the white brick structure. "I was about seven or eight. I used to come over every afternoon after school to see what had been done each day. You know, I was the first one to ring the bell when they hung it in the tower. Did you know the stained-glass windows were actually in the old frame church this one replaced?"

"I wasn't aware of it," Clements replied, "but do you remember what happened to the old church building?"

"Yeah," Coop answered, "it was moved over the tracks and is still being used by one of the Negro congregations. In fact, it was the church where Calvin Ross was saved and baptized. It is also where he was arrested."

"The Grace Methodist Church it's called now,"

the preacher noted as he turned away from the building and focused his attention back on Coop. "It might have been easier if we had just invited the black folks to come here rather than move the old building, but we didn't do it, because it is just not natural. Just like the animals, people like to be with their own kind. If a colored man gets in trouble, it should be a colored man who gets him out. Same thing goes for whites. And when it comes to worship, coloreds need to be with their people and whites need to be with ours."

"You're not like my father," Coop cut in, "he never went the long way when it came to making a point. He was a bit more direct."

"I'm not sure I understand," Clements said.

"I think you do," the lawyer returned. "Let me ask you a question. Are you the Jew or the Gentile?"

"I'm not following you."

Coop grinned. "The religious leaders in Christ's time separated themselves by tribes and races. Thus, they were shocked when Jesus crossed the lines. He saw Himself as loving, understanding, and being there for both Jew and Gentile."

"I don't see what this has to do with me," the now-confused preacher admitted.

Coop smiled. "Would Christ attend your church or the one on the other side of the tracks?"

A puzzled look came across the man's face as

he considered the question. "This isn't a matter of race, Coop. This is a matter of doing what is right. You chose to represent a man who murdered a member of our church. Therefore, you have turned your back on your people and on God. Thus, we have no place for you here. Once you acknowledge where you failed and ask those you have failed for forgiveness, maybe this flock will welcome you back in."

"So those people on the other side of the tracks," Coop said as he pointed off toward the south, "are not worth either saving or accepting." He then smiled and added, "But wait, didn't we just raise money to support a missionary in Africa? Aren't those we are trying to save over there Negroes? And didn't we have a Kenyan man speak to our church about his faith two months ago? What is the difference?"

The preacher shrugged. "You're lost, boy. You don't understand that God makes rules and we must play by them."

"God segregated this town?" Coop asked. He didn't get an answer and he didn't expect one. Though the man preached acceptance, he was really a person who inwardly embraced a concept of those like himself being a part of God's chosen few. In his mind, God loved the rest of the folks, too, but not as much as He loved white people. And for this reason Clements seemed like the Pharisees who debated Jesus;

they saw others' shortcomings, but never their own.

Coop glanced back at the building his father had helped build and smiled sadly. He then looked back at the pastor. "I think it's time for you to get inside. The Booths will need to hear some comforting words."

"I will do my best," Clements declared quietly. He paused, looking back at the church's steps before turning and laying his hand on Coop's arm. "And I'll pray for you, too. And I'll even pray for the boy. I will pray he will find grace before they execute him."

As Clements moved up the walk, climbed the steps, and disappeared inside the church, Coop shook his head and slowly strolled in the street toward his car. His head down, he didn't notice the dusty, blue Chevy pickup truck until it was almost upon him. His first clue was a backfire. When he finally spotted the vehicle, it had to have been going at least fifty and was weaving wildly down the street. As it neared the lawyer, it swung across from the far lane into the one Coop was using to walk back to his car. Calling upon his almost-forgotten athletic instincts, he leapt to his right and landed on the hood of a '62 Rambler. His back struck Detroit cast steel as the truck blew by. Rolling off the car and back onto the street, Coop watched as the male driver straightened his wheel, crossed back to the pavement's far side, and continued down Vine Street at a rapid clip.

The stakes had been raised again. No longer could Coop ever let down his guard or take even a short walk for granted.

22

The remainder of the day was relatively quiet. A few kids tossed racially themed insults at Coop as he got into his car and drove home, but otherwise most folks hadn't even acknowledged his presence. It was as if they were either looking around or through him. When he pulled the Studebaker into the driveway, he was surprised to see the family's blue Galaxie parked in the garage.

Pushing the home's back door open, he strolled into the kitchen and found Judy at the stove. She smiled and quickly covered the ground between them, opening her arms as she walked. He dropped his briefcase on the floor and embraced perhaps the only person on this side of the tracks who was still in his camp. After they kissed, he pulled back, moved her hair from where it had fallen over her left eye and smiled.

"Your smile seems a bit forced," she noted.

"It is," he admitted. "The world has changed dramatically since you took the kids north."

As she moved back to the stove to check the pinto beans, she asked, "How so?"

He watched as she went to the cupboard, pulled out a large glass, filled it with water from the tap, and then poured it into the pot. Once she had completed the task, he explained, "I think I can best sum up where we stand in Justice by telling you we are no longer welcome in our church. On top of that, our house has been egged, I've been kidney-punched, and even had a man try to run me down with a truck. John David Maltose has tried to buy me off, and one of my father's best friends has begged me not to involve him in this case. And unless there are calls threatening our lives, I'm not expecting the telephone to ring. Oh, and five of my clients sent me notes telling me they no longer want to use my services. It seems they didn't even have the guts to face me with the news. Or maybe they just couldn't stand the sight of me."

She considered his words before whispering, "Someone tried to kill you?"

"I don't think it was an accident," he admitted, "so I'm really glad the kids aren't here. And, in truth, I think you need to go back to Ohio, too. They might go after you just because you're my wife."

As he wearily dropped into a chair beside the table, she shook her head. "I signed up for better and worse." She moved gracefully over to the table and sat in the chair just to his left. "I can understand them turning on you, cancelling work, and even not wanting you to be a part of the church, but I don't understand why they would want to try to kill you. I didn't foresee this when I encouraged you to take the case."

"It's what doesn't make any sense to me," he muttered while leaning back in his chair and running his hands through his hair. "Oh, we have a trial date. It is July 13. Glad it is a Monday and not a Friday."

She tilted her head and observed, "I think you need a haircut. You look a bit shaggy."

"You'll have to do it," Coop returned. "I went into Floyd's today. There were no other customers, but he just went about cleaning up the shop and never even acknowledged my presence. It was as if I wasn't there."

"I used to cut your hair when we first got married," she said with a smile. "I probably still have the touch. But I hope you tip better now than you did then."

He forced a smile, rubbed his left hand across his mouth, and glanced toward the clock. His eyes stayed there, but his mind was a thousand miles away.

"What are you thinking about?" she asked.

He turned his eyes back to hers. "Nashville. I just wish we had never left."

"Coop?" she asked, her tone very serious, "do you still believe Calvin is innocent?"

"More than ever," he quickly replied.

Putting her hand over his, she continued her questions, "And do you think you can put together a case to prove it?"

"If he were white," Coop answered quickly, "I would have no doubt. But as he's black it means I have to find a lot more to save him." He looked into her beautiful but troubled face. "I think I have a plan, but having it work depends upon one man's sense of right and wrong. Not fair is it?"

"No," she admitted. "But it's why we aren't in Nashville. If we hadn't come back to Justice, Calvin wouldn't have had a chance."

She was right, if for no other purpose than the young man in the jail cell, they were supposed to be here. "Okay, I get it. Maybe, as my father would have said, God led us here. But there is something I just don't understand."

"What?"

"I can understand the hate, I can understand folks who have been taught prejudice since childhood shunning me for what I am doing. But why has it driven someone to the point where they would like to see me dead? I've been thinking about it all day, and it just doesn't make any sense."

"Someone's scared," Judy solemnly suggested. "If you prove the kid innocent, then it means someone else did it."

"Yeah," he replied, "and that person is likely

one of their own. Someone they trust. It might even be a friend or a family member. If I die, they hang a young man on a lie, while they also save the skin of someone they value."

He drummed his fingers on the table as he whispered, "Maltose."

"What?" she asked.

"Ten grand is a lot of money," he quickly explained, "but it was just a down payment. John David Maltose as much as said if I dropped the case he would make me rich. When he made the offer, I sensed he might want me to run for office, thereby owning a politician so I could steer things his way and influence legislation he wanted. But it makes no sense. He already has people in office who do those things. So he doesn't need me. He was simply spinning a yarn. I guess it was my time to be tempted in the wilderness, or in this case Lovers Park. So as I really offer him nothing of real value, why does it worry him if I'm on this case?"

"You think he murdered Becky?" Judy whispered.

"No," Coop replied. "He has no reason to. They are a generation apart in age, and I doubt the Booths have actually ever been to his home. Besides, he never does any of his own work. He has things done for him. Everything anyone has ever suspected his family of doing has never been proven."

The room suddenly grew silent. There had to be something else Coop was missing, something so hot it put a price on his head. This was far bigger than a high school girl's murder, but it was somehow tied to it. What was so important to John David Maltose that he'd kill rather than have it revealed?

Coop looked into Judy's eyes. "If you are not going back to Ohio, then I have a favor to ask."

"Anything," she said, as she leaned over and kissed his cheek.

"Since I fired Abby," he explained, "I don't have anyone helping me in the office. I wonder if you would mind applying for the job."

She smiled. "This offer wouldn't be due to the fact that no one else will talk to you, much less work for you?"

He smiled. "Well, plus the fact that I can't afford to pay you."

She got up, put her arms around his neck, grinned, and kissed his lips. One kiss led to another, and soon the two were making out like newlyweds. As he stood, swept her up in his arms, and headed for their bedroom, she wrinkled her nose.

"Uh-oh," she all but yelled. "Let me down."

Her feet had no more hit the floor, when she was racing across to the stove. Grabbing a potholder, she lifted the lid on the pan and frowned. "I scorched them."

The odor was rolling through the house like a stink bomb. Nothing like burned food to mess up a romantic situation.

"Sorry," Judy moaned, as she picked the pan up and headed toward the back porch. "I've got to get these out of the house, or we won't be able to live here."

He grinned, but his grin suddenly turned into a moment of illumination. Snapping the fingers on his right hand, he hollered out toward his wife, "Thank you, sweetheart, you've been on the job for less than fifteen minutes and you've already shown me something I missed."

As she reemerged into the kitchen, she said, "I have no idea what you're talking about, and now we have nothing to eat."

"Got any peanut butter?" he asked.

"A little," she answered. "But, Coop, where are we going to buy food? I don't have nearly enough to feed us for three weeks."

"Monday we are going to the capital and visit the state medical examiner. No one knows us there, so we can stock up and bring home the stuff we need. Glad Mom left us her freezer. But this weekend we have to eat whatever we can find in the cabinets and just put up with each other's company."

"I can think of worse things," she said as she kissed him.

23

Monday, June 29, 1964

It was just after one when Coop and Judy sat down in front of the desk of the Mississippi state medical examiner. Collins, an average-sized, silver-haired man with blue eyes framed by gold-rimmed spectacles, looked as though he was nearing retirement age. But in spite of his appearance, his baritone voice was filled with youthful power and enthusiasm. Wearing a light blue shirt and dark slacks, he'd been listening to rock-and-roll music blaring from a desktop radio when the visiting couple entered. After Collins turned the radio off and introductions and greetings exchanged, the trio gathered around the table in the corner of the ME's small office.

"You ever visit with Hyrum Metlock?" The host began the conversation on a seemingly light note.

Coop smiled. "Very recently, in fact."

"Old Hy," Collins continued, "beat me in the semis of the state amateur tennis tournament last year. I thought I had a lock on winning the whole thing in my age group until he graduated up. He cost me my chance at a silver cup. But at least he bought me a steak for dinner." The ME pushed his hands together, intersecting the fingers of his right with his left, before settling into matters at hand. "You have a long drive home, so I guess you need me to go over the report with you. As you called ahead, I have already pulled the files and spent some time refreshing my knowledge on the case."

Coop laughed. "As much as I would like to hear about Hy's backhand, there are more serious matters I do need to get your take on. So I am glad you are ready."

"I will do what I can," Collins replied, "and I enjoy talking about my work. Usually only my dog, Sam, shows much interest though. I find few folks want to hear about what I do. But before we get started, let me jump the rails and steer my train of thought in a couple of different directions. First of all, madam," his eyes falling on Judy, "the light blue suit is perfect on you. And the red scarf just sets it all off. I love those bright colors, but Kathryn, my wife, seems bent on wearing different shades of what she calls subdued hues."

"Thank you," Judy replied with a smile. "And subdued hues or colors can be very pretty, too. How long have you been married?"

"Be thirty-eight years this summer," came the obviously proud response.

"Congratulations," the visitors said in unison.

"I married way above myself," Collins admitted, "and, God bless her, she doesn't know it. I plan on keeping her in the dark, too. And by the way, I want to pass along a bouquet to Hyrum. I have never played against an opponent who was as honest as he was. He never once tried to cheat me on a line call. I'm sure his attitude is evident in the way he handles his cases as well." After smiling wide enough that both of his deep dimples showed, the ME continued, "Now to your questions."

"On the Rebecca Booth case," Coop began, relishing the chance to gain insight on information he needed, "you listed the probable cause of death as being a severed spinal cord."

"Without immediate treatment," the ME explained, "the wound would have likely caused a fairly rapid death. Though it would not have been instantaneous. And she might well have died of blood loss, too. Strangely though, as she had so many wounds, none actually pierced her heart or lungs."

"I noted on the photos some things that troubled me," Coop admitted. "You're the expert; can you tell me about the differences in the wounds? Some were deep and some shallow. The shallow ones seem to have caused more damage upon entry and exit. The edges are ragged. Meanwhile, the larger ones seem smooth."

"For an amateur," Collins smiled, "you have a

keen eye. I suppose you want me to give you my thoughts on those differences."

"I do."

The ME rubbed his brow before opening the file and leafing through the photos he had made during the examination. Handing the pictures and a chart he had filled out during the autopsy to Coop, he began his explanation. "These are copies, and you can take them with you. On your question, I am guessing the smaller wounds happened during the struggle. As you can see, those are mainly on the right side of the body. I would guess that soon after the attack started, when it was obvious Miss Booth could not fend off her attacker, she attempted to run from the assailant. When she turned, it was most likely the single blow to the back of the neck that severed her spine, probably paralyzing her immediately. As there were no other wounds on the back, I would guess she must have somehow ended up facing up or been turned over. At this point, with the victim unable to move, the wounds could have been deeper and smoother because the attacker could use his full force in delivering the blows. Or maybe the attacker used a different weapon because the first one broke, though there is no evidence the knife was damaged."

"Do you think she fought with her attacker?" Coop asked.

"She must have," Collins assured him. "At least

for a short while. I found blood and skin tissue under five fingernails and two of the nails on the right hand had been broken."

"Interesting," the attorney said. He took a final look at the photos and set them to one side. "I might need to call you to testify. Can I depend upon your story staying as it is?"

"Mr. Lindsay," he replied with a smile, "Hyrum isn't the only one who always plays within the rules."

"May I ask a question?"

Both men looked to Judy.

"Was Rebecca sexually assaulted?"

"No," Collins assured her, "but, as I am sure your husband read in my report, she was about fifteen weeks pregnant."

24

After a trip to the grocery store, Coop and Judy hit the highway toward Justice. He found a St. Louis Cardinals game on the radio, and both dismissed the world as they listened. Tired and a bit overcome with the task ahead, they might have remained mute if not for Coop's fascination with third basemen. As he spoke, Judy looked over and observed the man she'd married. It seemed like just yesterday.

"Have I ever told you how much I like watching Ken Boyer play third base?" Coop said, as they turned off a US highway onto the state road to take them home. "I mean, I know everyone in the world was a fan of Stan Musial. I was, too, but now since Stan the Man has retired, I'm hoping folks come to fully appreciate Ken's skills at the hot corner and in the batter's box."

She smiled. He so loved baseball and especially the Cardinals. He talked about them so much she not only knew that White, Javier, Groat, and Boyer made up the infield, but she could list the batting order for the whole team and who came in various relief situations on the mound. She had even grown to the point where she enjoyed listening to the games on the radio. But after what she had heard earlier today, baseball was now completely on the back burner.

The Cardinals were batting in the fifth inning when she shifted her body on the big Ford's bench seat and stared at her husband as he drove the car. In a tone meant to be accusing, she demanded, "Why didn't you tell me Becky was pregnant?"

He glanced her way before setting his eyes back on the road. "I didn't tell you because I didn't know."

"But you have a copy of the autopsy," she argued. "I saw you studying it this morning at the breakfast table."

"Wylie gave me the part I had," he explained. "He got it from Fredrick. Open up my briefcase and take a look. Then compare it to the copy Collins gave us this morning."

Judy grabbed the case, opened it, and hurried through the contents until she found the file. She scanned through the first report. By looking closely, she could see some writing had been covered up. It was obvious even on the copy. She then looked back at the one they had been given today. The line about her pregnancy was there and had not been blacked out.

She glanced back to her husband. "Didn't the fact that this part had been marked out on the first report you were given make you believe something had been covered up?"

He shook his head as he continued to stare down the lonely road. "Not at the time. I just assumed a mistake had been made during the write-up of the report and it had been cor-rected."

She reached down and switched off the radio. "So does this give you motive? Is this a way for you to open the door to finding the person really responsible?"

Coop shrugged. "I don't know what it does for the case, but today's trip was worth it for this and another reason. I have two more cards to play that K. C. Fredrick will not expect. I now have the information I need to shock everyone in this county when the trial opens. And I'm not even talking about the pregnancy."

He reached down and switched the game back on. As the voice of Cards play-by-play man, Harry Caray, once again filled the car, Judy leaned back and considered Coop's cryptic response. What else was he talking about? What other information had he gotten that she'd missed? She knew better than to quiz him, and at this moment, with his mind on baseball and off the case, she figured it was better to let him have some peace, as there would probably be little of it once they got home.

25

Friday, July 3, 1964

At a time when most folks in Justice were taking their morning coffee break, Coop moved from his inner office into the reception area. Judy was sitting behind the desk reading the morning paper.

"I see you're hard at work," he teased.

"You don't exactly have a lot of legal business," she replied looking up from the front page. "By the way, Mom called and says the kids are doing great. They're really enjoying being on the farm."

"Good," he replied. "Better than being here. And probably a lot cooler, too."

"When this case is over," Judy said, "and everyone helps us pack to move north, I will not miss the heat and humidity. Sure wish your office was air-conditioned."

"At this point," he noted, "we are lucky to have an office. I'm still surprised Mr. Jessup hasn't canceled the lease."

Walking over to the window, he looked down onto the square. Everything appeared normal. In fact, it seemed too normal. In the past few days, there had been no hostile words or threats. No one had spoken to them, either, but the fact that the wave of terror was over seemed strange. Were they waiting for the trial, or was there some other reason for the passive behavior?

"How was Calvin today?" Judy asked.

Without turning, Coop replied, "He's starting to heal up. They are letting Hattie bring meals to him, so he's eating better, too."

"How are his spirits?"

"Considering the odds against him," Coop answered while turning back to his wife, "they are amazing. Maybe it is Hattie, or maybe it is what I shared with him, but he seems to believe a miracle can happen."

"Maybe it can," she said with a smile.

The sound of heavy footsteps followed by a knock caused both of them to turn apprehensively to the door. She looked his way, and he shrugged. "First time we've had a guest since I took the case. Maybe I spoke too soon on Jessup cancel-ling the lease."

Moving across the room, Coop twisted the knob and cracked the door, relaxed, and smiled. "Hattie. Good to see you. In fact, I was going to come over and visit you this afternoon. So you saved me a trip."

The woman, dressed in a flower print dress and black shoes, dipped her head and stepped for-ward. She'd no more than crossed the threshold when she began an apology. "I is so sorry Mr. Coop. Here I go troubling you again."

"No trouble," Judy said before her husband could respond. Getting up from behind the desk, she made her way over to the visitor and stuck out her hand. "I'm Judy, Coop's wife."

"Why you is a pretty thing," Hattie answered, "and look at your figure. Coop tells me you have three young'uns, and your waist is so tiny I'll bet I could circle it with just my hands."

"Thank you." Judy beamed. "You need to teach my husband to talk like that."

"Oh, he's bragged on you to me," the visitor replied. "He powerful loves you, yes he does."

Feeling left out, Coop jumped into the fray. "Did you just come here to meet Judy, or is there something else on your mind? Is everything okay over at the jail?"

"Calvin's fine," she quickly answered. "Sheriff Estes makes sure. He's been real nice to us. Speaks real highly of you, too, Mr. Coop."

"Then what is it, Hattie?" Coop asked.

"Why don't you have a seat?" Judy suggested.

After Hattie took her place in one of the two round-backed oak chairs in front of the desk, Judy grabbed the other one. Coop then rested on the corner of the desk. As they did, their guest opened her large purse and pulled out a light pink embroidered handkerchief, dabbed her eyes, and then looked toward the attorney.

"I lost my home."

"What?" Coop demanded.

"It weren't my fault," Hattie explained with tears in her eyes. "I don't own the place, and the landlord just upped the rent on me. When I told his collector I couldn't pay, he ordered me out. I had just a couple of hours and had to move my stuff to a storage room in the church."

Coop nodded. This smelled clear up to high heaven, and he figured he knew who was behind it. "Hattie, who owns the house where you lived?"

The sad woman looked up. "Mr. Maltose. He owns almost all the houses over in colored town. I was renting another place from his daddy twenty years back."

"Yep," the lawyer spat out. He considered the strange move for a second and then asked what sounded like a bizarre question. "Did he give you any opportunity to pay any other way than by money?"

"Yes, sir," she quickly replied, "it was his hired help who came by to give me the news. He said if I'd tell the law Calvin weren't home that night, I could live in the house for free. Of course, I couldn't do it."

Coop glanced over to Judy and frowned. It was getting real dirty now. Looking back to his visitor, he asked, "Did this man hassle any of your other neighbors?"

"Well, he talked to Mamie Johnson, she's my closest neighbor, but when she told him she was at church and didn't know if Calvin was home or not, he didn't say nothing else."

"What about Mamie's husband?" Coop quickly asked.

"Oh," Hattie whispered, "he don't know about him. None of the white folks do. You see he's from Atlanta, and while Mamie's taken his name, Claude isn't legally married to her. I mean they went to a preacher, but never took out a license. So it is okay with God, just not the governor."

This news was a relief. He needed Claude on the stand, so he couldn't let Maltose put the scare in him. Besides, if Fredrick was sure Mamie was unable to say Calvin was home, the DA might put her on the stand to give a black voice to the case. Once Mamie was under oath, she could deliver for the defense, as well.

"Hattie," Coop asked, returning his gaze to the woman, "where are you going to stay?"

"I guess I could stay at the church," she explained. "Lots of folks have slept on them pews on Sundays; maybe I could take their spots the other six days."

"No, you're not," Judy said, jumping back into the discussion. "We're going to get your clothes and other needed items, and you stay in the same room my folks stay in when they come to visit."

"No," Hattie said, waving her hand, "you folks are in enough trouble right now because of me. If I lived at your place, there is no telling what might happen."

"You are staying with us," Judy shot back. "No ifs, ands, or buts. Isn't that right, Coop?"

"It is more than right; it is perfect." He smiled.

"But," Hattie argued, "what would your neighbors say about a colored living with you?"

The lawyer grinned. "They're not talking to us now, so I don't guess they will say anything. At least, not to our faces." He chuckled and looked back to his wife. "Do you feel comfortable driving over to Hattie's part of town and getting her things?"

"You know I do," she said, bouncing out of the chair. "Much better than being bored here."

"I'll stay at the office and work," Coop quipped. "The car's in the alley. You can go out the back and no one will see you. Get Hattie's stuff, take it to our house, set things up there, and call me. Let me know everything went smoothly. Then you come back to the office and let Hattie get some rest." He looked over to the visitor. "And don't you answer the door or phone—no matter what."

"Mr. Coop," Hattie moaned, "I'd be fine at the church. You don't need to take any more chances."

"You let me worry about that," he replied. "If the war does accelerate, I'd rather have you where I can keep you safe than living where it would be easy for Maltose to grab you." The attorney rubbed his chin and looked back toward the woman. "Hattie, one more thing. This man who came to see you, was he by himself?"

"Yes, sir."

"What kind of car was he driving?"

"It weren't a car; it was an old truck."

Coop grinned. "Was it blue?"

"Yes sir, a kind of a dirty blue."

26

Sunday, July 5, 1964

For much of his life, Coop had seen the way the Negroes were discriminated against and simply accepted it as not just fact, but as the way life was intended to be. Countless times he'd witnessed someone belittled due to his or her race. He'd also come to understand that the opportunities were few for those who were black. But until now, he had never fully gotten the hidden under-current of hate that bombarded these people on a daily basis. While some were patronized and a few even respected, none were fully accepted in any facet of Justice. Why had it taken Becky's death to open his eyes?

The poverty and despair he had seen when he'd made the trip across the tracks had dug into his heart like a baited hook in a fish's mouth. No matter how much he wanted to forget the haunting images of the children who were scared of the white man, he couldn't anymore escape them than he could the signs in town reading Colored Only. Why had it taken him so long to not just recognize it but to have it register for what it was? As Saturday dragged into Sunday and he, Judy, and Hattie, hid behind the walls of their "safe" house, he continued to beat himself up for not noticing the facts so much sooner.

Sunday morning, while Coop was sitting in front of the TV essentially lost in thought and ignoring a minister delivering a sermon, Hattie came in from the kitchen.

"Do you mind if I join you, Mr. Coop?" she asked.

He smiled. "You don't have to ask for anything Hattie. Our home is yours."

"And I surely appreciate. I do. Are you watching the preacher?"

As he eased back in his chair and glanced over to his guest now taking a place on the couch, he shrugged. "Watching, but not hearing. My mind is a hundred different places looking back at a thousand different things I missed. I guess I have finally realized in my more than thirty years of life, I have been kind of like the old hymn 'I was blind but now I see.' "

Hattie nodded, "We've all been there, but sadly, most folks never really take their blinders off. So they miss a lot of goodness all around them. And lot of other folks not only wear them blinders, but they is as stubborn as a mule. Stubbornness, more often than not, can make a person look real foolish."

Coop paused, studied the woman's ebony skin, and said, "It has to be tough being a Negro here in Justice."

"I ain't never known anything else," was her honest reply. "But life is no walk in the park no matter what color you is. If you are like me, you just come to accept the way things are and do your best to deal with what you've been given. And maybe it is when you are down, when you is like the child no one wants, maybe it is then you recognize the kindness of folks like you and Miss Judy. If I had everything I wanted, I'd have likely missed it. In fact, I feel sorry for

Mr. Maltose. He don't know nothing about kindness and how sweet it is to receive it from others."

He pondered her words for a moment before tossing out a comment he could have better left unsaid. "Hattie, if I had been born black, I think I'd have been angry. I think when I saw all the things I was denied, I'd have risen up with rage and tried to grab some of it. I don't think I could have ever accepted that living on the other side of the tracks was to be my lot in life."

She smiled. "We all feel it sometime. Can't tell you how many times I wanted to steal a drink from the White Only water fountain. In fact, I did once, but all I found out was the water weren't really any different and there are more of you people than my kind, so the line was usually longer, too. Yet, it's tough knowing the only time souls will ever really be equal is when we die and meet the Lord."

She nodded and then went on, "At some point most of the young folks just give up. They just don't see the use in working hard if they're never going to escape colored town. But what can you do? The rules are set, the lines are drawn, and we is what we is. You is white and I is black. Can't change the fact."

Pushing off the chair, Coop walked over and switched off the TV. As he did, Judy came in from their bedroom and kissed him. She then looked over to Hattie. "My, your breakfast was something special."

"Shucks," Hattie said, waving her hand, "it weren't nothing. But I do like your kitchen. I think I'd be happy just spending all day cooking in there."

Judy laughed. "And if you did, I'd be as big as a barn."

"Don't want to make you big," their guest said, smiling, "but Miss Judy, you could stand to gain a few pounds. You'd blow away in a good wind."

While Hattie's first visit to his office might have set Coop on the road to being rejected by those he'd known all his life, it also opened the door to better understanding what his father spent years unsuccessfully preaching from the pulpit. This woman was special, and Coop would have never fully known it if she hadn't come into their home.

"Mr. Coop," Hattie said, breaking into the lawyer's thoughts of the past and present colliding, "would you mind if I told you and Miss Judy a private story?"

"Please do," he answered quickly, sitting back in the chair while Judy grabbed a spot on the couch.

"My daddy was a really special man," Hattie began, her face glowing with pride. "I was one of seven kids, and my mama died when I was just six. Daddy raised us all by working, cutting down trees for the lumber mill. On Sundays and Wednesdays he'd preach at the same church I goes to now. But back then, it was just a log building. They hadn't moved the old white Methodist church across the tracks for us yet."

Hattie smiled, her eyes misting up, before dropping her chin and continuing, "He was a fine man, just as fine as any man, white or black, whoever walked this earth. He taught us right from wrong, and also taught us forgiveness was far more important than hating. He could quote Scripture, and my, how he could sing! And he was a good-looking man, too. Looked a lot like a darker version of Calvin."

"He sounds special," Judy chimed in.

"Oh, yes, and more," Hattie assured her. "Anyway, we kids was all grown, and most of my folks had moved up north to work in Chicago and Detroit when Daddy started to fail. It came on kind of sudden. He was just sixty-three, but something just grabbed him and wouldn't let go. One week he was preaching strong, and the next he could barely climb up to the pulpit. We didn't have no money, so even though folks kept telling us he needed to go, he didn't see no doctor. And one day he just didn't get out of bed. I could see in his eyes he knew the end was near, and we was both powerful scared."

She dabbed a tear from her eye before picking up her story. "I went to work that day cleaning up the Methodist church and told your daddy, Reverend Abe, about my father. We sat there on the front pew in the church and talked for at least an hour. I went back to work then headed down the street to clean two other houses before heading home. When I got to our little house in colored town, I saw a car parked out in front. Naturally, fear gripped my soul. I thought sure my daddy had gone to Heaven and I hadn't been there to hold his hand when he drew his last breath. So I almost had the chilling kind of shakes as I went running up the steps into our house and back to his room. And you know what I found?"

She glanced over at Coop. "Your daddy was there holding my daddy's hand. Reverend Abe came to the wrong side of the tracks to visit the bed of a washwoman's father. You don't know how much it meant to me. For five hours, Reverend Abe held my daddy's hand, and they talked about children and life and God. Your daddy kept telling my daddy what a blessing he'd been to the world."

Hattie, tears now streaming down her face, took a deep breath and whispered, "Reverend Abe sensed my daddy's time was near, and he leaned close to his old black face and said, 'I'll always be there to take care of any needs your family has. Don't you worry about it.' "

"Daddy's eyes opened big and he stared at me

and then back to Reverend Abe. He smiled, and it was like angels were in the room. I swear things got brighter than they had ever been, even in the middle of a summer day. Then just when I thought singing was going to break out from Glory, Daddy squeezed your daddy's hand, looked right in Reverend Abe's eyes, and smiled."

Hattie's throat tightened. She tried to catch her breath but couldn't. Dabbing her eyes with her dress sleeve, she whispered, "When my daddy died, the last person he saw was your daddy."

Hattie choked back a rush of tears and forced a smile as she said, "Your daddy came to the wrong side of the tracks to take the last earthly steps with a colored man he'd never met. It don't get no finer. And then, just by his actions, he showed my daddy that a white man can love a colored man and respect him, too. For maybe the first time in his life, my daddy felt like he was an equal in Reverend Abe's eyes. It was likely the best gift anyone ever gave him. He left this earth feeling like a white man thought he was just as good as him."

She paused, took a deep breath, and pushed herself off the couch. "If you will excuse me, I is going to make sure I got everything unpacked in the room you're letting me stay in."

When she was out of earshot, Judy looked over to her husband. "That pretty much tells me all I need to know about your father."

Coop nodded, but held his thoughts. His dad didn't just speak the lessons of life; he lived them. And it must have been why he preached the story of the good Samaritan so often. Maybe most of those who heard it never fully understood what he was trying to say back then, but for Coop the lesson had finally taken full root. And it was a colored maid who had been the instrument to his becoming what his father dreamed he would be.

27

Monday, July 6, 1964

He'd been at his desk for almost two hours when he heard footsteps on the stairs leading up to his office. Coop checked his watch, 10:24, got up and moved toward the entrance. The guest didn't bother knocking. As the door swung open, John David Maltose's tall, wide-shouldered form filled the entry.

"John David, what brings you to my humble side of the planet?" Coop made sure the visitor caught his sarcastic tone by adding a smug look.

Not waiting for an invitation, Maltose strolled into the office and took a short look at the modest surroundings before pointing to the open door behind Coop. "Is this where you do what bit of business comes your way?"

"It's modest," the lawyer quipped, "but I like it."

As if he were calling the shots, the visitor pushed by Coop and marched into the inner sanctum. After quickly surveying the office, he took a seat in one of the green leather chairs in front of the desk.

Coop was amused as Maltose drummed his fingers on the chair's arm while staring at the wall behind the desk. The lawyer, enjoying his control, intentionally waited almost two minutes before asking, "Would you like me to join you or is this a private dance?"

Without looking around, the big man barked, "I didn't come here to sit; I came to talk turkey."

"I guess it's better than talking to the turkey." Coop walked into his office and moved to the empty chair where his guest's eyes were fixed. After studying Maltose a few seconds, noting the starched white linen shirt and pressed gray slacks, he took a seat. "Now, John David, what can I do for you? Do you need someone to draw up your will?"

The man didn't waste any time. "I already have someone working on a new will. I don't need you to do it. But let me take a moment and lay my cards on the table. Cooper, you need to end the charade. You and I both know you can't get a jury here to find a Negro innocent of murdering a white person—much less a white teenage girl. So what you're doing is not just a waste of your time, it's political suicide. You'll never have another paying job in this county again. Besides, the boy will die and we don't want that to happen."

Coop picked up a pen from his desk and began to twirl it through his fingers. The writing instrument made three full passes between every finger on his right hand before he finally asked, "So?"

Shaking his head, Maltose continued, "You would commit career suicide over a black kid?"

"If it means seeing an innocent person get a fair shake, I sure would. Sleeping is very important to me, and I couldn't sleep if I didn't at least try."

The visitor's face defined frustration as he spat, "You're a fool."

"Maybe in the world's eyes, I am," Coop admitted.

Maltose shook his head in disgust. "I could give you all you have ever dreamed of. I have the connections to do so. I even have the power to get the kid out of the death penalty."

"And you have the power," Coop added, "to pay to have me killed. But I'll hand it to you, at least you warned me you were going to do it."

The words seemed to catch Maltose by surprise. A confused expression framed his face as he said, "I don't know what you're talking about."

Coop smiled, dropped the pen, leaned forward,

rested his elbows on his desk, and explained, "At Lovers Park you told me you'd kill me if I continued with this case. I wish I could remember your exact words, but the sentiment and the promise were clear. Then just a few days later, one of your men tried to run me down with an old blue pickup as I walked in the street in front the Methodist church."

The visitor leaned back in the chair, crossed his right leg over his left knee in a move revealing a pair of shiny eelskin loafers. After folding his arms across his chest, he spoke, "I was actually talking about your career being killed, not stopping your heart. And I don't know anything about a blue pickup truck trying to run you down."

"Are you denying that one of your workers drives one?" Coop asked.

"Maybe they do," Maltose shot back, "but I employ scores of people, and I certainly don't keep track of what they drive."

Coop raised his eyebrows as he leaned in further and drew a bit closer to his guest. "This would be the same guy who evicted Hattie Ross from her house last week."

"The woman was evicted?" John David asked.

"As if you don't know."

Coop leaned back and watched his guest seemingly attempt to come up with a way out of the trap the lawyer had sprung. As the seconds ticked by, it was obvious Maltose was at a complete loss for words. Finally, rather than pursue a verbal road he likely believed he couldn't successfully navigate, the man pressed on with his original agenda.

"Listen, Coop, I still have the power to make good things happen for you. I can still use my power to make you look noble for the work you have done. And I can get Calvin a way out of dying in the chair. And the money we talked about the other day is just chicken feed. I can do all of it and so much more if you will just drop this matter and accept a plea bargain today. That's all it would take."

"Why would you do all this for me?" Coop asked as he lifted his arms off the desk and leaned back in his chair. "What's in it for you? You own this county and a lot more, too. You even own enough legislators so you can get what you need at the capitol. You already have enough local stooges, and the lawyers you use are from New York City firms. Nothing I can give you would be worth anything. So why are you trying to buy me off?"

Maltose shrugged. "I see something in you I believe is worth saving."

"No, you don't," Coop barked as he rose to his feet. "What I am is just what you don't want in this town. I'll stand up to you. I will fight for the very ones you want to beat down. What you see as business, I see as evil. The fact that you're trying to make a deal with me means I've hit a nerve going much deeper than business. This is about something you are afraid will come out. This is about something that might just ruin you. I don't know what it is yet, but I might stumble across it, and therefore it might come out in the trial. It's why you're trying to buy me off, because you are scared!"

Coop wagged his finger toward his guest and grinned. "Imagine, a preacher's kid has a member of the Maltose family scared. No matter how you look at it, the irony is even funnier than a Jonathan Winters comedy routine."

Maltose leaped off the chair, turned, and quickly headed toward the door. Just as he was about to reach for the knob, he glanced back to Coop. "You're making a mistake! You're playing in a league you shouldn't be in. When all this is over, the money you could have had and the life you could have lived will haunt you for as long as you walk this earth." He paused before adding, "And the innocent colored boy, the one I tried to help you save with a plea bargain, will be executed. And his last few seconds in the electric chair will stick with both of us until our dying days."

The big man pulled open the door, stepped out into the stairwell, slammed the door, and marched down the stairs. Once more Coop was alone with his thoughts.

28

A blind man could see that the most likely key to unlocking this whodunit was finding out why John David Maltose was so interested in buying the lawyer off. Yet the information was not in any evidence files, and few in Justice were willing to visit with Coop about Maltose or anything else. So where could he look and who could he ask to dig a bit deeper into the millionaire's fear and motivation? As he mentally rolled over the big man's history, he remembered something he'd once overheard his parents speaking of in hushed tones when they thought he was asleep. Could his old childhood memory lead him to pay dirt? A short trip might well give him the answer he needed.

Locking his office door, Coop crossed the street, strolled into the courthouse and down the hall, and walked into the office of county records. When the secretary ignored his ringing the bell on the front desk, he simply invited himself into the adjacent file room and scanned rows of cabinets until he came to the one he needed. Five minutes later, he had jotted down the information and turned up the volume on his parents' almost-forgotten hushed words.

After a quick trip back to the office to make a call to the state capital and take a few more notes, Coop rang up Judy, informed her that he had to make a quick trip up to Brandice and wouldn't be back in time for supper. Jumping into the yellow and green Studebaker President, he eased out of his parking spot in the alley and pushed the car east. An hour later, he was at 607 Bellford Street in a small, sleepy town of 307 that time had seemingly forgotten. After ringing the bell, he only had to wait a few seconds for a redheaded woman in her midthirties to peek through the glass and then open the door.

"Whatever you're selling," she said, her tone registering somewhere between perturbed and apathetic, "I'm not buying."

"My name's Coop Lindsay, and I'm not selling anything. But I would like to visit with you for just a few minutes. If you don't feel comfortable letting me into your home, we can sit outside."

She considered his offer before pointing to the end of the porch where two white cane chairs had been set. He led the way and took the one closest to the railing; she grabbed the one nearest what was probably the living room window.

"Make it fast," she demanded. "I've got some soup on the stove I don't want to scorch."

He nodded and looked into her almost violet eyes. She'd likely been beautiful once, but time had not been kind. Though not heavy, she nevertheless was soft and out of shape. She had the skin of someone who spent way too much time in the sun. The rhythm of her speech gave hints that she was either extremely tired or sick. As a hacking cough suddenly grabbed her causing her whole body to shake, Coop assumed that maybe it was a bit of both. When she was finally over her spell, Coop had taken a full inventory of the woman and began his explanation of why he needed to speak with her.

"I'm from Justice."

"Too bad." Her tone indicated her revulsion for his hometown.

He smiled. "It can be a trying place to live."

"Tell me about it," she said. "I grew up there, lived there until I was twenty-five, then turned my back on it and I'm never going to look back."

Coop nodded sympathetically. "I understand. I believe your name was Molly Thornton before you got married."

"Yeah," she answered. "You know I was the homecoming queen my sophomore year." She paused and then looked over to her guest as if she was studying him real hard. When lightning suddenly struck, she snapped her fingers and happily exclaimed, "I bet you're Reverend Lindsay's son. Sure, I remember when you were a kid." She smiled, "Your folks were sure sweet people. How are they?"

He shook his head. "They're both dead now.

Dad died about seven years ago. Mom passed over the winter."

"I'm sorry," she said.

"A lot of folks miss them." Coop answered. "But I'm not really here to talk about old times; I want to know how you feel about the man you married."

"The man I was forced to marry," she bitterly corrected him.

"So you didn't love him?" Coop asked.

"As much as anybody could," she explained. "He was a couple of years older, from a rich family, and my folks didn't have anything. When he paid just a little bit of attention to me, I fell hard. He was a charmer and could talk me into doing anything and it's how I ended up pregnant. When I refused to get rid of the baby, his parents made him marry me. And it's how I become a Maltose. A few months later, Travis was born and I was convinced everything was going to be all right. We were going to make this work. But in spite of living like a queen and having servants cater to my every whim, it didn't take me too long to get tired of being trapped in luxury. You see, John David's dad was practically a jailer. I couldn't leave the house without his permission. His servants were spying on me all the time. I somehow stuck it out for nine years before I had enough and got a divorce. Old John David was more than happy to get rid of me, but freedom came with a steep price."

"And what was that?" Coop asked.

Molly sadly shook her head. "They bought me a house here in Brandice. As you can see, it is the nicest in town, and they gave me money, too. But the family kept Travis. I've only gotten to see him a few times since I left Justice."

"Sounds like you loved your son a lot."

"I did," she sobbed, "and no matter what folks say, I didn't desert him. It just became impossible for me to stay there watching him grow up and become just like his father and grandfather. And there was nothing I could do about it."

Coop leaned closer and in a soft tone asked, "If Travis meant so much to you, why did you give up?"

She shook her head while tightly folding her hands in her lap. "I couldn't look at myself in the mirror anymore. John David never beat me, he never laid a hand on me, but his family still broke my spirit. He was always having affairs and loved parading his mistresses in front of me. I know he got remarried to a gal from Gulfport who is young enough to be his daughter. Maybe money soothes her spirit a lot more than it soothed mine, or maybe she's as mean as John David and can dish out as much as he can, but I wasn't that way and had to get out."

"Molly," Coop asked, "how old is Travis now?"

"He's twenty. He's a junior at Mississippi State. You ever see him?"

Coop shook his head. "I've only been back for a short while. He would have been away at school."

"If you ever do see him," she almost whispered, "please tell him his mother loves him. I want him to know."

"I sure will," he assured her. "And thanks for your time."

She looked up as if disappointed he was leaving and asked, "Is that all you needed?"

"Yes," he said. "You have given me exactly what I was looking for."

29

Coop stopped and grabbed a bite at a Dairy Frost Drive-In before turning the Studebaker toward Justice. As he navigated the two-lane blacktop, he considered what he'd learned. John David had been a womanizer and likely still was one, but how did it tie to this case? And more importantly, how would it serve to help the lawyer spring his client?

As he hit a long, open stretch of highway with no other cars in sight, Coop pushed down on the accelerator and watched the car easily climb to sixty. For the next five minutes as Coop pondered what he just found out and tried to match it with what he already knew, the Studebaker effortlessly drifted along through the rural, wooded countryside. Then the road took the lawyer to a stretch of hills demanding his full attention. The first was an easy adjustment to the right and could easily be navigated without braking, but the second required a much sharper turn to the left. When he pushed down on the brake to slow his speed, the pedal dropped to the floor and didn't come back up.

It was just minutes before dusk and the car was now hitting seventy with a curve meant for half the speed looming just ahead. Gripping the steering wheel with both hands, Coop eased it to the left and prayed the already squealing tires would somehow hold the road. As the back end slid toward the ditch, he fully expected the Studebaker to go airborne and roll across the ground and into forest, but somehow he safely exited the curve and onto a long, downhill straight patch of asphalt. As the car's lights flashed down the highway, he noted a sign for what amounted to two consecutive U-turns at the base of the hill. The first went left and the next right. Locals called this a severe *S* curve, but as the Studebaker climbed to eighty, Coop sensed the moniker was about to change and this stretch of road would soon be named for the popular Jan and Dean song "Dead Man's Curve."

Reaching down to the dash, he switched the engine off, and as the motor died, all he heard was the sound of the air rushing by and his tires trying to keep a grip on the road. As he approached the first of the turns, he was greeted by an even larger problem. Just ahead in the oncoming lane was a logging truck beginning to chug up the hill.

As his speed was still climbing, Coop figured he only had one chance to avoid disaster. Saying a quick prayer, he reached down and yanked the emergency brake. As it grabbed, the car pulled hard to the left directly into the path of the huge truck. Letting go of the brake, Coop jerked the steering wheel to the right just in time to miss the big rig. One danger avoided, but an even more foreboding one loomed directly ahead.

The emergency brake slowed the car to about fifty before burning out. The curve sign said twenty-five. Could those Goodyear tires hold the road and guide him through the final half of the S curve?

Yanking back to the left and then quickly to the right, trying to stay in the middle of the highway, he somehow made it through the first part of the challenge, but the car simply couldn't move quickly enough to hold the road for the sharp bend that followed. Even while Coop pushed the wheel right, his passenger side tires lost the blacktop and found the shoulder, and there was no coming back. Hitting a pothole, the Studebaker dipped into the ditch causing the driver's side wheels to leave the ground. A split-second later the car was spinning like a ballerina. With Coop tightly gripping the steering wheel, the vehicle continued its wild dance until it crashed into a barbwire fence at the edge of the woods. It came to rest on its passenger doors with the driver's side tires reaching for the sky. Coop was lying against the passenger front door, his head in the floorboard, when everything stopped moving. Though physically sound, it took him a few moments to clear his mind enough to assess what had happened. He was still fighting mental fog when he pushed off the dashboard, managed to get to his feet, and came to a crouching position in the cramped quarters. Gaining a few more of his faculties, he checked for blood and found none. His legs and arms felt good, too. So with his body intact and his brain starting to come up to speed, it was time to pull himself out of what was left of the car.

Though it was sunset, there was still enough light for him to see that the windshield had popped out. At last, a break. It was a way to exit the crumbled, twisted mess once labeled with the grand moniker of President. Ducking his head, he stepped through where the glass had been and climbed over the fence into the woods. On unsteady legs, he made his way along the wire property boundary until he got to the car's nose and then crawled back over the fence and into the ditch. Just as his feet hit the ground, a car drove up and a man climbed out of a '62 Thunderbird.

"You okay?" He yelled as he sprinted over to the accident scene.

"Yeah," Coop shouted back, "I think so. Maybe a little bit bruised, but nothing more."

As he got closer, Coop noted the man was built like a linebacker, sporting a crew-cut and a hard, big jaw. He also wore blue jeans and a gray shirt proudly proclaiming Jim's Garage above the pocket. After visually checking out Coop, the man took a look at the Studebaker's now easy-to-view undercarriage.

"My name's Jim O'Banyon," he announced as he surveyed the wreck in the fading light. "What happened? Did you take the curve too fast?"

After brushing himself off, Coop replied, "Not intentionally. I pushed down and had no brakes."

O'Banyon was nearing the back of the car when he stopped, pulled a screwdriver from his pocket, and poked at something. After shaking his head, he glanced back to the lawyer. "You were lucky. Come back here and look at this."

As the still-shaking lawyer approached, O'Banyon pointed to a rubber line that appeared to have literally melted. "Do you see that?"

"Yes, but what is it?"

The mechanic smiled and then grimly noted,

"Some fool bent your exhaust in such a way that it was blowing on your brake line. I don't know who worked on your car recently, but whoever he is, if I were you, I'd give him a piece of my mind. You were lucky he didn't kill you. It might have taken days, but at some point, your brakes were going to fail."

Coop shook his head. Maltose had probably only come to his office to give one of his boys time to rig the car. But once more, the lawyer had somehow cheated death and lived to continue to shake up a man who usually couldn't be shaken.

30

Tuesday, July 7, 1964

John David Maltose slept little. Waking up at dawn, he dressed and made his way to the kitchen where one of his maids rustled up eggs and toast for his breakfast. After knocking down the food with two cups of coffee, he made his way into his office to fume.

Sitting in a chair beside the French doors overlooking the garden area of his estate, he looked out over a carefully manicured rose bush but never saw it. In fact, he was blind to everything at this moment other than his rage. He was the chess player; he moved the pieces at will and controlled the outcome of every game he played, but over the last few days, others had stepped into the picture, and the millionaire not only didn't know who they were, but he couldn't figure out what they wanted.

Drumming his fingers on the chair's arm, he considered those who might be horning in on his territory. Fields was too old, Lindsay was too noble, and Fredrick too stupid. So who was left?

Smoothing his mustache with his thumb and forefinger, he considered others who might want to become players. Yes, there were folks in the capital, and even in Chicago and New York, who would love to have some of his action, but they had no connections to Justice, and obviously whoever was pulling these strings knew something about the case. Maltose was so consumed by a mystery he couldn't come close to solving, he didn't even hear the door open or notice the beautiful woman walk into his private lair.

"What's on your mind?" Linda Maltose asked.

He glanced across the room to his second wife. Though it seemed out of place in the hills of Mississippi, she defined Hollywood beauty. She was five-and-a-half feet tall, a store-bought blonde, with huge blue eyes and a perfect body. She didn't as much walk as glide through a room. The lilt in her voice often hung in the air like perfume, tempting any who heard it to follow the woman wherever she went. He'd still been married when he first gave in to her voice and the temptation it offered. But she made sure he wasn't married for long. And when the first marriage officially died, Linda sunk her claws in so deep, he knew he wouldn't be free for long.

"Good morning," he said. "Is that the night-gown and robe set you bought on your trip to Atlanta a few weeks back?"

"No." She smiled. "This came from my last trip to New York."

She didn't seem to care much for spending time in Justice. At least once a month, she'd find an excuse to take off and go somewhere, and as she'd gotten older those trips had become even more frequent. Thus, she was hardly a mother to either their eight-year-old son or four-year-old daughter, but they had people for those duties anyway and those caretakers were likely much better role models and parents than he or Linda.

She frowned and waltzed over to where he sat. "You haven't been paying much attention to me lately. You found a new filly?"

"I've had things on my mind," he snapped. "Besides, you're the one who is never here." His eyes caught hers before adding, "It has just been a bit crazy the last few days."

"Are you caught up in the mess with the colored boy and Becky Booth?" she asked.

"Everybody's been thinking about it," he replied in an off-handed manner.

"Figured it might just be eating you up." She laughed. "I think you knew her pretty well, didn't you? I mean she had been to our house more than just a few times over the past few months."

Maltose looked back out the window, as he chewed on her words. As he thought, she rattled on, "And you need to do something about Travis. He is partying hard and not doing his work at school. He is becoming worthless. And he doesn't need to come home so much. He is a bad influence on Michael and Jodi."

She was baiting him. She always did. She didn't like Travis and was constantly trying to find a way to expose his flaws. And it wasn't hard. After all, she was spot on with her remarks. The kid drank too much, was a skirt chaser, and barely scraped by in his schoolwork. Plus, he was lazy and had a surly attitude. In other words, he was just like his old man.

"I'll crack down on Travis when he needs it," Maltose finally replied. "And you have no business worrying about him anyway. Travis isn't your kid. But I think it would be a fine idea if you spent more time with Jodi and Michael. Why don't you go see if Millie needs any help getting them ready for school?"

"You don't want me around?" It was more a dare than a question.

"Not now," he replied. "I have things I have to do."

"You always do," she shot back. She then smiled, "I heard a rumor going around, and you aren't going to like it."

He glanced back into the catty smile he had grown to hate. "I suppose you're going to tell me what it is."

She shook her head, spun, and headed back toward the door. Yet just before walking out, she looked back at her husband. "They say you're trying to make a deal to keep the colored boy out of the chair."

"Where did you hear that?" he demanded.

"It's all around," she assured him. "Folks are dreaming up all kinds of reasons for your soft heart, but there is one I've come up with that no one has guessed yet."

"Linda!" His calling of her name demanded an explanation.

She glared at him for several seconds and then announced, "They say you're going soft on coloreds, but I don't buy it for a moment. I think you're trying to keep this from going to trial because you think Travis did it." She took two steps forward and pointed a finger toward Maltose. "John David, you're protecting your son and you believe Cooper Lindsay might be able to figure things out in a court of law. Your son is going to bring your world down on top of you, and it might just cost Jodi and Michael their inheritance. Whatever it takes, you best never let it happen, or you won't live long enough to grow old."

She was gone before he had a chance to respond, but if there were rumors going around, he had no doubt she was at least partially responsible for them. Linda loved to stir things up and was always trying to find a way to exert some kind of control over him. Setting anyone and everyone against Travis was her favorite tactic.

31

Linda's words were still on his mind when Maltose picked up the phone and dialed a familiar number. It rang four times before the man he needed to speak with picked up.

"Main office."

"Melvin," Maltose said, "you still driving your blue pickup truck?"

"Sure, I love my old Chevy."

The millionaire took a deep breath. "I hear you've been using it as a weapon."

"What do you mean?"

"You tried to run down Coop Lindsay in front of the Methodist church."

There was no hesitation in the reply. "The

steering is a bit loose, and when I looked down to change the radio station, I lost it a bit. He jumped out of the way, so it was no big deal."

"So," Maltose said, "you didn't try to kill the lawyer?"

"Listen, John David, I've worked for you for a long time. I've done what you asked when you asked it. And over the past week, I've heard you complain about what Lindsay is doing on this case. So if the truck accidentally crossed a lane, and if it had managed to take the guy out of the case, I don't think you would have complained."

Maltose shook his head. Which way was it? Was it an accident, or was it one of his workers reacting too strongly to one of his rants and taking matters into his own hands? With the scruffy but powerful hired hand, he had no idea, so until he had something more concrete, he would let it go.

"Listen, Melvin," Maltose explained, "if Cooper Lindsay is taken down, I will make it happen. Don't jump the gun and try to anticipate what I want. Do you understand that?"

"Boss," the man replied, "I promise I won't take anyone for a last ride unless I have orders and am paid well for my work."

"Glad we got it cleared up," the millionaire quipped. "Now, what is this I hear about you evicting Hattie Ross from her home?"

This time there was a much longer pause before

the explanation came. "Listen, Boss, it was time to collect the rent, and I just figured I might be able to get her to give the testimony needed to get the case decided in the fashion the town wanted. But when I pushed the buttons, she didn't cave in."

"Hattie's not going to cave," Maltose assured his hired man. "She has more character than either one of us."

"I didn't know," Melvin replied.

"Listen, boy," the millionaire shot back, "I run this business, you work for me, and unless I give you a direct order, you don't do anything. Don't try to help me by thinking, because you're not very good at it. You've made two big mistakes, and the next one will be your last. Do you understand?"

"Yes, sir."

Maltose didn't bother with a good-bye before slamming the phone down. Melvin was walking on thin ice. If he kept taking matters into his own hands, he'd soon be washing someone else's dirty laundry.

32

After taking a final look at what had been his mother's pride and glory, Coop caught a ride back to town with the state trooper who had investigated the wreck. The final cause was chalked up to equipment failure, and thus, there would be no further investigation regarding who actually reworked the exhaust to slowly burn out the brake line. Nevertheless, Coop had a guess as to who was behind it, and it was the reason he actually made a trip to the place he had avoided for his entire life.

The Maltose mansion was anything but quaint. With its two-story columns, stained-glass windows, and twenty-foot-deep by fifty-foot-wide porch, it shouted Old South. The main part of the house was more than a hundred years old, and with the additions added since the structure's original construction, it likely was now in excess of fifteen thousand square feet. Yet Coop had little interest in studying the architecture or questioning if some of the more modern additions blended with the original work; he was here to face off against the man who seemed intent on killing him.

It took about twenty seconds for a black butler

to respond to Coop's knock. The finely dressed gentleman then led the visitor to the double-door entry where John David Maltose spent most of his time. After knocking, the servant pushed the right door open and signaled for the lawyer to enter. Taking three steps into the wealthy man's office, Coop fully realized he was completely alone. He hoped the butler was tracking down the man he'd come to see and that his solitude would not last long.

As impressive as the exterior of the home was, Maltose's private lair had taken it to the next level. The Queen of England likely had nothing comparable to this. Everything from the light fixtures to bookends reeked of history and money. Major art museums no doubt had less impressive paintings and sculpture. The book-shelves were lined with the greatest books ever written, and as Coop discovered when pulling out a few to examine, they were first editions and some were even signed by the likes of Mark Twain and Jules Verne.

"I take it you appreciate fine literature."

Replacing *The Adventures of Tom Sawyer* back on the shelf, Coop turned to face his host.

As always, the man looked as if he had stepped out of the finest New York men's shop. Maltose was dressed in gray slacks and a light blue shirt. His silk tie had stripes to perfectly match the rest of the ensemble.

"I didn't know you read the classics," Coop noted.

"I don't," Maltose admitted. "I just collect them. And before you ask, I care nothing for art, either. But I do like good whiskey. Would you like to join me?"

"Kind of early in the morning," Coop observed. "Besides, I don't drink."

"There are days when even mornings call for stiff drinks," Maltose replied moving across the room to his bar. After pouring a shot in a glass, he quickly tossed it down his throat and strolled back to his desk. "So, to what do I owe the pleasure of your company?"

As Coop watched his host sit down in the oversized leather desk chair, he smiled. "I guess you're surprised to see me still breathing?"

Maltose shrugged. "What do you mean?" The look on his face indicated confusion. "And why don't you take a seat? I hate talking to folks who are standing while I'm sitting."

"I'll stand."

"Suit yourself," Maltose replied. "Will you excuse me for a moment, I need to make a call."

"Sure," the lawyer replied. "It's not like I'm very important."

Maltose picked up the phone and dialed a single number. A few seconds later, he asked the operator to place a person-to-person call to a William Heights in New York. Within a minute, he had his party on the line and was demanding action.

"I pay big dollars for you to do my legal work. My new will should have been here a week ago. Where is it?" The big man waited, nodded, and replied, "It better be here tomorrow. I have to get this mess taken care of. And what about the other matter?" A few more seconds passed. "I don't want the work to be done locally. If it is, she will find out. Now get moving on it, or I will see you lose my business and I'll take a few others with me across the street to you-know-who." He slammed the phone down without bothering with a good-bye.

As Maltose drummed his fingers and stewed, Coop walked over to a wall where several dozen different firearms were mounted and displayed behind glass. He raised his eyebrows and quipped, "I guess you must be quite a shot."

"I don't fire them," Maltose answered as he sipped on his drink. "I accidentally shot my dog when I was a child and haven't touched them since. My wife is the expert. She has won a number of trophies for her marksmanship. So if you want to go hunting with someone, call her. Now, what is this about my believing you'd be dead?"

"I was out on Highway 24 last night and had an accident," Coop explained as he walked over to check out the views of the garden. "It seems someone tampered with my brakes. If you look at what's left of the Studebaker, you would wonder how in the world I managed to live through the crash, much less get out of the car with nothing but a few bruises."

From behind him Maltose said, "Glad you weren't hurt."

Coop slowly pivoted until their eyes met. "I doubt it."

"Listen," his host quickly replied, "I've told you a couple of times now, I'm not trying to kill you. It is not my style. Besides, I've kind of come to admire your resolve. This having someone actually stand up to me is refreshing."

"There is no way to prove who fooled with my car," Coop said as he stuck his hands in his pants pockets, "so you can admit it now without recourse. I just want the truth."

Maltose stood and slowly closed the gap between them. "I had nothing to do with it. And I didn't have anything to do with trying to run you down either. And even if you don't want to believe it, I had nothing to do with Hattie getting kicked out of her home. If she wants to move back in, she is free to do so."

The big man shrugged and walked over to the window. He looked out for a second and then noted, "I used to think I could fix anything, but over the last few days I have lost my touch. I'm in the middle of a game where I'm not pulling the strings. And it's not just you I can't control."

He turned back to his guest. "But I need to know something."

"You need to know something?" Coop grinned. "I thought you had all the answers."

Maltose's tone and body language seemed sincere. "Coop, I need to know two things. The first is, how sure are you that Calvin Ross will not be found guilty?"

The lawyer considered the question. Was this something he really wanted to answer? Wouldn't Maltose feed the information directly to Fredrick?

"What does it matter to you?" Coop asked.

"I don't want to see the boy die," came the reply. "That's all there is to it. From the moment Fredrick visited my office and told me of the arrest, it has been my goal."

"You're serious?" Coop asked.

"Yes, I am," Maltose replied, "but I ran into a roadblock when you got in the way. If you could have been bought off, this thing would have been worked out by now."

"But," the lawyer pointed out, "Calvin's not guilty. Thus, the jail time would not really offer any justice."

The host looked sadly back to the window and dug his hands into his pockets. "He wouldn't have served for very long. I'd have made sure of it. The locals would have celebrated getting vengeance against the black boy, and then after they moved on to something else, I would have stepped in, paid some folks off, and made things happen."

What was Maltose trying to sell now? What was this new act all about? Was the mask coming off and revealing the real man, or was this just another game?

"Why?" Coop demanded.

"Why what?"

"Why do you want to help Calvin?"

Maltose turned back to his guest. "I have always admired Hattie. She has courage and conviction. I don't want her to have to deal with the loss of the young man she raised. And in truth, she did a good job raising him, too."

Coop studied the other man's face. "You're actually serious about this, aren't you?"

"Yeah," he admitted. "I am. If you can actually get the locals to admit that this boy didn't kill Becky Booth, then fine. But I just cannot fathom how any lawyer can do so. I think the guilty verdict is already in, and he will be going to the chair just because you're too stubborn to give up on the idea of somehow the right will win out this time. After all, the right has never won in the past; why would it start now when racial tensions are as high as they have been in decades? This Martin Luther King guy has everyone stirred up. Passions are high."

Coop pondered the words, turning each of those

thoughts over slowly in his head before posing his next question. "You said you wanted to know two things?"

"Yeah," Maltose admitted, "I also need to know if you can finger the person who actually did it."

"No," the lawyer admitted. "I have theories, but nothing concrete. But I have to believe if you're not the one trying to kill me, then the person who is behind it is likely guilty or is protecting some-one who is."

Maltose jerked his hands from his pockets and moved back behind his desk. After sitting down, he nodded sadly. "That dog won't hunt. The guy who was out to get you was one of my over-zealous employees who took matters into his own hands. In other words, he was trying to impress me. I've talked to him and put a stop to it."

Maltose took a deep breath before asking, "So you really don't have a clue as to who did it?"

"Well, if you're off the list," Coop explained, "it does frame things a bit differently. But I never actually thought you did it; I just thought you knew who did and were protecting them. You aren't, are you? Are you sure it is not guilt driving you to save Calvin? The deal gets someone you know off the hook and you still manage to save the life of the man who was chosen to pay for the deed."

"No." Maltose sighed. "I don't know who did it. But for Hattie's sake, don't let Calvin fry. Don't mess this up."

"You into betting on long shots?" Coop asked.

"Sometimes."

"Then make sure Fredrick doesn't intimidate the witnesses I need to talk to and place your money on our side."

Maltose nodded. "I can do that, Coop, but I can't control the underbelly of this town. And there is one, and they are brewing up a real hate for you. If someone else lights a fuse and the rabble gets fired up, even my money and power can't do anything to stop them. In other words, quit worrying about me and start realizing it's your old friends who are the ones most likely to go after you now."

"Thanks," Coop replied. "My eyes and ears are open."

"Good."

The two men's eyes met a final time before the lawyer spun and exited. While he had no way of knowing if Maltose had gotten anything from their honest jawing, Coop was sure he had a much better idea of the millionaire's endgame.

33

The day had been uneventful. No one had come by the office, and the phone hadn't rung. On his ten-block walk home, no hateful remarks had been hurled his way either. But because of Maltose's warning, Coop was still on edge. There was less than a week before the trial and it was a lot of time for something to happen.

It was just past nine. Hattie sat in a rocking chair knitting and singing the old gospel song "Stand by Me." Coop held down his normal slot in the big chair while Judy was curled up on the corner of the couch watching *The Fugitive* on TV. During a commercial break she turned to him and asked, "So you actually now believe John David didn't have anything to do with the attempts on your life?"

"I'll never really trust him," Coop admitted, "but my gut tells me he didn't know about what had happened and was just as surprised as I was."

"So does it make you a bit more relaxed?" she asked.

"Not in the least." He quickly explained, "If it was Maltose, I'd know what to look out for. But if it is not him, then who is it, and what will they do next? I prefer the enemy I know rather than the one I don't."

As David Janssen's image flashed back on the TV screen, Judy rejoined the program, and once more the trio kept their thoughts to themselves. This welcome silence left Coop with time to once more go over how he was going to try the case.

Initially, he wanted to put the pressure on Fredrick. He'd let the DA set his case in motion and systematically call his witnesses. Upon cross-examination, there were four or five who Coop fully expected would offer him a chance to shake up the State's case. Depending upon who was called and what came out, it would allow him to decide how to proceed from there. There was nothing he anticipated in the testimony to scare him, and if necessary, he had some surprises he could easily throw to cast at least a shadow of guilt on others. But he hoped he wouldn't have to employ the scattershot method. If he did, he would no doubt bring even more pain and suffering to Brent and Martha Booth.

"My Lord," Hattie exclaimed from across the room, "I must have left the oven on. I stuck the leftover cornbread in there, and I think I smell it burning."

As she and Judy got up to check, Coop took a whiff. What he smelled wasn't burning bread; it was gasoline. Leaping from his chair, he spun and slightly pulled back the curtain. What he saw shook him to the bone.

In the front yard, just fifteen feet from the porch, was a burning cross. It was at least ten feet high, and the crossbeam was six to seven feet wide. Glancing beyond the flaming wood, he noted three or four figures standing in the shadows of an oak tree in the Giffins' front yard.

"Weren't nothing burning in there," Hattie explained as she and Judy came back into the room. "But I still smell something."

"It's out in the yard," Coop explained. He signaled for the two women to join him at the window. As they peeked through the small opening, they gasped in unison.

"I hadn't seen nothing like it since . . ." Hattie stopped, took a deep breath, and added, "since I was a little girl. A bunch of men on horseback burned one of those down the street from where we lived. They also grabbed a colored boy who lived in the house, and none of us ever saw him again."

"They're not grabbing anybody tonight," Coop promised. "Look at them over there hiding in the shadows. They are waiting to see us react, and we aren't going to give them any satisfaction."

"You're just going to let it burn?" Judy asked.

"No wind tonight," he explained grimly, "so nothing is in any danger. Let them have their sick joke. As long as it doesn't go beyond this, we are fine. Now, let's get away from the window and go back to what we were doing."

As they made their way to their seats, Judy asked, "Don't you think we need to call the sheriff?"

"No," Coop replied, "Wylie needs to stay out of this until we really need him. Right now I'm sure they believe he is on their side."

"Are you sure he isn't?" Judy came back.

"I'm willing to stake my life on it," he assured her.

As Hattie went back to humming and Judy turned her eyes to the TV, Coop considered what the latest event might mean. Burning the cross was a pretty lame way to scare him, but was this the first sign of the shadowy group Maltose had warned him about? And if it was, what would be their next play?

34

Wednesday, July 8, 1964

Coop woke up at six, not as much because he was an early riser, but because he wanted to see what was left of last night's blaze. Stepping out onto the porch, he glanced toward the burnt wood. It no longer looked like a cross; the horizontal beam's left side had burned completely while the right still had about two feet left. The vertical section was likely 20 percent as thick as it had been when it was set aflame. There was about a five-foot black circle of charred grass under the cross, so the damage to the lawn had not been too bad. The pine tree on the far side of the front lawn had not even been singed, and the rose bushes beside the house showed no signs of heat damage, either. He was about to go back in when he noticed something else peculiar at the least and downright strange at best. All around the base of the cross were what appeared to be partially burned newspapers. A few dozen more papers had been tossed just outside the burn zone. Why were they there?

Pulling his robe tightly around his pajamas, Coop hurried out in his bare feet to where one of the untouched papers set. Grabbing it, he took a quick look in both directions; spotting no one, he leisurely strolled back up the steps and into the house. He wandered through the living room to the kitchen before he unrolled the paper. Proudly the masthead declared *The Justice Bugle*. The date of publication was July 7, so it was yesterday afternoon's edition. The headline boldly announced, "Negro Awaiting His Day in Court." Coop shrugged. It could have been worse. After scanning the story, basically listing the facts in evidence, he noted a front-page opinion piece written by the paper's editor, James S. McMilliam.

McMilliam and Coop's father had been close friends when they were kids. The editor had also been a force in the church his father pastored. His wife, Jackie, ran a stationery shop and headed up the Garden Club. Their oldest daughter, Sandy, had been in his class before marrying and moving up north somewhere. So with those relationships working in his favor, Coop figured the editorial couldn't be that damaging.

In the history of Justice, few men have ever stood as tall in their convictions and courage as did the late Abraham Lindsay. Therefore, it is certainly discouraging when his own son, Cooper, has chosen to turn against the very people who have supported his family and this community for years. In representing a Negro —in a case where the evidence in the public forum assures each of us he is guilty of the horrible, brutal, and immoral attack on innocent Rebecca Booth—Cooper has proven himself to be a man who can't be trusted by whites in Justice or anywhere else. Why is he taking this case? Why is he going against his own kind? The only answer has to be that the man is seeking to stir up enough controversy to gain notoriety in the national media and therefore land a position in one of the large, liberal law firms in the North.

While what Calvin Ross did is vile and disgusting, a crime against humanity to shock each of us, we all know a Negro man often has no control over his animalistic urges, lust, or his temper. But Cooper Lindsay is an educated man. He was raised by Christian people. He should naturally side with those who embrace the values that have made this country great. But instead, he has sold us out in hopes of turning this horrible situation into a platform for fame and wealth.

This paper will not allow Cooper to use us in this fashion. As the trial goes forward, we will unmask who he is and what he is. And when the verdict comes down and Ross is led away to the gallows, it is my hope that Cooper Lindsay's law career is dealt a similar fate. While I don't wish harm on this man or his family, I do hope he never practices law again. A man who turns on his own people is a man no one should ever trust.

Tonight each of us needs to pray that real justice is served next week. We need to know and feel that revenge will be exacted on those who dare threaten the values we embrace in our town and should embrace in this nation.

Coop was visibly stunned. While he didn't figure the paper would support him, he never saw this kind of attack coming from McMilliam.

Perhaps this editorial led to the cross burning last night. The phone's ringing pulled his nose out of the paper.

"Coop Lindsay," he answered.

"It's John David. I guess you have seen the newspaper."

"Just read it," Coop replied.

"Now you know what I was warning you about," the millionaire explained. "This thing is going to get ugly, and I'm thinking Calvin might have problems living long enough to get to see your supposedly great legal work in action."

"Is this another warning?" Coop asked.

"No, at least not from me. But don't trust anyone from this moment until the end of the trial. McMilliam can stir up the mob mentality with his words, and he's likely going to keep them coming."

"Did you hear about the cross burning they had in my front yard last night?"

The line when silent for a few moments. "No, I didn't. But I'm not surprised either. Who did it?"

"They stood in the shadows last night," Coop explained. "I couldn't see them."

"They'll stay in the shadows," Maltose said. "They are afraid of the light. But their numbers will grow, and at some point one of those who joins them is going to be stupid enough to incite all of them into a riot. Just make sure you're ready for it."

"Why all the concern?" Coop asked.

"I don't want to see the innocent boy die."

Maltose hung up leaving the lawyer both mystified and amused. Had the big man always been on his side and he had misjudged him or was there something Coop might uncover that Maltose couldn't afford to have exposed? But what was it? Was it in the evidence files and Coop had missed it? And why did Calvin's living mean so much to him? Maybe Hattie knew!

35

The women both appeared in the kitchen around seven, possibly stirred from their slumber by the aroma of frying bacon. As they wandered into the kitchen, dressed in bathrobes and wearing confused expressions, Coop saluted them with a spatula and an order, "Take a seat, your breakfast will be ready in a matter of seconds."

It was actually a couple of minutes, but after a few bites the women agreed it was worth the wait.

"Honey," Judy observed as she took a second forkful of scrambled eggs, "these are amazing."

"And the hotcakes are pretty special, too," Hattie added.

"Why did you go to all this fuss today?" Judy asked.

"I was up, had nothing else to do, and I just figured you all might be as hungry as I was."

For a few minutes, the trio ate in silence before the lawyer posed a cryptic question to their guest. "Hattie, do you know any reason John David Maltose would take such a deep and protective interest in Calvin?"

After finishing a bite of a hotcake, the woman looked over to Coop and shook her head. "Not really. It's not like they shared any friends."

Coop nodded. "But what about when Maltose came to pick up rents or look at some of his rental property? Maybe he got to know Calvin then."

Hattie rolled her eyes and chuckled. "Mr. Maltose didn't soil his shiny shoes on our dirt streets. He always sent his workers over. He wasn't like his father; his father used to always come over three or four times a week. He knew everyone over in colored town."

Coop sighed. "Well, I was hoping for a connection of some kind. I can't come up with a reason why Maltose is so intent on making sure Calvin gets a fair shake in this matter. It just makes no sense at all."

Coop got up and took his dishes to the sink as the women finished their feast. After running some water and splashing in some dish soap, he was working on a cast-iron skillet when Judy sidled up to him.

"Let me do it," she insisted. "You cooked so I clean. Sound okay?"

"Just the opposite of the way we usually work." He laughed.

As he stepped away from the sink, Hattie came up to his place and picked up a dish towel. As Judy washed, Hattie dried, and Coop walked over to the table, more puzzled than he had been in days. He just hated it when actions defied logic. It simply wasn't natural.

"Mr. Coop."

He looked back at Hattie.

"You know, I does recall Mr. John David and Calvin did meet, but Calvin wouldn't remember it at all."

"When?" Coop asked.

"At the fire. Mr. Leeland Maltose had been in our part of town that day. He was there with a few black folks and John David when I gots home from my cleaning work. They was just watching the house burn. Mr. John David was just a boy then, maybe late teens, and he was asking why no one was trying to help the crying child. I think he wanted to go in, but his daddy wouldn't let him. It's then I ran in and saved Calvin."

"And it's how you got the burns?" Judy asked.

Hattie nodded. "Yep, but it was worth it. Wish I could have done more. I wanted to save my sister, too. Nancy wasn't worth much, I knew it; of all of Daddy's kids she was the onliest one didn't stick to the straight and narrow. Maybe it was because she was so pretty. She turned the heads of black and white men everywhere she went."

She paused, as if recalling something she had either forgotten or simply tried to forget but couldn't. "Nancy was in the house lying on the floor."

"Was she killed by the fire?" Coop asked.

Hattie shook her head. "No, sir, the fire hadn't reached her when I went in. She was on the floor just as dead as she could be. Her eyes was open, but she weren't seeing nothing."

"Wonder what happened?" Judy asked.

"She'd been shot in the head," Hattie sobbed, "at least that's what it looked like to me. I mean, she weren't no good, but she didn't deserve that."

Coop looked into Hattie's eyes. "Who did it?"

"Could have been anybody." She explained, "She slept around and made a lot of women angry because they had husbands who knew Nancy too well. And there were likely jealous men or those who got mad when Nancy asked for stuff."

Another sad story from the other side of the tracks! How many more did Coop have to hear? He was about to get up, change clothes, and head down to the office when Hattie continued her woeful tale.

"When I came out of the fire with the little one in my arms, I was hurting more than you could know. Some men splashed some water on me, because they saw my dress was on fire. And then one of the ladies ran and got some butter to put on my arms. There weren't no one around to hold the baby while I was getting doctored, until John David stepped forward. He held little Calvin for about twenty minutes until Maud White dressed my arms. Then Maud took Calvin, and the two of us went back to her house to stay the night."

Coop's jaw dropped. Could a simple act of kindness from twenty years ago be the reason John David Maltose was so interested in seeing that Calvin didn't die? Was that what this was all about? It might have been a stretch, but at least it was something.

Judy sat at the table, leaned close to Hattie, and asked, "Who is Calvin's father?"

"Don't know," the woman sadly answered. "Nancy never would tell us. She took the secret to her grave."

36

Thursday, July 9, 1964

James McMilliam sat in his office at the *Justice Bugle* and studied his latest opinion piece. Even more than the first tirade against Cooper Lindsay, this one was a blatant call to arms. McMilliam was demanding the city clean up colored town. The gray-headed, pot-bellied, nearsighted man had now gone so far as to suggest that the Negroes in Justice be sent packing and the area where they lived be burned to the ground. He ended his editorial with the words, "These actions are the only ones to ever bring security and safety to the good citizens of Justice and ensure our women and children will never again have to endure another crime like this one."

Since the edition's release the evening before, his phone had been ringing off the wall. Every caller, but one, had voiced their approval. The lone voice of dissent was John David Maltose. But as the big man owned most of the property on that side of the tracks and those colored folks paid him rent, he naturally wanted to keep things as they were.

Looking across the room, McMilliam noted the

clock. 9:45. It was time for him to come up with today's call to arms. Picking up a pad, he began to scratch down ideas and study them. He was about to center on suggesting a prayer vigil for justice be held on Sunday night at the court-house lawn, when a longtime friend walked into his office.

"Well, K. C., how are things going?" McMilliam liked the DA for a number of reasons, not the least of which was that Fredrick was about two inches shorter than the editor.

"Doing fine, Jim," Fredrick politely replied as he took a seat in front of the editor's desk. "Just wanted to tell you I appreciate you keeping the heat on Coop. We need to have some sense scared into him so we can get this nasty thing behind us. I want this thing settled before it goes to trial."

"Don't worry," McMilliam laughed as he tossed a pencil into the air. Only when it came down into his hands did he add, "I'm going to make it real hot for Mr. Lindsay. Before I'm done with him, he'll consider tar and feathering a good Christmas present."

"What a goal." The DA laughed. "But do me a favor. Don't turn up the burner where it gets so hot, we burn the town down. That would not reflect well on me or my office."

Before Fredrick's request could be answered, the phone rang.

"*Bugle*, this is the Editor-in-Chief, James S. McMilliam. What can I do for you?"

"McMilliam, this is Bob Taylor from CBS-TV. I am looking at the last two copies of your paper."

The editor lifted his eyebrows. How did they get copies of his stories in New York? No matter, he'd figure that out later. For now, it was time to bask in a bit of fame and glory as well as find out what the network wanted. "What can I do for you, Bob?"

"I'm sending a crew down there this weekend to follow the trial. I think ABC and NBC likely will follow our lead. I know the *New York Times* is going to send a photographer, and one of the best scribes, Jinx Lanthom, as well. So I was wondering where the crews could sleep. You got any motels or hotels in your community?"

McMilliam smiled. "Bob, are you telling me my little story has reached clear up to New York City?"

"We wouldn't have known about it otherwise. You are pretty much off the radar down there. Now that we know where you are, where can we stay?"

Feeling as if he had suddenly been crowned the King of England, the editor waved at Fredrick and pointed to the phone. With his grin expanding, he jumped back on the line. "I'd suggest the Southern Inn, but if it books up, then the old Riverside Motel is not too bad, either. Stop by the office when you get to town."

"Don't worry, we will." As the line went dead, an excited McMilliam jumped out of his chair and shouted, "CBS, NBC, and ABC are all sending crews down here to cover the trial. The *New York Times*, too, and who knows who else! And it's all because of what I wrote! The power of the pen, that's what it is, the power of the pen! You and I are big-time news!"

"What?" a suddenly distraught Fredrick screamed.

"The big boys are coming to Justice." The editor laughed. "I wonder if they'll send Dan Rather. I always wanted to meet him. You know, he's from Texas."

"You fool!" the DA growled. "Don't you see what you have done?"

"Yeah, I've put Justice on the map!"

"No," Fredrick yelled, "you just made us a target." The DA tossed his hands toward the ceiling before asking, "When are these folks coming down?"

A suddenly confused McMilliam leaned against his desk. "Sunday, I think, but why is it important?"

"Because," Fredrick hissed, "it means we've only got a couple of days to put this thing to bed before we get all kinds of bad national publicity. We have got to do something tonight or tomorrow night. It has to be something to scare Lindsay and the colored kid into taking a deal and not having this thing go to court. So when the New York media gets here there will be nothing to report. No story, no black eye!"

McMilliam moved back to his chair and slumped down. He'd never known good news to become bad news so quickly.

"So," Fredrick snarled, "you got us into the mess, what is your plan to get us out? You got any rabbits in your oversized hat?"

The editor shrugged. What could he possibly do in less than forty-eight hours to wrap up the case before the national news media arrived? As he considered his options, inspiration struck. Jumping out of his chair, he raced over to his files. Opening the third drawer of the second metal cabinet, he leafed through several folders until he came to the one he wanted. Marching back to the desk, he tossed it in front of Fredrick and rubbed his hands together as the DA opened the folder and looked at a series of news stories.

"The Klan?" Fredrick asked as he reviewed the material.

"Not just the Klan, but specifically, a group from a different city, maybe even a different state."

"How could you get them to Justice before the media gets here?" The DA asked.

"We can't," the editor laughed. "We don't need

233

them to come here, we just need the national media to think it is an outside group. If we report a KKK group from, say, Louisiana rolled in here and maybe kidnapped Ross while our local lawmen fought hard to save him but were overpowered, then the focus shifts to someplace else and we look good for our efforts to keep Ross alive. And the fact that some high school kids already burned a cross in Coop's yard really sets this up, too."

"You really think it could work?" Fredrick asked hopefully.

McMilliam smiled. "If it doesn't, it might at least get Coop and Ross to rethink going to trial and instead go along with the deal you told me you offered them."

"But who you going to get to be your Klansmen?" Fredrick asked.

"I have a few dozen folks in mind," the editor assured him, "but I will need cash to pay them off. And I have a source for that. So it's time for me to get to work."

"I'll leave you to it," Fredrick said. "The less I know the better. And don't even think about telling me your money source. I don't want to know."

As soon as the DA cleared the office door, McMilliam picked up the phone. With one well-placed call and a race to buy some sheets, he could put his latest plan into operation.

37

Friday, July 10, 1964

Not wanting to leave the women without access to a car, Coop walked to work. As the clock struck ten, it hit him that there were exactly three days until the trial started. He also figured it meant less than a week until Calvin Ross's fate was determined. The evidence the attorney had gathered offered little doubt that the young man should be cleared, but in this case, would it be enough? To guarantee his client his freedom, Coop might have to produce the person who really killed Becky Booth, and while he had theories, he had no concrete evidence linking anyone to the crime. Even after spending the day going over the short list of suspects, he still had no success connecting any of the dots. Finally, as the courthouse clock struck five, he closed up shop and made the ten-block walk home.

Being hated was one thing, but being ignored might be even worse. During his twenty-minute walk to his modest home on Elm Street, not one person as much as looked at him. Even worse, four different people actually crossed the street rather than meet Coop on the sidewalk. When he did pass people visiting in their yards, their conversations grew mute. The silent treatment and hateful stares got so bad he began to imagine that even the birds lost their voice when he appeared.

After finally making it to his house, he rushed quickly up the sidewalk to the porch, hurried up the steps, grabbed his keys, unlocked the door, and took a deep sigh of relief as he stepped into the modest frame home. Closing and locking the front door, he was incredibly grateful just to be in a place where people would acknowledge he was alive and look at him with loving, caring eyes.

"How are you, Dear?" Judy asked, crossing the living room and reaching up to kiss him.

"Too quiet," he replied. "Not only do they not talk to me, I'm pretty much ignored."

"I guess you is too black for them," Hattie noted as she stood in the door leading to the kitchen.

Coop smiled. "I don't know what you mean."

"White folks in Justice pretty much always ignore us black folks unless they catch us doing something they don't like. Even when I work in their homes, they pretty much talk as if I'm not there."

"Maybe that's it," he answered. "Another element of life I've missed that I should have corrected. I wonder how many times I've been guilty of it."

Hattie shrugged. "Just the way things are."

After their meal, when the evening shadows began to chase away the setting sun, Coop apprehensively made his way to the front window and pulled back the curtain. There was no one in the street.

"Any trouble tonight?" Judy asked.

"Doesn't look like it," he answered, "but it's early. Why don't we just watch some TV? Might take our minds off things."

Coop was reaching to turn on the Zenith when the phone rang. He looked to Judy and then Hattie before announcing, "Well, it seems there is someone who is still speaking to us."

"Maybe not," Judy announced, "we've had calls all day where when we answered, people just hung up."

"I'll let them hang up on me this time." He smiled.

Marching into the kitchen, he jerked the wall phone's receiver from its cradle and announced, "Coop Lindsay."

"Glad I got you."

Ironic, the one person still acknowledging Coop existed was a person he didn't like or even remotely understand. "John David, what do you need?"

"Just got wind the Klan is rallying in the city park right now and then marching to the jail. I know Wylie is there, but I don't see anyone else coming to help him. Thought you'd want to know."

Coop took a deep breath and looked back toward the women. As he studied their concerned faces, he softly said, "I didn't know the group had a chapter around these parts."

"I found out about this from Melvin," Maltose explained, "my employee who supposedly tried to run you down. I'm guessing this case must have stirred up enough hatred to get outside members of the KKK to rally in our quaint little town."

"I'd better get down to the jail, then," Coop replied. "I figure Wylie wouldn't mind some company tonight."

"Coop," Maltose cut back in, "they will likely be liquored up and nasty. You combine that with the mentality of the mob and you could be putting your life on the line."

"Yeah," the attorney answered, "but it is all in the line of work. Thanks for the tip."

After he put the receiver back in its place, Coop walked back toward the front door. A quick peek proved nothing was amiss outside their home. It was something to be thankful for, but it also gave a bit of validity to Maltose's warning. After all, those who wanted his neck had to be somewhere.

"What was the call about?" Judy asked.

"Not much," he lied. "Wylie has something he wants me to see, so I'm going to head down to his office and take a look at it."

"Is it necessary this time of night?" Judy queried. "Couldn't it wait until tomorrow morning?"

He smiled. "No, he's on duty tonight and will be sleeping tomorrow during the day. So this is my way of giving him a break." He grabbed the front door knob, twisted it, and stepped out onto the porch. Looking back over his shoulder, he added, "I'm taking the car, and please keep the doors locked." He didn't wait for a reply.

Hurrying around to the drive, he unlocked the Ford and slid into the front seat. After sticking his keys in the ignition, he paused. What if this was all a setup? What if someone had rigged a bomb in the car to activate when he turned the key?

Leaning back, he rubbed his lips with his left hand and considered his options. As the jail was at least twenty blocks away and there was a long list of folks who might just go after him at night, walking wasn't an option. There was no one he could call and ask for a ride either. It was either the car or stay home.

As the seconds ticked by, the eighty-degree heat combined with his nerves began to push sweat from his pores. As water began to trickle down his face and drop to his shirt, Coop recalled something his father had told him countless times, "When you can no longer trust in people, it is time to take a leap in faith and trust in God." Saying a quick prayer, he leaned over, grabbed the key, and flipped it to the right. The Ford's V-8 started effortlessly. Maybe John David could be trusted after all.

38

It was close to nine when Coop arrived at the jail. For the moment, things were quiet. After parking the car around on the side, he walked quickly through the shadows to the front door. He twisted the knob, but the door didn't budge. After he knocked, a familiar voice yelled out from inside, "Who is it?"

"It's Coop."

A few seconds later, the lock released and the door quickly opened. The sheriff stepped out, looked into the street, and then signaled for the attorney to enter. After locking the door behind them, Estes turned back to his guest and frowned. "Guess you heard what's brewing?"

"Yeah," Coop said, as his eyes locked onto his friend's face. His old baseball coach was tense, on edge, and solemn. By the worried look in his eyes and the way he clenched his jaw, it was apparent he was expecting the worst.

"You're here," Estes barked more than said, "but you don't need to be. This is my job. You need to get on home."

Ignoring the man's suggestion, Coop asked, "Where are your deputies?"

"I called them," came the quick reply, "but

they're not coming. They seem to have other things to do, and frankly, I don't blame them. They don't get paid enough to deal with something like this. I realize they've got families."

"You've got a daughter," Coop pointed out.

"Yeah." He sighed. "And I sent her out of town to my sister's in Little Rock yesterday. If anything happens to me, Blanche will do a good job taking care of her."

Coop nodded. He fully understood. If anything happened to Judy or him, her parents would do a good job with their kids, too. And it was time to admit that in this climate anything could happen.

"Coop," Estes grimly noted, "I hate to remind you of this, but I told you not to take this case because of what it might mean to you and your family."

"You did," came the almost silent reply. "Maybe I should have listened."

"No." Estes smiled. "You were right. What kind of father would I be to my daughter if I didn't live up to my responsibilities as a sheriff, a man, and a Christian? Doing the right thing sometimes has unpleasant consequences. But it doesn't mean we should avoid doing it."

"Yeah, we have to make a stand somewhere," the lawyer agreed. "Still, at this moment I kind of feel like the Texans at the Alamo."

Estes shook his head. "What we are going

through tonight might be a more noble effort, and perhaps we are facing even longer odds."

Coop considered the man's words before asking, "What are you expecting?"

The sheriff moved behind one of the outer office's desks, sat down, and leaned back. After locking the fingers of both hands behind his neck, he solemnly shared what he knew. "There are supposed be about thirty of them. They've been talking up a storm down at the park and quoting our local editor's words. Those pieces in the newspaper and some home brew have evidently gotten them pretty stoked up."

The man paused and grimly smiled. "They are supposed to march the ten blocks here, and then it's anybody's guess. But I don't think they intend on burning a cross and then just walking away. Tonight they are looking for real action, and the drunker they get, the thirstier they'll become for blood."

Coop shrugged. "So having them kind of parade around and then head back to wherever they are from is not likely."

"Yeah." Estes sighed.

"How's Calvin?" the attorney asked.

"I told him what's going on," the sheriff explained, "so he is aware of the way things are. He is nervous and praying, but he is not going crazy. The more I look at his reactions to things, the more convinced I am he is innocent. And dying for an innocent man, no matter his color, seems like a pretty noble cause to me."

As the confrontation would have to start at the front of the building, there didn't seem to be any reason to go back and see the prisoner. In fact, it might be better if Calvin wasn't aware Coop was here. The kid would likely just try to talk the attorney into going home. Yet no matter the cost, he wasn't going to let Estes go it alone.

"If this goes down bad," the sheriff noted, "I wonder if they will make a movie about it."

"A movie?" Coop almost laughed.

"Yeah," Estes continued, as he propped his boots on the desk, "if I'm going to die for a cause, I'd like to think it will at least make the big screen. And I wonder who they'd get to play me. John Wayne is too old."

"And too tall," Coop cut in.

"Whatever," the sheriff replied, "maybe they could cast Glenn Ford in my role, and George Hamilton could play you."

"George Hamilton?" Coop said, raising his eyebrows. "I was thinking more along the lines of Tony Curtis."

As Estes shook his head, the lawyer moved toward the other desk, pulled out a chair, and took a seat. He had no more than gotten comfortable when he heard a car's rumble. The vehicle stopped in front of the jail and went silent. Coop looked to Estes and then back to the door. All thoughts of movies evaporated. Perhaps the moment of decision was here. Maybe this was the time when their wills and courage would really be tested. But were they really ready?

One second became ten, and then twenty, before a car door slammed shut and heavy footsteps were heard on the sidewalk. A few seconds later, the doorknob twisted.

"You think one of the deputies had a change of heart?" Coop asked.

"No way," Estes replied soberly.

"So any guesses as to who it is?"

Estes shook his head and whispered, "But there is one way to find out." After pulling a shotgun from his desktop and cradling it in his arms, he yelled, "Who is it?"

"Maltose," came the blunt reply.

39

Coop remained in place and watched the sheriff unlock and open the door. As the sheriff stepped to one side, the big man entered. Estes and Maltose had never trusted each other, so it was not surprising that neither of them initially spoke. Their silent stare fest continued for almost a minute, before Maltose looked over to Coop and grimly smiled. "I was going to try to beat you here. I guess you must have left right after my call."

"Yep."

"Wait," Estes said, "you called Coop to tell him what was going on here?"

The guest nodded. "I figured he'd want to be in on the party."

"Strange choice of words," Coop noted. "Seems more like a wake."

Maltose chuckled. "Let's hope not." He turned back to Estes and in a firm but friendly tone asked, "What you got planned, Wylie?"

The sheriff lifted a bushy eyebrow. "Why, John David, you have never called me by my first name. In fact, the names you normally call me, I wouldn't repeat in front of a preacher's son. And other than making sure no one gets my prisoner, I've got nothing planned."

The millionaire shrugged. "We are outnumbered more than Custer was at Little Bighorn, so it likely doesn't matter if you've got a plan or not. They are on their way; I saw them back about eight blocks as I drove. Nothing short of a machine gun will likely slow them down, either." Maltose glanced over to Coop. "I drove by the park. They hung a pretty good-looking effigy of you from the old oak over by the band pavilion."

The lawyer shrugged. "Of course it was good-looking. How else would you have known it was me?"

Estes leaned against a desk and smiled. "John David, what do they look like?"

"Poorly dressed trick or treaters," Maltose quickly explained. "There must be about thirty of them, wearing white robes to 'look a bit like they belong to the Klan', carrying torches, and waving a Confederate battle flag. A few of them have rifles."

As the sheriff went over to gaze out the window, Coop chewed on one of Maltose's remarks. "John David, what do you mean they 'look a bit like they belong to the Klan'?"

Maltose moved his gaze from the now curious lawyer to the cop. "What I mean is this: my hired man told me the KKK had driven in from Louisiana to take this case into their own hands. Well, on the surface it made sense. But as I got to looking at this ragtag group, the story started to fizzle out. Any Klan group coming in from out of state would be very well-organized. Their uniforms would have been ordered and sewn according to certain specifications. What would be sewn onto their white costumes would signal such things as the rankings of the men who were wearing them. These guys are not wearing anything but sheets with a few holes to see through. They're not from Louisiana, and I don't think any of them is a card-carrying member of the KKK."

"In other words," Estes noted, "they're locals."

As the men considered this revelation, they

began to hear male voices shouting in the distance. Looking back toward the street side of the building, they sat silently as the voices grew louder. When they could see the flicker of the torches' flames through the office curtains, the now silent trio knew the moment was at hand.

Estes once more picked up the shotgun, walked over to the exit, then seemingly reconsidered and set the weapon down beside the door. He reached for the lock but, before unbolting it, looked back at his two uninvited guests. "You boys stay put. I'll deal with this mob."

Before Coop could protest, the sound of bottles breaking against the building's walls caused all three of the men to turn their attention outside. Though none of them could see the mob, they had a pretty good idea of what was closing in on them.

"You still thinking Glenn Ford?" Coop asked Estes.

The lawman grinned. "I sure wish Gary Cooper was a bit younger."

"William Conrad looks more like you," Coop shot back.

A confused Maltose glanced from one to the other before asking, "What is this all about?" There was no time for an explanation.

"Sheriff," a deep voice called out.

Estes glanced over to Maltose and whispered, "I think he's looking for me."

"Sheriff," the man called out again from the street. "This is the Grand Duke of the Louisiana Klan, and I'm not used to being kept waiting. Are you going to come out, or do we break the door down?"

"The Grand Duke," Coop noted, "sounds a great deal like one of the men who stopped me outside the church a few days ago when I tried to attend Becky Booth's funeral."

"Yeah," Estes said, "it's Bobby Sloan. You probably don't know him, Coop. Moved here when you were in law school. He owns an auto repair service."

Coop smiled. "Then he might have met the old Studebaker."

"Sheriff," the man shouted. "Are you coming out, or are we coming in?"

"Guess I'll go out," Estes announced. "I'm not really satisfied with the tune-up old Bobby did on my truck. Time I told him about it."

As the sheriff stepped back toward the door, Maltose waved and pointed to the shotgun. "Aren't you forgetting something?"

"No," Estes said, "it would make this bunch of drunks more dangerous. Only thing I'm going to shoot off is my mouth."

Coop watched as a now seemingly confident sheriff yanked the door open and walked out into the night air. As it closed, the attorney looked over at the other visitor. Maltose smiled and pointed to the door. After returning the smile, Coop joined him at the exit and followed Estes down the walk and into the street.

Maltose had been right; it was a ratty-looking group with costuming right out of a bad high-school play. About the only impressive element of their get-up were the torches. Those put off a lot of light, which once again showed just how quickly their sheets and pillowcases had been turned into uniforms. One of the men to the side seemed to be wearing a light pink robe rather than white, and another's seemed a pale yellow. If things hadn't been so volatile, this situation would have brought grins from the trio now facing the mob.

"We want the boy," the man snarled. "It's time the Booth family got justice. We've got a tree and rope; now step aside and let us take him."

"Not going to do it, Bobby," Estes boldly declared.

After a few mumbles, followed by a number of the torch bearers looking at each other, the man in charge yelled, "Who's this Bobby? We don't have anybody by that name in our band."

The sheriff shook his head, crossed his arms, and laughed. "It is harder to guess the identity of the kids who came to my door at Halloween than it is who is under those shabby-looking sheets." Estes took a step forward; now only twenty feet separated him from the mob. "Ricky," he said, pointing to a robed figured on the far right, "if you are going to play dress up, at least wear something other than those black boots I see you in every day. And, John Clark, your slacks are a giveaway as well. And you should have found a bigger sheet. You're the only one in town who would even consider wearing that shade of green."

As the mob nervously looked toward a man near the back, Bobby once more found his voice. "We don't know what you're talking about. We drove all the way over here from Louisiana to get the boy you're holding. Now give him to us or you, John David, and Coop will be sorry."

Estes chuckled and glanced back at the two men a step behind him before noting, "I didn't know folks in Louisiana would have any idea who those two are, much less be on a first-name basis with them. You boys need to drop the charade and go home and burn those sheets."

A few in the group actually started to turn, but one man in the back held his place and yelled out, "We won't leave until we get what we want."

Coop didn't recognize the voice. It was also apparent that Maltose and Estes were drawing blanks as well.

"You're going to have a long wait," the sheriff explained. "Calvin Ross is staying where he is until the trial."

"You aren't even carrying a gun," Bobby shouted as he regained his voice.

"Don't need one," Estes yelled back.

With no warning, the sheriff moved forward toward the mob and half of them immediately took a few steps back. Standing directly in front of the supposed leader, Estes reached out and ripped off the pillowcase covering his head. The man was too shocked to move.

"Now you look like the Bobby I know," Estes announced. After holding the pillowcase over his head like a flag, the sheriff tossed it to the ground. "Bobby, you did a lousy job tuning up my truck. I want a refund. Have it on my desk first thing Monday morning." He then turned and looked at the rest of the band. "Who else wants me to rip off their masks?"

No one moved, but sensing Estes might need some back up, Coop quickly walked to his side. Maltose followed the lead and stood to the sheriff's right.

"You're cowards," Estes shouted. "You spread rumors about where you were from and then hid your identities behind pieces of bedclothes. You have no respect for the laws of man or God. Now get moving before I take off my belt and whip you like the children you are."

Pointing a finger at Maltose, a man in the back shouted, "So you've joined the other side."

The millionaire shrugged. "So you know who I am? Guess you're not from Cajun country, either."

The man yelled back, "You'll pay. I'll see to it."

As Maltose laughed, Coop studied the man hiding under the pillowcase and sheet. He was short, but otherwise there was little to note except that his torch revealed a cut spot on the toe of his caramel-colored wingtips.

"Do something," someone yelled out from the back row.

Mr. Wingtip hesitated only for a moment before waving his torch and calling out, "Come on, men. They can't stop us."

A few of the crowd hesitated, but not enough. A dozen in the back row pushed the nervous members of the band forward. As Estes held up his arms to urge them to halt, one of the group brought the butt of his rifle across his forehead. The sheriff folded up on the street. The odds had now moved from 10:1 to 15:1, and Coop was suddenly not feeling good about things.

"Back to the door!" Maltose yelled, while pushing the lawyer ahead of him.

The mob, sensing they now were once more in control didn't run after the pair. Instead, they walked slowly toward their objectives. Once the lawyer and millionaire were at the jail's entry, Maltose turned, faced the white-clad band, held his hand up in the air like a traffic cop and shouted, "Stop!"

Coop couldn't believe it when they hesitated, stumbled another step or two toward the door, and finally stood staring at the man who had dared challenge them. Meanwhile, twenty or so feet behind them, Estes rolled over and got to his feet. He seemed as curious about the game Maltose was playing as were the fake Klansmen. With everyone's eyes on the big man, Maltose grinned.

"I really don't care what happens to you white-robed cowards," he announced while reaching inside his suit coat, "but I'd hate to see me suffer any injuries. And as I have a relative who owns the funeral home, it might be time for me to drum up a bit of business for him. Who wants to experience my cousin's work firsthand?"

Maltose smiled as he slowly pulled his hand from under his coat, "I saved this from a bit of construction work we did on our farm recently. It might look like a simple bottle of vodka to you, but in truth it has a little more kick. Remember those loud explosions some of you complained about last winter? If any of you have mastered reading, there was a story in the paper about them. Well, those blasts were caused by my men using this to get rid of a hill spoiling the view of one of my private lakes. It's called nitroglycerin. I'm sure even the stupidest among you knows what it can do."

Holding it over his head, he looked back at the mob. "There's enough here to take out most of you, and those who don't die in the blast will likely be missing some body parts you treasure.

So here's the deal. You walk away from this place and go home, and I'll not toss it in your direction. But if you stick around for ten more seconds, then I'll just have to test how powerful this nitro really is. Oh, and to make sure you don't try this again, I'm going to leave it with the sheriff so he will have a lot more firepower than you can muster if you come back. Now move and move quickly or my cousin is about to get a lot of business."

Maltose looked to Coop and then back to the crowd as he closed his fist around the bottle and barked, "One!" He never got to two. Led by those in the rear, the band began to quickly move back, and within seconds, every one of the mob was in full retreat. Still, the millionaire continued to hold the bottle as if ready to heave it until the band was halfway back to the city park.

"You came prepared," Estes noted as he rejoined the men at the door.

As a stunned Coop looked on, Maltose smiled, unscrewed the bottle, tilted his head and took a long swig. He then offered the bottle to the other two men, both of whom refused. Grinning, Maltose said, "Nothing but vodka, but as those folks remembered our using nitro, I figured my bluff would work." As he slipped the bottle back into his pocket he added, "Glad they didn't test it."

40

Saturday, July 11, 1964

"You got company," Coop announced as he followed Deputy Bob Smith up to Calvin's cell door. "I think you'll like this visit."

The county lawman wordlessly unlocked the door and stepped aside so Coop could enter. The lawyer was halfway in when he stopped and looked back to his escort. "Aren't you going to check what's in the basket?"

"Naw," the man answered. "It's just food."

"Well, you're right," the lawyer replied, "but I still figured you'd want to see it."

"No," he said with a shrug as he shut the cell door, "if his mother cooked it, then I don't want to see it. It would be a lot better than anything I get at my house."

"Hey, Smith," Coop called out. "You forgot to lock the door."

"No, I didn't," he yelled back. "I don't figure Calvin is going to try anything. He'd have to come through the office, anyway. I'll lock it when you are finished."

Coop shrugged. "Things are getting a bit lax it seems." He then smiled and asked, "You hungry?"

"Am I?"

The lawyer sat back in the metal chair and watched Calvin consume a hunk of roast, four sticks of cornbread, and a quart of potato salad. He didn't stop eating until there was absolutely nothing left. Once he'd put the containers back into the wicker basket, he leaned up against the wall and smiled. "I thought I was done for last night. But when you and Maltose showed up, things shifted a bit."

"What you sensed was the earth pivoting on its axis," Coop explained.

"What?"

"I mean when John David joined our side, everything on the planet went out of balance. I can't figure him out. For some reason, he is rooting for you. You have any idea why?"

The prisoner shook his head. "You kidding? I have only seen him a half-dozen times in my life. He's never done me any favors."

"It's got me buffaloed, too," Coop admitted. "But I'm going to find out what horse he's got in the race at some point. Right now, let me move on to Monday."

Calvin's smile faded as thoughts of the looming trial came back into the picture. He took a deep breath, pulled his feet up into the bunk, and crossed his arms over his knees. "I don't know whether to look forward to the day or dread it. For a few seconds last night, the thought of those guys stringing me up didn't sound so bad."

"Well," Coop calmly stated, "that was then and this is now. We stopped them from being the judge, jury, and executioner; now we have to face the real judge in a real courtroom." The lawyer licked his lips and leaned toward his client. "Let me be honest with you. If you were white, I think I could get the judge to toss the thing out based on a lack of evidence. But as you know better than I, this is about the color of your skin. It changes the parameters. Even though the law books tell me in this country it can't be the case, the rules seem different for a Negro and a white when it comes to justice in Justice or anywhere else."

"You don't need to tell me," Calvin replied. "I've known it all my life. But what about this time? Do we have enough evidence so I can walk out of here a free man?"

"I think so," Coop said, trying to convince both himself and the boy. "But I'd feel a lot better if I just knew who actually did have a motive for killing Becky. I can't find anyone to point a finger at and make it stick."

"I'll be praying for a revelation," Calvin assured him.

"You do it, son. You do it."

Coop looked into the other man's eyes, trying to reassure him before adding, "And if things don't go our way, I know I can get an appeal. I have no doubt about it." He paused before standing and asking, "Anything else you need?"

"No, sir."

"Calvin, I'm going to lay low tomorrow. I've got to make one visit, and once I'm finished, I think it would be wise for me to stay in the house and make sure nothing happens to frighten or harm Judy or Hattie. So I won't see you until the trial. But if you need me, just let the deputy or the sheriff know, and I will get here quicker than you can bat an eye."

"I'll be fine." Calvin smiled. "After all, Mr. Maltose did leave his bottle of nitro. I don't figure anyone will come gunning with the image of it in their heads."

Coop grinned. "You mean he left it, and Wylie has it in his desk?"

"Oh, no, sir." The prisoner laughed. "The sheriff gave it to me. I have it right here in my cell. Why do you think the deputy is being so nice to me? He thinks it's real, too."

"Wylie's a good man." The lawyer laughed as he opened the door. After swinging it shut, he glanced back in between the bars and said, "I'll do my best."

Calvin pushed himself off the bunk and walked over to the door. "I trust you." He then paused, nodded, and stuck his hand through the bars. "I'd appreciate it if you shook my hand, Coop."

As their hands met, a tear streamed down the lawyer's cheek.

41

Sunday, July 12, 1964

One day left and nothing to do. He was as ready as he could be. He had the evidence and his game plan down pat. He'd played over every possible surprise the DA might toss his way. Coop even had the autopsy report memorized. If he had any artistic talent at all, he could have drawn each of the crime scene photos in minute detail. Thus, with nothing left to do but allow things to play out and react to them, he should have been relaxed. But how could he relax when he knew a man's life depended upon his work?

"Can I get you anything?" Judy asked as she came into the living room.

He glanced up at his wife. Even though she was dressed casually, she still looked like a New York model. And she was smarter than she was beautiful. He had married well!

"I'm fine," he answered. Glancing up to the wall clock, he noted it was almost three. His eyes were still on the clock when he asked, "Would you mind if I get out of the house for a while? I don't think anybody will bother us during the daylight hours."

"Where you going?" she asked in a reserved, if not concerned, manner.

"Just driving out to the cemetery to visit with Dad," he explained. "I kind of want to give him the insight into what I'm doing, tell him I finally figured out the sermon he kept giving two or three times a year, and then pose a question."

"Will it be safe?" Judy asked.

"In the daytime, it should be," he assured her, "and I won't be gone long."

She swept across the room, sat in his lap, and kissed him. Laying her head against his shoulder, she sighed. "I'm looking forward to moving to Ohio. If we don't get there soon, the kids won't remember who we are."

"I think a new start would be good," he agreed. "And I miss the kids, too. But I don't want Clark becoming a Redlegs fan. He has to stick to the Cardinals like his old man."

She stood, smiled, and said, "I'll see what I can do."

Most folks were home from church and enjoying a lazy afternoon, so the drive to the old Justice Cemetery was uneventful. Parking on one of the two gravel lanes cutting through the grounds, Coop eased out of the Galaxie and walked over to the twin plots where his folks were. He hadn't been here since his mother's funeral and was surprised to see someone had placed fresh flowers on her grave. At least one

member of the family was still loved by someone in Justice.

On the far side of the plot, nearest his father's
grave, was a bench under a dogwood tree. Coop
walked over, took a seat, and then glanced back
at his parents' resting place. He silently studied
the gray granite marker for a few moments before
beginning what he knew would be a very one-
sided conversation.

"I guess you know I've gotten myself into a
big mess, and it likely means the Lindsays won't
be welcome in these parts for a long time. I'd be
kind of surprised if they even let my grandkids
come and visit your grave. But I'll tell you what,
Dad, it is really your fault. If you hadn't beaten
the good Samaritan message to death, I might
have made a different choice, and life could have
stayed like it always was. But if I had taken the
easy road, you wouldn't have been proud of me
and maybe I would have messed up the promise
you made to Hattie's father on his death bed."

Coop stood up, looked behind the cemetery to
the tree-covered acres all the way down to the
Peerpoint River. All things considered, this
wasn't a bad place for a body to rest. Glancing
around at the familiar names around his parents'
graves, he smiled. So many of these people who
had gone on had been so good to him. They had
bought the things he sold to raise money for Boy
Scouts and class projects and had cheered him

on in sports. Some of them had taught him in Sunday school, and others had been his teachers in public school. As the names brought back memories, another thought fought its way through the warm, fuzzy feelings and bubbled to the top.

Looking back at the hundreds of tombstones, a stark reality set in. This cemetery was just as segregated as the town. Where was it the black folks rested? He had no idea. He shook the thought from his mind long enough to find the question he needed to ask his father.

"Dad, I don't know who marked out the line on the autopsy proving Becky Booth was pregnant. I wish I knew if Brent and Martha knew. Even if they do know, what will it do to them if I bring it up at the trial? What if I have to share a piece of dirty laundry with the people of Justice? Would you understand? I mean you married Brent and Martha and you christened Becky."

There was no answer; Coop hadn't expected one, but the fact was, exposing the pregnancy and uncovering who the father was might be the trump card in this case. He just prayed he didn't have to make the play to open the door to freedom for his client and in the process to more deeply damage two other already broken hearts.

He looked back at his father's name etched into the stone. Stepping forward he traced it with his fingers—Abraham Lindsay. He studied the name and then read the words written at the top of the marker. "He left this world a better place."

"Okay, Dad, I won't use that bit of evidence unless I absolutely have to. Let's pray I don't."

Ten hours later, when Judy and Hattie had gone to bed, Coop sat at the table with a pen in his hand. In front of him was one of a series of journals he'd kept since he was twelve years old. In each of those now eighteen volumes, he'd written the highlights of each day. The last few weeks had seen the entries grow in size and detail. Tonight, for the first time since he began this tradition, he couldn't think of anything to write. Maybe it was because he'd already poured his soul out and it was now empty.

42

Monday, June 13, 1964

There had never been a scene like this in the long history of Justice. The courthouse lawn was filled with people. They were standing shoulder to shoulder. Around the grounds were news trucks from the nation's three major television networks and another half-dozen local television vans from as far away as Atlanta. Just to get into the building required either press credentials or spectator passes issued by the court. To get one of those, you had to know someone very well.

In spite of arriving thirty minutes before the designated starting time of nine, Coop had to shove his way through the mob hurling insults and tossing out questions. He ignored all of them as a deputy escorted him up the stairs and into the district courtroom. Taking a place at the defense table, the attorney opened his briefcase and tried to ignore those behind him. With all the whispers and cold stares, it wasn't easy.

At a few minutes before the top of the hour, Wylie Estes escorted Calvin in via a back entrance and placed the young man at the table with the attorney. As the defendant sat down, the crowd grew hushed. Coop smiled and nodded. Calvin did the same as he adjusted his dark tie and glanced back to Hattie seated just behind the railing separating them from the gallery. The woman smiled and mouthed, "God bless you." Judy, seated on the other side of Hattie, dipped her head and whispered, "I love you."

As the moments ticked down, Coop reached back into his past and set his jaw. Just like he had when he was getting ready to play an important basketball game, he focused on the task ahead. He called it putting on his game face, but in truth, it was actually more about setting his mental game in place. As his eyes fell on the American flag, he went back over all the details of the case and considered what the trial meant.

To Calvin it was about life. If Coop did his job, then the young black man would have one to live. But to Coop, it was about setting something right today, which had been wrong for more than a century. If he played his cards right, then the endgame might just open up a new world where Martin Luther King's vision would be a bit closer to being realized. If he played the wrong cards at the wrong time, then a man would die and a dream would be pushed back a bit further.

The bailiff's voice pulled him from his thoughts and turned his attention to the appearance of Judge Hyrum Metlock. As Coop and the rest of the court rose, the judge walked in and took his seat. It was time!

"Is there any business before we go about the process of interviewing prospective jurors?" Metlock asked.

Coop stood. "I have something we need to address, Your Honor."

"Go ahead, Coop."

Stepping out from behind the defense table, Coop buttoned his navy blue suit coat and looked to the defense table. With every eye in the court focused on him, he began, "As is my under-standing of the law, the defendant in this case should be judged by a jury of his peers." Turning to the judge, he posed a question, "Am I correct, Your Honor?"

"Of course," Metlock quickly replied.

Standing, DA Fredrick spat out, "We all know the rules. We learned them in grade school. Can we please just move along and not turn this proceeding into a circus?"

"What's your point, Coop?" Metlock asked from the bench.

Grabbing a paper from his table, Coop waved it in the air. "There are no Negroes in the jury pool. Where are the peers who are supposed to judge my client?"

"Your Honor," Fredrick protested, "we don't use Negroes in cases like this."

Before the judge could explain, Coop posed a question, "If a white man, let's say K. C. Fredrick," the attorney smiled, as he pointed to the DA's round belly, "was to be tried for murder, would the jury pool be made up only of Negroes?"

"What in the world?" Fredrick asked, tossing his arms in the air.

"If," Coop continued, "Calvin's peer jury is all white, then it only makes sense to me that those involving white defendants should be all black. And yet, my study of the county court records indicate it has never happened." Coop glanced from the judge to Fredrick and then to the reporters covering the trial. "It is obvious when you visit the area where Negroes live and how they are treated by whites in this community, they do not consider them their peers. Therefore, how can a jury pool made up of only whites from this side of the tracks be considered a jury of my client's peers?"

"Your Honor," Fredrick screamed.

As the press hurried and scribbled notes, the crowd murmured, and Coop looked back to the bench. The judge pounded his gavel once to bring silence before asking, "Coop, while your point might have some validity, the jury pool has been created and you must choose your jury from the pool."

Moving closer to the judge, Coop smiled. "Actually, it is not my only option."

"It isn't?" Metlock asked, while raising his right eyebrow.

"No, sir," Coop continued. "You see, in cases where a jury of one's peers cannot be seated, the defense has the option to have the case judged solely by the judge."

Metlock's shock registered not just on his face, but in his body language. He considered the suggestion for a few moments before scratching his head and sighing. It was obvious he had not anticipated Coop's move. Looking back to the two attorneys, Metlock said, "I need to visit with both of you in my chambers. Court will be recessed until this issue has been discussed in private."

Coop and Fredrick headed to a side door leading into the judge's chamber. Their robed host was waiting for them when they arrived. As the men formed a standing triangle, the DA spoke.

"What are you up to, Coop?"

"Trying to get my client a fair trial, and I won't get it by picking from the jury pool."

Metlock chimed in, "This is highly irregular. I can't even think of the last time a man on trial for murder gave up his right to be judged by a jury."

Coop nodded. "But when a Negro is on trial for his life in a courthouse where every Negro is found guilty no matter how scant the evidence, what choice is there?"

"You've put me in a horrible spot," Metlock argued.

The attorney smiled. "If placing you in a position where you have to weigh the evidence and make a fair ruling is putting you in a difficult spot, then you have no business being a judge. It is simple; if K. C. can't produce the evidence needed to convict Calvin Ross beyond a shadow of a doubt, you have to rule not guilty."

"But," Metlock argued, "I have to run for reelection. If I rule in such a way that the majority of voters turn against me, then I lose my job. And this job is important to me. I'm putting two kids through college."

"I realize what I'm asking," Coop replied, "but a man named Collins who has played tennis against you swears you are the most honest person he has ever met. So I feel I can be pretty sure if I keep the ball in between the lines and Fredrick goes out of bounds, you will make the right ruling. To do otherwise would fly in the face of everything you stand for."

Metlock shook his head and turned to the DA. "Do you have any objections to this?"

"No," Fredrick replied quickly, "in fact, I like it. It lets us move much more rapidly in presenting the evidence."

The judge sighed. "Well, I guess you've got what you want, Coop. But with the media circus out there and the way this town feels about this case, this is not going to be fun for any of us."

Coop smiled. Part one of his plan was in place. He was sure he could get a fair verdict. Now his attention could shift to exposing a series of lies and perhaps revealing the actual killer.

43

Coop listened to Fredrick's opening remarks carefully, but as the man introduced nothing new, the attorney's attention for details didn't matter. And when he stood to share his thoughts, Coop offered little more than a promise to prove his client innocent. As he sat down, the real trial began.

"Your Honor," Fredrick began, "I wish to call to the stand Linda Maltose."

John David was not in court to see his second wife stand up, smile, and make her way to the stand, yet everyone else, including the New York media, got an eyeful as Linda sashayed from the back row, down the center aisle, and through the swinging gate. Her outfit was a robin's egg blue suit tailored to hug every one of her curves. The skirt was tight and short, and her heels were expensive and tall. Her blonde hair was held in place by at least a half can of spray, and her makeup was as carefully applied as if she had been making an appearance in a Hollywood film. In other words, she was ready for her moment in the spotlight. After she was sworn in, the DA smiled smugly and began.

"Mrs. Maltose, I know you were one of at least six different people who witnessed the confrontation between Brent Booth and the defendant on Saturday, June the twentieth. Would you share with us in your own words what happened then?"

The woman smiled and looked to the crowd. "Well, the boy over there"—she pointed to Calvin—"was flirting with Becky. Brent saw it and asked the young man to quit. Then the Negro got nasty, cursed Brent, and moved back toward Becky. At that point Brent, in trying to defend the honor of his daughter, pushed Calvin Ross against the wall at the Western Auto. I guess the boy was a coward, because he ran off just cussing up a storm and mouthing something about getting even."

Fredrick smiled. "Your witness."

Coop got up and moved slowly toward the woman. He studied her for a moment before asking a very simple question, "Mrs. Maltose, why is it no one else heard Calvin cuss and no one else reported Calvin making any threats? I mean, we can call several other witnesses who will refute what you just said."

The woman's smile evaporated, replaced by a hateful glare. "Are you accusing me of lying?"

Coop replied quietly, "Are you? After all, in their statements to police, none mentioned the things you noticed."

Maltose snapped, "Well, they must have not had as good an angle as I did. And everyone knows I have the best hearing in town."

Coop turned toward Fredrick and softly said, "Will the Cardinals win today?"

The DA looked confused and shrugged, as Linda Maltose demanded, "What did you say about me?"

Coop pivoted back to the woman and smiled. "I thought your ears were the best in the county." He then looked to the judge. "No more questions of this witness."

The parade of those who observed the downtown altercation continued until noon. None of their stories were alike, but none was as damning as the one offered by Linda Maltose. Early in the afternoon, Fredrick moved the case in a new direction and called Mamie Johnson to the stand.

The Ross's neighbor explained that Calvin had been home before and after she and Hattie had made their trip to the church, but she could not say if he had stayed home in the evening. When Coop stood up to question the woman, he posed a question and baffled those in the courtroom.

"Mrs. Johnson, do you and your husband have a new camera that can print its pictures one minute after taking them?"

"We sure do," came the quick reply.

"And on the night of Becky Booth's murder did you take a photo of Calvin and Hattie and give it to them?"

"We sure did, and it was a really good likeness of them, too."

"Your Honor?" Fredrick asked, "what is this all about?"

Coop smiled, retreated to his table, retrieved a photo, and brought it back to the witness. "Is this the photo you took that night?"

Mamie studied it for a few moments before shaking her head, "No, it's the one we took the next morning before church. I know because of how dressed up Calvin and Hattie are."

Coop grinned, showed the photo to the DA and judge, and asked for it to be entered into evidence.

He then went to the table and retrieved a second photo. Giving it to Mamie, he noted, "This must be the picture you took on Saturday night."

She glanced at the black-and-white shot and confirmed it was.

"No more questions," Coop announced.

Fredrick's next witness was Wendy Adams. The girl walked shyly to the stand, adjusted her ponytail, smoothed her gray, pleated skirt and pink blouse. After taking the oath, she shared what she had seen at Lovers Park on the sad night in June. There were no surprise revelations. When the DA finished, Coop posed only one question.

"Wendy," he asked from his table, "you shared with us what you saw, including the blouse and shoe on the ground. Now, I want you to think long and hard about this; did you see a large knife on the ground about five feet away from the body? Judging from your testimony and the crime scene photos it would have likely been about where you were standing?"

"No, sir," she answered, "but it was dark."

"Thank you," Coop replied, "and I am finished with this witness."

Next came Sheriff Wylie Estes. Using photographs from the crime scene, Fredrick led the lawman through what he saw at the crime scene. Estes often referred to his comprehensive notes in framing his answers.

"Wylie," the DA continued after entering the photos in evidence, "is this the knife found at the crime scene?"

"It is," came the reply.

Fredrick held the weapon up to the judge, smiled, and then continued, "Wylie, I noticed two things stand out on this knife. The first is the name carved into the handle. What is the name?"

"Calvin Ross," the sheriff quickly replied.

"And the stains?" the DA asked. "Were they made by blood?"

"Yes," Estes replied, "but—"

Fredrick cut him off, "Just yes or no." He smiled and added, "And I am finished with this witness."

Coop sat at his table studying the smug grin on Fredrick's face before slowly getting up and going over to the evidence table. He looked at the photos for a few moments and then moved back to the witness.

"Wylie, when asked about the stains on the knife, Mr. Fredrick did not allow you to finish your explanation of his question about the blood. I think it would be interesting to hear what you were going to say."

Estes nodded. "Well, there was blood on the knife. And as part of my job, I had it tested by the state lab."

Coop smiled. "And what did those tests show?"

The sheriff explained, "It was pig's blood."

"You didn't tell me that," Fredrick called out from his table.

"You didn't let me tell you," Estes shot back.

The judge pounded his gavel once, and the DA eased back into his chair. As he did, Coop walked over to the evidence table and picked up four items. Returning to the witness, he handed an eight-by-ten photo to the sheriff.

"Wylie, is this the picture you took of the knife at the crime scene?"

Estes looked it over and replied, "It is."

"Why is the light so different," Coop asked, "than it is in this shot of Becky's body?"

"Because," the sheriff explained, "it was actually taken the afternoon after we found the body."

"Why didn't you take this photo at night?" the attorney asked.

"The DA didn't spot the knife until we went out to take a look at the scene the next afternoon."

"I see," Coop replied, as he handed the sheriff another shot. "Wylie, this is one of more than a hundred photos taken the night Becky's body was found. From this angle, can you see the spot, about five feet from the body, where K. C. Fredrick found the knife?"

The sheriff studied the picture. "Yes. It would be right here." He pointed to a place on the eight-by-ten.

"Is the knife there?" Coop asked.

"No," Estes replied.

Coop quickly moved back to the evidence table. "And it is not evident in any of a dozen other photos showing the exact spot in those pictures taken on the night Wendy and Frank discovered the body."

As murmurs filled the courtroom, Coop looked back to Fredrick. The DA seemed more than a bit uncomfortable. He studied the man for a moment and then returned to the witness.

"Wylie, here are the two Polaroid photos Claude Johnson took of Hattie and Calvin. They were both taken on the porch of the Ross home. This one was taken on Friday night about six. What do you see on the porch floor next to the railing and just above the top step?"

Estes studied the photo. "Looks like the knife, resting on top of some jeans or coveralls."

"This one," Coop explained as he gave the picture to the sheriff, "was taken the next morning before church. What do you see in this photo?"

The sheriff looked at it and shook his head. "The knife is there in this one, too."

"And," Coop said as he once more turned back to face Fredrick, "if a knife can't be two places at the same time, then how did it get to the crime scene by the time you and K. C. went there the next day?"

"I don't think it is possible," the sheriff replied.

"I have one more thing I want to clear up, Wylie, and I hope you can help me with it." Coop turned back to face the witness. "You shared with us when questioned by Mr. Fredrick that you believed Becky was murdered somewhere else and then taken to the place where Frank and Wendy found her. Is that true?"

"Based on the evidence," he replied, "I believe it to be true. There was not enough blood at Lovers Park for her to have been murdered there."

"Okay," Coop said, "did you ever find a primary scene?"

"No, we didn't."

"When was the last time Becky was seen alive?" Coop asked.

"A photo taken at the VFW dance shows her standing with a group of other kids at 9:30."

"When did Wendy spot the body?" Coop asked.

"It was about 10:45."

"Giving a gap of one hour and fifteen minutes for the murderer to kill Becky, move her body to Lovers Park, and then get away."

"Actually," Estes corrected the attorney, "only about an hour, as Wendy and Frank had already been at the location for about fifteen minutes when they discovered the body."

"Okay," Coop continued, "how far is it from the VFW Hall to Lovers Park?"

"Five miles or so."

Coop nodded. "How far is it from Lovers Park to the Ross home?"

"Maybe eight miles."

Coop moved from the witness box back to the defense table and picked up a sheet of paper. He studied it for a few seconds and then looked toward the judge.

"My client does not have a car or have access to one. He walks wherever he goes, and his friends do as well. Hattie Ross does not have a car, and the neighbor's car, a yellow Dodge, was at the church all evening where Mamie Johnson had driven it. So, Wylie, this brings up some inter-esting parameters we need to discuss."

Coop moved back toward the witness as he continued, "Did anyone see Calvin at the VFW dance?"

"No, sir," Wylie replied, "I questioned everyone who was there, and no one saw him."

"It was a whites-only dance," Coop observed. "Is that correct?"

"It was," Estes confirmed.

"Do you have any confirmation from any source of Calvin being seen with Becky after she disappeared from the dance?"

"No, I don't."

"Okay, Wylie, I need you to consider this care-fully and answer based on your experience as a lawman. Is there any way a man could carry a body from the VFW hall to Lovers Park on foot in an hour?"

"I don't see how," the sheriff replied. "I mean, it would take more than an hour to walk the distance, even if you weren't carrying anything."

"I have no more questions," Coop announced as he walked back to the table to join his client.

"Any cross?" Metlock asked.

Fredrick got up and slowly moved to Estes. Rubbing his brow, he glanced over to the evidence table and asked, "Could the knife have been hidden by the grass enough that it was missed on Friday night?"

"If it was lying on top of the grass," Estes replied, "as it was when you discovered it, I don't see how."

Scratching his head, the DA sighed. "Could Becky have been taken to Lovers Park in the hour window if Ross had access to a car?"

"Yes," Estes assured him. "But what car would it be?"

The DA didn't answer the question. Instead, he frowned and went back to his table. Coop could read on his opponent's face that the first day of the trial had not gone the way he'd expected.

44

After the smooth day in court, Coop sent Judy and Hattie back home while he reviewed a few things at the office. Satisfied he had his ducks in a row, he then headed over to the jail to visit with Calvin. He was sitting in the cell going over his plans for the next day when a concerned Wylie Estes joined them.

"Coop," the sheriff announced quietly, as he unlocked the door and took a seat on the bed beside the prisoner, "this just came for you." The look on his face gave way to the fact that it wasn't good news.

Coop took a badly wrinkled piece of yellow paper that appeared to come from a school note-pad from Estes. With a confused look, he opened it and read the pencil scribbling on the note.

We got Judy Lindsay. If that boy is found innocent, she's dead.

As Coop looked up, Estes sadly explained, "Someone had this wrapped around a rock and tossed it through a window in the front office. By the time I found it and looked outside, they were gone. I did check with Hattie. Judy is not there. She went out on the back porch an hour or so ago and never came back in."

Now the real nightmare had started. The stakes had been raised, and it was no longer just one life hanging in the balance. Glancing back to the note and then to the sheriff, Coop sighed. "So this is the way they are playing the game now."

The three men remained silent for a few seconds before Calvin quietly offered, "Let's call the judge and tell him I'll plead guilty tomorrow. Then your wife won't have to die. It's the only thing we can do."

"Maybe not," the sheriff cut in. "Judge Metlock is in my office. He was here discussing a different matter when the note came in. Let's talk to him about this before we make any rash decisions."

Estes hurried down the hall leaving the two shocked men alone.

"You got to let me plead guilty," Calvin said. "You have proved I couldn't have done it. No matter what happens after this, Hattie will be sure of the truth. And you've been pretty noble through this whole thing; now it is time for me to return the favor."

Coop didn't answer. He couldn't. He didn't know what to say. After all, this wasn't Calvin's fault; it was his. Why hadn't he insisted Judy stay in Ohio? Why had he allowed her to come back to a place where she would be in danger? But those questions were now moot. They didn't matter. What did matter was making sure his wife didn't die. It just wasn't an option. But he couldn't let Calvin die either.

"Coop," Metlock announced as he and the sheriff approached the cell, "I know what is going on, and Wylie and I have a plan that might work."

"What is it?" Coop asked rising from the chair.

"Okay," the judge explained as he entered the cell, "Judy won't die until an innocent verdict is announced. K. C. is about to finish with his evidence, but you still have to present yours. Then we have the summations. At that point, I will deliberate. I can slow things down enough by calling for additional lab tests, breaks for me to examine evidence, a trip to the crime scene, a visit to the state crime lab, and other random delays, including a tennis injury. If we need to do so, we can stretch this thing out for more than a week. During this time, Wylie can figure out who is behind this and find Judy. Only when she is free, do we make the ruling."

"But what if we don't find Mrs. Lindsay?" Calvin asked.

The judge put his hand on the prisoner's shoulder. "Then it falls on you, son. If you want to be the silent hero, you can plead guilty. But as Coop has already torn holes in the case a mile wide, let's only use it as a last resort. It is time to let Wylie go to work, and the rest of us must act as if nothing has happened. Can we do it?"

"I'll try," Calvin softly answered.

"Just go on like I planned?" Coop asked.

"Yeah," the judge replied.

"Okay." He sighed as he eased back down on the metal chair. "I guess it is time to trust someone who has my fate in his hands." It was anything but a comforting thought for a man who claimed to have faith, but only when he was in complete control of the situation.

45

Tuesday, July 14, 1964

The *Bugle* had gone to press late on Monday night and the editor's coverage of the trial read much differently than what had been printed in the *New York Times*. For those in Justice who didn't get a chance to witness the proceedings and didn't read the out-of-town papers, their only point of view came from the pen of James McMilliam, and McMilliam slanted his coverage to favor Fredrick and prosecution. In his editorial, McMilliam called for the local citizens to rally in the city park for a prayer meeting to show their support for the Booth family and the District Attorney. They also were to pray that Judge Metlock would be given the wisdom to do the right thing. It did not take reading between the lines to understand what the *right thing* meant.

In a second feature piece, McMilliam went after Coop for his lack of sensitivity to the Booth family. The latter is likely the reason the courtroom crowd was surly when the attorney arrived just before nine.

As Coop walked across the lawn, scores tossed insults his way and a few even spit at him. Focused on the case at hand and on what had happened to his wife, the attorney barely noticed the hate pouring from people who had once been his friends. In fact, he perceived or heard little until Fredrick finished the prosecution's case and turned the proceeding over to the defense.

The first witness Coop called was A. J. Collins. After the representative from the state office took the stand, the lawyer pulled his concern from his wife back to the case.

"Mr. Collins, what was the actual cause of Becky Booth's death?"

"A stab wound to the back of the neck severed her spinal cord."

"In looking through your report," Coop continued, "I noted there were several different wounds of varying depths and size." After picking up Calvin's knife from the evidence table, the attorney handed it to the examiner. "Could this weapon have been used in the attack?"

Collins studied the knife. "Seven wounds fit

this knife's profile, but as I looked back through my notes and examined the sheriff's report I have come to the conclusion that this knife was not involved in the wounds leading to Becky Booth's death."

"I'm not sure I follow you," Coop announced.

"In the last few days," Collins explained, "I went back and looked at my photographs and notes. I had always believed because of the type of wounds, their depth, and the lack of blood, the larger ones had been postmortem. I am now sure of it. I can categorically say this knife was not used in the attack that killed Miss Booth, and my new report, which I have with me, presents information to verify the fact."

"I'm not sure I understand," Coop replied. "Where is this new report?"

"I have a copy with me today," Collins announced, holding up a file.

"But why did you go back over your original and make changes?"

"Because of your visit, Mr. Lindsay," Collins explained. "Then, the depth and size of the wounds bothered me enough to wonder if there was not one, but two different attackers. So I called Mr. Bryson Tillman, who was at the funeral home when the body arrived, and asked him a few questions. He swore to me, and will swear to this court, the larger wounds were not on the young woman's body when it arrived at the funeral home. Yet those larger wounds were there when it was brought to my lab on Monday. The only explanation is someone using the knife in evidence placed those wounds on the body between those times."

This frame was much more elaborate than he believed possible. Someone with access to the body had put some thought into this. Coop glanced to the judge and then to Fredrick, who looked stunned, then turned back to his witness. "Dr. Collins, did your examination reveal anything else to help in identifying a possible suspect?"

"One thing," the examiner quickly replied, "due to the position of Miss Booth's defensive wounds and where the other wounds done with the first knife were inflicted, her attacker was left-handed."

"And you know this how?" Coop asked.

"The direction of the blows, the angle, and the fact that the wounds on the front of her body were on the right and when she turned the wounds were to the left. The only other wounds were made by the large knife, and they were spread on both sides of the body."

Coop considered the information, glanced over to Calvin, and nodded. As Calvin was right-handed, this pretty much sealed the deal. But Collins's new, updated report offered another element to possibly open an even larger hole. But should he go there? If he did, it might make Calvin's suddenly pleading guilty to save Judy impossible.

"Do you have any more questions, Coop?" the judge asked.

The attorney nodded. "I may, but first I need to look at my notes. There is some new evidence revealed today I had not anticipated."

Coop moved back to his table and opened his briefcase. With everyone looking on, he pretended to scan some documents, while in truth, he was stalling for time, trying to balance his job as an attorney against his role as a husband. Whose life was more important? In his mind, even as much as he had grown to like Calvin and Hattie, it had to be Judy's. She was the mother of his children and the only woman he'd ever loved. But if she could talk to him right now, she would tell him to save his client and let the chips fall where they might. It was how strongly she believed in justice and was one of the reasons he had fallen in love with her. And if Calvin were executed, she would never be able to live with the fact that her living had cost him his life.

Setting the papers down, Coop slowly made his way back up to the examiner. After running his fingers across his lips, he finally spoke, "My client is right-handed. How likely is it he could have delivered the killing strikes?"

"Very unlikely."

"We have already established the blood on the knife was from a hog," Coop continued, "did you also test the blood on the defendant's clothing?"

"I did not," Collins replied. "But if they have not been washed, I could conduct the test today and then provide the court with my findings. I have what I need in my car to do that."

This was a window he needed. It would buy him some time. Coop looked to the judge, took a deep breath, and announced, "I would like to request the test."

"Any objections?" Metlock asked Fredrick.

"No," came the flat reply.

"Could you have it finished and ready to present by two this afternoon?" the judge asked Collins.

"If I can be provided with a place to work," the witness replied, "I can."

"I will secure you a place in one of our doctor's offices," Metlock answered. "So I guess we can dismiss until this afternoon."

"Actually, Judge," Coop cut in, "I do have one more question."

"You may ask it."

"Mr. Collins," the attorney continued, "the local newspaper and gossip mill has trumpeted the information that Becky Booth was sexually assaulted. Your examination would prove it either right or wrong. So as painful as it is for me to ask this question, was the victim raped?"

"No, she was not."

"Thank you." Coop looked back to the judge. "I can continue my line of questions this afternoon after the tests have been completed."

46

Wylie Estes initially had little to go on in trying to pin down who kidnapped Judy and where they were holding her. But he did have one theory. Whoever was involved was also likely a part of the group pretending to be Klansmen. So the first thing he did Tuesday morning was stop by Bobby Sloan's garage. Sloan was not happy to see the sheriff, but as he had been unmasked the night of the supposed rally, he couldn't deny his involve-ment.

"Now listen, Wylie," he began, "I was paid to do what I did. It was just a job. I got fifty bucks and some booze. That's all. As I think of it now, I was stupid."

Estes sized up the short man in the greasy bib overalls before grabbing him by the shoulders and pinning him against an old GMC pickup. "Listen, Bobby, what you did the other night was against the law. I can arrest you and make enough stuff stick that you will get to work in a prison garage for the next five years."

"Wylie, please."

Leaning closer and pushing hard, the sheriff got right into the little man's face and snarled, "Who was behind this? Who paid you?" He almost asked him about Judy's kidnapping but stopped short. Bobby might not know, and if he blabbed the information to someone else, the woman might get hurt.

"The money was given to me at night," Sloan stammered. "A man gave me money when I showed up at the park."

"What was his name?"

"I don't really know; he was wearing a hood and he never spoke."

Estes eased his grip and stepped back. As Sloan took a deep breath, the sheriff made another demand. "Who else was in the group you did know?"

"There were a bunch of folks," came the quick reply.

"Then let's go over to your desk, and you are going to write down every one of them. When you are done, I think it might be time for you to take a vacation . . . a very long vacation."

"What do you mean?" Sloan nervously asked.

"What does it usually mean when someone disappears and is never seen again?"

"You wouldn't?" the man whispered.

"It depends on who is on the list of names. If you leave one out, then you might as well have an address where mail can't be forwarded."

47

As the *State v. Ross* was called back into session, A. J. Collins once again took the stand and Coop picked up his questions.

"Dr. Collins, were you able to determine the source of the blood on Mr. Ross's clothing?"

"Yes, I was."

"And was it human?"

"No, it was pig's blood. There was only one place I found any human blood, and it was a very small amount and not the same type as the victim's."

Coop smiled. "I have one more area I hope to clear up before I turn you over to Mr. Fredrick. You said Miss Booth had defensive wounds. So it means she must have put up a fight. What did you find to indicate she did?"

"Well," Collins began, "wounds to the palm and arm where she likely tried to fend off the blows, and there was blood and flesh under three fingernails on her right hand where she scratched the attacker."

"Did you examine the skin?" Coop asked.

"I did," Collins replied, "but there was not enough to link to a person's sex or race."

Coop walked to the table and pulled out the

series of photos he had taken of Calvin in the jail. Returning to the stand, he handed them to Collins.

"Doctor, my client's face and body were worked over by the authorities in an attempt to gain a confession." Coop strolled over to the witness table and grabbed the photo Calvin Johnson had taken on the Sunday morning after Becky was murdered. "Here," Coop continued, "is a photo taken after Becky's death but before Calvin was arrested to prove what I told you. Now, look at the photos I took in the jail cell and see if you see any wounds that might have been caused by a young woman trying to fight off her attacker."

Collins studied the shots and shook his head. "None of the shots here show any scratch-like wounds created by fingernails. This work was likely done with a blackjack."

Coop grimly smiled. "We have already established the attacker was left-handed. I have also read in knife attacks that the attacker's height can sometimes be determined by the angle of the wounds."

"It is true," the examiner explained, "and it is my belief the person who delivered these blows was likely no more than five-and-a-half feet tall, maybe less."

"Your witness," Coop announced as he moved back to his chair.

Fredrick slowly rose and walked toward the witness box. He fiddled with his thinning hair for a moment before asking, "Would it still be possible for a person who was taller than five-six to commit the crime?"

"Yes," Collins replied, "if the crime scene was set up where Miss Booth was on elevated ground. But unless we have an actual crime scene, I can't say for sure one way or the other."

"Thank you," Fredrick replied, "I have no more questions."

48

In a period of four hours, Wylie Estes met with and scared half of the fake Klansmen, but none of them had given him the information needed to track down Judy Lindsay. He was returning from the Ashburn farm and on his way back to his office when he came across Reverend Martin Clements parked alongside Route 227 changing the front passenger-side tire on his maroon and black 1958 Olds. Estes parked his police cruiser just behind the minister's vehicle and got out.

"How you doing, Martin?" he asked. The temperature was in the low nineties, and the humidity was almost as high. So the question didn't deserve a reply. The preacher was obviously miserable.

Looking up from the wheel, lug wrench in hand, Clements shrugged. "I've been better. This wouldn't have happened if I hadn't decided to be a good Samaritan."

"What do you mean by that?" the sheriff asked as he leaned over to examine the preacher's work.

"Well," Clements explained while twisting the last nut tight, "I was coming back from seeing Missy Walters out on her farm—she's been kind of sick and has missed church the last three weeks—and on my way back, I noticed a guy whose truck had broken down. I stopped and offered him a ride back to a garage, but he'd have none of it. Instead, he asked me to take him to an old shack way out of town. It was ten miles out of my way."

The preacher stopped his story long enough to snap the car's hubcap back in place, let the jack down, and take it and the wrench back to the trunk. Only after retrieving and stowing the flat did he continue.

"Anyway, I took the guy out there, and we drove by a spot where they'd torn down the old Watkins home. There were nails all over the road, and I must have picked one up. I got this far back, and the right front just gave out."

"Was the guy you helped a member of your church?" Estes asked.

"Naw," Clements replied, "he was just a scruffy guy who needed a lift. More of a drinker than a choir member. Anyway, I need to get back to town. I'm already late for a committee meeting."

Estes went back to the squad car and slid in. By the time he had the Ford started, the preacher was half a mile away. Taking a look at his suspect list, he opted to next pay a visit to Troy Bedlow. He figured the big man would still be at the lumberyard.

After easing the police cruiser back onto the highway, the sheriff drove three miles before noting a dusty blue pickup parked on the side of the road. He almost drove by it before the preacher's words hit him. Did this belong to the guy Clements helped?

Pulling in front of the truck, Estes stopped and got out. Wiping his brow, he peered into the cab. It was as dirty as the outside with the floorboard littered with soft drink and beer bottles. A box of shotgun shells was on the seat along with a large Big Chief writing pad displaying Elizabeth Taylor's picture on the front. Stepping to the bed, the sheriff spotted a few more cans, some loose tools, including wrenches, screwdrivers, and a couple of knives, as well as a tackle box and a fishing reel.

Moving to the front of the car, Estes yanked up the hood of the old Chevy. There was a crack in the six-cylinder's block, and what oil had been in the crankcase was now mostly spilled on the ground. This vehicle was not going to get anywhere before a tow job and some major work. As it was already more than a decade old, it likely wasn't worth the price it would cost for the new motor.

His curiosity satisfied, the sheriff jumped back into the car. Five minutes later, he was at the lumberyard and ready to dress down Troy Bedlow.

49

It was nearly four when Coop called Claude Johnson to the stand. The big man with the even bigger smile eased into the witness chair with all the grace of a water buffalo. Even if he was the only black man in the courtroom, other than the defendant, he didn't seem to care. Dressed in a blue serge suit and bright red tie, he seemed willing and eager to actually deal with some serious questions, even if he was in front of a hostile audience.

"Mr. Johnson," Coop began, "I understand you were home the night of Becky Booth's murder."

"I was," Johnson answered in a booming voice.

"Were you alone?"

"Naw," he replied with a smile. "Three of my friends stopped by and stayed at my place until about eleven."

"And what were you doing?" Coop asked.

Johnson scratched his head, looked over to his wife who was sitting in the audience alongside Hattie, and took a deep breath. After a few seconds, he smiled and explained, "We was involved in a study of sin. We often get together to visit about the ways we can be led astray by temptation. I feel you have to know about these things in order to avoid them."

"I understand," the lawyer replied. "And what sin were you studying on this particular evening?"

"Gambling," came the quick answer. "We was trying to figure out why it is men seem to love to play dice."

For the first time since the trial began, a few chuckles could be heard in the gallery. Coop waited for the laughter to fade away before asking, "Did you figure out the answer?"

"I think we did," Johnson answered. "It is the lure of perhaps rolling for a big win. The temptation is often just too strong to resist."

Coop shrugged. "I will try to remember the lesson. Now, during the night did you see Calvin Ross?"

"Saw him early, even took a picture of him and Hattie, and I saw him later when my wife and Hattie got home. I didn't see him during my meeting with my friends, but I did hear him turning on the kitchen water tap; their pipes make a terrible racket, and heard him walking about a few times, too. But it wasn't what I saw made the real impact on me and the boys. It was what we smelled."

"Smelled?" Coop asked.

"Yes, there was a ham roasting in the oven and some pintos cooking, too." Johnson stopped and licked his lips. "They both smelled so good, it was almost a bigger temptation to go sample them than it was to play with, excuse me, I mean, study the dice."

"I see," the lawyer replied. Coop glanced back to Fredrick and then over to Hattie before continuing. "Now, Mr. Johnson, as your houses are so close, the windows were open and you could smell the food cooking, did you happen to notice if anything had scorched or burned?"

"No, sir," the witness answered, "everything smelled so good, I had a yearning to make some cornbread to go with it."

"Well," Coop replied, "I guess you mean Calvin had to keep putting water in those beans or there would have been a terrible smell all through the neighborhood."

"You would be right." Johnson laughed. "I've dealt with burned beans a few times, too."

"Now, Mr. Johnson, did you slip on something on the Ross porch the next morning?"

"I did," the man said with a smile. "It was Calvin's butchering knife. Hattie warned him the night before to put it up, but I guess he just plum forgot."

"Thank you, sir," Coop said. He then turned to the DA and said, "Your witness."

"I have no questions," Fredrick replied.

"If that is the case," Metlock announced from the bench, "and as the hour is late, let's dismiss until one tomorrow afternoon."

"One?" Fredrick asked from his table.

"Yes," the judge replied, while rubbing his right shoulder, "I have a doctor's appointment to check out a tennis injury. So I will be out of commission until after lunch." Metlock smiled before pounding his gavel. As everyone rose, the judge said, "Mr. Lindsay, I would like to see you in my chambers."

A minute later, the judge and defense attorney were standing side-by-side looking out a window at the courthouse lawn. The judge quietly opened the discussion.

"Wylie hasn't tracked down who grabbed your wife or where she might be yet."

"I was afraid of that," Coop whispered.

"And you are doing far too good a job," Metlock said. "I would have dismissed the case and already found your client innocent if we didn't have this kidnapping hanging over our heads." He turned to face his guest. "You realize there is no way Ross can plead guilty. It is as plain as the nose on your face—he is innocent. Therefore, we have a problem."

"I know," Coop grimly replied, "but Judy

wouldn't be able to live with the fact that she had been responsible for Calvin being found guilty. I couldn't throw the case, because she would never forgive me either. There are times when having integrity is a real pain."

"Tell me about it," Metlock grumbled. "When I rule the way I have to on this case, I'll be looking for a new job come election time."

50

It was just past nine when Wylie Estes knocked on the door of the Methodist parsonage. Martin Clements, dressed in old khaki pants and a white dress shirt, pulled the entry open.

"What are you doing here this time of night, Sheriff?"

"I need your help," Estes explained. "Can I step inside?"

"Sure," Clements replied. "My wife is out of town, so why don't we just sit in the living room. I'll turn the TV off."

The living room was small, less than 150 square feet and decorated like something from the prewar years. The wallpaper was a dark flower print and the carpet well worn. The couch and matching chairs were covered in light green fabric. The coffee and end tables were stacked with magazines and showed signs of water rings. The Clements must not have used coasters.

The sheriff took a seat on the couch, while the preacher, after cutting the power to the television, eased down in a wooden rocker. After a few seconds of studying one another, Estes opened the conversation.

"The man you picked up today, do you remember his name?"

"I think he said his name was Mel. I had seen him around, but until this afternoon had never talked to him."

"What did he look like?"

"I'd guess him to be in his thirties, light brown or reddish hair, ruddy complexion. He had really deep green eyes."

Estes nodded. "After the trial had adjourned for the day, I took Coop out to look at the truck this afternoon. He thought it might be the one that tried to run him down."

"Really?"

"Did you look in the truck?" the sheriff asked.

"No," Clements replied, "I didn't. I just gave him a ride to where he told me he wanted to go."

"Did you tell him you were a pastor?"

"Wylie," Clements cut in, a confused look on his face, "what does this have to do with anything?"

The sheriff shrugged. "Did you tell him you were a preacher?"

"Yes."

"Now," Estes said, "how brave are you?"

"What do you mean?"

"I mean, will you make a step on faith?"

"Yeah," Clements said, "I guess so. But what is this all about?"

Estes leaned back in his chair, crossed his right leg over his left, and folded his hands over the raised knee. "Judy Lindsay has been kidnapped. There is no ransom; the only demands are for Calvin Ross to be found guilty. If he is found innocent, the kidnapper or kidnappers have promised to kill Judy."

"Oh, my Lord," Clements whispered.

"I have struck out finding who is responsible for this crime. Every lead I have had has turned up dry. Then I got to thinking about the blue truck. When Coop and I went back out to look at it today, I picked up a notepad resting in the seat. Upon examining it at the office, I discovered it matched the paper of the note alerting us Judy had been taken. And I could make out the impressions of the original note on the top blank page of the pad."

"So the guy I helped," the preacher asked, "is the person behind the kidnapping."

"I don't know if he is the person behind it," Estes explained, "but I am sure he is connected." The sheriff paused for a few moments, then shared the real reason for his visit. "If I go out and try to enter the place, odds are pretty good Judy will be killed. But with your connection as the good Samaritan, you might have a chance to get in."

"But why would I go out there again?" Clements asked. "What reason would I have that would not tip him off I was being used?"

"To give him this," Estes announced as he pulled a billfold from his pocket.

"Where did you find it?" the preacher asked. "Was it in the truck?"

"No," the sheriff admitted, "it was one my daughter gave me on Father's Day. I just pulled it out of a drawer and put five ten-dollar bills in it."

"I don't see how this can help," Clements replied, a confused look framing his face.

"You," Estes explained, "being the good preacher you are, will make the trip out there and tell him you found this in the seat of your car where he had been sitting and wanted to know if it was his."

"But it would be a lie."

Estes grinned, "Not if I take it out to the car and drop it there right now."

Clements shook his head. "And if I walk into a place where a woman might well be held, I might get killed."

"I doubt it," the sheriff assured him. "The guy will just want the money. And while you are taking care of business, I'll work my way around to the back of the building. Then I can figure out if Judy is there and what I need to do to set her free."

"But," Clements asked, "what if she is not there?"

"Then I've lost fifty bucks."

"When do you want to do this?" the preacher asked.

"So you're on board?"

Clements shook his head. "If Calvin Ross is innocent then what Coop is doing is right. And it means I have got to admit my thinking is all wrong. It's time for me to start making up for it."

"We'll make our move tomorrow morning," Estes explained. "Even though I'd prefer the cover of darkness, if you made your move tonight it might spook him and put you in danger. I will meet you at the church at ten. Meanwhile, is your car unlocked?"

"Yes."

"Good, I'll put this in your seat," the sheriff said as he waved the billfold in the air, "so you can find it when you go out and lock your car in a few minutes."

51

Wednesday, July 15, 1964

From the backseat of the preacher's Oldsmobile, Wylie Estes nervously viewed his surroundings. It looked like the place good ticks and chiggers go when they die. The road was little more than a washed-out trail, and the woods were so thick they could hide the Soviet Army. Once they had turned off the main road, the travel had been slow. It now took five minutes to cover a mile, and thus, the ten-mile trip to where Clements had taken the stranded motorist took almost a half hour.

"We are close now," the preacher said. "I think the house or barn or whatever you want to call it is just over the next rise and around the bend."

Estes's original plan called for Clements to let him out just before arriving at the place. The sheriff would then work his way through the woods and to the back of the building. But he then considered the way sound traveled in these woods. Melvin and whoever was with him would hear them before they saw them and they would know if the Olds had come to a stop. They also might suspect the driver was not on the up and up. So Estes decided to ride all the way with the preacher and then sneak out the back door while the men were talking.

"I see it," Clements whispered, apprehension obvious in his tone.

"Is there a place you can park kind of off to the side?" Estes asked. "I will need some cover to get out and move to the back."

"Yeah, there is a stand of cedar trees. I can pull in there and it should make it hard for them to get a good look."

"Great," the sheriff replied, "do it. And don't stall getting to the front door. Look like you are on a mission. If you fiddle around, he will suspect something. And don't go inside. Stay at the door where I can hear and see you. You got it?"

"Yeah."

"You okay?"

"I guess so." Clements sighed. "Up until now I thought the toughest job in my life was preaching a funeral."

Estes laughed. "This is not a walk in the park for me either. I'm not used to ever pulling my gun. You know, as a sheriff I've never even shot at anyone, much less walked into a situation where I might have to kill somebody."

"I'm about to pull in," the preacher whispered. He chuckled and then added, "I guess God does have a sense of humor. He is pretty much showing me that my life and Calvin Ross's life are equal in His eyes. Just not real crazy about the way the Lord opted to prove it."

"Okay, no more talking," Estes warned. "They have to believe you are alone."

Clements pulled the car off the road and into what the sheriff presumed was the yard. From the way the long grass skimmed the underside of the car, it was obvious no one had mowed for a long time. From his position on the floor, Estes could see the cloudless sky and the tops of the cedars. He judged them to be about fifteen feet tall.

"Don't forget the billfold and don't answer me," the sheriff warned. "And I will be there to protect you."

Clements opened the door and slid out of the car. Estes heard the man take a deep breath and begin a walk he didn't want to take. Ten seconds, fifteen, thirty, and finally a knock. When no one answered, the preacher knocked again. This time there were results emphasized by a rusty hinge's squeal.

"Yeah, you lost or something?" The voice was rough, deep, and ragged.

"I picked you up yesterday," Clements explained. "Your truck had given out on the highway."

"Yeah, I remember now. You're a preacher, aren't you?"

"Sure am," Clements replied.

"Well, I don't need saving, so just move along."

"It's not that. I found a billfold with fifty dollars in my car and thought you might have dropped it."

This was as good a time as any. Opening the back passenger door, Estes slid out, landed on his belly, and crawled to the front of the car. Peering around the bumper, he assessed the situation.

The building had likely once been built as a barn and then converted to a house. Judging from the appearance, it probably hadn't been in use for twenty years or more. The roof was tin, the walls unpainted slab side wood, and the front door was the same material. There might have been two rooms, but likely no more. About thirty feet behind the shack was an outhouse. There were no power lines, so the place had never known electricity.

The man framed by the entry was maybe an inch over six feet in height, about two hundred solid pounds, and had shaggy light brown hair. His eyes were large and expressive, and his complexion pitted. And from the smile on his face, he looked ready to claim the billfold. The trap had been set and was about to be sprung.

With the preacher holding the man's attention by waving the wallet, Estes made his move. Staying low, he sprinted behind the cedars and raced quickly to the rear of the home. As he took a deep breath to slow his heart rate, he surveyed the backside of the building. There was a single window and a door. If he went in at an angle, it would be hard for anyone to spot him; he could then crouch down until he got to the window and take a quick peek.

It took five seconds to cover the ground and make it to the window, but those five seconds seemed like an eternity. Using only his right eye, he snuck a look into the home. There was only one room and a loft. He could see a pot-bellied stove, a rocking chair, a cane-backed chair at a small table, and a bed in the far corner. A ladder led up to the loft. On the floor, perhaps five feet beyond the ladder, was someone or something. The light wasn't good enough for him to make out if it was Judy Lindsay, but his gut told him it had to be.

Glancing back to the front door, he noted Clements handing the man the wallet. Moving quickly to the back door, he gently tried the knob. It was locked. Though he'd seen it done a hundred times in the movies, Estes wondered if he could manage to knock the door open with his shoulder. There was only one way to find out.

Backing up, he readied himself for the charge. Holding his gun in his right hand, he raced forward twenty feet and hit the wooden entry with his left shoulder. He was completely unprepared for what happened next. The old door didn't just give way; it splintered into a hundred pieces. As it did, Estes tripped and fell to the ground. It gave the suspected kidnapper all the time he needed to reach for a shotgun he'd set beside the front entry. As the sheriff rolled over onto his stomach, the other man steadied his weapon and took aim. A second later, the room was filled with smoke, fire, and the noise created by the blast.

52

Estes closed his eyes as the other man pulled the trigger, but he opened them again a second later when he felt nothing. Rolling to his knees and looking up, he noted Clements standing between him and the shooter with blood seeping from a wound in his stomach. Behind the preacher, Mel had already yanked out a shell, reloaded, and was pulling the gun up to fire again.

It was more a reflex than a planned action, but either way it was effective as the sheriff steadied himself on his knees, aimed, and fired two shots from his forty-five. Both hit the man in the chest. He wobbled for a moment before falling to the floor.

Estes pushed to his feet and covered the ground between them. He picked up the shotgun and tossed it through the front door. He then looked back to the preacher. Clements was holding his hands over his gut, but it was not doing much to stem the blood flow. Somehow, the man was still managing to stand.

Glancing over to the ladder, the sheriff holstered his firearm and hustled up the rungs. There in the loft was Judy Lindsay. She was tied up and gagged but appeared all right. Pulling a knife from his pocket, Estes cut the ropes binding her wrists behind her back.

"You all right?" he asked.

As she turned over, she nodded.

"Good," the sheriff said as he handed her his knife. "Cut yourself free and hurry down. I need to help Reverend Clements. Then we have to get him back to town and to the hospital."

Scurrying back down the ladder, Estes put his arm around the preacher's shoulder and guided him to a cane-backed chair. He then pulled the injured man's hands away and studied the wound.

"What's the verdict?" Clements asked with a wry grin.

"Seems the bleeding is slowing down," Estes answered.

"I hope I manage to live through this," the preacher replied as he gritted his teeth to fend off the pain. "There is too much sermon material here to waste it."

"Let me know when you preach the message," the sheriff replied as he pushed the wound closed with his hand, "and I might wander over from First Christian."

"You got it," Clements said with a forced laugh, "and I managed to save your fifty dollars for you." He paused a moment and then asked, "Is he dead?"

"Yeah, and Judy is fine."

"I sure am," the woman confirmed as she made her way down the ladder. She studied the bleeding pastor for a moment before reaching down and tearing a part of her dress. As she used the material to help control the bleeding, she glanced to Estes and said, "We need to get moving and get Reverend Clements some help."

"Yeah," Estes agreed, "you stay here and I'll pull the car up to the door."

"There is an irony in all of this," Clements noted as he reached up and grabbed the sheriff's arm.

"What?"

As the men's eyes met, the preacher explained, "After your visit last night, I dug out an old county map. The muddy, rutted-out dirt path we drove on to get to this house is called the Jericho Road."

53

Coop walked into the courtroom in a fog. The judge's visit to the doctor had bought him the morning, but there was still no word on Judy. Closing arguments were about to begin, and then it would be up to the judge to study the evidence and render a plea. Metlock might be able to stall for day or more in making his decision, but it was likely all he could do. Then they would be out of time.

As the bailiff announced the judge's entry, Coop rose. A shudder went through him as he realized in front of a packed house, he was going to plead for one life while silently praying for another.

Metlock looked out at the gallery, then to both lawyers, and asked Fredrick and Coop to approach the bench. When they both were in front of him, he spoke in hushed tones.

"Gentlemen, there was one matter standing between me and making a suggestion concerning the fate of the defendant, and the matter has been cleared up." He stopped, glanced over to Coop and winked. "She is fine, Coop."

"What's this all about?" the DA asked.

"You will learn soon enough," Metlock answered. "Wylie will be here in a few seconds.

As this case has been nothing but strange from the beginning, I am going to delay closing arguments until our sheriff retakes the stand. He has found some new evidence with a direct bearing on this case"—the judge looked toward the back of the room—"and he is here now. So both of you go sit down."

Though he had no idea what had happened, a now completely relieved and smiling Coop made his way back to his table. Judy was obviously safe, and he was free to finally put all his cards on the table. Justice would be served, and maybe, when the details of this episode came out, he might be able to even win back some of the trust of the locals on both sides of the tracks. And even if he were still hated, everything was still downhill from now on in. He'd met the challenge, done the right thing, and Wylie and God had both rewarded him for his efforts.

"What is it?" Calvin whispered as Coop sat down beside him.

"Judy is free," he explained, as they leaned their heads close together. "So you don't have to worry about pleading guilty for something you didn't do."

"Thank God she's okay," Calvin breathed. "Do you know who was behind it?"

"Not yet," the attorney answered.

"Ladies and gentlemen," Metlock announced from his bench, "this has been a very strange case from the beginning. In the past two days, it has taken a turn, making it even stranger. Because of this, it is time for us to depart from normal courtroom procedure in order to present evidence vital to this case. Therefore, I am calling Sheriff Wylie Estes back to the stand."

Coop watched as the sheriff, who had been standing in the back entry, slowly made his way toward the witness box. He stopped a few rows from the front to study a shoe sticking a few inches out in the aisle. It was caramel-colored with a deep scuff on the toe. He looked at its owner, smiled, and remarked, "Mr. McMilliam, I suggest you get those shoes shined. You might be able to do it with the sheet you once wore." Estes waited until the editor's eyes caught his, then moved forward.

Coop caught McMilliam's eyes and shook his head. The cat was out of the bag.

Meanwhile, the sheriff opened the gate and wearily made his way to the witness box. He more fell into than sat in the chair and took a deep breath.

"Wylie, you are still under oath," the judge explained. He then looked the witness over and added, "I note you have stains on your uniform. Would you like to tell us how you got those stains and what happened earlier today?"

The courtroom was at rapt attention as the sheriff spilled his story of the kidnapping and the rescue of Judy Lindsay. As he finished the tale, the judge opted to ask the question everyone present wanted to ask.

"Wylie, how are Judy and Reverend Clements?"

"Judy Lindsay is fine. Hungry, but has no injuries. The preacher had to undergo surgery, but somehow the shotgun blast did not do enough damage to kill him. They feel he will be all right after a couple of weeks in the hospital."

"Good," the judge said. "Now, in looking at the notes from our phone conversation just before court began this afternoon, I have a few questions. The man at the house where Judy was held, did he tell you anything?"

"No," Wylie replied, "he died before he could talk. But I returned to the cabin about an hour ago and found one of Becky Booth's bracelets there. I showed the bracelet to Martha Booth a few minutes ago, and she confirmed that Becky had worn it the night of the VFW dance. I then went back to where Melvin Forest's truck had been left. In pulling down the tailgate, I discovered blood on the right hinge and on the part of the bed not exposed when the tailgate is in the upright position. There also a short-bladed knife in the truck covered with blood. So it seems pretty clear how this played out."

"What do we know about Mr. Forest?" the judge asked.

"He has worked for John David Maltose for a

decade or so. Beyond that, we know precious little. He did not socialize in town and seems to have no relatives here."

Metlock nodded before turning to the two attorneys. "Do either of you have any questions for the sheriff?"

Fredrick shook his head, but Coop stood. After approaching the witness, he asked, "Wylie, with Forest dead and your investigation really just beginning, I doubt if you can answer this, but as this is an unusual proceeding now, do you have a theory as to why this man might want to kidnap my wife in order to influence the outcome of this case?"

"The only thing that makes logical sense," the sheriff explained, "is if Melvin Forest was afraid if Mr. Ross was proven innocent, the case would be reopened and he would be exposed as Becky Booth's murderer. I know, from photos taken at the dance, he was there at the VFW on that night."

Coop nodded, ran his hand over his lips, crossed his arms, and continued, "Could someone have put him up to it? Or could Forest have been working with someone else to throw the blame on my client?"

"I guess it is possible," Estes replied.

"We know Calvin's knife was not placed at the scene where Becky's body was found until a day later. Once again, who found the knife and pointed it out to you?"

The sheriff smiled as his eyes went to the prosecution's table. "K. C. Fredrick."

The DA leapt from his seat and yelled, "I did find it there!"

"Are you sure you didn't place it there?" Coop asked.

"No," Fredrick shouted, "I didn't place it there."

"Then who did?" Coop demanded.

"I don't know," the DA stammered, "I got a call early Sunday afternoon telling me where to look for the weapon. Either the caller disguised his voice or it was someone I didn't know. But I didn't place it there. How could I? I'd never been to the Ross's home."

Coop glanced into the gallery to John David Maltose. As their eyes met, the big man stood up. "You have something you want to say, John David?"

"Right," Fredrick barked, as he pointed a finger at the millionaire, "it was John David who didn't want Calvin Ross to die in the chair. He was the one trying to pull the strings to give the kid a break. Maybe he was a part of this."

Maltose smiled. "Judge, I will be happy to take the stand and tell what I know under oath. But I doubt if it is necessary. I can assure you I had nothing to do with Becky Booth's murder or Judy Lindsay's kidnapping. Melvin Forest had become somewhat of a wild rogue, and I was about to fire him. So he was not working for me in this matter. As to my wanting to make sure that Calvin Ross was not executed, well, it was because I pretty much guessed he was not guilty, but I figured he had no chance of proving it in this town. I guess I underestimated the courage and skills of Cooper Lindsay. If I had realized how sharp an attorney Coop was, I wouldn't have gotten involved. I'm not a saint, and I am certainly no hero."

As the crowd murmured, Metlock pounded his gavel. When he had put the focus back on the bench, he spoke, "At this time, I don't know who killed Becky Booth, but I know who didn't. The evidence offered by the prosecution in this case has been so full of holes, it should have never come to trial. The work by the defense has proven beyond any doubt the defendant had nothing to do with this crime. What appalls me is how the people of this town and the city's newspaper turned this case into something ugly. Rather than seeking the truth, they were ready to trot out age-old prejudices in order to hang the crime on someone whose skin was darker than theirs but whose soul is likely a lot purer."

Metlock paused and looked toward those from the national media. "I would like to tell you what you have seen is not a picture of the real Justice, but sadly it is. All I can promise is that my personal thinking and behavior will change, and I hope others will seek to open their eyes as well.

"Now, Mr. Fredrick, do you have anything else to present? Are there any more witnesses you can call or anything you can say in the summation you have planned that can give us a clue as to why you went after Calvin Ross?"

The DA pushed his finger under his shirt collar and shook his head. He then rose and meekly suggested, "I think all charges against Calvin Ross should be dropped."

"So you believe he had nothing to do with this crime?" Metlock asked.

"Correct, sir," Fredrick replied.

"I trust," the judge said, "those of you in the courtroom heard this and took it to heart and there will be no more Klan rallies or cross burnings." Metlock looked from the gallery of shocked citizens to Calvin Ross. "Mr. Ross, I won't act upon the suggestion of the prosecution to have all charges against you dropped."

Coop was shocked. What was Metlock up to? Why wouldn't he dismiss the charges?

"Simply dropping those charges," the judge continued, "would not be enough. This court needs to go on record as representing the full measure of the fair and balanced justice system of this nation. Therefore, I want you to stand. And, Coop, you stand with him."

Calvin and Coop stood at their table and looked back to the bench. As they did, Metlock smiled.

"Mr. Calvin Ross, as judge in this court and speaking for the State of Mississippi, I find you not guilty on all charges. You are free. And on behalf of this court, I want to apologize for the way you have been treated.

"This court is dismissed."

54

"Thank you, Mr. Coop," Hattie cried as she reached over the railing separating the gallery from the defense table.

"We did it, Hattie." Coop laughed, as she embraced him. "Justice has been served!"

As the big woman let him go and she reached over to hug Calvin, Coop eased down into his chair. What a few weeks this had been! And in spite of all that had happened, it was worth it. He'd lived up to be the man his father had wanted him to be and, in the process, had somehow done what most thought was impossible.

"Coop."

The attorney looked up into the tear-filled eyes of Brent Booth. "Coop, I'm sorry for the way you were treated. I just believed the worst."

"I probably would have, too," Coop assured him.

"Who did it?" Brent asked. "Who killed my little girl? Was it Forest or someone else?"

Coop shook his head. "I wish I could tell you, but I can't. Maybe Wylie can piece things together in a few days and give us the answer."

"But," Brent sobbed, "my baby didn't know Forest. I mean she might have seen him when she went over to the Maltose's home or at the dance, but why would he want to kill her?"

Coop shrugged and watched the brokenhearted father make his way back to the aisle and out of the courtroom. It was over, but as happy a day as it was for Coop and Calvin, there were many whose wounds were now reopened and bleeding. After all, Becky Booth was still dead. Nothing could change that fact.

"Congratulations!" Estes boomed, as he approached the attorney.

"I couldn't have done it without you," Coop said, standing to take the sheriff's hand. He then leaned closer and asked, "Is Judy really okay?"

"She is tough." Estes laughed. "She likely saved Clements's life with some first aid she applied on our way to the hospital, and then she went home to get something to eat and change clothes. I'm sure she is waiting for you now. By the way, the judge has already called her and told her the good news."

"Great!" Coop grinned. "I need to go with Calvin to sign some papers and get his stuff from the jail, and then both of us will head home." The attorney looked over to Hattie and then back to the sheriff. "I know you're tired, Wylie, but I have a favor to ask."

"Anything."

"Could you take Hattie to my house?"

"No problem," Estes assured him. "I need to head that way to go home and get cleaned up, anyway."

"Thanks."

After shaking Calvin's hand, the sheriff escorted Hattie from the room. Coop watched them leave then put his notes back into his briefcase. A few seconds later, an officer of the court brought the papers for the defendant to sign. When they finished, Coop looked to Calvin and asked, "Are you ready to walk out of here?"

"Yes, sir." Calvin paused and added, "I can't believe you did it, but do you think the folks in Justice will let you stay here?"

Coop smiled. "I don't know. But I think I might be headed to Ohio, anyway."

"Coop," Calvin asked, "who do you believe really killed Becky Booth?"

The lawyer pushed his hand through his wavy dark hair, "I'm not ready to say, but I don't believe it was Melvin Forest. Yet for me to actually prove who did it, I need one more piece of evidence. And I know where I can get it." He smiled. "Let's go to my office first; I have a couple of things to file away, then we will go over to the jail and get your stuff."

2014

55

Monday, July 14, 2014

He was six-foot-two, with a strong jaw, high cheekbones, gray eyes and dark, wavy hair. Dressed in a white shirt and charcoal slacks, he stepped out of a blue Ford Fusion, made his way across Front Street and to a bench just in front of the old courthouse. Taking a seat, he studied the second-floor windows above what was now an antique store. As he viewed the white stone building, he leaned forward and, after rubbing his lips with the forefinger and thumb of his right hand, set his elbows on his knees. It would be twenty minutes before someone stopped to ask the stranger what was on his mind and what he was doing in Justice, Mississippi, and the solitary time was well spent getting a solid grip on his surroundings.

"Are you here about the murder?" an elderly black man, dressed in big overalls and a white shirt and blessed with a friendly face and friendlier manner, inquired. "I mean it's the main reason there are so many strangers in town this week. Just thought you might be a reporter or crime blogger or something. I met three folks from CNN yesterday."

Looking up at the tall man with the gray hair and thin face, the stranger shrugged. "What murder are you talking about?"

"LaDerick Jenkins," came the quick reply. "He was run down and killed a few months back after the prom. It was a hit-and-run. They're going to start the trial this week and thought you might be in town to watch it or write about it. It has been kind of like a circus, and they are about ready to raise the big top."

The stranger shook his head. "No, not here for the murder trial but am here to revisit another one that happened a long time ago." He paused before pointing to the building he'd been studying. "Do you know what's on the second floor above the antique store?"

The old man turned, rubbed his lower back, and watched a new Mustang drive by before finally nodding. "Nothing's been there for a long spell. In fact, the last time it was used was when I was a young man. A lawyer named Lindsay had his offices in there. And what a man he was! The bottom half was a drug store back then, and it was owned by a Ralph Jessup. He was a good man, too."

"Who owns the place now?" the visitor asked.

"You're looking at the guy who owns the building." The old man laughed. "And two or three more on Front Street, too. Bought them back in the nineties before the downtown started coming back to life. I have been kind of a wheeler and dealer all my life. Made some money in music in Nashville and Los Angeles and then invested it here."

The visitor grinned. "Is there any way you could show me the old law office?"

After studying the stranger on the bench for a moment, the thin man nodded. "Guess I could. I got the keys in my pocket; just follow me."

After waiting for a Dodge truck hauling a few hogs to motor down the street, the pair crossed Front and stepped up onto the walk. After the old man pulled a set of keys from his pocket and a door was unlocked, the pair walked up fifteen steps to another door. Before unlocking it, the owner turned back to his guest.

"Except for me and a cleaning lady, no one has been in here in a long time. In my mind, you are about to tread on holy ground. So step lightly."

The guest nodded. Fifteen seconds later, the door opened and the men entered. The stranger spent only a few seconds in the empty outer office before moving to the other door and twisting the knob. The now-opened door revealed filing cabinets across a back wall, a large oak desk, a swivel chair, and two more green leather-covered chairs. There were family photos on the desk, as well as a varying number of items, including diplomas hung on the walls. Stepping closer, the visitor noted a calendar, one of those that flipped over each day to change the date. It read July 15, 1964.

"You look like him," the old man solemnly announced from the door. "You're almost the spitting image. Though you might be an inch or so taller. All of us around town thought he looked a lot like the actor Clark Gable. You do, too. But I bet you don't even know who I'm talking about."

The stranger turned back to the building's owner, raised his eyebrows, and smiled. "I guess you knew Cooper Lindsay?"

"Never actually spoke to him," came the quick reply, "but saw him often enough those last few weeks before he disappeared. He walked tall when few men had the courage to do so." The old man smiled. "My name is Mike Morgan. They used to call me Big Mike, but when I lost a lot of weight, I lost the handle, too."

"I read your name in his journals." The stranger smiled. "I'm Clark Cooper Lindsay."

As the two men shook, Morgan grinned. "I guess you must be Mr. Coop's grandson."

"Yeah, I am. And they call me Coop, too."

"And," Morgan asked, raising his mostly white eyebrows, "why are you back in Justice, Coop?"

"I need to find some answers," he explained moving over to the desk and looking more closely at the calendar. After tracing the date with his finger, he glanced back to his host. "Why is this place so neat and clean?"

"I guess because we've been waiting for someone to come home," Morgan explained. "For a long time, it was your grandfather we were waiting for. You see, he was the man who really changed Justice, but in time we realized he and Calvin weren't coming back. John David Maltose bought the building about a year after Coop and Calvin vanished; John David ordered his people to keep it clean. For years, he used to come up here by himself and just stare out the window over there. I used to watch him from the square. And though he had several offers, he wouldn't rent it out or change anything. I bought it from him with the understanding I would do the same. Why don't you try out the chair for size? Nobody has sat in it for a long time . . . maybe fifty years."

Coop looked at the antique wooden chair and spun it around before slowly dropping into it. It could have used a cushion, but it felt pretty good.

"The room looks like it should now," Morgan quietly announced.

Coop nodded, his eyes moving resolutely to every corner, trying to fully grasp this snapshot of another age. And it was exactly like his grandmother had described it. It was amazing. It was as if his grandfather has just left.

Coop once more turned to his genial host and

asked, "No one knows what happened, do they?"

The old man shrugged and leaned against the doorframe. "Lots of people think they do. Some blame the Klan, and others a couple of local businessmen. A lot of folks pointed to the guy who ran the newspaper. But all we know for sure is your grandfather and my friend walked into this office just after the trial ended and then disappeared. They never found any part of them or the blue Ford your grandfather drove. It was like they just evaporated."

"My grandma told me," Coop replied. He leaned forward and put his elbows on the desk.

"What do you do?" Morgan asked.

"I'm a lawyer," Coop answered.

"You coming back to Justice to practice?"

Coop glanced back at the calendar and shook his head. "No, Mr. Morgan, I'm not here for that. Though I could. I have my Mississippi license." He pushed out of the chair and strolled over to the window overlooking the square. Sticking his hands in his pockets, he tried to picture what things must have looked like five decades ago. It was not easy. The cars were new, the lawn had been relandscaped since the photos he'd seen, and they had added a new wing onto the courthouse.

"I guess you must just be passing through," Morgan noted from across the room.

Without turning, Coop replied, "No. I'm here to put the ghosts of the past to rest. I'm here to find out what happened and give my grand-mother some closure before she dies. I'm here because I have read my grandfather's journals; I have studied in depth his last case and the trial, too. I'm just hoping there are enough folks still alive to give me the answers I need to fill in the final pieces of the puzzle that has haunted my family for fifty years."

"I guess you're going to need an office for a while then." Morgan's announcement was framed by a grin.

Coop smiled. "I'll need a base of operations for a few days or maybe a few weeks."

"Then, this place is yours," Morgan announced. "There is a set of keys to the front door and the street entry in the desk. Just open the middle drawer there. They're in the tray beside your grandpa's pens and pencils. And I'll bring in a couple of window units so we can air-condition this place, too."

"Thanks," Coop said, more than a little over-whelmed.

"If you need anything else, let me know."

Coop watched the man leave before turning his gaze back to the street. This was not what he expected—not at all. He had planned to just wander around unnoticed and make the motel his headquarters, but then Big Mike had come into his life. It had given him more traction than he could hope for. But what about the reason for his visit? Could he manage to find anything to reveal answers hiding for five decades? He knew from the journals, the whole case likely hinged on a couple of things not introduced at the trial. One of those was Becky Booth's pregnancy. The first thing he had to do was try to find out who was the father. After all these years, was it even possible?

Pushing his hands deeply into his pockets, he rolled his shoulders and walked back to the desk. Leaning up against the massive desk, he whispered, "Justice is still here waiting on you, Grandpa."

56

Tuesday, July 15, 2014

It was just past 8:30 and Coop was checking his e-mail when someone knocked on his door at the Justice Holiday Inn Express. Getting up from the desk, he strolled across the room and opened the door. On the other side of the entry was a tall, distinguished, middle-aged, African American man dressed in gray slacks, a light blue shirt, and shiny black shoes.

"Mr. Lindsay?" the visitor asked.

"Yes," Coop returned.

"I'm Austin Reed, the mayor of this community. I was hoping we could visit."

"I'm dressed and ready for breakfast," Coop suggested, "is there a place close by that serves a good pancake?"

"Right across the street," Reed replied with a large smile, "and the meal is on me."

After Coop grabbed his iPhone, the two men strolled across a parking lot, down a shady side street, and into the Mississippi Mud Diner. With its colorful booths, chrome trim, and long counter, it looked like something out of the 1950s. The menu pretty much read from the era, too, but the prices were definitely up-to-date. After both men ordered, Reed picked up the conversation.

"Been a long time since we have had a member of your family visit. I guess the last time was when your grandmother left about five weeks after Cooper Lindsay and Calvin Ross disappeared. It was a solemn time and a different time, too. Justice was caught in the past and having a tough time stepping into the present. It took another generation before things really began to change. During that time, your grandfather moved from being a hero in the black community to becoming a legend embraced by a new generation of whites as well."

Coop nodded. "I kind of figured it out about ten years ago when my grandmother told me they had named the new elementary school after him."

"I wish she would have come back for the ceremony," Reed noted.

Coop shrugged. "She doesn't want to come back until they find and bury my grandfather. There are simply too many negative memories here. She just can't handle them."

"I'm sure." The mayor sighed. "But when Mike called me last night to tell me you had come back, it did make my heart race a bit. The news spread fast, too. Everyone in the town likely knows about it by now. Everyone is anxious to meet you, too."

"Everyone?" Coop asked as he raised his eyebrows.

"There are a few that might still be holding old grudges," Reed admitted. "But most have moved on. I'm not saying race isn't still an issue. But look, I'm mayor; we have a black police chief, and a black woman, Lillian Adams, is the school superintendent. I could go on, too. There is no 'other side of the tracks' anymore, either, and except for a few areas of town, whites and blacks live together pretty well. So you came to a much different place than your grandfather knew."

"Yeah," Coop said, "but I didn't come back to see how Justice has changed; I came back to try to bring some peace to my grandmother. The only way to do it is to find out what happened to her husband."

Reed frowned. "I wish I could help. I wish anyone could. The sheriff at the time, Wylie Estes, worked his tail off for years trying to figure it all out. The FBI even came in. Not even one clue ever showed up. It was like they vanished into thin air." He paused, took a deep breath, and sighed. "The man who got them wasn't just a murderer; he was a magician."

As they contemplated this chilling thought, a thin, tall, blonde waitress brought their meals. As there was no reason to open more doors leading nowhere, the conversation steered to local achievements and the effects of the long-term drought on the area's farms, wildlife, and water systems. As they finished their meal and Reed paid the check, he turned to his guest.

"You come visit my office," he said. "I have some things I'd like to show you."

Coop nodded as the mayor walked away. His first morning in Justice had brought him a full belly but an unsatisfied mind.

57

Using the keys he had been given the day before, Coop let himself into his grandfather's old office. True to his word, Mike Morgan had already installed two powerful window unit air-conditioners, and they were doing yeoman's work on a day when the temperatures were predicted to hit one hundred. Setting his briefcase on the desk, Coop pulled out his namesake's final journal. He was going over the last entry, centering on the effect of his grandmother's kidnapping and his grandfather's resolve, when there was a knock on the outer door. Looking up, Coop waited until the visitor rapped again to make his way across the room through the outer office door and to the main entry. Twisting the knob, he pulled the door open and found himself looking into the eyes of a good-looking, well-dressed man, perhaps five-feet-nine, likely in his fifth decade, sporting a concerned expression framed by reddish hair, a weak chin, and deep green eyes.

"I understand you are Cooper Lindsay," the visitor almost barked. "I've been told you're a lawyer, and that is fine because I need one. But it only matters if you have your grandfather's grit."

Coop studied his uninvited guest for a few seconds before replying, "I am who you think I am; I do what you have been told I do, but as I never knew my grandfather or faced the kind of challenges he did, I can't really comment on the grit part."

"I'm Michael Maltose," the man shot back. "I pretty much own this town. At least the parts that matter and make money. And I need a lawyer to defend my son."

"I'm not here to practice law," Coop replied. "So it looks like you have wasted your trip up those steep stairs."

"Maybe not," Maltose replied. "Every man has his price, and I am willing to pay yours." He didn't pause long enough for Coop to join the verbal dance. "You see, my son, David, has been accused of murdering a black kid, and he didn't do it. It is as plain and simple as that. But this town is run by blacks, and there is no way a white boy, especially my son, is going to get a fair break in Justice."

Now this was irony at its best or worse. Coop couldn't decide which. Pointing to a chair, he looked back to his guest and said, "Would you like to sit down?"

"Yeah," Maltose replied, pushing by, and heading through the open door and into the inner office. He glanced around for a moment before lighting on the worn green leather. Coop followed slowly behind him, made his way around his desk, and eased down into the swivel chair. After running his fingers over his lips, he posed his first observation.

"Mr. Maltose, this might be my first trip to Justice, but I know enough to realize you have the money and influence to bring in any trial lawyer in the country. And while you might not have the power your father did, you still have enough to buy a big hunk of justice whenever you want it. And I mean that both legally and locally . . . if you get my drift. I am only four years out of law school; my experience is nil in criminal matters. Therefore, if I have grit or not, I'm the worst choice you could make to defend your son." Coop raised his eyebrows. "Besides, I read in today's paper that this case goes to trial in just a couple of days. You would be best served to keep the team you have. If your son is innocent, they can no doubt prove it."

"You don't understand," Maltose shot back, "my team wants to toss in the towel. They want to make a deal to get David twenty years or perhaps more."

"Why?" Coop asked. "If your son is innocent, why not just present the facts and prove it?"

The expression in the visitor's eyes fully represented the man's desperation. "Because my son messed up and made himself look guilty. This was a hit-and-run, and David drove his truck up into Arkansas. While there, he had bodywork done on the vehicle, changed the color, and then sold it to a used car dealer in Smackover. So it looks like he was trying to hide his guilt. Even though he is only seventeen, he is being tried as an adult and he seems intent on doing nothing to prove he has been framed. In fact, by staying mum, it is like he is participating in the frame."

Coop grimaced, "Why would any seventeen-year-old kid want to take a rap for something he didn't do? I can see why your lawyers are trying to cut a deal. Sounds like the smart move to me."

"Maybe smart," the visitor admitted, "but not right. I know he didn't do it, even if he won't say so. No one saw who hit the Jenkins boy, no one actually saw David driving the truck that night, and there was no reason for him to go after the kid, anyway."

"But the evidence must say he did," Coop suggested. "This sounds more like a father just not willing to admit his son messed up."

"No!" Maltose screamed, bringing his fist down on the desk. If it was meant to shake Coop up, it failed to work, but it did prove just how solid the old hunk of oak was. Nothing on the desktop even rattled. "David would have reported the accident the moment it happened if he had been at fault. He wouldn't have run. I might be an unscrupulous jerk, but he isn't. And he is not a racist, like my mother. I don't know how, maybe it has been Amy's influence—she's my now-divorced third wife—but David's the kind of kid who is, or at least was, going places. This has to be about honor, something I don't understand much or care for, and that is why it confounds me."

Coop leaned back in his chair and studied his visitor again. The dark circles under his eyes and the drawn lips showed a man driven to exhaustion with worry. The man's expression also seemed to prove he wasn't playing mind games with himself. He actually believed his son was not guilty.

"So what is your defense team trying to do?"

"They want to prove it was an accident while the DA is determined to prove it was murder. It seems David and this Jenkins kid had a fight a few hours before they found the kid's body. It wasn't much, just some kind of childish thing at prom, but there were witnesses, and both boys left the scene angry. So it messes up the accident theory."

"A good lawyer," Coop suggested, "can likely bring into play your son's past character and defuse the bomb."

"Maybe," Maltose replied, "but not in this town. You see, my mother has done pretty much everything she can to stop any kind of black advancement in Justice. She has fought every-thing from integrating schools to combining the black and white proms. She has put up huge chunks of money to defeat black candidates and proudly, to this day, flies a Confederate flag at the home she built after my father went off the deep end with alcoholism."

"When was this?" Coop asked.

"When my older brother Travis died in a car wreck back in 1965," Michael explained. "Dad started sliding downhill soon after. Then Mom built the new house up on the hill about five miles outside of town and made a special room for him. Basically, her property is like a fortress. My sister lives in the old family mansion. I built a place here in town."

"So," Coop interjected, "you believe in 2014 someone like your family won't get a fair shake in Justice. And the evidence collected, combined with five decades of a town wanting to put your family in its place, pretty much dooms your son."

"Yeah," Maltose admitted, "and my lawyers don't care to fight it. They are ready to sacrifice the boy and walk away. They say it will be better for family business. I'll pretty much pay you anything to jump on board and at least fight for David's freedom."

"This makes no sense at all." Coop almost laughed. "You are doing nothing more than grasping at straws. I mean there is nothing I can do."

"Yes, there is," the visitor argued. "Your name means something in the black community. You handling this case might mean they would take a second look, a deeper look, at the evidence. Maybe you could cancel out some of the hatred folks feel about my family."

"Based on what I have been able to read from afar," Coop solemnly said, "as well as what my grandmother told me about your mother, I'm not sure Abraham Lincoln working alongside Jackie

Robinson and Martin Luther King, Jr., could do it."

Maltose looked Coop solidly in the eye. "Would you at least try?"

Coop brought his hands together and glanced over to the window. He could see the courthouse spire. As he studied it, he considered what he knew of his grandfather from the stories he'd heard and the journals he'd read. A man was in trouble, a part of his life was on the line; if he were innocent, then someone needed to be in his corner. But what if this was all just a lie concocted by a man intent on using the Lindsay name to purchase a verdict?

Coop turned back to face his guest. "Listen, I cannot just shrug off my grandfather's legacy. I cannot come across as a man who will choose money over justice. I cannot sully our family reputation." He patted the leather-bound book on the desk before continuing, "My grandfather could not be bought by your father. No amount of money could get him to compromise his position. I can't be bought, either."

"I see," Maltose replied dejectedly, while pushing off the chair and moving toward the door. He'd just about gotten to the outer office when Coop's voice brought him to a stop.

"Listen, I won't take your money, but I will go over to the jail and visit with your son. If I feel he is innocent, then I'll see if I can help your team prove it. But you have to let me do it my way."

"How?" Maltose asked as he turned back to face the lawyer. "If you don't want money, then what do you want?"

"You stay out of this unless I call you," came the quick reply. "And you set up a meeting between me and your mother."

"My mother?"

"Yes," Coop said, "if she is the reason your son can't get a fair trial, I need to get to know her. I can't do it secondhand. I have to sit down in her house and meet her face-to-face. Can you arrange a meeting?"

"I can," Maltose assured him.

"And," Coop added, "I need access to your father."

"He's off his rocker," the visitor shot back.

"Maybe, but he knew and respected my grandfather. I need to at least get a chance to visit with him, without anyone else in the room. Will you arrange both of those things?"

"I will," he promised.

"Okay," Coop shot back, "you get the ball rolling, and I'll head over to the jail to visit with David. Make any calls you need to assure I will get to see him."

Maltose nodded, pulled his cell from his pocket, and hurried out the door. As it closed, Coop stood and moved over to the window. This was hardly what he had expected, but it might just open the door to his speaking to people who could shed some light on events from two lifetimes ago. So there was no way he was going to turn down the chance that had fallen into his lap.

58

The jail, built just a decade before, was a much different place from the one where his grandfather had visited Calvin Ross. From the outside, the two-story brick building looked more like a hospital or school. The inside was just as clean and bright.

As he called ahead, Coop was immediately taken from the front desk down a long hallway to the chief of police's office. The man sitting behind the desk looked like an NFL linebacker. Bill Miles was at least six-four, a solid 220 pounds with shoulders an axe handle wide. If it hadn't been for his generous smile, he would have been one of the most intimidating figures Coop had ever met. Yet his smile and the warm greeting put the visitor completely at ease.

"I understand you are here to see David Maltose." Miles said from behind his desk in the small, but efficient, office.

"I see his father has already called you," Coop shot back from his chair.

"He did," the chief announced with a grim smile. "So does this mean the grandson of the great Cooper Lindsay is about to switch sides?"

"I haven't taken the case," Coop replied, "and I'm not sure I would call it switching sides. I would hope I would have the courage to do what my grandfather did. I have read his journals and fully realize what he went through. And those journals assured me it wasn't about sides, but about right and wrong and innocent and guilty."

"Yeah," Miles replied, his face no longer wearing the large smile, "I knew of your grand-dad but never actually met him. One of my earliest memories is of seeing him come over to the wrong side of the tracks one day. I was a little kid and scared of white folks, especially white men. I ran into the house and hid when he came to visit Hattie Ross. The more I have found out about him, the more I wish I had climbed up on Hattie's porch to listen to him speak."

"He is why I am here in Justice," Coop admitted, "and likely why I am here in your office. If this kid is innocent of the actual crime, then, like Calvin Ross, he needs someone to believe in him and help him."

The chief leaned forward until his elbows were sitting on his desk. "You have to understand something. The people in Justice don't really care if David Maltose is innocent. They just want the family to pay for some of what they have done. For generations the Maltoses have used their money to hold others back while they maintained a viselike grip over everyone and everything. Over the past generation, their powerbase has shrunk. They are losing some control, they can't rig elections anymore, but the old wounds still seep and the old anger still remains. Folks, both white and black, are looking for a way to bring grief and pain to the evil old woman who lives in her fortress outside of town, and they see this as their best way of doing it."

"You don't paint a pretty picture," Coop noted.

"If I could actually paint," he replied, "it would be much darker than my words. You can't fully conceive of what bringing the Maltoses to their knees would mean to so many. About the only ones who would like to see David walk are those bigots who look upon Linda Maltose as the final bastion of the way America should be or used to be, whichever viewpoint you want to take."

"What about the kid?" Coop asked. "Is he anything like his grandmother?"

"I've got a son his age," Miles replied. "Marcus tells me David is all right. When you get him away from his family, it's obvious he is not his father's son or Linda's grandson. But it doesn't mean he is perfect. Until this year, he partied hard and sometimes acted like a rich jerk in public but nothing racially motivated. He seems to have matured a bit recently, too."

"But," Coop asked, "could he be innocent?"

The chief shook his head. "I don't think so. While there are no witnesses, the case stacks up pretty solid. He got into a fight with LaDerick Jenkins at the prom. Several kids caught it on their iPhones. So we have video. He left the prom early, and when he was seen later, he had a spot of blood on his shirt. We got the shirt from the tux rental place, and the blood matched Jenkins. He drove out of town the next day, got his truck repainted, and then sold it to a used-car dealer in a town where his father owns an oil fracking company."

"Hence the charge of premeditated murder," Coop noted, "using the truck as the weapon."

"Yeah," Miles said, "it's what the DA is going for. I don't actually think the jury will see it that way; I think it will likely be second-degree murder, but with the way folks feel about Linda Maltose and her son, who knows?"

The chief paused for a moment, and when he picked up, he sounded like a preacher caught up in a moment of soul-saving inspiration. "Look, Coop, you will be up against a black DA, there will be a black judge, the jury will be at least fifty percent black, and though folks like me, old Mike, and the mayor will understand why you are doing what you are doing, the community won't. Both black and white working folks want the Maltose family to pay. There won't be any crosses burned or a Klan march like your grandfather faced, but no one is going to make you comfortable either. And there is simply nothing you can gain for yourself or the kid by taking the case. I'm telling you, this is a mountain you can't and shouldn't climb."

Coop rubbed his lips and went mute. Miles might be right. The odds here could be even longer than those his grandfather faced. No matter what Michael Maltose believed, his son simply looked like the perfect fit for this crime. Of course, Coop couldn't be sure of that until he had seen the case file and talked to the boy. And there was one positive the chief didn't know about: by looking into the case, he would get a crack at Linda and John David. That was what he'd hoped for when he came to town, so maybe this case, no matter the odds or how folks would feel about him taking it, was actually an answered prayer. He looked back to his host. "You're probably right, but I at least need to look at the evidence and speak to the kid. I wouldn't be cut from the Lindsay cloth if I didn't do so."

59

Coop sat at a table in a small conference room using one of the eight chairs. Initially, he was so caught up in looking through the case file, he barely noted the photos lining the room's walls. It was only when he set his briefcase on the table to retrieve his iPad that he saw a photo of his grandfather. In the shot, likely taken by a member of the press, the first Cooper Lindsay was leaning over talking to Hattie Ross.

Getting up and crossing the room, Coop studied the image more closely. He did look like his grandfather; the expression on the man's face was one he had seen in the mirror many times. And my, how young Hattie appeared! She'd been so much older when she'd practically raised him.

"Here is the flash drive with photos of the evidence and crime scene," Miles announced as he entered the room.

Coop turned back to the big man and smiled. "The woman in the picture was practically my mother. You see, my own mother died of cancer, when I was just six. I don't remember much about her, but Hattie Ross made sure I toed the line. She stayed after me when I strayed and hugged me when I did good."

"She left with your grandmother to move to Ohio," Miles noted as he handed the drive to Coop. "I was really young then, but I do remember her pretty well. As my mama always said, 'Miss Hattie was fine!' And she was."

"You know," Coop smiled, "everyone has been comparing me to my grandfather, but I think there is more of Hattie in me than anyone else."

"Not a bad thing," the chief noted. "Now I will leave you to go over the materials. Just let me know when you want to visit with David. I'll bring him in here."

After the door closed, Coop took another long look at the framed photo and then returned to his chair. Within a few moments, he had loaded the flash drive onto his laptop and powered up his iPad. Even though he was obviously not friends of any of the kids who had been interviewed about the crime, he did have access to most of their Facebook pages and the photos on them. The only shots he cared about were the ones centered on the prom. As he studied those captured moments, he made detailed notes on each, taking down information about everything from the time each photo was posted to what those in the pictures were wearing.

After over a half hour of study, he singled out a half-dozen shots he viewed as vital to the case. In one, David Maltose wore a traditional black tux, light green shirt, and bow tie. He looked a bit like his father but more athletic. His date, Heather Wills, small and, judging from her muscle tone, athletic, had opted for a blue gown. The photos of them together appeared more like best friends hanging out, rather than two kids who, according to Facebook, were in a relationship.

LaDerick Jenkins looked much different in these shots than he had in those accompanying the autopsy Coop had just reviewed. Here, the six-foot-one young man sported a Hollywood smile and bright eyes. Like Maltose, he had chosen a traditional tuxedo and had topped it off with a white shirt and blue tie. His date, Cindy Reed, who was tall and thin, had chosen a light green number with a low back. It really showed off her dynamic chocolate-almond complexion. There was no doubt she had to be the mayor's daughter, as she looked just like him.

One thing the prom photos did prove was that as the night began, Jenkins and Maltose had gotten along. In most of the shots taken before the altercation, the two boys and their dates always seemed to be together. They even sat at the same table during the country club dinner, and he spotted them dancing almost side by side in other shots. So what set off the fight?

Turning from the iPad to his computer, Coop looked through the evidence photos and videos. After studying the crime scene, complete with stark images of a muddy road and Jenkins's body lying in a ditch, he turned to five different videos of the fight between the two boys. As the footage was taken outside, at night, and by students using cell phones, it wasn't very sharp or crisp, but it still clearly showed neither kid would have made it as a prizefighter. Their three minutes of rolling around looked more like angry eight-year-olds than high school seniors. When Lillian Adams showed up and broke up the fight, ordering the boys to go home and not come back, both kids shot a couple of lame insults at the other and walked off in opposite directions. And that was it.

So what were they fighting about? Nowhere in the police report was a single motive given by those at prom as to what prompted the two to duke it out. For some unknown reason they challenged each other in front of a dozen witnesses and then moved outside to settle it. He needed to know what the ignition factor was that set off their rage.

Coop glanced from the video back to Cindy Reed's Facebook page. He studied the photos for a few moments and then turned back to Heather Wills's pictures. There were scores of the two couples together, not just at prom, but throughout their senior year, and there were no hints of any friction. So what had set off the events ending in LaDerick Jenkins paying with his life?

60

"Here's your boy," Miles announced as he escorted David Maltose into the conference room.

"Thanks," Coop replied.

"Just call my cell," Miles said, tossing a card on the table. He then shrugged. "I meant cell phone, not cell. Just call me when you are ready to leave. I'll come back and get David and take him back to his cell." The chief exited, locking the door behind him.

Unlike in the prom photos, Maltose was now pale from his weeks behind bars. He also appeared a bit thinner. And his garb had changed as well. There was no longer a *GQ* look about him; he was now outfitted in a black-and-white-striped, ill-fitting prison uniform.

"I'm Coop Lindsay; your father sent me over to visit with you."

"I know," Maltose replied, "but it doesn't make any difference. I realize the score, and I'm ready to take what is coming to me."

"You're gallant," Coop noted. "You don't hear that trait much in prison or the outside world these days. Why don't you sit down and we can discuss why you feel so noble?"

Maltose took a seat opposite Coop. He then cast his eyes at the table and became a statue. It was obvious he didn't want to talk.

"Okay," Coop began, "I've reviewed the evidence, and I must say, the State has a pretty solid case against you. And as you were a big enough coward to run away and try to get rid of the evidence, that must mean you're a cheat and liar, too. I would also suggest, because you ran down a black kid, you're a bigot. After all, it's your family legacy."

The words were harsh, and they stung enough to bring the kid's eyes up to meet Coop's. Just as the lawyer had planned when he launched his attack, the kid was a solid stone figure no more.

"I'm not a bigot," he almost snarled.

"How about a liar, cheat, and coward?" Coop shot back. "You want to claim those titles or toss them to the side, too?"

Maltose opened his mouth as if trying to relax his jaw before looking toward the far wall. He kept his gaze there until the lawyer issued his next challenge.

"Okay, by not speaking, you've admitted to me what you are. You're scum, you are the filth of humanity who wears hate as its cloak and can't wait to lash out at those you feel are beneath you. You're nothing more than a rich kid with no morals or regard for others. You are so egocentric you couldn't love anyone but yourself."

"No!" Maltose yelled. "I can love. I don't hate, and I'd like nothing better than to escape my legacy."

Coop smiled. "I got a feel for you over the last hour as I looked through Facebook. You are in NHS, you work with Special Olympics, your classmates like you, you have a slew of black, brown, and Asian friends, and you have earned special compliments for your teamwork. In spite of your legacy, you have built relationships transcending racial lines. And do you know what also hit me while studying you online?"

The kid shook his head.

Coop leaned closer. "You're not reckless. You are careful. You don't make rash judgments, and you don't panic. I even understand, according to several posts, you performed CPR on a woman who had fainted at a basketball game."

"Yeah," he admitted, "it was an out-of-town game. I knew how to do it and just jumped in. It was no big deal."

"It was probably a big deal to her," Coop replied. He paused and looked back toward his iPad. After licking his lips, he stared right into the boy's eyes and observed, "You know, it is amazing what you can find out from Facebook. Yeah, I've even found out you're not guilty. I don't care what the evidence says; you couldn't have done it. This isn't your style."

"I did it," the boy said quietly. "So don't waste your time."

"Why was LaDerick out near Lovers Park?" Coop asked.

"I don't know," Maltose replied.

"Why were you out there?"

"You know why people go there," the kid replied.

"By yourself?" Coop asked. "Then where was Heather Wills? She was your date. She must have been there, too."

"She wasn't," Maltose quickly shot back. He then added more forcefully, "She wasn't anywhere around there."

Coop rubbed his lips. "So I guess that means you and LaDerick are gay."

The boy's eyes shot back at Coop with a look of disbelief. "No way."

"Then, why were you out there?" Coop demanded. "Why did you go to Lovers Park with another man?"

"Because he called me and challenged me to finish our fight where no one would get in our way."

"That's not what you told the cops."

"No," Maltose shot back, "I didn't tell them anything!"

"And there is one other problem with your story," Coop noted.

"What?"

"You never got a call from him on your cell." The lawyer smiled. "Plus a hundred other things right here in the evidence files. And besides, LaDerick didn't have a cell phone. His family was a bit poor, at least it says so here. His mom didn't even know where he got the money to rent the tux. So, what is this all about? Why all the lies?"

The room again went silent as Maltose set his jaw and looked down at the table.

"Fine," Coop said, "don't talk. But there is a lot more to this than you're saying, and I'm going to find out what it is."

"The trial starts in two days," the kid said. "You don't have the time to find out anything."

"We'll see," Coop replied. "In the meantime, if you get ready to tell me the whole story, let your dad know. I'll be glad to come over here and listen."

61

Coop drove his car from the jail to his grandfather's office. After climbing the steps, he unlocked the door and made his way through the outer office and to the old family desk. After setting his briefcase down, he eased into the chair. From outside his window, barely audible over the air conditioner, the courthouse clock struck three. It was then he realized he hadn't had any lunch. He was about to retrace his steps, get back in his car, and head over to a Sonic he'd passed between the office and jail when his cell rang.

"Coop Lindsay," he announced.

"It's Michael Maltose. I understand you saw my boy. You going to take the case?"

Coop's face erupted in a smug smile. How should he play this? Should he eagerly say yes or just toss out a teaser and let the bait buy him some time and power. He opted for the latter.

"I'll let you know after I talk to your mother and father. If it goes well, I might be able to help out your team."

"Okay," Maltose quickly agreed. "Why don't you drive out to Mother's place tonight? Say about 6:30. But don't expect supper. She might visit with you, but she won't serve as a host. She still holds a big grudge against your grandfather for the way he treated her on the witness stand fifty years ago."

"Nice to know she's the forgiving type." Coop chuckled. "And I will be there."

He'd no more than put the phone down when someone rapped on the outer door. It seemed lunch was going to turn into supper before he had a chance to look at a menu.

"It's not locked," he hollered.

A second later, the hinges squeaked and the door opened. Standing in the entry, framed by the stairwell light, was a woman, perhaps twenty-five, auburn hair, high cheekbones, and a square chin. She looked to be just a bit over five feet tall, and even in her T-shirt, jeans, and tennis shoes, it was obvious she had an athletic build. To go with it was a million-dollar smile exuding incredible confidence.

"I'm Charli Shane," she announced.

Coop got up from his desk, strolled toward the entry, and smiled. "I guess you are."

"You've heard of me?" she asked.

"No," he admitted, "but something tells me I should have."

"I'm from Justice," she announced with a grin, "graduate of Vandy, about to finish my law degree. Taking the summer off to come home and spend some time with my mother. She works at the police station. She called and told me you might be taking on the Maltose case."

He laughed. "News gets around in a hurry."

"Well," she noted, "Mom did put it on her Twitter feed. And everybody in town follows her."

"So I guess my popularity is on the down-swing."

"No doubt," his guest laughingly admitted. "But while everyone else is bailing on you, I came to help. I know the case, I know my way around, and no one knows more about your grandfather than I do. I've been studying all I could find on him since I was a kid."

"Listen," Coop replied, "I'm not sure I need much help, but I do know I need a guide. So here's the deal, I haven't eaten lunch. Let's visit over a meal."

"Sounds good," she responded.

"And this job doesn't pay," he quickly explained. "I won't touch the Maltose's dirty money."

"Good," she answered. "Let me text Mom and share your news with her. Once folks read this tweet, your standing just might reverse a bit."

62

The late lunch consisted of hot dogs and tater tots from Sonic. Coop and Charli chose the city park to consume the repast. It was a typical small town park with tables, grills, playground equipment, and several dozen ancient trees. But as the temperature was close to the century mark, the pair had the whole forty acres to themselves. As they ate, Charli filled the attorney in on a few facts he didn't know, and she delivered all she knew in a machine-gun barrage of rapidly paced words.

"So," she explained, "Linda Maltose's bigotry is based on something that happened when she was nine. Her father was killed in a robbery attempt at their house. A black man named Jupiter Jones was convicted of the crime and was executed. Linda actually saw Jones as he ran out of the back of their home. When she went into their home, she found her father's body."

"Okay," Coop grimly admitted, "there is a reason for her motivation. It is good to know, so I can use it as I get ready to visit with the woman. Boy, when bitterness sets in early, it is hard to shake."

"Ah," Charli continued, while dipping her tot into catsup, smiling, and taking a bite. After swallowing, she added, "There is more. Because of writing a research paper in high school on the Calvin Ross case, I became fascinated with all the players. So I went back to try to find out more about Jupiter Jones."

She sipped a bit of her Dr Pepper before continuing, "He was a huge man, former boxer, but a gentle soul. He claimed he had only gone into the home because he'd heard someone call out for help. His final words as they executed him still proclaimed his innocence."

"So do you think he did it?" Coop asked.

"What I think is unimportant," she replied. "It is really all about what Linda Maltose thinks. By the way, as a little girl, she watched the state execute Jones. Can you imagine what it would do to a child's mind? And within a year, her grandmother, her only living relative, died and Linda was taken to an orphanage. She was never adopted. She grew up dirt poor, living on whatever she could manage to find in Gulfport, depending upon others for help, until she met John David. With her good looks and charms, she'd learned how to con men for meals and special favors, and she snared him in a hurry. Combining street smarts and good looks can take you a long way."

Coop took a final bite of his hot dog, wiped his mouth, and gazed off into the sky. He kept his eyes there for a few moments before looking back at Charli. "Was their marriage happy?"

"No," came the bluntly honest reply.

"And did you find it out through your research?" he asked.

"No," she admitted, "just hearsay. The old-timers told me the two were rarely seen together, and when they were together, they fought like cats and dogs."

"Interesting," Coop noted, "and yet she has taken care of him all these years."

"Well," Charli added, "in this case, you take care of your husband and you get to take care of his wealth."

"What about the death of Travis Maltose?" Coop asked.

"No one was with him," Charli said. "I've seen the accident report, even got a chance to view the photos. He was likely drunk and just didn't make a curve."

"Is it what put John David over the edge?" Coop asked.

"Evidently," she agreed. "It took a while. He slowly lost it. It wasn't like it happened all at once."

"Not surprising," Coop replied. "Hattie never got over losing Calvin. It is kind of like cancer, just comes back and eats at you from time to time. If it eats deep enough, it will destroy you."

"So," she asked, "am I on the case?"

"Can you show me the murder scene?" he asked.

"Let's go." She grinned. "It's only about five minutes from here. Not much to see, but you do get to go by Lovers Park."

On the drive out, Coop studied the terrain and compared the way it looked now to the way it was described in his grandfather's notes. Meanwhile, in the passenger seat, barely taking time to breathe, Charli rattled on about the workings of Justice. As they passed Lovers Park, she paused and pointed to her right. "This is where generations have gone to make out. Even finding Becky Booth's body there didn't stop them."

Coop slowed and glanced to his right. There

was a lot of his family's history tied to this spot. It was everything he could do not to stop and take a closer look.

"About a half mile up the road is where LaDerick was killed," Charli explained, drawing Coop's attention once more back to the road. "That was the last time it rained here, so you will still be able to see the ruts made by David's truck and then later by the cop cars. The storm dropped so much water so fast the place must have been a bog at night."

She was right about the ruts; they were deep and clearly defined. They made the clay a nightmare to navigate.

"How far now?" Coop asked.

"A hundred yards or so," she answered.

"I don't want to damage my car," he explained, as he slowed to a stop. "So let's walk the rest of the way."

Leaving his Fusion in the middle of the road, the two got out and strolled up the rutty, packed, rock-hard soil to the place where a soul had departed from Mississippi to parts unknown by mortal men.

"It's right there," Charli said, pointing to ruts made by the truck's wide tires. She then turned to her right and gestured to a ditch. "His body was found in the grass over there by the edge of the road. The ditch was surely filled with water in the evening. Sadly, all the rain we had at night did little to quench the ground's thirst. Even ponds that never go down are drying up."

Coop walked over to study the place where the body was found. There were lots of footprints, likely made by the cops who investigated the scene. Kneeling in the ditch, he looked back down the road.

"Where does the road go?" he asked.

"Nowhere," she replied, "just a dead end."

"The truck was coming from there," he asked. "Why?"

"I don't know. But it dead ends in about a half mile. We could walk up if you want to see it."

Coop checked his watch. He had enough time to study it and then get back to town, shower, and change clothes before heading out to visit Linda Maltose. "Let's go."

Ten minutes later the two were looking at a fence marking the end of what had become little more than a trail. The only tracks found here were obviously made by the truck.

"He got stuck," Coop pointed out. "He got this far and tried to turn around and was almost buried in the muck."

"He sure did," Charli noted. "If he hadn't have had four-wheel drive, he might not have gotten out."

"And then there would have been no crime," Coop said. "Look at the steps leading down the road and back toward Lovers Park. Someone must have been walking back for help. Yet no one could have pulled him from this mess without leaving tracks, too. So help didn't get here. He had to have gotten out himself. But where are the tracks coming back to the truck?"

"Were the photos of this in the evidence?" she asked.

"No," he assured her, "but I think it is time I put my camera to use. He pulled out his iPhone and began to click away. He snapped a dozen shots of both the tire tracks and the shoe prints and then glanced back to Charli. "Put your foot in one of these prints."

He watched as she did. Her shoe fit easily inside the preserved footprint. "What size do you wear?"

She shrugged. "These are six and a half."

"My foot is an eleven," he noted, and mine won't fit into the tracks. "Therefore these were made by someone who was likely in the nine-ten size range." He studied the tracks again before asking, "Do kids own their tuxedoes or rent them?"

"Everyone rents them," she explained.

"From where?" he asked.

"There are two places in town," she answered. "Anderson's Men's Clothing and Gerrard's."

"Let's get back to town," he announced as he began to move quickly down the road. "And I need for you to do a favor for me. I want to find out who rented tuxes, from where, and if any of them came back muddy. Also, I need to know if they rented shoes and what size they were."

"Got it," she announced when she caught up with him. "I guess I am working for you."

"I guess so," he said, not even bothering to look back.

They were hurrying past the place where the body was found when Charli said, "Hey, wait a minute. Look at this!"

Coop stopped and glanced toward the woman. "What have you discovered?"

"Look," she said, pointing to the side of the road.

"Yeah," he replied, "tracks, and lots of them."

"But see these?" she asked, pointing to a set of imprints appearing much different from the others. "Some woman was out here in heels. Can you imagine? One of the off-duty cops, maybe Janis Records, must have rushed to the scene, probably from church the next day. It was about the time they found the body. And she didn't bother changing out of her dress shoes. I'll bet those were ruined."

"No doubt," Coop acknowledged as he turned and pushed back toward the car. "Now I have a date with someone I've wanted to meet all my life, and you have some work to do before the stores close."

63

He was fifteen minutes early for his engagement, so rather than driving up to the large metal gate and ringing the buzzer, Coop stopped his car outside the fence and studied the Maltose estate security system. The walls were eight-foot-high stone topped with razor wire. If you managed to climb over without cutting yourself to ribbons, there were likely more security cameras in place than were used at the White House. The gate was massive, thick, and imposing. And the rural road's pavement ended just past the turn into the estate. Within a hundred yards, it became little more than a deer trail. Linda Maltose obviously enjoyed her solitude and was willing to pay a fortune to maintain it.

Coop was trying to figure how much the native stone fencing and security system cost when his cell phone rang, interrupting his rudimentary figuring. Retrieving the iPhone from his pocket, he studied the caller ID and smiled. It was a number he'd only recently loaded into his address book, but it might have already worked its way into being his favorite.

"So, what do you have for me, Charli?"

"The only tux not returned was the victim's,"

she quickly explained. "They are holding it for evidence. About fifteen guys rented shoes fitting the size we need."

"What about David Maltose?" he asked.

"He wears an eleven," she replied, "and his were returned."

"Did the place have to clean up Maltose's shoes?"

"Not too much," she quickly replied. "His were pretty clean. The owner remembered. Of course, it might just mean he took care of them in order to not put himself at the scene. But the shirt did have blood on it matching LaDerick's. The police have it."

"Thanks," Coop replied. "You did good. Now let me see what I can find out here. It is time to go behind the gates, and that's a little scary."

"The dragon woman has you jumpy?" Charli asked.

"Yeah," he admitted. "If she is only half as mean as I have heard, she'll be a challenge. Hey, I need another favor."

"Name it."

"Just watch my grandfather's office tonight. Don't let anybody see you, but just keep your eyes on the place. And don't stop anybody if they go to it. I'll call you later."

"Got it, Boss," Charli replied. "You're kind of cute when you give orders."

He grinned as he hit the end-call spot on his

touch screen. Sliding back into his car, the lawyer drove up to the gate, pushed a call box button, and waited. About a minute later, a man appeared and the imposing entry opened.

The lane was two cars wide and wound through oak and maple trees until it came to a hill. The property appeared to be nothing more than a well-maintained park minus picnic tables until he rounded a bend and the two-story abode appeared. No wonder folks in Justice called this a compound. The structure looked much more like a prison or mental institution than it did a home. It was white block and its styling would never make the cover of any design magazine unless it was *Prison Monthly*. It was little more than a thick-walled rectangle with barred windows topped by a red tile roof.

Parking the Fusion in front of the house, he made his way up the steps to an imposing, metal front door. Spying a button, he pushed it and waited. Michael Maltose opened the entry a few seconds later.

"Nice to see you," came the greeting.

"Warm place you have here," Coop noted.

"This is not my home," he corrected the guest. "It is my mother's. Just like the flag out there, everything in this place is her idea."

Coop turned and glanced toward the hill. Flying from the pole was the largest Confederate battle flag he had ever seen. The lawyer shook his head and asked, "Where do you buy something like that these days?"

Michael sighed. "It has to be specially made. She has dozens of them. Now, come on in; she's in the library and hates to be kept waiting."

As Coop followed the man inside, he was amazed at how dark it was. Funeral parlors had more warmth. The walls had been painted in deep earth tones, the tiled entry was midnight blue, and even the paintings on the wall captured a certain gothic feel.

"This way," Michael advised as he pointed toward the back of the home. Coop followed him toward a large oak door at the end of the fifteen-foot-wide hall. As they walked, their footsteps literally bounced off the stone walls and high ceiling. His host knocked once, twisted the knob, and signaled for the attorney to enter. Michael did not follow. Instead, he closed the door and disappeared. He was obviously a coward!

The stern woman sitting in a straight-backed Victorian chair eyed her guest carefully. She might have been in her eighties, but Linda Maltose remained attractive in a cold, Joan Crawford kind of way. Her blue eyes were clear, her skin youthful, and her face surprisingly free of wrinkles. As he stood there waiting for instructions, she got up easily and strolled his way. When she was about ten feet in front of him, she pointed her long, thin fingers to a wooden chair and sternly announced, "You may sit there. I will take my place in the chair on the other side of the table." She waited for him to follow her instructions and then made her way gracefully to her assigned seat.

"My son tells me you want to see me."

"I do," Coop replied. Then moving his eyes to the room's walls, he made an observation, "You have an impressive collection of books and art."

"They are my husband's," she replied. "I have little interest in them other than their value." She lifted her rounded eyebrows. The words following her icy stare had the bite of a cobra. "You didn't come here to ask about my house or my hobbies, so what do you want to know?"

He turned his eyes back to Linda Maltose. Her stare burned through him, and he suddenly felt as though he was in the room with an evil and powerful sorceress rather than a woman of advancing years. This was not going to be easy.

"I don't believe your grandson is guilty," Coop began.

"You didn't have to demand a meeting with me to give me *that* information," she spat. "You could have told Michael, and he would have informed me. So get to what you want to say."

"Okay," he replied, "I didn't come out here to talk about David. I came out here to talk about my grandfather."

"He was a menace," she shot back. "He was the

beginning of the end of what made this town special. People like him ruined this country for decent people. He had no breeding and no sense of loyalty."

"Thanks for being up front," Coop replied. He brought his hands together in front of his face, drawing her gaze to his. He tried to match her harsh expression but failed, yet still managed to deliver the words he came to say. "What do you know about what happened to him?"

Her cold eyes never left his. "Why should I know anything?"

"He had something on you," Coop explained.

"He had nothing on me," she snapped. "Nothing!"

Coop smiled. He'd hit a nerve, and now was the time to push against it a bit harder. "You weren't aware he kept journals, were you?"

She tilted her head but didn't reply. As she continued to study him, the corner of her upper lip twitched.

"No one knew about the journals, not even my grandmother," Coop continued. "She discovered them after he died."

"So?" Linda Maltose demanded. "What is that to me?"

"On the last night before he disappeared," Coop explained, "the day before my grand-mother was freed by the sheriff, my grandfather wrote several interesting things about you. My grandmother was too heartbroken to read those journals for decades. She never has been able to read the last one. But she gave them to me last year, and I read them all. They were fascinating!"

"I care nothing for your family history," Linda hissed. "Quit boring me and get out."

Coop smiled. "The journals allowed me to get to know my grandfather much better than I would have. It is like I sat down and he shared with me everything important to him. I learned not just about his life, but his values."

"I care nothing about his values or his life," she cut in.

Coop's eyebrows shot up. "Judging from what he wrote about you, that fits." He paused and then added, "And he did write about you. In fact, if I can find one more bit of evidence combined with the code in the final journal entry, I can tie you to my grandfather's disappearance."

"Rubbish," she shot back. "If this is all you came out here to say, then get out."

Coop grinned, got up from his chair, and moved to the door. Grabbing the knob, he turned back to the old woman and smiled. "So nice to get to visit with you." He added, "I only need to find out one more thing."

As those final words sunk in, he thought he saw Linda Maltose blink.

64

Michael was waiting in the hall as Coop exited and closed the door to what was evidently Linda Maltose's sitting room. As their eyes met, the woman's son must have noted the attorney's smile. "I guess you got what you wanted."

"I set the hook," Coop noted without explanation. "Now I need to see your father."

"He is crazy," Michael explained again.

"Is he violent?"

"No," Michael acknowledged, "but he doesn't make any sense. He just babbles."

"So do brooks," Coop replied, "but you can still catch a fish in them from time to time. Lead me to him and then leave us alone."

The room reserved for the family patriarch was on the second floor. Michael unlocked the door and ushered Coop into a fifteen-by-fifteen chamber with white walls, a connecting bath, and a double window looking out toward a lake. Because of the drought, it was only half filled with water. John David was dressed in gray pajamas, sitting in a high-back chair, looking through the window and bars at land he had likely bought during his days of being the most potent man in this part of Mississippi. The titan Coop's grandfather had written about in his journals was no more. Now closing in on ninety, Maltose was frail and drawn.

"He sits staring like this for hours and hours," Michael explained. "He always looks the same way. It's like he is seeing something that isn't there. Or maybe he is waiting for something to appear. None of us have ever figured it out."

Coop nodded.

"And when he talks," Michael whispered, "he just says things that make no sense."

"Like what?" Coop asked.

"A brother he never had," Michael announced with a lift on an eyebrow, "or Travis being taken too soon and the water."

"Water?"

"Yeah, he just goes on and on about water. Stuff like, 'If only it could talk.' I guess the drought has even affected his mind. You see, he really is off the deep end. You sure you want to do this? You can look at him and tell he's not there."

"Yeah," Coop replied, "I want to do it. In fact, I have to do it."

Michael shrugged. "Okay, I'll tell him you are here."

"No," Coop suggested, gently grabbing his host's sleeve, "let me take care of it. You just leave us alone for a while."

The attorney waited for Michael to exit before slowly walking over to the window and standing beside an empty chair. He studied the scene in front of him, noting the setting sun reflecting off the lake before speaking to a man who had yet to even notice his presence.

"It has been a long time, John David."

The old man moved his gaze from the window to his guest. He studied Coop for a few moments, saying nothing.

"John David," Coop continued, "I still owe you for bringing the nitro to the jail that night. It was one crafty move."

A confused look crossed the patriarch's face, followed by a glimmer of recognition as his dark, brooding eyes suddenly locked onto the attorney with the power of an industrial vise. Perhaps there was still a bit of the hungry lion hidden in the old man.

"Listen, John David," Coop continued, "I left too quickly to really thank you for protecting me long enough to get Calvin off the hook. And I know you had nothing to do with Judy's kidnapping. I believed you when you told me in court on that day so long ago."

The old man finally found the word to frame his obviously troubled revelation. "Coop?"

"Yes," the visitor answered, "I'm Coop."

"But you're dead," he weakly argued. "You died a long time ago."

"But not to you," Coop replied, continuing the game he was playing only out of desperation and need. He leaned closer and whispered, "You never forgot me, did you?"

"No," John David answered, his eyes opened wide and his jaw agape. "I never did."

Coop nodded. "When I came into your room tonight you were looking out the window hoping to spot Calvin and me coming back to Justice. Weren't you?"

John David's lips trembled, and his eyes grew moist. "I've been praying for it. I really have. I kept your office just like it was. Big Mike owns it now, but he has instructions to keep it up for you."

"He has," Coop assured the old man as he eased down into the vacant chair. "It looks just like it did."

"Someone kept a promise," John David replied softly. "It was important to me. So few promises are kept anymore. Maybe they never were." He paused, a confused look framing his thin face as he quickly turned to the door. "Where is Calvin? I need to tell him something."

"He's not with me," Coop explained sadly.

"Wish he had come," the old man whispered, his gaze returning to his guest. "It should be his."

"What should be his?" Coop asked.

"Everything," John David replied.

Coop leaned closer. "I don't get it. What do you mean?"

"Not important," he answered and weakly waved his hand. He paused, glanced back out the window, and asked, "Did you work up those divorce papers?"

Coop leaned back and rubbed his lips with his fingers.

"Doesn't matter." John David sighed. "My only son died a long time ago." He stared at Coop for almost a minute before whispering, "It is under the bottom desk drawer on the right. You make it good. Please?"

"I will," Coop assured him even though he had no idea what the man was asking.

"You know," John David whispered, "you always did that."

"What?" Coop asked.

"Rub your lips with your finger and thumb," he explained. "It's how I knew you were thinking." John David smiled, his thin lips opening enough to show his yellowing teeth, and then his chin fell to his chest and his eyes closed. Coop studied him for a few seconds before placing his finger on the man's neck. There was no pulse. John David Maltose had taken whatever secrets he had left to the grave.

65

It was just past nine when Coop returned to town. He thought about going directly to his hotel but instead made a side trip to his grandfather's office. He was hardly surprised that the door was unlocked. Sitting down at his desk, he yanked open the bottom drawer and grinned.

Footsteps echoing from the stairwell were followed by the entry of an attractive redhead, waltzing in dressed in jeans and a Vanderbilt T-shirt. "What up? Did your bait work?"

"Sure did." He laughed. "Who came to get it?"

Charli took a seat in front of the desk, crossed her legs, and said, "Linda Maltose's driver. But why did he come to your office, how did he get in, and what did he take?"

"A journal," Coop explained. "And getting in was no problem; I was sure Linda had kept some keys to fit the door. After all, the locks have likely never been changed. I'm sure John David saw to it. And Linda had to have the book to find out what my grandfather knew."

"What book, and what did he know?" Charli asked, her dark brown eyes growing wide along with her curious smile.

"He didn't know much," Coop admitted, "and

I'll show you in his own words after we grab something to eat. Anyplace open late?"

"I can scramble some eggs and fry up some bacon at my mom's," she replied. "But how can you show me something you don't have?"

"What Linda Maltose has by now is a journal I wrote." He laughed. "And there is a lot of stuff in there to scare her to death. By now she believes my grandfather knew things no one else did. And thanks to my conversation with John David, my guesswork was accurate enough to likely push her into action. I still have my grandfather's journal. Linda wouldn't find it nearly as scary or interesting as the one I wrote."

"Are you setting yourself up as a target?" she asked.

"Yeah," he answered. "And she will likely feel the need to do me in, but her husband dying tonight buys me a bit of time."

"You're awfully calm for a man with a bull's-eye on his back." She paused, shrugged, and then asked, "Whoever named it that—I mean a bull's-eye? Why does it stand for the middle of a target? Why not pig's eye or a picture of the moon?"

The lawyer laughed. "If a bull is mad and charging you, the eye might be a good place to aim."

"Whatever," she argued, "it still makes no sense

to me." Her tone suddenly much more serious, she added, "You aren't playing this safe at all. You must have nerves of steel. Linda Maltose is not only a cold, conniving woman who relishes inflicting pain, she is also a crack shot."

"I can be calm," Coop explained, "because Chief Miles will have a man shadowing my every move. I was smart enough to ask for protection when Miles came out to the Maltose compound to investigate the old man's passing."

"Good for you," Charli said with a relieved tone. "Now can I text my mother?"

"About my coming over for a late breakfast?"

"No, Coop." She laughed. "She'll want to know about John David so she can tweet the news before anyone else."

"No problem," he said. Pulling his briefcase up on the desk, he popped the locks and opened it. He yanked out the journal and smiled. Setting it to one side, he then pulled out the rest of the file on the Calvin Ross trial and the disappearance that followed. As he leafed through those familiar pages, his eyes latched onto a photo he'd barely noticed in the past. Melvin Forest had a distinctive look about him. His grandmother had often described her kidnapper as cocky and aloof. Though kind of shabby and rough, he was not ugly. In fact, he seemed to have a bit of roguish charm. And then it hit him.

Tossing the paper to the desk, he looked over to

Charli. "Quit texting. We may not be sleeping much tonight. We have some information to find out that might rewrite an obituary or two and change the balance of power in this whole area!"

"Okay," Charli shot back, "but I have a news story I'm doing for an agricultural journal on the drought. I've written the piece, but I have to go through the aerial images they shot yesterday to pick out photos to best show the devastation. We're doing a side-by-side photo layout to present what the area looked like last year and what it looks like now."

"I'll give you time to do it," Coop assured her. "In fact, I'll help you over supper. We can't get access to what I need until tomorrow. And it likely means we will have to skirt a few legalities to pull it off. Hope you don't mind."

She shrugged. "Is it for a good cause?"

"Yeah," he assured her, "I think it will keep your mother tweeting for months."

"That's not a good cause," she laughed, "it's a great cause. If she is tweeting, she won't be in my hair."

66

"I don't understand why the will was so important." Charli noted. "There is nothing surprising in it. We did a lot of digging to find out the obvious. Michael and Jodi get everything."

"And Linda gets nothing," Coop added from his office desk chair.

"But her kids aren't going to kick her out on the street," she argued.

"No," he agreed, "they won't, but it means a lot more than you think. For the moment what I need is some hair from John David Maltose."

"What?" she asked.

"How are your connections with the funeral home?"

A baffled look crossed her face, but it didn't stop her from speaking, "I went to school with his daughter."

"Get me anything with John David Maltose's DNA on it. We have to have it tested."

"Why?" she asked. "We know who John David is. Unless you think the old man was an imposter."

Coop grinned. "We just need to get a DNA sample."

"Do you think the dragon lady did in John David and this guy has been a ringer standing in for him?" she asked, her eyes popping from her head.

"Just get me something, so I can get the DNA test," Coop insisted.

"Boy, oh boy," she sighed. "But we never got around to picking out the best photos for my story. I need to do it. I have a deadline, and they pay." She raised her right eyebrow and added, "Unlike some folks who expect to get their work done for nothing."

"Leave your laptop here," Coop suggested. "I'll go through the pictures and find the best ten, and you narrow it down from there when you get back."

"Fine," she replied with a shrug, "they're in iPhoto. They are in the last import. But stealing DNA is the most bizarre thing I've ever done." Grabbing her phone and keys, she ran out the door, down the steps and to her car. Coop walked over to the window to watch her drive off and then returned to his desk and opened her laptop. True to his word, he began to go through the images on the screen. He had already pinpointed seven good ones when his eyes locked on something very familiar. It was the Maltose compound.

Moving a bit closer to the screen, he studied the image. He was now even more impressed by the wall. It went around the whole property. If it had been any longer, it might have been known as "The Great Wall of Mississippi." The home's huge size was also best appreciated from above. It might have been a cube, but it was one of the biggest he had ever seen. Yet the drought had taken a toll on the trees making up a majority of the acreage. The leaves were brown and gold, and many of them had already fallen to the ground. Some of the timber even looked dead, especially the pines. The lake had receded at least a hundred feet from its natural shore, proving it had been a dumping ground over the years for all kinds of things. He was about to go in for a closer look in Photoshop of the trash along the shore when his cell rang.

"I got what you needed," Charli assured him. "Now, have you fulfilled your part?"

"I have seven picked out," he replied, "and I'll have the other three ready for you when you get back. Once you send these off, I need for you to drive down to Montgomery. There's a lab there I trust to run the DNA test for us."

"And what are you going to be doing while I'm using my gas?" she demanded.

"Maybe the toughest thing I've ever done," he replied. "I'm going to talk to a man about his dead daughter."

Coop had no more than hung up on Charli than his phone buzzed again. This time the other party was a Maltose.

"What can I do for you, Michael?"

"Are you taking the case?"

"I might," Coop assured him. "And if I opt to help, I won't take a dime for doing it."

"Because of Dad's death," Michael explained, "the opening of the trial has been moved back to Monday."

"Good," Coop replied, "It gives me time to do some work I need to do. Alert your legal team that I will meet with them on Sunday. And make sure you and your mother are in court when things begin the following morning."

"I'll be there for sure," he assured him. "But I doubt if I can get Mom to leave the compound."

Coop shot back, "After tonight, I'm thinking she is going to want to keep her cold eyes on me all the time. Now, when is the funeral?"

"Friday," Michael answered. "But it is only a graveside service."

"I'll be there," Coop replied. "I'm not going for you or your mother. I'll be attending for a man my grandfather grew to respect."

67

Brent Booth was a year short of ninety. He was stooped, bald, and had almost lost his sight, but he was still sharp. It was evident from his first words that his mind worked as well as it had back when he last spoken to Coop's grandfather.

"You know," the old man announced from his recliner in the living room of the modest ranch-style home, "I hated your grandpa when he took the case. I couldn't stand him. If I'd had the chance, I'd have shot him." He paused, as if reliving and then regretting a moment from another time and place, "But when he proved Calvin didn't do it, I suddenly realized the boy was almost as horrible a victim as our Becky. He could have lost his life just like she did. And both of them would have been innocent."

"I know," Coop replied from a well-worn, green couch. Looking around the room he noted faded photographs of a daughter who had been lost in time. In fact, it seemed the Booths had quit taking pictures when Becky died. There were none on the shelves or the wall from the last fifty years. Whoever had killed Becky had murdered a big part of this man and his wife, too.

"Martha died more than twenty years ago," Booth explained. "The doctors couldn't really find anything wrong with her; she just died. In fact, I'm not sure she didn't die on the day your grandfather disappeared."

Coop nodded. "You mean not finding Calvin guilty put her over the edge?"

Booth looked up, pointed his right index finger at his guest, and almost violently shook his head.

"No, not at all. We spoke that night and she was actually relieved your grandfather had exposed the lie the DA had championed. We wanted justice and we wanted revenge, but we wanted it for the person who did the evil thing to Becky." He paused, took a deep breath, and looked down before whispering, "You see, she was all we had. We never had any other babies."

An uncomfortable silence descended on the room, dropping a wall between the men. For the moment, it was a barrier Coop didn't know how to climb over or get around. It was the same kind of wall keeping his grandmother and Hattie from ever coming back to Justice. It was the kind of wall he sensed when he visited with John David. Its darkness, sadness, and hopelessness combined into something almost with a life of its own. And yet, it was still as dead and cold as the people who'd been taken so long ago.

Finally, summoning the courage to speak, Coop asked, "Did you ever read the autopsy report covering your daughter's death?"

Booth nodded. "I've got it memorized. And I have those blasted pictures of the crime scene memorized as well." He looked directly at his guest, shook his finger, and spat, "Do you know how many times I wished I'd get Alzheimer's just so I wouldn't remember those things? I prayed for it. I actually prayed to lose my mind, and I couldn't do it. My whole body is shot, but my mind is still sharp. And I think there is a reason for it."

"What would it be?" Coop gently probed.

"I have never believed, not back then and not now, Melvin Forest did it. And because of my feeling sure about that, I needed to hang on and find out who really killed her. I needed to see the person at least found guilty. So I just stubbornly lived day after day, year after year, decade after decade. And here I am, almost blind, bent over like a pretzel, and barely strong enough to pick up a phone book. I can't even drive my car anymore. And I'm still waiting. It still hasn't come. Maybe it never will. Maybe I'll just have to keep on breathing forever."

It wasn't fair. It shouldn't have taken this long for this man to have a taste of justice. But now Coop might be able to give Booth what he so longed for. Yet in doing so, he might also break the man's heart into even more pieces.

"I think," Coop softly said, "I know who killed Becky. And I think my grandfather did as well."

The old man jerked his head forward but said nothing.

"And," Coop explained, "I believe the reason Calvin was framed was tied to it. The person responsible intended both of them to die. It is warped logic, but logic nevertheless. It is evil, oppressive, and locked in greed. But it's there and is what took your daughter's life."

"You really know?" Booth asked. "So I was right. It really wasn't Forest?"

"No, it wasn't. And Mr. Booth, I'm pretty sure I know who did it. But there is one fact I need to give me the evidence to bring the person to justice."

"They are still alive?" Booth whispered.

"Yes," Coop explained. "But I can't give you a name unless you allow me to do something that on the surface sounds very strange."

"What?" Booth asked.

Coop pushed off the couch and looked out into the quiet street his host had called home for all of his adult life. The houses had aged, and most of the Booth's neighbors were dead. And it was likely none of them had known what he knew and what he dreaded sharing with this old, weary man. Perhaps no one did. There was something yet to be spoken, something Brent Booth might not know, and if he didn't know it, then a life-time image as well as myriad faded memories of his daughter would likely be tainted, if not destroyed. Having that happen was not something easy to stomach.

"Mr. Booth," Coop softly asked, "did you see the autopsy report with the line blocked out, or the other one?"

The old man looked up as if trying to understand the question. It was more than obvious from his expression which report he had memorized. Coop's task had just gotten much more difficult. In laying out the needed information, he was about to break what was left of an old man's heart.

Coop moved back to the couch. He was now fully aware of the dilemma his grandfather had faced fifty years before and why he'd written so many emotional thoughts about it in his journal. After rubbing his lips, he took a deep breath, and forged ahead.

"Mr. Booth, someone, my grandfather did not know for sure, marked out a line on the original autopsy to hide certain information. My grandfather got ahold of the original report, and I have a copy of it as well. As you don't know what was beneath the marked-out passage, it pains me more than I can say to tell you. In fact, my grandfather couldn't bring himself to share the news with you or anyone else. But as there is no easy way to say this, I'm just going to lay it out and hope you can handle it."

Coop's eyes locked onto Booth's; he took a deep breath and hesitantly announced, "Your daughter was fifteen weeks pregnant when she was killed."

"No." Booth sighed.

"I'm sorry," Coop said quietly, "if there had been a way I could have accomplished what I need to accomplish and not given you this information, I would have. But my grandfather believed, as do I, the fact that Becky was pregnant is why she was killed."

"I'm so glad Martha never knew," the old man whispered, his words all but catching and lodging in his throat.

Coop nodded. "My grandfather was not going to allow the information to come out at the trial unless it was the only way he had of freeing Calvin. So he protected you back then."

Booth put his face in his hands and looked toward the floor. He remained frozen in position for a long time. Finally he glanced back at his guest and mumbled words he would have likely rather kept to himself. "Who was the father?"

"My grandfather thought he knew," Coop explained, "and I'm more sure now than he was back then. But I don't want to say until I am certain. And it's why I need to ask you to okay a court order to have your daughter's body exhumed. I believe tests can be run on the fetus to give me the information I need."

"Need to what?" Booth demanded. "To make my daughter look like a tramp?"

"No," Coop assured him. "I need information in order to bring the truth out about who killed Becky. And I will use it. I have to. I want you to know that! But if you say no to the exhumation, then it will never come out. It's your call."

The old man nodded and leaned back in his chair. He studied his guest through his teary eyes for at least a minute before admitting, "I need justice. I really do. I need to know why she was brutally murdered and who did it. So, I'll sign the request." He hesitated. "But please, protect her better in her death than I did in her life. Please try to do it."

"I will do my best," Coop assured him. "As soon as I've spoken with the judge and DA, I'll send Chief Miles to you with the documents you will need to sign. And in order to keep it as quiet as possible, we will do it at night and arrange for it to appear to be something other than an exhumation. I think I know a way to accomplish it."

"Thank you," Booth replied. "And when you find out who it was, will you tell me before you share the news with anyone else?"

"No," Coop explained. "It might put your life in danger. As long as I'm holding the information, I will be the only one they might go after."

"It still means that much?" he asked in an astonished tone.

Coop rose and nodded grimly.

Booth stood on unsteady legs and said, "Don't take the news to the grave like your grandfather did. I need to know." He shook his head and then whispered, "I have to know."

68

The paperwork had been finished and filed by midnight, and two large, walled tents were erected at the cemetery over about a dozen graves, including Becky Booth's. In the still of the night, four members of the FBI went to work quietly digging up the girl's grave. By five, the body was on its way to the state forensic lab. Now it was a matter of just waiting to see if the information Coop needed could be retrieved. If successful, he would be a step closer to giving Brent Booth and his own grandmother some sense of closure.

Satisfied he had done all he could for the moment, Coop grabbed a few hours of sleep before heading to the office. It was ten when he walked in and found Charli waiting for him just outside the door. She had her iMac in her lap.

"Those photos you picked out were great!" she exclaimed. "They were a perfect fit with my story on the drought. And the shot of the Maltose compound was amazing! The place is huge! The editor wondered if he might be able to buy the old tractor that was uncovered when the lake subsided. And the graphic designer wants the car and the old boat. They both look too rusty to be any good to me, but they still wanted to take a look at them."

Coop smiled and shook his head. "Fat chance! Linda Maltose isn't going to let anyone on her property to look at anything. It'd be easier to view the graves hidden away on the property at Fort Knox."

"There are graves there?" she asked. "Whose?"

"There are some family plots," Coop explained. "They date back to before the US bought the property. A couple of times a year relatives get to go in and visit where their loved ones are buried, but they are watched pretty closely when they do."

"Wow." She sighed. "How do you know?"

"Because I have some ancestors who call that ground home," he explained.

"You've been there?"

"Once."

"Speaking of graveyards," Charli chimed in, "did you hear about what's going on at ours?"

"What?" Coop asked, hoping she was not talking about the same cemetery he thought she was.

"My mother tweeted that the whole area was roped off and a big tent had been brought in to cover a sinkhole. The mayor made the announcement this morning on the radio. Nobody is allowed into the area until they get things stabilized."

Coop smiled. "Well, my guess is it won't take too long."

He moved over to his desk, took a seat, and opened his briefcase. Pulling out his laptop, he went back to work looking through the recent crime scene photos. It still boggled his mind how well the drought had preserved the site. He clicked on the next file to look at the photographic evidence found and retrieved at the scene and noted something he'd missed before.

"Charli."

"Yes," she said from the other office where she was sitting on the floor answering her e-mail.

"You said you figured a deputy must have worn her heels out to the crime scene."

"It was my guess."

"Can you call her and find out?"

"Sure," she replied.

As he studied the photo, she made the call. Within two minutes, she was in his office and ready to report. "Janis was at the scene then, but she changed into her uniform before heading out. She doesn't remember anyone there in heels."

Coop nodded, slapped the laptop shut, and rose to his feet. Glancing over to Charli he said, "Stay here and sign for any reports sent to us. I need to head over to Chief Miles's office."

"You have something?" she asked.

"Maybe," he quickly replied.

"Which case?"

"The hot one," he announced as he walked out the door.

69

It took only about ten minutes for Coop to look at the one piece of evidence everyone else had seemingly ignored. Now the overlooked and dismissed item would be the key to his defense of David Maltose. He'd left police headquarters and was heading to his car when a smiling Mike Morgan waved him down.

"You got a second?"

Coop nodded. "Sure."

"I heard you were helping Michael Maltose."

"I guess it doesn't please you too much," Coop replied.

"If his son is innocent," Morgan replied, "he deserves to have someone prove it. And, as I think you're like your grandfather, I'm giving you the benefit of the doubt on this case. In fact, almost everyone I know is. But it doesn't mean a lot of folks aren't praying you're barking up the wrong tree."

"Thanks," Coop said with a smile. "I'll try to live up to your confidence."

Morgan looked over to make sure they were out of earshot of any bystanders and explained softly, "There is a woman who needs to talk to you. She was just a bit older than me when the trial took place. And she saw something you might want to hear about."

"I can meet her," the lawyer assured Morgan. "Where and when?"

"Coop, there's a map I drew and stuffed in the door of your car. The woman's name is Billie Horn. She lives in the same house she was raised in. Listen to her story. It hasn't changed a bit since she first told it to me fifty years ago, when I was just a young man trying to figure life out."

"Okay," Coop replied. "Should I go now?"

"Yeah, I told her I'd get you to come out today. But there's something you need to know."

"What, Mike?"

"She's not all there," came his quick explanation. "Folks used to call her retarded, but they got a nicer name for it now. Either way, she is simple minded. But she doesn't make things up, and she doesn't forget anything. And ever since she was a kid, she has watched the road where she lives like a hawk. Rain or shine, cold or hot, day or night, nothing drives by that she doesn't see. So you go talk to her."

"I will," Coop assured him. "And Mike, I have a question for you."

"Sure."

"Do you always wear bib overalls?"

He laughed. "I have a suit in the closet; I bought it just in case I ever win an award or something. He grinned. "But, I am who I am and I love things soft, comfortable, and easy to take care of. With that in mind, you need to meet my wife."

70

Billie Horn was sitting on her front porch when Coop arrived. She was an inch or two short of five feet tall, didn't weigh ninety pounds, her skin was blue-black, her eyes were like two black chunks of coal, and her fingers long and bony. She was dressed in a flower-print dress likely made in the 1950s. Her hair was graying and bushy and her smile quick. The place she called home was little more than a shack. The paint had all peeled away except for a few places on the east side giving evidence it had once been a pale yellow. A few chickens ran loose in the yard, and a hound rested in the shade of an oak tree. As the dog didn't even flinch when the car arrived, he evidently believed it was too hot to get up. And with temperatures nearing triple digits, the hound should have been cited for his intelligence.

"You Mr. Coop?" Billie hollered as he got out of the Ford.

"Sure am," mixing in a big smile and wave with his reply.

"I'm Billie Horn," she announced as she waved back. "I is pleased to meet you. Come up here and sit a while in my chair. I'll just up and move over to the swing."

Coop marched up the steps and waited for the tiny woman to take her seat before making himself at home in her chair. After he was as comfortable as he could get on a windless, hot, humid summer day, he glanced back her way and found her eyes fixed on him. It was as if she was memorizing every one of his features.

"Big Mike says you is special," she noted with a grin.

"I don't know if that's true." He laughed.

"I seen you before," she said.

"Really?"

"You drove by here yesterday."

He nodded and glanced back to the road. He may have missed this place when he was going to visit Linda Maltose, but Billie sure had not missed him.

"You looks like your grandpa," she added. "Almost the spitting image. But I thinks he was a touch darker."

"You knew him?" Coop asked.

"I saw him twice," she replied. "That's all, just twice. The first time was when my mom took me to the courthouse to watch folks parade in during Calvin's trial. He had a gray suit on and looked mighty fine."

Mike was spot on. She obviously had a good memory. How many people could recall so many details of something from fifty years ago?

"The other time was when he, Calvin, and someone else drove by here," she explained. "Yep, your granddaddy were driving, Calvin was in the passenger seat and someone wearing something dark and a hat was right behind the first Mr. Coop. It was strange, too."

Coop studied the woman closely as she stopped talking in order to peer off toward the road and watch an old truck pass by. She observed it for a few moments, only returning her gaze to her guest when the vehicle had disappeared.

"That was Jim Tate," she explained. "He works in town. He's ten minutes late today. I guess he got something at the store. He and his wife live in the next house up the road."

"Billie," Coop cut in, trying to push the woman's mind from the present to the past, "you said something was strange when you saw my grandfather and Calvin the last time."

She nodded and then spoke, "Yeah, whoever was in the back seat was holding something in their hands. I could see it just above the window line. It was like it was all but up against the glass and, boy, was it shiny! It caught the sun like a silver soda can. You know, flickering like a diamond in light. Or maybe it was more like sun shining off a big chrome car bumper."

She stopped and turned her attention to a yellow kitten that had jumped up beside her. She petted the ball of fur for a few seconds and sighed. "Sure don't seem like so long ago."

"You never saw him again?" Coop asked.

"You mean the first Mr. Coop?"

"Yeah."

"Nope, he never came by our place again."

Coop got up off the chair and stuck his hand out to the woman. "Thanks, I appreciate you telling me what you saw."

She smiled as they shook. "Weren't nothing. I ain't got nothing more to do but see. I guess it's the Lord's gift to me—just seeing stuff and remembering it."

"I guess it is," Coop replied. "I sure am glad He gave you the gift, too."

71

As Coop rolled out of Billie's driveway and pushed the car back toward town, he pulled out his cell. The first call he made was to Charli.

"Where are we going to eat tonight, Boss?" she asked.

"It will be someplace you pick out, I'm sure." He laughed. "I'm on my way back to town. Does Miles know you?"

"We go way back," she cut in. "The chief was once my softball coach."

"Good deal," Coop replied, "but as we are now playing hardball, find out if David Maltose had a DNA test. I'm talking David, not John David. Now, let me warn you, the results might not be overly important to the case, but it still could be helpful."

"Got it," she answered. "Anything else?"

"No, I'll meet you back in the office in a bit. Still have a couple of things I need to do."

As the call ended, Coop quickly hit another button and waited for someone he dearly loved to pick up. A few seconds later, Judy Lindsay answered.

"Hello, Coop, I was wondering when you would check in."

"Didn't want to talk until I had something to say."

"Ah," she noted, "you do sound like your grandfather. Do you have any answers?"

"Well," he solemnly replied, "yes and no. I don't know where grandpa is, I haven't figured it out, but I think your suspicions as to who killed him are correct. But I also think I know the reason, and it had nothing to do with racism. At least, not in the sense you thought. Meanwhile, even as I have tried to sort it out, another strange thing has happened."

"Strange things are not things I need to hear

about," Judy quickly replied. "I find they lead to horrible tragedies for those I love."

"In this case," Coop assured her, "it's actually working out to our benefit. They are holding John David Maltose's grandson on murder charges. I have kind of joined the defense team, and it has given me access to people I otherwise wouldn't have gotten to talk to and places I wouldn't have been able to go."

"Did John David wrangle this?" she asked.

"No," her grandson explained, "it was his son Michael who made this request. Initially, I turned it down, but after talking to the son, David, I opted to stay in. I really think he is innocent and taking the rap for someone else."

"Interesting how what goes around comes around," she noted. "When do you take the case to court?"

"It was supposed to be today," he replied, "but John David died. His funeral is tomorrow. So they have moved the case back to Monday. That works best for me as I need to get a few test results back, and I've found labs don't work nearly as fast in real life as they do on TV."

"John David died?" She sounded shocked.

"I was there when it happened," Coop explained. "He was just a shell of a man. For decades, he lived in one room of Linda's new home. He was basically a prisoner. Everyone thought he had gone crazy. And maybe he had.

He actually believed I was grandpa. But if I can just decipher what he was trying to tell me, I believe it has a bearing on what happened fifty years ago. I'm rolling it over in my mind, and in time I may figure it out. It had something to do with water."

"Water has cleansing power," Judy pointed out.

"As I remember my Scripture," Coop replied, "so does blood."

"I taught you that, too," she grimly noted. "I think you learned it well. But whatever you do, I don't want any more of my family's blood spilled in Justice."

Coop looked up ahead and took in the scene before him. After turning down a lane on his right, he shut the car off.

"I just got to the cemetery," he explained. "I'm going to visit old Abe's grave."

"I never met him," Judy noted sadly. "But he was a good man." She paused before asking, "How much are you being paid to represent Maltose?"

Coop didn't immediately respond; instead he opened the door and stepped out of the Fusion. The spot he wanted to visit was just a few feet away on his left, but to his right, up on a hill, the large tent was still in place, and two men were guarding the spot as if it were the White House. Almost a football field's distance farther to the right, close to the creek, a grave was being prepared for John David. As he observed two men working under a small canopy, he finally answered his grandmother's question. "I was pretty much offered the sky but took nothing. I'm doing this work for free."

"The good Samaritan." She chuckled.

"Maybe." He laughed. "Nobody believes in the kid, and with Justice now being run by folks who have a deep hatred for any and all things Maltose, the odds are stacked against him."

"Well," she replied, "John David might have saved your grandfather's life one night, so we owe him; God rest his troubled soul."

"You take care," Coop replied. "I'll tell you more when I can."

"Love you, Coop."

"You, too."

After sliding the phone back into his pocket, the young man moved forward to a grave he had never seen but knew well. After all, it had been described in great detail in the journal. Studying the marker, he nodded and spoke, "I understand it was your sermons that pretty much got this family into thinking a bit differently from others in these parts. My own dad, Clark, went through life not liking you much. He felt like you set in motion the thinking that killed his father. And maybe you did."

Coop stopped, took a deep breath, and glanced back to where the workers were preparing another grave. "But I think I've got a different take on this whole thing. The good Samaritan thing you harped on, well, there is more to the story than most realize. The real moral might be that it is better to live a short life standing for something important and making an impact than it is to live a long life letting things just continue as they are."

Coop rubbed his lips before adding, "I wanted to tell you that, just like the ancient Samaritan and Christ, I'm here to shake things up. And I think I'm doing it for the right reasons. I hope you understand if I have to reveal a long-buried secret; it'll be for the right reasons, too. I'm not doing any of this for glory or even revenge. I'm just trying to right a wrong."

He looked from the grave to the Peerpoint River and then back. "Oh, I also need you to know, there is another reason I might be here. Been looking for the right girl for a long time. Just never found one with the right combination of spunk, brains, and energy. Well, your town seems to have at least one woman with all those qualities and a whole lot more. Now, my question is, did you have a hand in sending her my way? If you did influence this in some way, then I sure do want to thank you."

After bowing his head and saying a short prayer, Coop moved back to his car, turned the key, and headed to town.

72

He had no more than gotten back on the main road than his cell begged for his attention. Pulling it out of his pocket, he glanced at the caller ID and grinned. "What do you need, Charli?"

"I have a report; there was a DNA test on David, but the reason it was not in the evidence files is anyone's guess. And it seems to have disappeared. Miles contacted the lab, and they have lost the file as well. Their system crashed, and when a tech restored it, David's results were not recovered. So I had them check the backup to the backup, and they finally found it."

"I'm not surprised someone tried to hide it," Coop assured her. "And good work, too."

"There's something else," Charli noted. "Not sure this means anything, but it is filled with irony."

"I find the ironic interesting," he said. He was not ready to admit it to her, but he also found the woman on the other end of the line interesting as well.

"I went back and traced through the murder of Linda Maltose's father," she explained. "Though it's not easy to find them, the records can be viewed online. It seems none of the money or jewelry stolen then was ever recovered. Now, here is the really strange part. They tore Jupiter Jones's place apart and found nothing. There was no record of him or any of his family spending any cash, either."

"So what happened to it?" Coop asked.

"There was one really unique and interesting piece," Charli noted. "It was a small star-shaped pendant made for Linda's grandmother by her grandfather. It was one of a kind. I did a search for it and discovered that it somehow showed up about thirty years ago. An old man was wearing it when he was admitted to a charity hospital in Atlanta. He gave it to one of the nuns, telling her he had killed someone to get it."

"How did you find this story?" an astonished Coop demanded. "I mean this is some sleuthing!"

"Not really," Charli admitted, "the nun, Sister Angela Freeman, has the picture and story online hoping she can unite the piece with its proper owner and solve the mystery haunting her since she heard the confession."

"So," Coop replied, "Jupiter Jones was innocent. All Linda's hate and bigotry were born out of a lie."

"So it seems," she answered. "And thanks for leaving the doughnuts for me. I was starving, so it was fortunate. I was not a fan of the icing. Had kind of a strange taste. But had to eat something. It is almost like you paid me for doing my job."

He was about to respond when his cell vibrated. "Got to go, I have another call." After pushing a button, he announced, "Coop Lindsay."

"Good day, Mr. Lindsay, I'm calling from the Premium Life Insurance Company . . ."

73

Coop silenced the telemarketer's voice and slid the phone back into his pocket. The work had been done; now it was a matter of waiting on others. When the results came back from the various labs, he could set in motion the final steps needed to finally solve the old mystery. But unless he could actually find his grandfather's body, the victory would ring hollow. The story's ending would remain forever open. It was also likely his killer would never see a day behind bars. So, would the knowledge of the who and the why be enough to bring his grandmother some peace, or did she need to know the where, too? It was a question he couldn't answer and one she probably couldn't either. At least, not yet.

After dropping by a Dairy Frost and scarfing down a burger, Coop drove downtown, parked his car, and walked up the long flight of stairs to his grandfather's office. The door was unlocked.

As he swung it open he sang out, "Charli, I'm home."

There was no response.

Setting his briefcase down at the entry, he glanced around the outer office. There was no one there. Five long steps took him into the inner office, and the scene took his breath away. Charli was lying on the floor in front of the window. Beside her body was a half-eaten doughnut.

Rushing to her side, Coop checked her neck for a pulse; there was one, but it was weak. His eyes searched for a wound or injury. Except for a small knot on her forehead, there was none. He pulled his phone from his pocket and called 911.

"I've got a woman, barely breathing in my office. When I came in, she was unconscious. You need to get EMTs here in a hurry." He listened to the operator before assuring her, "Yeah, your GPS is working fine. I'm on Front Street, right above the antique store on the east side of the square. Coop Lindsay's old office. And, yes, I will stay on the line."

As he waited for more instructions, Coop once again checked Charli's pulse. It had slowed even more.

"What's your name?" the operator asked.

"Clark Cooper Lindsay," he replied. "And Charli is getting weaker."

"My Lord, her mother works at the station."

Gathering herself, she fell back into her professional mode. "Do you know CPR?"

"I do," Coop assured her, "and I think it might be time to put my learned skill to work, too."

This was not the way he had envisioned giving this young woman a first kiss. What he now feared was their first kiss might be the last kiss. What if he never got to know her any better than he did now? Suddenly a million different what-ifs were bouncing all over his mind, each demanding consideration, but now was not the time. There would be time in the future, if Charli had a future.

As he bent down to put his lips to hers, he recalled her last words to him. Looking over to the half-eaten donut, he figured it out. The icing had tasted strange. She must have been poisoned, and it had been intended for him. As he again lowered his mouth toward hers, something else hit him. The poison might still be on her lips. Depending upon how powerful it was, just trying to save her life might doom his. He reached up to once again check her pulse. It was now almost too faint to detect.

Without meaning to or knowing she was, she had taken his place on the floor. He was the one who was supposed to be there. He was the one who should have been dying. Yet she was here instead. And Coop now watched a woman he thought he might learn to love die before he had gotten to really know her. It seemed that the curse from fifty years before, the hate that wouldn't die, was back. He drew closer and stared into her face. Her lips were parted, eyes closed, and skin pale. She almost looked like a corpse. Her chest pushed upward and fell down, and then there was no movement at all. Had she just died? Had he watched it happen? Five seconds became ten, and ten became twenty, and she didn't move. And there were no sirens blaring outside. The EMTs were not going to make it in time.

How much faith do you have, Coop? It was a question he'd been asked a few times in church, and he always answered it very simply, "I have enough." But did he? Was faith just a word to him? Did he have what it took to make a real leap of faith? In fact, did he have what it took to make even one step on faith? Suddenly, he wasn't sure. After all, he'd only known this woman a few days, and what good would it do for both of them to die? Then the mysteries he needed to solve would continue to haunt so many people. Now thirty seconds had evaporated into thin air.

It was time for a leap of faith. He was not ready to give up on Charli or on love this quickly. Saying a quick prayer, Coop leaned down, opened Charli's mouth, and put his lips to hers. Pushing his breath into her, he went to work. Then putting his hands on her chest, he pushed in. For the next three minutes, he repeated what he had learned so many years before. Thirty pushes two breaths, thirty pushes two breaths, and in between each there was a prayer. He was soon concentrating so hard on trying to save Charli that he failed to hear the siren. His only clue help had arrived was when two uniformed men pulled him away to begin their work.

Pushing off his knees, he looked down at the trained professionals and the once strong person they were trying to save. Pulling out an IV, one of the men asked, "What do you think happened?"

"My guess is there was poison in the dough-nuts she ate," he explained. "I don't know who brought them up here, but I do know someone is after me."

The man reached over and grabbed the half-eaten pastry, dropping it into a sack. His partner started oxygen. "Let's get her rolling," he barked.

"You better come with us, too," one of the men announced. "If you're right and it is poison, you likely got some doing CPR. Can you walk okay?"

"I'm fine."

A minute later they were in the truck and headed to the hospital. But were they in time? If they weren't, could Coop ever find a way to live with himself?

74

Friday, July 18, 2014

It was just past midnight, and the Common County Medical Center was painfully quiet. Only a third of the rooms were occupied, and just a few nurses were walking the halls of the fifteen-year-old white stone, one-story building. Coop was only slightly affected by the poison he'd contacted while doing CPR but not enough to make him any more than a bit queasy. But Charli had consumed so much of the stuff that she was in a deep coma. There was no guarantee she would pull out, either.

"You can go home, Mr. Lindsay," a tall, thin nurse informed him as she stepped into room 117. "All your tests look fine."

"And Charli?" he asked as he eased out of the bed.

"We're hoping for the best," she assured him. "If she makes it, then Miss Shane owes you her life."

"Actually," Coop replied, "I'm the one who owes her."

"Chief Miles is in the waiting area," the nurse continued. "After you get dressed, he'd like to speak with you."

"Thanks."

Five minutes later, Coop and Miles were in a deserted hospital cafeteria sitting across the table from each other. It was the chief who began the conversation.

"The whole bag was poisoned," he explained. "We know where they were bought, but there was no poison there, and there is no reason to suspect Chan Ho. He and his wife own the doughnut shop and have a solid reputation. Besides, they would have no reason to want to harm you."

"So," Coop replied, "you're saying that whoever bought the doughnuts applied the substance."

"Has to be," came the quick response. "And as scores of folks bought a half-dozen donuts yesterday, there is no way to pin down who it was. Besides, the building has no security cameras. So there is nothing to check out. And, sadly, no fingerprints."

"What about the type of poison used?" Coop asked.

"Essentially it was medicine," he explained. "There is a long name for it in my notes, but pretty simply, it is kind of like a beta-blocker. It is not hard to find, and it is safe when used in the proper dosage. Too much, though, and it slows the system down to a crawl. You literally found Miss Shane in the nick of time."

"So, there is no way to trace this back to anyone?" Coop asked.

"No." Miles paused before looking at the lawyer. "Okay, who do you think did it?"

"You don't have any clues?" the lawyer shot back.

"There are people who don't like you working with the Maltose clan," the chief admitted, "but none of them are likely willing to kill you to make such a statement."

"Same as I figured," Coop replied. "And the guys you have shadowing me saw no one?"

"They were watching you," Miles said, "not your grandfather's office or Charli."

"Okay," Coop said, "let's consider this. The only possible people who might want to push me out of the way have the last name Maltose. But the timing seems all wrong! Why would they try to murder me now before the trial and before I have the chance to get David off of the murder charge? Why not wait until afterward?"

"So," Miles asked, "you're saying you have no real suspects either?"

"Maybe," Coop admitted with a shrug, "but none I could actually finger yet. Because I still have a question as to who is the person behind the death of LaDerick Jenkins."

The chief smiled. "Well then, I guess I'd better keep my men on your trail for a while."

Coop sadly sighed. "Well, they won't have to go far. I'll be camped outside Charli's door until it's time for John David's graveside service."

"You going?" Miles asked, his tone indicating his obvious shock.

"Yeah, I wouldn't miss it."

75

The service began at precisely 2:00 and was over by 2:15. There were no songs, no prayers, and no message. Michael and his sister muttered a few words while their mother remained mute. When offered the chance to speak, the fifteen or so mourners said nothing. It seemed the once mighty lion had gone out like a lamb. Still, Coop's attending had not been a total waste. He had discovered a few things he hadn't previously known.

The first was that Jodi Maltose Cone looked almost exactly like her brother. Their features were beyond similar; it was almost as if the same sculptor had cast them, with one image being male and the other female. Even the way they walked and moved their hands were eerily alike.

The next interesting observation came from Coop studying Linda Maltose. When Coop walked up, her clear blue eyes all but shot flames. It looked to be all she could do not to lash out at him. But somehow she restrained herself. It might well have been only because of the uniformed deputy at his side. The woman also did not wear black or even pretend to be interested in the proceedings. It was as if her mind was in a different place.

The funeral director did a wonderful job in preparing the body. John David looked a decade younger and much healthier than he had in his room. The suit he took to his grave, black silk, likely cost a few thousand. And his hair was perfectly combed with a part on the right side. The most troubling aspect of his final presentation was his expression. He appeared to be grinning. What was this all about? It was something Coop had never seen from the star of a funeral. Had his grin in death been too pronounced to wipe off? Was it a message John David was leaving to the world about finally being released from the grip of a wife he had grown to hate?

As soon as the service broke up, Michael approached. The eldest male in the family waited until the other mourners were out of earshot before asking, "So can you get my boy off?"

Coop nodded. "You should sleep pretty well the next couple of nights. I not only have the information I need to get David a free pass out of jail, at least for the murder, but I think I can actually point to the real culprit. You might want to inform your mother that she will not want to miss the fireworks when I pin this thing on a family member of one of her most visible enemies. I think she will enjoy the moment immensely. Of course, she probably enjoys picking the wings off flies, too."

"Really, you can get him off?" Michael asked.

"Yeah," Coop said. "And based on how easy it was for me to figure out what really happened, I'd fire the team you brought in to work this case and never use them again. I mean, they have to be at the table on Monday—they are your official attorneys on this case—but afterward, they should never get another dollar of the Maltose fortune. In fact, I'm betting they never get to touch another dollar your father or his father made and passed down to you."

"Thanks." Michael nodded. "Thanks a lot. I need to catch up with my mother and sister and ride back with them. So I'll see you later."

"Aren't you going to ask about Charli Shane?" Coop quizzed.

"Who is that?"

The seemingly sincere response told the lawyer all he needed to know.

76

Saturday, July 19, 2014

Coop had slept little in the past two days. The only time he left the hospital was for the memorial service. It was now close to eight, and there was still no word on Charli's condition. The fact was, things hadn't really changed at all. They were keeping her in a coma, using new rounds of drugs to counteract the drug that created this mess and hoping and praying her body had the strength to heal any damage done. As the hours moved on, frustration and guilt ate at the man. With each second, he felt more and more responsible for what had happened to the young woman.

"Mr. Lindsay?" He looked up into the eyes of a nurse he'd seen the night before but whose name he didn't know. "You really can't be comfortable in the waiting room. Miss Shane's mother just left to go home and get some sleep and suggested you might find the chair next to Charli's bed a better place to pass the night. Would you like to?"

"Yes," he almost whispered.

"Then come with me."

She led him past the doors and into room 124. The lights were low, and there were several monitors providing information on Charli. Except for her being pale and sporting the bruise where she'd hit her head when she fell, she looked pretty well. The nurse pointed to the chair on the patient's left, smiled, and stepped out the door. Coop took a deep breath, moved across the room, and dropped into the empty seat. Reaching out, he took Charli's hand and placed it into his own. He couldn't get over how his hand all but swallowed hers. She was such a small creature; no wonder the drug had hit her so hard.

Looking up to her face, so still on the slightly elevated pillow, he spoke, "You're one crazy kid. I mean, I've never had anyone get under my skin as quickly and as deeply as you have. I guess this kind of gives credence to the whole love-at-first-sight thing. I mean, you walked into my life, took over, and in the process somehow stole my heart. And I don't want it back."

He shook his head. This was stupid. Why was he pouring out his soul to a woman who couldn't hear him at all? Instead, maybe he needed to be talking to a higher power. But what good would it do? After all, as his father had pointed out a few times, God didn't really care enough to save the first Cooper Lindsay or Calvin Ross. And God didn't do much in healing the hearts of his grandmother or Hattie either. So did He really ever listen? If this was the case, then the good Samaritan parable left out another major plot point: those who reach out to the persecuted and neglected often don't live to see their good deeds take root. Maybe it was time for a Bible rewrite with a warning attached for all who make helping others the primary focus of their lives: do so at your own risk!

Essentially, Charli had caught the bullet intended for him. She had taken his place in this bed and might even take his place in a grave. And for what? He hadn't paid her a dime. If fact, had he even once said thank you? She had done it all because she just wanted to help him put some demons to rest. And now, just at the moment it was about to happen, he had met other demons ready to take their place. If Charli died, then those newly introduced demons would haunt him for the rest of his life, and another generation of Lindsays would be running from their past.

For hours he studied her face, happy for each breath and hoping to see another, and during the time Saturday became Sunday, fatigue eventually closed his weary eyes and shut down the conflict raging in his mind and soul. The only thing better than sleep for an escape might have been death. And it is what he dreamed of— trading his life for Charli's.

77

Sunday, July 20, 2014

Though he didn't know what it was, something awakened him at 9:30. Shaking the cobwebs from his mind, Coop looked at the woman in the bed. It seemed nothing had changed. Was it good? Was just holding her own a chance she was closer to becoming well? He didn't know and was afraid to ask.

Out of a sense of a need to make intimate contact, he reached forward and patted Charli's hand. "Listen kid, I'm going to be gone for a while. Got something I need to do. When I come back, we have to talk about a few things." Once more he wondered, why was he explaining himself? What good did it do? Frustrated and lost, he leaned over, kissed the young woman on the forehead, and hurried out of the room. After a shower and a change into a gray suit at the motel, he drove across town to the church his great-grandfather had helped build. Parking the Fusion in the lot, he studied the scene playing out in front of him. People of all ages, sizes, and races were walking up the steps to go inside the brick building. They were smiling, talking, and even hugging. The divisions his grandfather had written about in his diary were breaking down. Justice was a different place. With each new birth, there was a sense of optimism and brotherhood taking root. And while it was a good thing, he simply couldn't celebrate it now when the ghosts of the past had risen up to claim another victim.

Stepping out of the car, he straightened his blue tie, pulled the sleeves down on the suit, and made his way up the walk. Stepping into the sanctuary, he took a bulletin from an usher and found an empty seat on the back row. To his left sat an elderly gentleman with gray hair and a distinguished white mustache. He was dressed in a blue sport shirt and khaki pants.

"Welcome, young man," the stranger said with a smile. "You look familiar, but I don't think I have seen you here before. Of course, I'm a touch over ninety, so maybe I have forgotten. Anyway, my name is Martin, Martin Clements."

Coop took his hand and noted, "You used to pastor here, didn't you?"

"Yes, I did," he laughed, "but how did you know? That was years before your time."

"I'm Clark Cooper Lindsay"—he paused— "you saved my grandmother's life."

The old man shrugged. "I wouldn't go that far, but I will tell you this: your grandfather might well have saved my soul."

As the organ began playing, Coop leaned closer. "I don't understand."

"Old Coop," the man whispered, "held a mirror up to my face one day, and I came to understand that I reflected the world and not God. It's a pretty sobering image for a preacher. I'd hate to think what I'd be now if it wasn't for him. Probably just another bitter old man."

The music director's signaling for the congregation to stand and sing all the verses of "Victory in Jesus" brought a halt to the conversation. But over the next fifty minutes, as old hymns were sung, prayers were said, and a woman pastor named Bethany Lucas shared a message about the amazing grace shown on the Jericho Road, a sense of peace fell over the visitor. His grandfather had written in those journals that he had really wanted to run away from his legacy. He didn't want to be his father's son. And yet, it is just what he needed to be. He needed to continue to do the work his dad had begun. And this morning, in a church filled with people of at least three or four different ethnic backgrounds, the dream was being realized, at least partly because his grandfather and a few others had found the faith to stand tall and do the right thing in the face of overwhelming odds.

When the final song was sung, a closing prayer said, and a last amen recited, Coop got up to make his way out the door. He was halfway down the steps when Clements caught him by the elbow. "I need to talk to you, if I could."

"Sure," Coop said.

"Let's step over in the shade of that elm," Clements suggested. "It's already awfully warm." Once they had found some relief from the noon sun, the old man shook his head, looked at the church building, and said, "During the time we first integrated the schools here, there was such great strife. This church led the way to finding peace and understanding. While others were preaching how God wanted to keep the races apart, we sponsored a service with the church Hattie Ross once called her spiritual home. I guess you know who Hattie Ross was."

"Yes, sir," Coop replied. "She all but raised me."

Clements nodded. "For a decade, our two churches would come together and worship together twice a year. It took years, but in time, there wasn't a reason for two churches, only one. And it would not have happened without your grandfather. I would have never seen fit to even suggest such a thing. Do you understand?"

"I think so," Coop assured him.

"And let me tell you," Clements continued, "it took a lot of forgiving on the part of the folks on the other side of the tracks before it happened. The government should get some credit for forcing us into doing the right thing in schools and public places, but it took God sending someone like your grandfather to really put what needed to be done into a spiritual perspective."

Coop nodded.

"You never met him," Clements continued, "but look at those people on the lawn. Look at how different they are but how much they are the same. They are God's quilt come to life and stitched together by faith, grace, and a bit of courage. It is what happens when a good Samaritan decides to step up and do what is right. It is your grandfather's legacy and yours, too."

"Thanks," the attorney replied. "I needed to hear that today. There is someone in the hospital fighting for her life who is there because she was my good Samaritan."

Clements nodded. "So you are the young man Tammi Shane told me about this morning. Well, let me tell you, Charli is a member here; she knew what she was doing. She saw it as a cause."

"She's special," Coop noted.

The retired pastor nodded before adding, "But not everyone always saw her as something special. She had to fight to be accepted, and some still don't accept her."

"I don't understand," Coop replied, his face framing his confusion. "She's about the most wonderful person I know."

"You read her right." The preacher smiled. "But do you know about her dad? Has she ever told you about him?"

"No," Coop said. "I've met her mother, but never her father."

"It's because Charli doesn't know who her dad is." The preacher shook his head. "Charli's mom never married, and she has never told anyone about the man who got her pregnant."

"Being born out of wedlock doesn't hold the stigma it used to," Coop argued.

"I know," Clements replied, "but not knowing who one of your parents is, and not knowing the reason why your mother won't tell you, does carry a huge stigma with it. And if she pulls out of the coma, if she does recover, you will likely have to address the issue at some point. God bless you, son."

Clements shook Coop's hand and moved over to visit with some of the others who were still milling around the lawn. The lawyer turned and looked back in the direction of the hospital. Now there was a new mystery begging to be solved.

78

Coop returned to the hospital to keep Charli's mother company. As they sat by the bed, Tammi told him everything, from when Charli learned to walk to the time she won the lead in the high school play, and all about the little redhead as the star of basketball and softball games. Among a thousand memories, from proms to skinned knees, the only thing seemingly left out during those hours was the young woman's father, and Coop had no intention of digging into it—at least not now.

A text from Michael Maltose gave Coop the time and place for the meeting with the defense team. Although he didn't want to, at 6:30 he leaned over, kissed Charli's forehead, and marched out to his car. Ten minutes later, he walked into the office of Maltose Properties. There an attractive woman in her late thirties greeted him with a forced smile. She was brunette, dark eyed, olive skinned, and all business.

"I'm Marie Tasker, Mr. Maltose's assistant. I am guessing you are Cooper Lindsay."

"I take it you don't get Sundays off," Coop shot back.

"I'm paid well enough that working weekends from time to time doesn't bother me," she explained. "Now, follow me to the boardroom." If Tasker enjoyed her job, she didn't show it in her unenthusiastic manner, but the expensive pumps and nicely tailored red suit did hint she was paid very well.

As they strolled from back to front, the office setup was nothing like the woman. It did not cry out money or power. If anything it was

433

simply generic. It had no theme or style. The boardroom was the same. There were twelve chairs surrounding a rectangular table, and they all looked like they had come out of an office supply catalog; nothing, not even a calendar, hung on the walls.

"Coop," Michael announced, as Tasker showed him in and then promptly turned and departed. "This is my team. The man on the left is Branford, Showers is next, then Smith, and finally White. They are from the New York firm of Branford and Smith."

Coop didn't bother stepping forward or shaking the men's hands. Rather, he just sized them up and smiled. They were the typical "suits" he had met in the big firms in Nashville and Cincinnati. They dressed well, worked hard, and had little use for humor. And they were likely experiencing extreme culture shock in small-town Mississippi. Served them right; they needed to get out more, eat a chicken-fried steak, and drink some sweet tea.

"Gentlemen," Coop began as the quartet sat down. "What are your plans in this case?"

Branford, a short, squatty man with badly dyed but wonderfully groomed black hair, spoke for the group. "We think we can make a deal and get vehicular manslaughter and driving under the influence. If we do and we play our cards right, David will likely be out in less than ten years."

"Interesting," Coop observed while walking over to a window. He studied the final rays of the setting sun for a few moments and then turned back to Branford. "Do you have any evidence David was drinking at all that night? I mean real evidence. You know, photos, blood tests, and the like?"

"Of course not," the lead attorney answered.

"And," Coop continued, "do all of you feel the young man is guilty?"

"If I were on the jury, I would," Smith admitted. "And with the feelings of this town toward the Maltoses, it will be a hostile jury at best. So we just need to cut a deal and get what we can."

Coop rubbed his lips before smiling. Turning toward his host, he said, "Michael, who is in charge, me or them?"

"Do you want to be?" he asked.

"No, I don't," Coop replied. "You let the suits do your dirty work and sell your kid up the river. I want no part of it."

"But," Michael argued.

Coop held up his hand. "I'll be there. And I'll help David, but I will not help you or any of your clan. When I speak, it will be in a way no one expects, and it will give me the latitude to kill two birds with one stone." He smiled at the quartet of shocked faces, waved, and headed for the door.

79

Monday, July 21, 2014

Just like any other visitor, Coop sat in the gallery section of the old courthouse and watched as the defense and prosecution went through the process of choosing juries. Observing paint dry would have been far more interesting. It was just after 11:00 when the seven women and five men were finally picked and the real show began. Branford gave the opening argument for the defense. He was smooth but uninspiring. Jerome Foster, tall, dark, and handsome, then spoke. When the DA finished, all the jury needed was an altar call to step forward and be saved. He was that good! Bearing the speech in mind, David Maltose didn't have a chance. By the look on Michael and Linda's faces, they realized it, too.

Over the lunch break, Coop dropped by the hospital to sit with Charli. While he kept watch beside her bed, her mother stepped out to grab some lunch. He watched the young woman just breathe for a few minutes and then turned his attention to a new magazine sitting on the nightstand. On the first few pages was the story Charli had written on the drought.

Picking it up, Coop began to read the copy. It was not just informative; it was actually interesting, and it took real talent to make a story on a drought good reading. After finishing the five-page feature, he glanced at the photos he'd helped pick out. The before-and-after views were amazing! They fully showed the damage inflicted due to the long period with only one major rainstorm. One especially jumped out showing the difference in the Maltose compound last summer and the way it looked now. The most pronounced difference was how the lake had lost almost half its water. He was trying to come to grips with how much rain would be needed to once more fill the lake when something else in the photo stole his attention. As he realized what he was seeing, he looked over to Charli and shook his head. "It has been there all along and we didn't notice it, girl. What were we thinking?"

Pulling out his cell, he tracked down the police chief.

"Chief Miles, I've got a favor to ask, and it will likely clear up the most famous cold case you have on your files. And I need a rush job on it, too. I have a photo in my hand giving us an indisputable reason to obtain a search warrant, enter the Maltose compound, and search their lake for a car. As the vehicle can be seen from the air, we will have no problem making our case. I believe you'll find that the vehicle exposed by the drought is my grandfather's 1963 Ford Galaxie 500."

"Are you serious?" Miles asked.

"Dead serious," he quickly replied. "You'll need to get the FBI involved as this will be classified as a kidnapping and hate crime. Also, take a forensics team with you. If possible, I need to know the cause of death before tomorrow morning. Don't let word of this slip out. I want to keep Linda Maltose in the dark until you get to the lake."

Coop leaned forward and kissed Charli on the lips, grimly smiled, and whispered, "Thank you, sweetheart." A few seconds later, he was out the door and jogging down the hall where, in his haste, he almost collided with the doctor in charge of her case. After both men stepped back, Dr. Anderson smiled and happily announced, "Charli seems to be getting better. The vitals are up. We're going to bring her out of the coma starting today."

Coop grabbed the man by his shoulders and almost yelled, "That's great! By the way, did you do any DNA work on Charli?"

"We have some in the lab," he replied. "We also have a lot of other tests we ran to assure we were ready for any emergency, including possible organ failure and transplanting."

"Great to know," Coop replied. "Have her mother call me if there is any change."

A few seconds later, the lawyer was out the door and racing for his car. If Charli really was getting better, this was shaping up to be the best day of his life.

80

The afternoon session of the trial saw Foster parade a short list of witnesses to the stand to provide motive for the crime. The jury and court also watched four different phone camera–recorded videos of the fight. Once again Coop marveled at how ineffective the young men's blows were. The medical examiner's report came next. It was pretty cut-and-dried. Jenkins had suffered blunt force trauma when the truck hit him, but his death was caused when the vehicle ran him over. He likely died within seconds from massive internal injuries. When the medical profes-sional's testimony concluded, Judge Rachel Adams called it a day.

Before racing back to check on Charli, Coop stopped by his office to run through his private e-mail. Three messages popped up in his e-mail giving him all he needed to ask the judge for permission to dramatically alter the trial's course. After jogging across the courthouse lawn, he strolled into the office of the tall, refined Judge

Adams and after exchanging greetings, explained his plan. The African American jurist listened, made several calls to assure the legality of what Coop wanted to do, and then gave him the okay. The ball was rolling.

After leaving the judge's office, Coop hopped into his car and made the three-mile trip to the hospital. As he walked into the room, the solemn faces of Tammi Shane and Dr. William Anderson greeted him. No one had to inform him there was something very wrong. His balloon burst, his knees grew weak, and his throat dry. It took him almost a minute to find the courage to ask, "What is it?"

"Things have changed radically since lunch," Dr. Anderson solemnly explained.

Coop swallowed hard and looked over to the woman whose only daughter was evidently dying, thanks to him. "Miss Shane, what happened?"

She shook her head and turned toward the wall, and after composing herself whispered, "In the brief time she knew you, she thought a lot of you. I know she'd like to have you with her now." She paused, then added, "This is all so overwhelming, I need to step away from this for a few minutes." She never turned to face him; instead, she just hurried from the room.

Coop looked back to Charli. He thought her color actually looked better; her breathing seemed steady as well. But what did he know?

The doctor placed his hand on Coop's shoulder. He let it rest there for a moment before just nodding sadly and saying, "She looks the way I imagined Sleeping Beauty." Anderson then walked out of the room, leaving Coop alone with the woman he had known for less than a week but had somehow loved all his life.

He mournfully sighed as he moved up beside her. "Charli, it's not right. It should have been me, not you. I should be the one where you are."

As he studied her placid features, a chill ran down his spine. She would likely look this way at the funeral, and folks would probably say she appeared so normal. And yet it wasn't true. Not at all! She was a dynamo of energy. She walked into a room and owned it. In her diminutive form, she packed a heavyweight's punch. The life in her eyes and the crooked smile generated more electricity than Mississippi Power and Light ever would. And none of it would be evident at her funeral.

He traced her smooth forehead with the fingers of his right hand and continued on through her soft auburn hair. He then smiled grimly and whispered, "Sleeping Beauty should have had red hair. It'd have made for a better story." Leaning closer, he cupped her cheek in his right palm and lowered his lips slowly to hers. He let them linger there for a moment and, with tears filling his eyes, turned away. As he did, he licked his lips and tasted something familiar. What was it? Colgate!

Whirling around, he looked into the twinkling eyes and grinning face of a woman now sitting up in bed. Shaking his head, he laughed. "My kiss did it."

"You're denser than I thought," Charli announced with a smile.

Coop studied her face and said, "You have makeup on."

"You just noticed?" she asked. "Your powers of observation are anything but perfectly tuned. We need to work on them."

He licked his lips again. "You brushed your teeth."

"I didn't want Sleeping Beauty to have bad breath," she shot back.

"I was set up!" He laughed.

Charli giggled. "The kids call it being pranked. And you were pranked really good, too."

"When did you come out of the coma?" he asked moving back to her side.

"About two hours ago. And I feel good, too. Just a bit of headache and a big hunger that a Sonic hot dog might help cure."

He smiled. "I'll get you anything you want."

She returned the smile. "Good. Now, the first thing I want is a real kiss where I get to kiss back. Think you can manage it?"

"You have no idea!"

81

Tuesday, July 22, 2014

Just before court came into session, Coop met with Judge Adams to go over his plans for the day. Unlike yesterday, when his request caught her off guard, she was now completely schooled in the interesting and unusual way today's events would likely play out.

It was almost nine when Coop took his place at the back of the gallery and studied the faces of those in attendance. Chief Miles had done his homework; everyone Coop needed seemed to be in place. Linda Maltose, finally dressed in mourner's black, was sitting beside her dark-suited son. They were in the first row behind the defense table. Off to the right was Martin Clements. Behind him was Mayor Austin Reed. Reed's daughter, Cindy, was to her father's right. Three rows behind them was Heather Wills. Though he hadn't met them, Coop figured the two middle-aged people on each side of the young woman had to be her parents. On the far side were three stern-looking individuals dressed in black suits and white shirts. Coop had already been briefed on who they were as well. Finally, Brent Booth had made his way into the room with the help of a nurse.

With everyone in place, the court was called to order, and Judge Rachel Adams entered and rapped her gavel. As soon as she did, the defense's lead attorney, Branford, stood and asked to be heard.

"What is it, Mr. Branford?"

"Based on the evidence presented yesterday and after a conference with our client and his father, we would like to enter a new plea."

Adams smiled and shook her head. "I don't think I will grant your request just yet."

"But, Your Honor—"

"Trust me," the woman jurist cut him off, "you will need to sit on your hands for a while. When I think the time is right, I will then allow you to make your motion and I will consider it. Meanwhile, something else has come to my attention and needs to be addressed before you get to open your mouth."

She paused to look at her notes and then explained what was about to happen, "Ladies and gentlemen, there are times when regular procedure in a courtroom can be dismissed in order to bring evidence into a proceeding with a direct impact on a case. When this happens, an outside person, who is neither a part of the defense nor the prosecution, is allowed to present evidence and question witnesses. Legally, this person is known as an *amicus curiae*, which means 'friend of the court.' This morning, Mr. Clark Cooper Lindsay has petitioned me to grant him this privilege. After visiting with Mr. Lindsay, I believe this is in the best interest of this case, as well as another cold case that remains fresh on the minds of many in this room."

Adams paused to observe the reactions of the curious throng as well as the media. Seemingly satisfied she had everyone's full attention, she continued, "While it is not always necessary on these rare occasions when we turn the proceedings over to the *amicus curiae*, I have chosen to hold the jury in the deliberation room. This is why they are not in the court at this time. If any of the evidence presented by the *amicus curiae* is needed to assure a proper verdict, we can bring the jury back in at a later time and go over it."

Looking toward the back of the room, she nodded and announced, "Mr. Lindsay, the floor is yours."

Coop smiled, stood, buttoned his dark blue suit, adjusted his red tie, picked up his briefcase, and strolled up the aisle through the gate to the prosecution table. He set his briefcase down, popped the latches, and opened it. He then turned and faced the gallery.

"In the matter of the *State versus David Maltose*, I have evidence to clearly show who is at fault in this death, how it happened, and why

Mr. Maltose has refused to work with his illustrious team of attorneys." Coop winked toward the defense table and moved on, "Essentially, David has placed himself in the role of a martyr. And what has transpired is the direct result of a series of lies and deceptions begun long before the night of the Justice High School prom and the accident in the area by Lovers Park.

"To begin to unravel what really happened, I need to call back to the stand some of the prosecution's witnesses from yesterday. The first person I must question is Cindy Reed."

The teen looked to her father who shrugged and smiled. Nervously, she got up and walked through the gate to the witness box. After she took her seat, Judge Adams reminded her that she was still under oath.

"Miss Reed," Coop began, "what was the fight between LaDerick and David all about? They were good friends, they were teammates, and they were both leaders in the school. I have seen scores of photos from prom night, and the two of them, along with you and Heather Wills, were inseparable. So why did they suddenly make a scene on the dance floor? And remember, you are under oath."

Cindy's dark brown, almost almond-shaped eyes found her father. She looked for all the world like a deer caught in headlights.

"Cindy," Coop said in a soft tone, "I can tell the

court what happened then if you would like me to do so. Or maybe it would be best if I just asked a series of yes or no questions. Okay?"

"Yes," she whispered.

"Your official prom date was LaDerick Jenkins. In fact, you and Mr. Jenkins had supposedly been dating for months. Am I correct?"

"Yes," Cindy said, and then nodded as if to reinforce her answer.

"Who did you always double date with?" Coop asked.

"David and Heather," she replied.

Coop moved back to the table and retrieved a photo. He brought it back and handed it to the young lady. "This is a shot of the four of you together. You have on green and so does David. The two of you match. Heather is wearing the same shade of blue as LaDerick's tie. This pretty much says it all. Your dating LaDerick was all a front. Your real date, not just this night, but for the whole semester, was David Maltose. And Heather had been going with LaDerick. Am I right?"

Cindy's eyes fell to the floor, and she went mute. The judge waited only a few seconds before demanding, "You must answer the question."

The witness nervously looked back at her father and then to Coop before whispering, "It's true."

"Why the charade?" Coop asked.

"It wasn't because he was white," Cindy quickly explained. "It was just that my father wouldn't have allowed me to date anyone from the Maltose family. He wouldn't give David a chance."

"Thank you, Cindy," the attorney said. "You may step down." He watched the petite young woman make her way to her place in the gallery before he looked back to the judge. "Now I need to have Heather Wills return to the stand."

He turned and watched as the redheaded, green-eyed young woman slowly stood and cautiously walked to the stand. During the girl's short trip forward, Heather's mother looked at the floor, while her father's face had become as red as a stoplight. As he followed his daughter's path, his blood must have been close to boiling. Everyone in the room could easily see she was scared to death. As Heather took her seat, the judge again reminded her of the oath she had taken the day before.

"Miss Wills," Coop began, leaning on the rail in front of the witness, "this is not going to be easy for either of us. You heard what Cindy said. Is it true?"

"Yes, sir."

"And," Coop continued, "I'm guessing the two young men staged the fight to actually get kicked out of the dance so each of you could be with your true dates. Am I correct?"

"Yes, sir." Heather wrung her hands as she waited for the next question.

Coop walked over to the railing and signaled to Chief Miles. The policeman came forward and handed a small paper sack to the attorney. Coop looked into the sack and then slowly moved back to the witness stand.

"Heather, you had a beautiful blue dress at the prom. I noticed in photos that you somehow found matching shoes. Do you still have those shoes?"

She shook her head.

"You will need to verbally answer the questions, Miss Wills," the judge cut in.

"No, sir," Heather said. "I threw them away. They were ruined by the mud."

"How did you manage to find shoes the same bright blue as the dress?" Coop asked.

"The cleaners dyed them for me," she explained. "It's how most of the girls do it."

Coop reached his hand into the sack and pulled out a blue high heel from a woman's shoe. "I think this is called a stiletto heel, correct?"

"Yes."

"You know where you lost this one, don't you?" he asked.

Heather brought her hands to her face and moaned. As she sobbed, Coop turned back to face both the DA and the defense team and grimly explained, "No one realized this was a part of what happened then. It was retrieved by the crime scene team, but it was so covered with mud that most folks just assumed it had nothing to do with what had played out. And yet a boy died because of this broken heel. I finally realized it when Chief Miles and I took it to the lab and had it cleaned."

Setting the heel down on the evidence table, Coop moved back to the witness box. He studied the broken young woman for a few seconds and then softly suggested, "We need to move on, Heather. After all, you don't want or need David to pay for something he didn't do, do you?"

She looked up, dabbed the tears from her cheeks, and shook her head.

"Heather," Coop continued, "I'm going to try to lead you through what I think happened. If I have guessed wrong, you let me know. Otherwise, just answer yes or no. Okay?"

"Yes, sir."

"I'm thinking your family wouldn't have approved of you dating an African American. Correct?"

"My mom was cool with it, but Dad would have killed me."

Coop looked back at Heather's parents, moved his hand over his lips, and continued, "So what happened after the fake fight? I think David and Cindy likely took Cindy's car, and you two borrowed David's truck, right?"

"Yes, sir," Heather admitted. "LaDerick didn't have his own car. It had to be that way. David worked it out. David also gave LaDerick the money to rent the tux."

Coop sadly nodded and pushed on, "Had you ever been to Lovers Park before?"

"Only once," she quickly replied, "and it was in the daytime. LaDerick had never been there."

"And because of the storm," Coop continued, "you missed the turnoff point."

"Yes, sir."

"When you tried to turn around at the end of the lane, you got stuck?"

"Yes, sir," she admitted sadly.

"Why didn't you call for help on your cell phone?" Coop asked.

"I'd taken so many pictures and videos at the prom, the battery was dead. And LaDerick's family couldn't afford to buy him a cell."

"I'm reaching here," Coop informed the young woman, "but after he got stuck, I believe, by looking at footprints left at the scene, LaDerick decided to walk back for help, right?"

"Yes, sir," she meekly answered, her nervous eyes doing any and everything but looking into her father's face.

"You must have scooted over into the driver's seat and gotten it going," Coop continued. "And somehow, you managed to get the truck unstuck."

"I just kind of rocked it back and forth," she

explained. "My dad taught me how to do it."

"And," Coop continued, "when you got out of the mud, you drove forward to pick up LaDerick. But your heel somehow got caught in or by the accelerator."

She shook her head sobbing. "I guess the mat had slipped, and when I looked down to see why my foot wouldn't come up, I hit him. I panicked and couldn't stop, and I ran over him."

"When you got outside, you lost your heel in the mud," Coop noted.

"And he was dead," Heather cried. "So I got back into the truck and drove to where I knew David and Cindy were. David took over from there."

Coop looked to the bench. "I have no more questions of this witness, Your Honor."

The judge glanced to the DA and then to the defense table. She studied each for a moment before announcing, "I believe this case as it currently stands is over. I fully expect the State will use the evidence presented today to file new charges against the three people involved in this cover-up."

She paused and then added, "But there are two other related and pending cases our *amicus curiae* can help put into perspective. So I order no one to leave this room until he presents this new evidence. And, as you just saw in the matter of the *State of Mississippi versus David Maltose*,

Mr. Lindsay is free to call any witnesses he chooses to the stand. Those called must answer the questions or plead the fifth. This is still a court of law, even if its only purpose at this time is to help clear up two other cases by presenting new evidence and testimony.

"Mr. Lindsay, I am giving you incredible latitude; don't abuse it."

"I won't, Your Honor," Coop assured her. As he turned to call his next witness, he was shocked to see his grandmother walk through the door and sit in the chair he had vacated thirty minutes before. Judy Lindsay, dressed in a green suit, had finally returned to Justice.

82

Coop looked from his grandmother to the chief of police. Miles smiled and nodded. The last piece was in place. It was time to go back fifty years and, in the process, shake up the present and dramatically alter the future.

Coop slowly walked across the courtroom and stopped just in front of the defense and prosecution tables. With every eye locked onto him, he looked at his now captive audience and began.

"I came back to Justice with the mission of trying to find out what happened to my grandfather and Calvin Ross. I am not sure it would have been possible without a series of seemingly unrelated events coming together and providing me with the perfect storm. The first was when my grandmother, Judy Lindsay, gave me my grandfather's journals. The second was showing up in Justice in the middle of an incredible drought. The third was having David Maltose decide to be noble and try to save two young ladies from feeling their fathers' wraths. Ultimately, David's noble though misguided gesture led his family to seek me out to help on the case. It gave me the chance to dig deeper into the matter that brought me here. The fourth element to open the door to my uncovering new evidence was having a young law student jump onto my team. If I had come here during the school year, I would have never had Charli Shane's research at my disposal. And finally, there was the matter of John David Maltose's death. The fact that I was with him when he died, coupled to . . ."

Coop froze as a mental bolt of lightning struck. He finally understood what the old man was trying to tell him. Turning back to the judge, the attorney asked for a favor, "May I have a moment to speak with Chief Miles, and then would you allow him to retrieve something from my office?"

"Does it pertain to the matter we are now discussing?"

"It does, Your Honor," he assured her.

"Then get on with it," Adams suggested.

Coop waved Miles up to the railing, leaned over, slipped some keys into his hands, and whispered into the chief's ear, "Go to my grand-father's office, pull out all the desk drawers. Something should be hidden under one of them. Then bring what you find back here to me. If I am remembering correctly, you will find it under the bottom right drawer. But if it is not there, keep looking."

"What if I can't find it?" Miles asked.

"I don't think it will be a problem," Coop assured him.

He watched the lawman hurry down the aisle and out the guarded door before continuing. "I always find it interesting as to what triggers one person's hate or mistrust. In Linda Maltose's case"—he made eye contact with the woman just fifteen feet from him—"it began because her father was murdered in a robbery attempt. Isn't that right, Mrs. Maltose?"

As she nodded, her cold, clear blue eyes almost burned through Coop. He could tell by her expression, she was likely reliving one of the most horrible moments of her life. He let her stay in the past for only a few moments before posing a question.

"You almost collided with a man named Jupiter Jones as he ran from your house, and then you saw your father's body. It changed your whole life, didn't it?"

"Yes," she barked. "Of course it did."

"And you had a hate lit in you at that moment that is still burning today," Coop continued, his eyes never leaving hers. "You didn't want to just get Mr. Jones for what he had done; you also wanted to inflict pain on every man who looked like him."

Linda Maltose didn't move or say a word, but her glare spoke volumes. The hate born when she was a child was still there.

"You were the sole witness for the prosecution in his trial," Coop continued. "Your testimony was damning. And it was also likely embellished, much like the testimony you gave fifty years ago when you falsely claimed Calvin Ross cursed and threatened Brent Booth."

"In both cases, I only told what I saw and heard," Linda shot back.

"I doubt it," Coop continued, "and when it comes to the first case, I'm guessing rules were much different back then. You were a minor, and yet I found out you were allowed to watch Jupiter Jones being executed. He went to his grave proclaiming his innocence, and you heard his pleas for mercy."

"He didn't deserve mercy for what he did to me," she snarled.

"Actually," Coop explained, his voice calm and

emotionless, "he did. A few decades later, a sick man stumbled into a charity hospital. He was dying a slow death and carried a great deal of guilt with him as he looked at his final days. A nun in the hospital visited him every day. In time, he showed her a piece of jewelry; it was star-shaped with a small red stone in the middle. Engraved on the back were three words: *Given in love.*

Coop pulled his iPad from his briefcase, powered it up, and opened the photo file to display an image. He flipped the electronic tablet over and showed it to Linda Maltose.

"That was my mother's," the shocked woman gasped.

"Yes, it was," Coop replied, "and it was stolen on the day you fingered Jupiter Jones for murdering your father. The dying man told the nun the real story: how he had tried to rob your family's home, how your dad had surprised him, how he had hit your father with a heavy bookend and ran out with the loot. But his mind was too far gone to remember the actual date or your family name."

Linda Maltose shook her head in disbelief.

"Oh, Linda," Coop announced, irony dripping with each word, "he was white. His name was Richard Oates. He was a career criminal. Always pulling small jobs and never getting to the big time. He simply stole enough to get by." Coop sat the iPad down and allowed the news to soak in for a few more moments before adding, "So it was not a black man who made you an orphan and plunged you into a world of poverty. It was a white man. All your hate has been built on a lie. So every time you opposed any initiative for blacks, it was because you were wrong."

The balloon had burst, but the old woman said nothing. Her eyes still clearly displayed her hate. But she was not going to stop Coop. He took a deep breath, pointed a finger and proclaimed, "Jupiter Jones died because of what you imagined, not what you saw." He waited a few seconds for those gathered to grasp the meaning of knowing that a man had died for a crime he hadn't committed. He then moved forward.

"What happened almost seventy years ago set Linda Maltose's life on a rocky course. After being raised in an orphanage, she survived by her wits and the help of her friends in Gulfport. None of us can fully blame her for the things she did because we all understand the need to eat and survive. Charms she learned as she made her living allowed her to work her way into John David Maltose's head and heart. Think about it now, John David was a man trapped in a marriage he hadn't wanted and haunted by the actions of a cruel father who let him down in ways few of us could understand. I will explain that later. John David was therefore an easy target for Linda's wiles."

"John David loved me," she shot back.

"I won't argue his motivation," Coop replied, "but whatever he was looking for and saw in you, it allowed you to escape a nightmare. And magically, like a twisted Cinderella, you were suddenly gifted with power and money. Which leads me directly to legal issues I am going to lay out for the district attorney."

Coop stopped, walked over to the prosecution table, poured a glass of water, took a sip, put the glass down and, as he stepped back to a place in front of the witness box, nodded to his grandmother. "Fifty years ago, my grandfather felt a need to repay the debt he owed John David for saving his life the night of the KKK rally. He also wanted to give the Booths the answer to why their daughter had been killed. But even though he had an idea as to what happened, he simply couldn't prove it. Science was lagging behind. It would be decades before DNA was used in cases like this, and it is what my grandfather actually needed to show both motivation and action."

The opening of the back doors and the appearance of Chief Miles caused Coop to stop speaking and move toward the railing. After the policeman handed over a file, Coop looked back to the bench and announced, "Your Honor, I need to review this for a few moments."

Judge Adams nodded and announced, "Those in the audience may feel free to relax and converse. But keep it down. And when you hear me call this unusual proceeding back to order, please remain seated and quiet." She then glanced back to Coop. "Let me know when you are ready."

83

It took ten minutes for Coop to fully study the pages of the file Miles had brought him. Satisfied with what he had read, he signaled the bench that he was ready to continue and Adams once more brought the gavel down.

"First of all," Coop began, "my grandfather heard about the new will John David Maltose had ordered. He actually was in the Maltose home when John David demanded in a phone call that the will be delivered within the week. My grandfather believed this new will was specifically written to coincide with a second bit of legal action John David had planned but never actually executed. Though I have no proof, Linda must have found out about her husband's plans, because the new will was somehow lost."

Linda Maltose stood, pointed a finger at Coop, and shouted, "There was no other will!"

"Actually," Coop replied, moving toward the woman and staring her in the eyes, "there was. The one filed the other day giving your children and Travis the estate was written in 1962."

"And it is the legal document," Linda shot back.

"No," Coop argued, "not anymore. The legal will was written and signed in 1964. You must have destroyed what you thought were all copies of the document. And you were almost successful, too. It wasn't until a few minutes ago that I realized what John David was telling me during our visit just before his death. He said, and I believe these are his exact words, 'My only son died a long time ago.' And then he added something I didn't get at the time, 'It is under the bottom desk drawer on the right. You make it good. Please!' "

Coop walked back to the table and picked up the file Miles had brought into the courtroom. He glanced to the chief. "Where did you find this?"

"Under the bottom right drawer of your grandfather's desk."

"Thank you," Coop said. "You know, when I arrived in Justice, I must admit I was confused by John David Maltose's making what seemed to be a shrine of my grandfather's office. And when Mike Morgan purchased the building, he did so with the provision that one floor not be used and the office be maintained as it was. Why? Now I know, it was a hiding place for a document John David knew would someday be found and would tell a story he needed to be told due to its contents. Hiding this will might have been the last thing John David did before his wife locked him up and took full control of his life."

Coop walked over, picked up the will, and flipped through the first few pages. Holding the document up, he explained, "This will is very similar to the previous one. The subtle changes are these: As in the previous one, Linda Maltose is completely left out. But in this document, the estate is left to only those who are John David's blood heirs." Coop smiled as he looked directly into Linda's eyes. "And it is the latter clause that so scared you."

The woman shook her head. "My kids would have taken care of me. I had no fears. I just didn't know the will existed. It changes nothing. It divides the property just like the one from 1962."

Coop set the will back on the table and looked over to Michael. "Actually, it changes a great deal." Pulling a newspaper out of the briefcase, he held it up for the audience to view. "Can anyone tell me who this is?"

"I can," Judy Lindsay called out. "The man who kidnapped me fifty years ago. His name was Melvin Forest."

Coop dropped the paper back on the table and shook his head. "My grandmother is right. And Melvin worked for John David Maltose. In fact, he began his time with Maltose within a month after John and Linda were married. He came from the same city where Linda had once lived. I'm sure the two of them knew each other long before Melvin came to Justice."

Coop stopped, took another sip of water, and continued, "And you will see why it is so important in just a few moments. But first, I want to go back to the reason my grandfather did not have the means to solve this case. And to do so I need to call Wayne Plymonth to the stand."

A tall, powerfully built man, with a solid jaw, dark eyes, and a clean-shaven face stood. After adjusting his dark suit coat, he moved confidently to the witness box.

"Mr. Plymonth," the judge said, "this is a very strange way of presenting evidence, but I still believe you need to be sworn in." After the man took the oath, Coop stepped to the box to pose a few questions.

"What is your profession?"

"I'm a medical examiner for the FBI."

"You were initially brought in on this case to do what?" Coop asked.

"When the body of Rebecca Booth was exhumed," Plymonth explained, "I was asked to conduct a second autopsy."

The crowd could no longer remain silent as a gasp went from the front to the back of the room. During the day's early testimony, they might have been a little surprised, but now almost all of those present were deeply shocked.

Coop looked back to Brent Booth. The old man nodded.

"And the purpose of your work?" Coop asked, now with every set of eyes focused on the agent.

"To do a DNA test on the unborn fetus Miss Booth was carrying at the time she died."

"Did you compare those results to any others your lab tested?" Coop asked.

"We did, and we found that the fetus carried DNA linking it to two known people."

"And who were those people?" Coop asked, continuing to look at the gallery rather than the agent.

"The first was John David Maltose."

Coop allowed those words to hover for just a few moments before he turned and asked, "And the second person?"

"A woman who lives in Brandice, Mississippi," Plymonth explained, "Molly Thornton Maltose."

Coop whirled and looked back to Linda Maltose. "When did you find out Becky Booth was carrying Travis's baby?"

"What are you talking about?" the woman hissed.

"You had to be aware that John David was planning to divorce you," Coop explained. "You were aware, probably by overhearing his phone calls or talking to servants, he was changing his will to include only blood relatives. And somehow, you found out Becky was carrying Travis's child. I'm guessing you likely discovered it the weekend she was murdered."

"You can't prove any of this," Linda stood and shouted.

"So far," Coop admitted, "you are correct." He moved toward the railing with just a few feet separating them, he reached into his pocket and tossed a small rubber ball at Linda. The woman's reflexes defied her years as her left hand shot up and caught it. Coop smiled and moved back to his briefcase to pull out an old report.

"The person who did the original autopsy indicated that Becky Booth was killed by someone who was left-handed and not very tall." He turned to the FBI agent and asked, "I know you have studied the report; do you agree, Mr. Plymonth?"

"I do," he replied.

"You can't prove I killed her," Linda taunted from her seat. "And I didn't know it was Travis's child."

"My Lord," Coop gasped, as he finally understood the woman's motives. "You thought it was John David's child?"

"He was always messing around," she shot back. "But like I said, you can't prove anything."

"Maybe not at this moment," Coop admitted, "but thanks to the work of the late Wylie Estes, I feel we will be able to do so with a couple of simple tests. You see, my grandfather's journal talks about how meticulous Wylie was. He wrote about what he observed, and he kept every piece of evidence, too. Melvin's old pickup had blood on a tailgate hinge, and there were several old knives in the bed as well. Sheriff Estes sealed those and other things away in an evidence room. They remained sealed until this morning. They are on their way for testing right now. And the knife contains fingerprints."

"Why weren't these tested at the time?" Judge Adams asked.

"Because," Coop turned and explained, "it was assumed Melvin Forest was Becky's killer. He might have been an accomplice, but he wasn't small or left-handed, and therefore, he didn't fit the killer's profile. Yet back then folks just wanted to put the case to bed, so Forest became the man folks believed killed Becky."

Coop turned and stared into Linda's blue eyes. She shook her head and hissed, "I don't have to stay here."

"Actually you do," DA Foster announced from his table. "You are a murder suspect. So either sit down or we'll book you right now and put you in jail."

The woman angrily took her seat.

"I think we have cleared up one matter," Coop announced, "but what was her motive in framing Calvin Ross?"

84

"In this matter, motive is a bit confusing," Coop explained as his eyes went from Linda to the crowd. "Why frame an innocent black man? I think there were three reasons. The first was Linda Maltose's bigoted mind. The second involved the fact that her accomplice, Melvin Forest, likely knew of Calvin's knife and could therefore easily get it. After all, once the murder had been completed and the body moved to Lovers Park, they needed to frame someone who worked with knives. Calvin was known as someone who helped others butcher hogs, and Melvin, who spent a lot of time in the area of the Maltose rental property, was aware of the fact and had likely seen the knife with Calvin's name carved on the handle. And Linda, because of her relationship through marriage, did have access to the funeral home, so it would have been easy to sneak in and use Calvin's knife to deliver the extra wounds. But there was a third reason making this frame perfect for Linda to use, and it is, by far, the most important."

Coop looked back at the woman as he asked, "When did John David tell you Calvin was his brother?"

All eyes went to Linda. She just shook her head.

Coop shrugged. "It doesn't matter if you admit it or not, but I know it and my grandfather figured it out. It is why John David wanted to get a deal cut for Calvin. It is also why John David carried so much guilt. You see, his father actually killed Calvin's mother and set the house on fire to kill his illegitimate son as well. John David watched Hattie risk her life to save Calvin. And then John David held the baby while Hattie's wounds where tended to. The last thing a bigot like Linda wanted was to have to claim a black man as a brother-in-law and have the young man share in the estate." Coop paused and smiled. "Remember the clause in the new will? It stated that all blood heirs would share in John David's estate"—Coop bore down on Linda with his stare—"and it would include Calvin."

She wagged her finger. "You have no proof that nig—" She stopped, glanced around the room at all the people watching her before saying, "that that boy was a Maltose."

"We'll have it soon," Coop replied. "You see, a search warrant was issued yesterday. You would have known about it, but you stayed in town with your son. Your workers at your compound were ordered not to share the news with anyone. Yesterday afternoon, my grandfather's car was found in your lake. The drought had exposed half of it, and it was spotted in a recent aerial photo taken to examine the drought's effects."

Coop turned back to the stand. "Your Honor, I need to call Mr. Nathan Revera to the stand."

As the short, lean man stood, Linda Maltose's face went ashen white.

85

"Mr. Revera," Coop began after the witness had taken his oath, "What is your job?"

"I'm a forensic anthropologist employed by the Federal Bureau of Investigation."

Coop turned back to the gallery before asking, "Were you at the scene when the FBI and local police pulled a 1963 Ford Galaxie from the lake at the Maltose compound?"

"I was."

"And what did you find in the trunk of the car?" Coop asked, while looking at his grandmother and slowly nodding.

"Two bodies," the witness solemnly replied.

"What do you know so far about these bodies?" Coop continued as he turned back to face Revera.

"Well, an autopsy will be used to confirm it, but personal effects found in the trunk along with clothing still on the bodies make us ninety-nine percent sure they are Calvin Ross and Cooper Lindsay."

"Can you guess how they died?" the attorney asked.

"I don't have to guess, sir," Revera replied. "They were shot. Bullets were found in my initial inspection of the bodies and also discovered in the car's trunk."

Coop slowly moved back to the railing and fixed his eyes on Linda Maltose before asking, "Can you do DNA tests on the bodies?"

"We can and will," the agent confirmed.

"Good," Coop smiled. "It will allow us to verify that Calvin Ross was indeed John David's brother and is why John David told me that the truth was in the water. When he said it, I thought he was talking figuratively, but he actually meant it literally."

The door at the back of the courtroom opened, and Dr. Alexander stood at the back and waved toward Coop. "Excuse me, Your Honor." The attorney walked back and took the file the doctor had delivered. After setting it in his briefcase, Coop looked back at Linda Maltose.

"Mrs. Maltose, I have a witness who will testify that someone was in the backseat of my grandfather's car on July 15, 1964, and holding what appeared to be a shiny object in their left hand. My grandfather was driving, and Calvin Ross was riding in the front passenger seat. The car was headed toward where the Maltose compound is right now."

"We didn't own the property then," she shot back.

"No," Coop admitted, "but John David had fished on the lake many times and was trying to buy it. The deal was actually completed in 1965. Within a year, the stone walls had gone up, the house was built, and your fortress was complete."

The old woman stood, made her way past her son and to the aisle before sticking her finger in Coop's face. "What does any of it prove? Can you tie me to the scene? Can you put the gun in my hands? Can you prove any of this? Even the blasted will you found only means my two kids get everything."

She turned and faced those in the gallery. "You can hate me if you want. You always have anyway, but when this is finished, I'll go back to my fine house and count my money and you will go back to your pathetic little lives." She turned back to Coop. "Are you satisfied?"

"Not quite," he assured her. Stepping back, he pulled an empty chair from behind the prosecutor's table, moved back to the gate, held it open, and made a suggestion, "Why don't you take this seat? I think you will want to watch this next performance up close and personal."

Before stepping through and taking the place she'd been offered, Linda shot him a glance indicating she wanted to feed the attorney piece by piece to a flock of starving vultures. If given the opportunity, he was sure she would, too.

86

"Mr. Revera," Coop asked as he turned away from a boiling Linda Maltose and back to his witness, "what caliber was the gun used in the murders of my grandfather and Calvin Ross?"

"It was a thirty-eight."

"Could you match the bullets fired to the gun if you were able to find the gun?"

"We could and we have," he answered. "The gun used was in a display case at the home of Jodi Maltose Cone. As she did not have a key to the cabinet, we had to use a locksmith to open it. We then tested the thirty-eight and it was a match."

"Who is the gun registered to?" Coop asked.

"Linda Maltose," came the man's quick reply. "The director of the local gun club supplied us with a photo of her using it to win a shooting competition in 1963. The framed picture was hanging in their clubhouse."

"Interesting," the lawyer said as he looked back to Linda. "Well, we have the gun now. What do you have to say for yourself? You ready to admit what you did?"

She shook her head. "So you have the gun, what does it prove? Do you have witnesses? And if my prints are on the knife from the early case, so what if I touched it? Melvin worked for us. I was around the truck a lot. You couldn't convict me of anything."

Coop smiled. "What if I told you the cartridges still in the gun match those used in the shooting of my grandfather and Calvin Ross? What if I explained that your fingerprints are on them? And what if I proved they came from the very same ammunition box? As we have motive, I think it would be all I need."

He watched her wilt under his gaze. It also appeared the strength had oozed from her body as she almost melted into the chair. For the first time since Coop first met her, she looked her age. Her beauty was gone, too, replaced by an ugliness only evil could create.

"It doesn't matter," she whispered.

"What doesn't?" Coop asked.

"It doesn't matter you figured it out," she hissed as she again brought her eyes to meet his. "I did it for my kids. I wanted to make sure they were able to have their father's legacy. And they have it, so whatever happens to me is fine. I had a good fifty years watching everyone wonder what had happened. I almost pulled off the perfect crimes."

Coop sadly nodded. "And you hurt so many innocent people in your life during the time as well."

"It would have never happened," she said, "if

your father had minded his place and those people had just stayed in their place."

"What happened to John David?" Coop asked. "Did you drug him? Is that why he went crazy?"

"He drank too much," she replied. "I just mixed in some drugs with his booze. After Travis died, he really went over the edge. He became easier and easier to control."

"And the drugs saved you from divorce," Coop noted.

"He was no longer competent," she laughed. "I was given control over the estate. I had the right as his wife."

Coop looked back to Revera. "I'm finished with this witness, but I would like to have Mr. Plymonth return to the stand. There is one other matter we need to address."

Coop stood next to Linda Maltose as the two men swapped places; he then took a deep breath and strolled over to the witness box. "Mr. Plymonth, earlier in the day we established you are a DNA expert. I obtained and asked you to run two other DNA profiles for me. Do you have them?"

"They are in a file in my briefcase."

"I'll retrieve it for you," Coop offered, while moving quickly through the gate and to Plymonth's empty chair. Picking up the black case, he briskly strolled to the witness box and handed it to the agent. Within seconds, the man opened the case and pulled out the reports.

"This is the test you sent marked unknown person A," Plymonth explained. "And this is the test for person B."

"Are these two related?" Coop asked.

"No doubt about it," he assured the attorney. "They are likely siblings."

"I know you ran another test," Coop continued. "How did the test compare to these two?"

"Test subject C is either the parent or an identical twin of the parent of both A and B."

Coop moved back to his own briefcase and retrieved another DNA test result. He then returned to the box and handed it to the agent. "Can you tell me if the markers in this test lead you to believe this profile, let's call it person D, is any relation to A, B, or C?"

Plymonth studied the report and compared it to the other three. "There is no possible connection."

"Do you have the report on John David Maltose?" Coop asked.

"Yes, sir," came the quick reply, "it is in my case."

"Could you tell me if John David is related to either A, B, or C?"

"What about D?" the agent asked.

"We will table that for the time being," Coop replied.

The agent pulled out the report and compared

it to the other three before looking up at the attorney. "There is no family connection between the late Mr. Maltose and either A, B, or C."

"Thank you," Coop replied. Turning back to where he faced Linda Maltose, he shrugged. "You've had a bad day. First, you had to admit to the crimes you committed. Now I'm about to reveal the reason John David wanted to divorce you."

Linda swallowed hard and shook her head. After taking a deep breath, she whispered, "No."

"John David figured out who the man was you had him hire." Coop paused and looked back at his grandmother. Her jaw was set as she nodded. She had already guessed what he was about to reveal. Letting his eyes fall back on Linda Maltose, he dropped the other shoe. "A and B in that DNA profile are your children, Michael and Jodi. Test C was the hired man who tried to kill my grandfather with his truck, kidnapped my grandmother, and helped you place Becky Booth's body at Lovers Park, Melvin Forest. And because you thought she was carrying your husband's child, you posed her body in the shape of the letter A."

Coop shrugged. "I guess you were a fan of Hawthorne's *Scarlet Letter*. The irony being the proved adulterer was in fact you, not John David."

Coop shook his head. "John David figured it out, didn't he?"

"Yes," she snarled, "he threw it in my face, just before the trial. It suddenly dawned on him who Michael and Jodi looked like."

"You realize," Coop noted, "your kids will now be cut off from the family fortune. They will get the same as you received: nothing."

Linda smiled. "But no one else will either. There are no more left in the Maltose line."

Coop glanced back at the witness and smiled. "Mr. Plymonth, thank you, and please leave the report with the judge on DNA test D."

Coop shook his head and, after nodding to the DA, looked back to the judge. "Your Honor, I now give up my role as *amicus curiae*. This court is yours."

It was finally over, and even though a host of those living in Justice had likely initially resented Coop for taking the case, he had now given them exactly what they wanted. The Maltose power was dead. The family no longer had a hold over Justice. From the look on the faces in the crowd, the lawyer wasn't sure they knew what to do with the gift.

"Mr. Foster," the judge announced, "I'm guessing you will be having Mrs. Maltose arrested and filing charges."

"I will be doing so posthaste," came the response.

"Then, Chief Miles," Adams continued, "I suggest you take the woman into custody."

"My pleasure," Miles replied.

The chief quickly crossed the room, and as Linda Maltose stood, he snapped the cuffs on her wrists and led her out.

"And before I close this hearing," Adams announced after Linda Maltose had been ushered out of the courtroom, "I have one question for Mr. Lindsay."

Coop's eyes met the judge's. "What's that?"

"I was unaware you could actually trace bullets and cartridges in the manner you stated. How did you figure out the unspent rounds in the gun matched those used in the crime? You mean to tell me the FBI can actually match them and link them to a crime, a gun, and bullets found in a body?"

"Not that I am aware of, Your Honor," Coop admitted. "Let's just say, when it came to that point, I might have been using a bit of deception."

She laughed. "I guess it is why all three FBI agents and Chief Miles raised their eyebrows when you made the statement."

Adams looked to the crowd. "This court is adjourned."

87

It had perhaps been the most unique double funeral ever conducted at the Justice Methodist Church. Two men, one black and the other white, dead for over fifty years, shared the attention of an overflow crowd of mourners, as well as media from all over the world. Perhaps Martin Clements said it best in the closing line of his message, "They not only changed Justice; they changed the world!" And maybe they did at least change a corner of it.

After the memorial at the graveside, when everyone else had left, Coop stood under the shade of a tree with his grandmother, Tammi Shane, and a now-recovered Charli. As the three women studied the hundreds of floral displays, he looked toward the western skies and called out, "We don't need to linger much longer; a big storm's coming."

"Hallelujah!" Tammi cried out. "It has been way too long getting here."

"Yes, it has," Charli agreed. She looked from the threatening clouds back to the graves and noted, "It seems appropriate to have Calvin and your grandfather resting side by side."

"Calvin broke the color line," Judy pointed

out. "He is the first African American buried in this cemetery."

"Won't be the last," Coop proclaimed. He put his arm around his grandmother and declared, "Justice is a much different place now than it was when you lived here."

"I know," she sighed, "and it all started with a sermon about the good Samaritan. You know, Coop, you are your grandfather's grandson." Judy turned away from the grave and studied the coming storm. She watched the clouds and listened to the distant rolling thunder before adding, "You're going to stay in Justice, aren't you?"

"I think so," Coop replied. "There is work Grandpa began here, and it needs to be finished. And I feel at home in his old office."

Judy patted his arm. "I'm glad John David kept it for you." She paused and then said to no one in particular, "I wonder what the state will decide to do with the Maltose fortune."

Coop glanced over to Tammi. As their eyes met, he said, "It won't be left up to the state of Mississippi."

Tammi tilted her head and looked from Coop to her daughter and then back to Coop.

"It's up to you," he whispered to Tammi.

The woman stared across the cemetery to another fresh grave. Crossing her arms, she looked into her daughter's eyes and admitted, "It is time for the truth to come out. I know it wasn't right, but he was a lonely man. He needed a friend. And when they hired me to help with their accounting, I got to visit the compound and got to know him. And things just happened. He never knew and neither did Linda. I would have taken the secret to my grave as well."

"Mom?" Charli asked. "What are you talking about?"

Tammi moved her eyes from her daughter to Coop. "You tell her."

Coop pulled Charli to the side and looked into her deep, brown eyes. He kissed her gently on the forehead and ran his hand through her auburn hair. "I told you about the DNA testing done to prove Michael and Jodi were not John David's children?"

Charli looked up and nodded.

"Well, the last DNA test subject," he explained, "the person D, was you. Your father was John David Maltose." He smiled. "It seems your dad not only saved my grandfather's life once, but he gave me someone to love."

"Wow," she whispered.

He laughed. "Yeah, the amount of money can be a bit overwhelming."

"No," she grinned. "I was talking about the fact that you love me."

Coop shook his head. What had he gotten himself into?

Discussion Questions

1. In taking the case in 1964, Coop was faced with a difficult decision. Would it have been easier for him to make that decision today? Why or why not?

2. Do you think Coop put his job ahead of the safety of his family? What do you think of his decision, and what would you have done in his place?

3. In 1964 the races were obviously divided, today things seem different but do you believe that there is more trust between African Americans and whites now? How have things improved and how have they stayed the same?

4. Why did so many whites fear blacks in 1964? What was at the root of this fear?

5. Hattie's attitude seems strange as we view her in today's light. Why do you feel she was so shy and apologetic when dealing with whites?

6. The newspaper editor incited a great deal of the violence in this book. Does that still happen today? If so, do you see this as a problem?

7. Coop's trip to the other side of the tracks was an eye-opener. What things did he see there that might have convinced him to take the case?

8. Coop's grandson finds Justice a much different place. How has it changed, and why do you think this happened?

9. It is said that the most segregated places in America are its churches. Why do you suppose churches have been so slow to integrate? Is this a sign of the continuing mistrust between races or something else?

10. John David Maltose kept Coop's office just as it was when the lawyer disappeared after the trial in 1964. What do you think were his reasons for doing this?

11. Hate is an obvious emotion that is seen in various characters throughout the book. Why was Linda Maltose so driven by hate? Why couldn't she let it go? What effect do you

believe it had on her life and her ability to be happy?

12. Did Coop Lindsay and Calvin Ross die for nothing? If not, what was gained from their deaths?

Want to learn more about author Ace Collins?

Be sure to visit Ace online!

www.acecollins.com

About the Author

Ace Collins has written more than sixty books that have sold more than 2.5 million copies. His home on the web is AceCollins.com.

Center Point Large Print
600 Brooks Road / PO Box 1
Thorndike, ME 04986-0001 USA

(207) 568-3717

US & Canada:
1 800 929-9108
www.centerpointlargeprint.com